NEW MEXICO

NEW MEXICO

Heartbreak of the Past Draws Couples Together in Three Historical Novels

JANET LEE BARTON

BARBOUR PUBLISHING

ISBN 978-1-59789-362-6

All scripture quotations are taken from the King James Version of the Bible.

Cover art by Corbis/Getty Images

Published by Barbour Publishing, Inc., P.O. Box 719, Uhrichsville, Ohio 44683, www.barbourbooks.com

Our mission is to publish and distribute inspirational products offering exceptional value and biblical encouragement to the masses.

Printed in the United States of America.

Dear Readers,

While I've lived all over the South, and we have just moved from Mississippi to Oklahoma—my husband's home state—New Mexico will always be special. I was born and raised there, and it's where my deep faith in the Lord and my Christian walk began and grew.

When the idea for *A Promise Made* came to me, I knew right where I wanted to set it—in my home town of Roswell, NM. After delving deeper into the town's history, the scenes of my story began to form. When the characters seemed to come alive to me, one story led into another as *A Place Called Home* and *Making Amends* also took shape, with the Lord's help.

I hope you enjoy New Mexico and Emma's story as she strives to keep a promise, Beth's as she fights with giving up the children she's come to love as her own, and finally, Darcy's story, as she struggles with letting go of pain from the past and learns to forgive. As in our own lives, it's only with the Lord's help that they are able to find the way to true happiness.

Trusting in Him always,
Janet Lee Barton

A Promise Made

To my Lord and Savior for showing me the way.
And to my family, whose love and encouragement keep me at it.
I love you and thank God for you all each and every day.

Chapter 1

Roswell, Chaves County, New Mexico Territory, 1897

Emma finished cleaning the dining room of her café, trying not to worry about Annie, the young mother who worked for her. Annie hadn't seemed to be feeling well on Saturday, and she wasn't in church yesterday. When she didn't show up for work this morning, Emma couldn't help but be concerned.

At the time she hired Annie, she hadn't really needed an employee, but the seventeen-year-old girl was trying so hard to create a new life for herself, Emma felt compelled to help her. Over a year ago, Annie had knocked on the back door of Emma's café asking for a job. She'd explained that after the death of her parents several years before, when she'd been too young to realize what she was getting into, she'd become a saloon girl. She was living with the consequences of her decision and wanted a better life for the child she was expecting, but she was having a hard time finding decent employment. Emma's heart went out to the young woman, and she'd hired her on the spot.

There were quite a few raised eyebrows from some of her customers when they found a young, unmarried, pregnant woman working at the café, but Emma didn't let that bother her. There were others who reached out to help Annie, too.

Emma's best friend Liddy had moved into Cal's place with her little boy after their marriage a year ago, so Liddy's small but comfortable home had sat empty—until Emma told them about Annie's plight. The couple had generously allowed Annie to move into Liddy's old place, but it was a little way out of town.

Emma was worried about her being out there all alone with the baby, especially if she was sick. If she didn't come in to work tomorrow, Emma would ask the deputy to check on her. He stopped by the café most nights to have a bite to eat before making his rounds.

Emma wished *she* was the reason he came by each night, instead of her cooking. But she'd given up on Deputy Matthew Johnson months ago. She had taken his supper to him at the sheriff's office several times, but he always insisted on paying for it. Said he didn't want to be beholden to anyone. Humph. Emma didn't want him *beholden* to her—she'd rather they be *betrothed!*

She sighed. It just wasn't meant to be. So they shared an easy friendship of sorts. He ate most of his meals at her café, they had common friends around town, and when he came by before starting his rounds at night, they sometimes shared a cup of coffee and conversation. But she realized there was no future for her and Deputy Johnson other than friendship, and her mind had come to terms with it—over and over again.

As the bell above the door jingled and Matthew Johnson entered the café, Emma realized her *heart* hadn't come to the same conclusion. It still beat erratically each time she saw the tall, green-eyed, rusty-haired deputy.

Trying to hide her reaction to his presence, Emma poured him a cup of coffee and dished up the piece of apple pie she'd saved for him. "You weren't out by Annie's place today by any chance, were you?"

Deputy Johnson hung his high-crowned Stetson on the post by the door and crossed the room with long strides. "No. She didn't come in to work?"

Emma shook her head. "I'm worried about her. I think she might be coming down with the influenza that's going around town. If she doesn't come in tomorrow, will you ride out and check on her and Mandy?"

"Certainly." Matt took a seat at his usual table.

"I hate to ask you to go out of your way, but I don't like the idea of her and the baby being out there by themselves, especially if Annie's sick." Emma brought his dessert to the table and sat across from him. "I hope the baby isn't ill."

"I'll ride out tonight just to make sure." Matt took a sip of the hot coffee.

"Thank you, Deputy. It's not like her to miss work."

"She's lucky you gave her a job and that Cal and Liddy provided her with a place to live. Not many around town were willing to do that." Matt forked a piece of pie into his mouth.

"She's an orphan, and I know firsthand how hard that is. I've been on my own a long time, and it can really be a struggle. With a baby on the way, my heart just went out to her. Annie never complains about her lot, though. She tries to make the best life she can for the baby." Emma brought her cup to her mouth and blew away the steam.

"I never thought about it before," Matt said, "but who watches the baby while Annie's working?"

"Oh, Mandy comes with her. We've set up an area in the kitchen for her to play in, and she takes naps upstairs in my apartment. She's an adorable baby. She'll be talking and walking soon. It's no problem to have her here."

"You're a generous woman, Emma."

"I've only done what any good Christian would do," Emma said. "After Annie got baptized in the Hondo River last spring, she really changed. She acknowledged that she'd made some mistakes in her life, and she asked the Lord for His forgiveness. Cal and Liddy and I have only been trying to help Annie make a decent life for herself and Mandy."

Matt snorted. "You three are the only folks I've seen offering to help."

Emma winced inwardly at the bitterness in Matt's voice. "That's not true. The minister and his wife check on her quite often. And the ladies' group made baby clothes for Mandy."

"But you're the only one who offered her a job."

"I don't think she went many places. I mean, how many jobs are there for women in this town?"

"I guess you're right. But I've seen a lot of people around here go to great lengths to cross the street so they wouldn't have to come into contact with Annie."

Emma had noticed the same thing. But those folks would have to answer to the Lord for their actions. Personally, Emma would rather not have some of them in her café at all. She was sure their uppity airs hurt Annie. Not that she ever said anything, but Emma had seen the pain in the girl's eyes.

Matt took a last swallow of coffee and rose to his feet. "Guess I'd better be making my rounds. I'll run out and check on Annie after I finish."

Emma followed him to the door. "Thank you, Deputy."

"You lock up behind me, you hear?"

He put on his Stetson and tipped the wide brim before taking his leave.

Emma locked the door and pulled down the shade. She ambled to the kitchen, rubbing the small of her back and rotating her neck to get the kinks out. It had been a long, busy day. While she may not have needed the help when she hired Annie, business had grown in the last few months, and she sure noticed a difference in the workload when Annie wasn't there. But Matt's assurance that he would check on the young mother and baby relieved her anxiety a bit.

After pumping fresh water into the dishpan, Emma added some of the steaming water that had been simmering on the stove to the dirty dishes, wondering if she'd be by herself the next day. She'd sent home her kitchen helper, Ben, over an hour ago. He hadn't felt well all day, and she hoped he wasn't coming down with the influenza she was afraid Annie had. Emma said a quick prayer that Mandy wouldn't come down with it, too. Maybe she already had, and Annie had stayed home to take care of her. She prayed for them both.

Emma left the dishes to soak while she started her preparations for the next day. She fed her sourdough starter so she would have enough for the next morning's baking, then made sure she had plenty of eggs. She did all the same things she'd been doing for the past several years—but tonight, it suddenly hit her that she was tired of doing it. Tired clear through.

Would she ever have any other kind of life? Here she was twenty-four years old, and it didn't appear she'd be getting married anytime soon. She no longer held out hope that she'd ever become Mrs. Matt Johnson, and she wasn't interested in anyone else.

She might as well give up on having a family. She'd just be Aunt Emma to all of her friends' kids. She adored Annie's baby and Liddy's little son and Cal's two daughters. Still, she longed for children of her own. It had been her dream ever since she'd been orphaned so long ago.

Emma had just started washing the dishes when she heard a loud knock on the back door. Hearing her name called out, she recognized Matt's voice immediately. Though she was sure this wasn't a social call, her pulse began to race and her heart beat double time. She rushed to open the door. "Is Annie all right?"

Matt stood there, tall and handsome, his hat in his hand. "Doc needs you, Emma. Annie's real sick with the influenza. She's asking for you."

Emma grabbed her shawl off the hook near the stairwell and hustled out the door into the chilly mid-September air. "You brought them back with you?"

"No." Matt's expression was grim. "I met her and Mandy on their way in. Sick as she is, she somehow managed to hitch the wagon and start toward Doc's."

"Oh, my." Emma imagined Annie struggling to get into town with Mandy. Hot tears stung her eyes. "How's the baby?"

"She seemed fine."

They scurried down the boardwalk to Doc Bradshaw's office, Emma praying silently all the way that Annie would be all right.

Doc must have been watching for them because he opened the door before they got to it. His thick white hair stood on end, as if he'd been running his fingers through it every which way. Worry clouded his eyes. "I'm glad you're here, Emma. She's been asking for you."

"Where's Mandy?" Emma asked as he led them into his office.

"She's in the kitchen with Myrtle. So far she's not sick, and I'm hoping we can keep her that way. Here, put this on." He helped Emma place a mask over her nose and mouth, then gave another one to Matt. "We don't need you two coming down with this, too."

Doc led them up the hall and into a room where Annie lay flushed with fever, quietly moaning. Matt stayed just inside the door, but Emma rushed to Annie's side and gently brushed aside the thick auburn hair clinging to her damp brow. Annie opened her big brown eyes, and Emma was startled by how bright they were.

"Miss Emma. . .please. . ." Annie's voice was a gravelly whisper.

Emma leaned in close. "I'm here, Annie."

Annie tried to talk again. "Please, take Mandy. . . ."

"Of course. I'll be glad to watch the baby while you're sick."

Annie grasped Emma's wrist and clenched it tightly. "Forever. Promise. . ."

"Shh." Emma covered the young woman's white-knuckled hand with her free one. "You're going to be fine. Just rest so you can get well. I'll take Mandy home with me and care for her until you're feeling better. Don't worry about anything."

"Not going to make it." A sudden spasm of coughing racked Annie's slight body.

Doc rushed to her side and listened to her breathing. He looked up at Emma and shook his head.

When the coughing spell receded, Annie squeezed Emma's hand and continued her plea. "You'll raise Mandy? You are the only one I trust to love her and to raise her to love the Lord. Promise me. Please, Emma."

Emma's heart twisted at the thought that Annie might not make it. She quickly gave the only answer she could. "Yes, yes, I promise. Don't worry about a thing."

"Thank you," Annie whispered before closing her eyes.

Doc listened to Annie's breathing once more, then motioned Emma back into the hall, where Matt had gone to wait for them. Doc closed the door softly. "If she makes it through the night, she may have a chance," Doc said in a low voice. "I'm just not sure she can do that. She's awful weak."

The sob Emma had been holding back finally escaped. "I should have ridden out and checked on her today, or sent Ben, or asked Matt or the sheriff to go out and see if she was all right. If we could have got her here sooner—"

"I don't think it would have made any difference." Doc patted her shoulder. "Annie's been dealing with this for more than a few days. She just couldn't fight it off."

He handed Emma a handkerchief, and she dabbed at her eyes. She tried to pull herself together as they made their way down the hall. In the kitchen, Doc's wife, Myrtle, was sitting at the table, holding Annie's ten-month-old baby in her arms and trying to coax some food into her.

When the baby spotted Emma, she broke into a smile and held out her hands. Emma gathered the child close. "I'm here, sweetie."

The baby nestled her face into Emma's shoulder.

"Would you like a cup of tea?" Myrtle asked. She gathered her robe around her plump body as she padded to the stove in her slippers.

Emma took a seat at the table and fought tears as Mandy patted her arm. "Yes, please."

Myrtle brought her a cup of tea, then poured coffee for Doc and Matt.

Emma gathered the baby closer. "I should have checked on Annie sooner."

"And I should have gone right out there instead of having dessert first," Matt added.

"Stop blaming yourselves, you two," Doc said. "It probably wouldn't have changed a thing. You aren't doctors. I can't even do anything about this, except make her as comfortable as possible. We don't have medicine to cure this kind of thing. It comes on fast and hits some people harder than others."

Emma rocked back and forth. When she gazed down at the sweet face framed by strawberry blond curls, she found the baby sound asleep. Emma kissed her head. "Myrtle, do you have a blanket I can wrap her in to get her back to my place? The air is mighty cool tonight."

"She can stay here with us," Myrtle suggested. "I'll be glad to take care of her for a few days."

"Oh, no, thank you," Emma said. "I promised Annie. I'll take her home with me."

Myrtle nodded. "I'll go get a blanket. What about clothes? I might have some of our grandchildren's things."

Emma shook her head. "I already have a few outfits of hers. Since Annie often brought her in to work, we kept several things there. I may have to go out in a few days and get some more. . .if Annie doesn't get better soon."

As Myrtle left the room, Doc got up. "I'll check on her one more time before you leave."

When they were alone, Emma looked up to find Matt watching her.

"Are you all right?" he asked.

"I'm fine. I just. . ." She cleared her throat. "I have to be strong for Mandy's sake."

Matt fingered one of the little girl's curls. "She's sure a pretty baby, isn't she?"

"She certainly is," Myrtle answered for Emma. She came bustling into the room with a blanket, which she handed to Emma. "And a good baby, too. She sure took to you better than me, though."

Emma draped the blanket around the baby. "She's just more used to me, that's all."

"She's still feverish and sleeping fitfully," Doc said, returning from Annie's sickbed. "I wish I could tell you some good news."

"I'm sure you'll do all you can, Doc." Emma rose to her feet. "I'd better go get Mandy settled in."

Matt stood and opened the front door for her.

"It's awful dark out there," Emma observed. The boardwalk was terribly uneven, and as they'd hustled over to Doc's, she'd almost tripped trying to keep up with Matt. She didn't want to take a chance of falling with the baby in her arms. "Would you mind carrying Mandy for me until we get to the café?"

Matt hesitated for a moment, then awkwardly took the baby into his arms. Emma was sure he felt uncomfortable, like most single men would. But she felt just as inexperienced. *At least he's familiar with the streets at night,* she thought. Mandy would be safer with the deputy than with her.

Emma turned to Doc and Myrtle. "Thank you for taking care of Mandy until I could get here."

"No thanks needed, dear," Myrtle said, walking them to the door.

Matt led the way down the street to her café, and once inside, he followed Emma up the stairs and into her apartment. He quickly transferred the baby into Emma's arms. "I'll wait downstairs until you get her settled. . .unless you need me to do anything up here?"

Emma could tell he felt uneasy in her living quarters. "No, we're fine. You don't need to stay."

Matt backed out the door. "I'll wait for you to lock up."

Emma pulled her bedcovers down with one hand and laid the baby in the middle, surrounding her with every pillow she could find. She was thankful that Mandy stayed asleep. *The poor baby must be exhausted having others take care of her,* Emma thought as she brushed a kiss over the child's forehead.

Aware that Matt was waiting for her, she made her way downstairs and was surprised to find him at her kitchen sink washing the dishes. "You don't have to do that."

He grinned as he scrubbed a pan. "I figured I could do something useful while I was waiting."

Emma grabbed a clean towel and began to dry the dishes he'd washed. "It helps a lot. Thank you."

Matt rinsed the pot and placed it on the drain board. "You're welcome. The baby's all settled down?"

"She never woke up. Maybe she'll sleep through the night."

"I hope so. . .for both your sakes." After handing the last pot to Emma to dry, Matt emptied the dishpan and wiped it out.

Emma set the pot on a shelf beside the stove and spread the towel over the edge of the sink while Matt retrieved his hat from the hook. "You've been real good to Annie," he said, fingering the brim. "She obviously thinks a lot of you."

Emma followed him to the door. "Please pray for her. . .and for Mandy."

"I will," he promised. "You try to get some rest, you hear? And lock up as soon as I leave."

"Thank you for coming to get me and for helping me bring Mandy home." Emma was sure he'd only assisted out of a sense of professional duty, but that didn't matter. She was grateful she hadn't had to deal with all this alone.

"I'm glad I could help. Good night."

"Good night." Emma closed the door behind him and locked it. She glanced around the kitchen to make sure there was nothing else she needed to do for the next day, wondering what tomorrow would bring.

Expelling a deep breath, she climbed back up the stairs to the bedroom. Emma gazed down on the innocent little face, so peaceful in slumber. It hurt to think about the possibility that Annie might not make it—that this sweet baby could become an orphan. Emma understood all too well what that was like. Because she did, she fully intended to keep the promise she'd made to Annie, if it came to that. She might not have the first idea how to be a mother, but she'd do her best for this precious baby.

Dear God, please help Annie. And help me be strong for Mandy. In Jesus' name, amen.

Matt waited to hear Emma lock the door before he started his rounds. When she'd looked up at him with that worried expression, he'd been sorely tempted to pull her into his arms, kiss her furrowed brow, and tell her everything would be fine. But he didn't have the right.

Did she have any idea how his pulse raced whenever she blushed at him? He'd been attracted to her for longer than he wanted to think about. Tonight, he couldn't seem to get her out of his mind.

Matt jiggled the doorknob of the barbershop down the street from the café, checking to make sure Homer Williams had locked up. He did the same thing to half a dozen other businesses, not really thinking about what he was doing, just working out of habit.

Emma was one of the prettiest women he'd ever met, with her dark hair and blue eyes. She was also one of the kindest women he knew. She'd help anyone in trouble, and that was a fact. If his mind could be changed about taking a wife, it would be by Emma Hanson. Of course, he wasn't going to change his mind, but she sure would be a catch for some lucky man. The thought left a bad taste in Matt's mouth.

Matt vividly recalled the day his father had died from being shot in the line of duty. His mother had grieved deeply over his death. But she'd worked her fingers to the bone, taking in wash for everyone in town, in order to raise Matt and his brothers until they were all grown and on their own. She was the reason he'd promised himself he'd never marry. Having taken up his father's line of work, he was well aware of the dangers inherent to his profession. He would not leave a widow behind to work herself to death.

Matt strolled into the Oasis, one of the two saloons at the end of Main Street and the only one with lights still on inside. "How's it goin', Sam?" he asked the burly manager.

"Oh, pretty good," Sam said, wiping down the highly polished bar. "Nobody cheated at cards tonight, and I didn't have to throw anyone out."

"That's good to hear."

Other than Sam, the bar was unoccupied. Matt felt grateful for the quiet night. He already had too much on his mind.

"I'm about ready to close up here," Sam said. "Can I get you anything?"

"No, thanks," Matt said. "You go on home to that pretty wife of yours."

Sam grabbed a jacket off the wall peg. "Think I'll do just that."

After saying good night, Matt resumed his rounds along the opposite side of the street. The town was peaceful, with crickets providing the only sound.

He passed the fire department, which was across the street from Emma's café. Then, at the next building, he opened the door to the sheriff's office. Matt poured himself a cup of thick coffee and took it outside to lean against the hitching post. The large front window with *Emma's Café* etched in gold was dark, but light still shone from the window of her living quarters upstairs. He wondered if the baby was awake.

That sweet woman would be taking on a huge responsibility if Annie didn't make it. Emma had never had a child of her own, never even been married. It certainly wasn't the best situation. Yet tonight, when she took Mandy from him, the expression on her face was so tender, so protective.

He'd never thought of Emma as maternal or domestic. She was one of the best cooks around, but he considered her more of a businesswoman than a homemaker. He'd been surprised at the cozy feel to her apartment—so much so that he'd hightailed it out of there as fast as he could. No, after tonight, he could never think of Emma Hanson in quite the same way again.

Chapter 2

The first night was a long one. Although the baby stayed asleep, Emma woke often, afraid she'd roll over on Mandy or wouldn't hear her if she woke up. Mostly she tossed and turned, wondering if she'd lost her senses.

How could she have promised Annie she would raise Mandy? What did she know about taking care of a baby? Emma prayed even harder that Annie would get well.

Emma tried to remember everything she'd seen Annie do for Mandy during the day, and all she'd seen Liddy do with her and Cal's children.

She was glad Annie had weaned Mandy early so she wouldn't have to worry about that. The ten-month-old baby could drink out of a cup and was already trying to feed herself with a spoon. But it wasn't feeding or changing or clothing Mandy that had Emma so frightened. It was the responsibility of teaching Mandy to love the Lord and to live life the way He and Annie would want her to that overwhelmed her.

When Mandy woke before dawn, needing to be changed and missing her mama, Emma didn't have time to worry about the kind of job she was doing. She simply saw to the baby's needs, then cuddled her close until her crying subsided. She was glad the baby was used to being around her.

Emma dressed quickly and pinned her hair up in a knot on top of her head, then picked up the baby and descended the stairs with Mandy on her hip. She'd have to get one of those new telephones installed as soon as possible, she decided, so she could call Doc regularly to check on Annie, and to get in touch with him if Mandy got sick.

She hoped Ben would be well enough to come to work. She should probably try to find someone else to help out so she could pay more attention to the baby.

As she slipped Mandy into her high chair and donned an apron, Emma thanked the Lord that Annie had been bringing Mandy to work with her. Ben had fenced off an area in one corner of the kitchen for the baby to play in, and several of Mandy's favorite toys lay scattered throughout the space.

Emma took a deep breath as she prepared Mandy's breakfast and fed her before starting preparations for the café. She set the baby in her play area, and for the moment she seemed all right, occupied with her toys. But Emma was sure she'd start missing her mama soon.

Emma mixed up a batch of biscuits and cut them out, telling herself over and over that she could do this. With the Lord's help, of course.

A knock on the back door startled her, but when she opened the door and found Matt standing there, she braced herself for bad news.

"Annie made it through the night, but Doc still doesn't hold out much hope."

Emma's heart sank, and she fought the urge to cry.

Matt peeked into the kitchen. "How's Mandy doing?"

Emma stepped to the side and motioned Matt to come in. "She slept through the night but woke up crying. Bless her heart, she doesn't understand what's going on." Emma poured two cups of coffee. As she handed one to Matt, she noticed him watching her closely.

"You didn't get much sleep last night, did you?" he asked.

"Not much," she admitted.

"How are you going to run the café and take care of Mandy?"

Emma shrugged. "Ben will help. And I can hire another person. I promised Annie I'd do this, and I will."

"But—"

There was another knock on the back door, and Emma was glad to have the conversation interrupted. What little confidence she'd been feeling was quickly deteriorating.

Emma was relieved to open the door to Ben.

"Mornin', Miss Emma. How are you today?"

"Better now that you're here. We've got a problem."

"Oh?" Ben tied on his apron. If he was surprised to see Matt or Mandy in the kitchen, he didn't show it.

"Annie is real sick. Deputy Johnson says Doc doesn't think she'll get better. And I promised to take care of Mandy."

Ben nodded. "Don't you worry, Miss Emma. You can do it."

At least Ben thought she could handle things. "Thank you, Ben. Are you feeling all right? I was worried you might have come down with the influenza, too."

"I'm fine. Sure am sorry about Miss Annie, though. I hope Doc is wrong. She's a nice lady." Ben began to slice the bacon for the customers who'd be coming in soon.

Matt drained his cup and put on his hat. "I'd better be getting back to work. I'll check on Annie later and give you an update. Is there anything you need me to do?"

Emma couldn't keep the cool tone out of her voice as she answered, "No, thank you."

He watched Mandy play for a moment. "If you do need anything, just have Ben find me."

Emma released a deep breath as he walked out the door. She didn't have time to worry about what Deputy Matthew Johnson thought about her keeping Mandy. She had a full day ahead of her.

As if Ben could read her thoughts, he said, "Don't you worry, Miss Emma. I can work the front and the kitchen while you take care of the baby. We can do it."

Emma smiled at the man who'd helped her for the past five years. "Thank you, Ben. I'm sure you're right."

Matt almost shivered as he walked away from Emma's. She'd become distant as soon as he asked her how she was going to handle everything. He hadn't meant to make her feel bad, but he honestly had no idea how she was going to run her business and take care of Annie's child at the same time.

Matt made his morning rounds, glad he'd be off duty soon. It had been a long night.

He watched portly Douglas Harper open up his bank down the street. The morning train's whistle could be heard in the distance.

"Mornin', Deputy," Homer Williams greeted as he unlocked his barbershop. "Looks like it's going to be a nice day."

"Indeed it does," Matt said, glancing up. The sky was a clear blue, with only a wisp of a cloud floating in it. The sun shone brightly, promising a warm day.

Matt ambled over to the sheriff's office. He hoped Annie would be feeling better today. But deep inside, he doubted that would be the case. Doc had said she'd been sick for longer than any of them realized.

The morning passed in a blur as Emma balanced her time between taking care of the breakfast crowd and checking on Mandy. The baby had played herself to sleep in the middle of the rush, just as she always did. Emma hoped she'd be able to check on Annie when things slowed down.

By the time the morning crowd thinned out, Emma was beginning to feel the effects of her sleepless night. When her best friend Liddy McAllister came in with the cakes and pies she baked for the café, Emma made a valiant effort to greet her in her normal, cheery way.

"Emma!" Liddy cried, leading her to a table and insisting that she sit. "Myrtle told me about Annie. Did you get any sleep at all last night? You certainly don't look like you did."

Emma couldn't help but chuckle. Usually it was Liddy who possessed a bushel full of tact, while Emma sometimes spoke before she thought. . .but not today. "Thank you, Liddy. Now I realize why my customers were staring at me strangely."

Liddy poured them each a cup of coffee and sat across from Emma. "I'm just concerned. Have you had any news about Annie?"

Emma took a sip of the hot coffee. "Not since this morning. I should go over and check on her."

"I'll do that. You should take a nap."

Emma stifled a yawn. "Mandy will be awake and hungry soon."

"Em. . .I saw Matt. He said you're planning on keeping Mandy if Annie doesn't make it."

Emma lifted her chin. Obviously Matt didn't think she could do it. Was that how her friend felt, too? She peered into Liddy's eyes. "I am."

Liddy rested her jaw in her hand. "I see that."

"And?"

"And nothing. You'll do a wonderful job. It won't be easy, but you know that from watching me. And I'll help in any way I can."

"Thank you, Liddy. I am a bit scared."

Liddy patted Emma's hand. "You'll do fine. Don't you remember how frightened I was about raising a baby? You were there."

"And no help at all."

"You were more help than you realize," Liddy said. "When I was alone with my son, I fell apart. But Cal helped me with my fears and assured me that God would give me the right instincts, and I just needed to follow them."

"But you are your son's natural mother, Liddy. I'm—"

"You are a woman who will be a wonderful mother. . .whether the child is given to you or if it's your own. I would trust you with my children in a minute."

Emma blinked back tears. "Oh, Liddy. Thank you. I really needed to hear that."

The next few days were some of the hardest Emma had ever gone through. She got a telephone installed on the wall next to the stairs, so she was able to check on Annie several times during the day. But the news was never good. Annie didn't get better. She slipped into a coma, and Doc said it was only a matter of time.

The first night taking care of Mandy was easy compared to the next two. She was a good baby, but she missed her mama, and she woke up crying several times each night. Emma cried with her as she rocked, cuddled, and bonded with the child. She'd loved her as Annie's child. Now she was beginning to love her as her own as she took care of her needs and gave her the attention Annie would if she could.

Emma realized it was only with God's help that she made it through each day. She and Ben managed to run the café without too many snags, but she didn't imagine it would get any easier.

"Miss Emma," Ben said as he swept the floor at the end of the day. "I know someone who needs a job, and we could sure use the help. You've got your hands full with that baby, and you have to get some rest."

"You're right. I've been thinking about putting up a help-wanted sign, but I kept thinking Annie was going to get better."

"It ain't gonna happen, Miss Emma."

She sighed, her heart heavy. "Who do you have in mind?"

"Well, you remember my brother died last year? His widow, Hallie, has been takin' in wash, doin' cleanin' at the hotels, and whatever she can to make a livin', but they only use her when one of their regular helpers is sick. She'd be glad to help out here, and she could sure use some steady work."

"Your recommendation is good enough for me. Tell Hallie to come see me tomorrow."

Ben grinned. "You won't be sorry, Miss Emma. Hallie's a hard worker."

But Hallie didn't come in the next day. Annie died during the night, and Emma closed the café in her honor.

The following day Emma stood at the grave site, holding Mandy tightly, weeping silently while the minister officiated. She thanked the Lord that Mandy was too young to understand the heart-wrenching changes going on in her little life.

Deputy Johnson stood behind her, giving Emma comfort, although she was sure he was unaware of it. She was pleased at the good turnout of church members and a few customers Annie had waited on regularly. But Emma had never felt more relief than when she'd been able to leave the graveyard behind.

The band of mourners made their way back to town, and most everyone came to the café for the noon meal. Several church members had brought in food before the funeral. Emma's heart was touched when Ben shooed her out of her own kitchen, and, along with some of the women from church, made sure everyone was served.

Cal and Liddy's children entertained Mandy. While the baby enjoyed their attention, her gaze constantly sought out Emma, as if to make sure she was still there. Emma made certain to say something reassuring to the baby or reach out and touch her head each time she passed by their table.

As people began to leave, Douglas Harper, head of Harper Bank and one of the town's councilmen, approached Emma with hat in hand. "Miss Emma, it's a wonderful thing you did, taking in that little girl. We'll make permanent arrangements for her in the next few weeks."

"What do you mean?" Emma frowned, immediately suspicious of this man.

Several years back Mr. Harper had tried to buy her place of business. Her café was in a prime location, near the train depot, across from the sheriff's office and just a couple of blocks from the Roswell Hotel. But she had no intention of selling her property. Harper had been persistent, and Emma'd had to work hard to convince him that her *no* meant *no*.

Just a couple of years ago, Harper had caused no end of trouble for Liddy, too, trying to foreclose on her farm after her first husband died. Why, that horrible man had even gone so far as to try to blackmail Liddy into marrying him!

Emma considered Douglas Harper a real snake in the grass. She wondered what he was up to now.

"We'll have to try to find a family to take her in, or get her into the orphanage in Santa Fe," he said.

"There's no need for that, Mr. Harper. I promised Annie I would raise Mandy, and I intend to do just that."

"No one is going to hold you to a deathbed promise."

"I hold myself to it."

Matt crossed the room to stand at her side. His nearness provided a sense of relief.

"Miss Emma," Harper said coolly, "you're a single woman. It doesn't seem fitting for you—"

"Mr. Harper," Matt interrupted him, "perhaps this isn't the time to discuss this. Miss Emma has had a long few days."

"There won't be a good time to discuss this," Emma said.

Liddy McAllister appeared at Emma's side. "Emma, I haven't seen you eat a bite. Come on. You need to—"

"I'm not hungry."

Liddy took hold of her arm and gently pulled her away from the banker. "I understand. But Mandy needs you now. You have to keep up your strength."

That was all it took. "You're right." Emma turned back to Matt and Councilman Harper. "Excuse me, gentlemen. There are some things I need to take care of." With that, she allowed Liddy to lead her to a table where a plate of food sat waiting for her.

"Well!" Harper said. "If she thinks the town leaders are going to let a single woman keep that child, she's sadly mistaken. This isn't the end of things by a long shot." The banker stomped off.

Much as he hated to agree with Douglas Harper on anything, this time Matt felt the man was right. It would be a huge responsibility for Emma to take on, as busy as she was with the café.

But it was going to be really hard for Emma to give up Annie's baby. And today was not the right time to press the issue. Matt took a plate of food and made his way over to Emma's table, where Cal and Liddy were keeping her company.

"No one is going to take Mandy away from me," Emma was saying. "No one."

Liddy patted her shoulder. "Of course not. Don't you give it another thought, Em." But her eyes held a worried look as she glanced at Matt and Cal.

Matt had never felt so confused in his life. He wanted to support the woman he cared so much about. But how could he do that? This baby wasn't even Emma's. She didn't know what she was letting herself in for, trying to raise someone else's child and running a business on her own.

Perhaps if the idea came from him instead of Harper, Emma would at least consider it. "If they could find a couple to take her in," he asked hesitantly, "wouldn't that be better for Mandy?"

The silence that fell on the table was deafening. Emma stopped pushing food around on her plate, put down her fork, and glared up at Matt. "Annie asked *me* to raise Mandy. She didn't ask me to find a couple to take her. She didn't ask anyone else. You were there, Deputy Johnson. You heard her. I can and I *will* give Mandy love and security. I will keep my promise."

Emma stood and gathered the baby in her arms. "If you don't mind, it's been a long day. I think I'll put Mandy down for a nap."

Matt felt as if he'd been slapped as he watched Emma leave. Cal and Liddy shook their heads at him.

"Are you two going to tell me you don't think a married couple wouldn't be better for Mandy?"

"I will tell you that your timing is really bad," Cal said. "And that Emma will make a wonderful mother for that baby. Annie believed that, or she never would have asked her to take Mandy."

Matt had never felt so confused in his life. Even Cal and Liddy didn't seem to realize he was only thinking of Emma.

"Raising a child alone is hard," Liddy said, "but it can be done. Happens all the time. And Emma won't be single forever," she added, raising her eyebrows at Matt.

Liddy sent her two girls to work in the kitchen, gathered up her toddler son, and hurried upstairs to check on her friend.

Emma was rocking Mandy to sleep when Liddy entered the sitting room. She brushed at her wet lashes.

Liddy hugged her friend. "Aw, Em. It's going to be all right."

Emma sniffed. "I hope I stop all this weeping soon. I don't know when I've cried so much."

A Promise Made

"Losing a friend is heartbreaking. And when a child is left behind, it's even more so." Liddy rubbed her friend's shoulders.

"I'm afraid I'm going to lose Mandy. Harper wants to take her away from me. And judging from Matt's reaction, Harper's not alone in his opinions." Emma held Mandy closer and kissed the top of her head. "I've grown to love this little girl. I can't let her go. I won't—no matter how hard I have to fight to keep her."

Chapter 3

Much to Emma's relief, Hallie came to work the next day. Her ready smile and sparkling eyes told Emma she'd be crazy not to hire her. Hallie would work on a part-time basis, coming in most days to help with the noontime rush. From the first day, she assisted Ben in the kitchen and also helped watch the baby, leaving Emma free to take care of the front. Ben was right. She was a hard worker, and she was wonderful with Mandy.

Emma tried to get used to the changes in her life. Caring for Mandy and running a business was a challenge, but Emma had always met the challenges in her life head-on. This time would be no exception.

She had a feeling it was only a matter of time until Councilman Harper would make trouble. The next town meeting was scheduled for the following week.

She'd noticed several of her patrons whispering when they didn't think she was paying attention, and she'd overheard her name and Annie's several times. Some of the people expressed concern about her raising the child "all alone." Everyone had advice to give. Emma was learning to ignore most of it.

She and Mandy were adjusting to each other more quickly than Emma had expected. The baby was sleeping better and began calling her "Em-mama." Emma promised herself she would keep Annie's memory alive for Mandy as best she could, but it would be several years before Mandy could begin to understand what had happened to her mother.

Liddy and Cal brought in Annie's few personal belongings from her house. It wasn't much, but someday the items would mean a great deal to Mandy. There was a picture of Annie, a Bible the church had given her on the day she'd been baptized, several hand-crocheted items, including a beautiful tablecloth, and Annie's clothes. Emma packed everything away carefully.

There was very little clothing for the baby, and Mandy was quickly growing out of what she did have. Emma wasn't much of a seamstress, but a new dry goods store had recently opened in town, so she and Mandy went shopping together during an afternoon lull at the café.

Emma also went to Jaffa-Prager Company, Roswell's large general store, to order a baby carriage and a crib. She was quite pleased with her purchases and was eager to show off the new clothes she'd bought for Mandy.

But the only patron in the café when she returned made her heart beat triple-time, betraying her emotions. She wasn't inclined to brag to Matt about her purchases. Still, she couldn't bring herself to be rude to him, either.

"Afternoon, Deputy," Emma said.

"How are you two today?" Matt asked.

Emma juggled Mandy on her hip as she filled a cup with milk for the child. "We're fine, aren't we, Mandy? We've been shopping for new clothes, haven't we?"

Mandy bobbed her head, and Emma wondered how much she understood.

"And you are going to look just beautiful in everything, aren't you, darling?" Emma tickled the baby under her chin.

When Mandy giggled, Emma and Matt both chuckled, and the tension between them seemed to ease.

"How is she adjusting?" Matt asked, reaching out to touch Mandy's cheek.

"She's doing well. Sleeping better. Not crying so much." She watched Mandy grin at Matt's overtures.

"That's good." He peered at Emma. "How are you doing?"

She shrugged. "I'm doing well. Sleeping better. Not crying so much."

Matt chuckled, and so did Mandy. "I'm glad."

Emma laughed outright when Mandy echoed, "Gad."

Matt raised an eyebrow. "She's talking?"

"Only a few words here and there." She bent to kiss the top of Mandy's head. "She calls me Em-mama."

Mandy pointed at her. "Em-mama."

"That's sweet," Matt said.

"I think so."

Hallie came in from the kitchen. "Do you want I should take her, Miss Emma?"

"No, thank you, Hallie. I need to go up and change clothes. Just refill the deputy's coffee cup."

Matt shook his head. "No more for me, thanks. I have to get back to work."

"I'll be in the kitchen if you need me, Miss Emma," Hallie said as she returned to her work.

Emma stood with the baby while Matt drained his cup and put his hat back on. He ruffled Mandy's hair. "I'm glad she's adjusting well. It's obvious you're taking good care of her. But you seem awful tired. Try to get some rest, won't you?"

"I'm fine, thank you," Emma returned coolly.

Matt left money for his pie and coffee on the table, then walked to the door. "Bye-bye, Mandy," he said at the doorway. "See you later."

After the deputy left, Emma slowly climbed upstairs, holding Mandy. She *was* tired. But she wasn't about to admit it to Matt. After all, he might be in cahoots with Harper. Her heart twisted at the thought.

She held the baby closer. She might never have the complete family she'd dreamed of, but because Annie trusted her child to her, she would be a mother to this precious child, and they would be a family. Emma kissed the top of Mandy's head, praying that she would be able to keep this child she'd grown to love.

On Sunday, Emma said a silent prayer for guidance as she entered church with Mandy on her hip. It was one thing to disregard the hushed comments of her patrons, but quite another to ignore those same stares and whispers from some of her church family.

She held her head high and gathered Mandy closer, overwhelmed by the protective feeling that rose in her chest. She quickly made her way down the aisle to sit in the pew behind Liddy and Cal. Their daughters, Amy and Grace, waved and grinned at Mandy, and they received a small giggle in return.

Liddy leaned over the back of the pew. "You will be having dinner with us, won't you, Em? The children can't wait to play with Mandy again."

Emma smiled at her friend, thankful that businesses in this town all closed on Sundays. "Thank you, Liddy. We'd love to come out to your place for dinner."

She did have some loyal friends in this town, and she had no doubt they would stand beside her in her fight to keep Mandy. As the service got under way, she reminded herself that the most important thing was that God was on her side in this. He had brought Annie into her life, and He'd heard Emma's promise. She was sure He would help her keep it.

When she left the church, the minister, John Turley, stopped her. "Emma," he said, his arm wrapped around his wife, Caroline, "we just wanted to tell you we're proud of the way you stepped in and agreed to take Mandy for Annie."

"And if there's anything we can do to help you," Caroline added, "please call on us. We'll be praying for you both."

"Thank you," Emma said. "That means more than I can say."

Several other members of the church expressed similar sentiments, and their encouragement strengthened her. In fact, that afternoon was one of the most relaxing she could remember since before Annie passed away.

Emma sat on Liddy and Cal's front porch, enjoying a cup of coffee and a slice of Liddy's apple pie while the children played together. It warmed Emma's heart to hear the baby's chuckles as the older girls played patty-cake and sang songs to her. She knew there would be tough times ahead, but spending the day with supportive friends did much to strengthen her resolve.

Emma wasn't a bit surprised when toward the end of the next week; she received a personal invitation to attend the town council meeting scheduled for the upcoming Monday evening.

"To discuss the custody of Mandy Drake," the letter said.

Humph! They could discuss all they wanted to, but she was keeping Annie's baby and that was all there was to it.

Emma tried not to worry about it. She was much too busy to fret, anyway. When the situation did enter her thoughts, she gave it to the Lord and got on with taking care of Mandy and her business.

The night of the meeting, Cal and Liddy showed up at the café to escort her and give her their support. Emma was thankful for their presence. She'd prayed all day, but she was still nervous to the point of feeling sick to her stomach. She trusted the Lord to get her through the evening and to give her the strength to handle whatever happened. Still, she felt as if she were fighting for her very life... and for that of her young charge.

Hallie offered to watch Mandy during the meeting, but Emma didn't want to let the child out of her sight. After donning her Sunday best, a two-piece navy brocade, she dressed the baby in one of her new outfits and cuddled her close as she walked down the boardwalk, with Cal and Liddy flanking her protectively.

When they entered the town hall, Emma gathered Mandy close. She raised her chin a notch as she realized all eyes were on her and the baby she held. It seemed half the town had shown up for this meeting. There must have been at least fifty chairs set out in rows, and most of them were already taken. Several men stood next to the windows that lined each side of the room.

Sheriff Haynes, a tall, middle-aged man with dark hair and alert brown eyes, stood at the back of the room. Matt leaned against the wall near the side door with Deputy Carmichael, a young man with blond hair and blue eyes. Matt tipped his hat as her glance caught his. Determined to ignore the thumping of her heart at the sight of him, she turned her head and looked for a seat.

Doc Bradshaw waved at Emma from the front row. His wife, Myrtle, patted the empty seat beside her. Emma joined them, adjusting Mandy on her lap, and Liddy and Cal took the seats next to her. She was confident these four people would stand up for her, but as the meeting was called to order, Emma wasn't sure their support would really help.

Four council members sat at a rectangular table at the front of the room. Harper stood beside the table, talking to the men in hushed tones. Homer Williams, the owner of the barbershop down the street from Emma's café, would probably vote whatever way Harper did.

Carl Adams sat beside Homer. He owned a big ranch outside of town but lived in Roswell because his wife hated the country. He came into the café fairly often, and Emma thought he might vote for her to keep Mandy, but she couldn't be sure.

Emma didn't know the other two councilmen, Ed Bagley and John McDonald, well enough to speculate what they might think.

Emma wondered why the other three town councilmen weren't in attendance. Then she remembered that the mayor had gone back East to settle his parents' estate, and the other two members were out of town on vacation.

Harper peered at his watch and took the podium. He immediately launched into a plea of help for Emma, telling the citizens that as a single woman running a business, she shouldn't be "saddled" with a baby. "What we really need is a couple who is willing to take the child—just until we can make arrangements to get her to the orphanage in Santa Fe. Surely one or two of you couples can come forward to do that?"

Emma gathered Mandy in her arms and stood to her feet to address the crowded room. "It appears Councilman Harper isn't quite clear on Mandy's situation. I promised Annie I would raise her, and I intend to do just that. I can run a business and raise a child. I do not want anyone to take Mandy." The baby fidgeted and Emma sat back down, rocking her.

"But Miss Emma," Mr. Harper said, "you are a single woman. This child needs two parents."

Doc Bradshaw stood. "Harper, this baby was doing just fine with the one parent she had. And I heard Emma promise Annie she would take her."

"Yes, well, she didn't leave a will, Doc. A deathbed request does not constitute a legal declaration of intent."

Doc grunted and took his seat.

Minister Turley, who was sitting with his wife two rows back, spoke up. "I'd venture to say that most of us don't have a written will. A deathbed request is often all there's time for."

"That brings another thought to bear," Harper interrupted. "We don't really know much about Annie Drake. Since the child comes from an uncertain background, it's even more important that she be placed into a stable home with two parents."

"Harper, what's gotten into you?" Doc sputtered. "What have you got against this child?"

Harper pointed to Mandy. "She could be the daughter of an outlaw, for all we know. Her character is, at best, questionable."

Emma jumped to her feet, startling Mandy a bit. "Are you saying that *my* character is questionable as well? After all, I was an orphan, too." She stroked the baby's head as she glared at Harper.

"No, of course not," the councilman said. "We all know you. But we have no idea who the father of this child was. . .and there's no telling what kind of person she'll become."

"I can tell you right now, Mandy will grow up to be a fine Christian woman if I am allowed to raise her in the way Annie asked me to."

Homer Williams stood. "Miss Emma, we understand your intentions are honorable. But we are concerned that you might be taking on more than you are able—"

"Mr. Williams, with God all things are possible," Emma asserted.

Homer cleared his throat and focused his attention on the rest of the group. "We need a married couple who is willing to take this child for a few weeks. Surely, that's not too much to ask."

Emma scanned the crowd, making eye contact with as many as would meet her gaze. She saw Jim Harrison nudge his wife, Nelda. Nelda glared at her husband. Harold Ferguson started to raise his hand, but his wife, Beatrice, quickly pulled it back down. Several silent conversations took place between husbands and wives. After what seemed like forever, Emma breathed a sigh of relief. Not one hand stayed up. She promised herself she would thank these women as soon as possible.

Homer sat back down and crossed his arms.

Harper raised an eyebrow. "No one? Surely one of you fine, upstanding women could take the child for a few weeks."

Liddy spoke up. "Emma Hanson is perfectly capable of taking care of Mandy. There is no need to do this."

"The town leaders believe there is, Mrs. McAllister." Harper's sinister gaze shifted from Liddy to Cal.

Cal stood. "The town leaders need to rethink, then," he said, his hand on his wife's shoulder as if protecting her from whatever the rude banker might say next.

Harper turned his focus back to the men at the table. "We have discussed this at length, haven't we, gentlemen?"

Homer and Ed nodded. The other two councilmen kept their heads down. Emma began to wonder just who ran this town.

"If you were a married woman," Harper continued, "there would be no question of you keeping the baby. But we feel it would be in the child's best interest to have two parents. We are contacting the orphanage in Santa Fe. When we hear back from them, we will make arrangements to take the baby there. In the meantime, since no one has come forward. . .we will allow you to take care of the baby."

Emma bit her tongue and prayed for guidance. But she couldn't keep the sarcasm out of her voice as she said, "Thank you so much, Councilman." She started to leave, but stopped mid-aisle and whirled back around to face the council members. "I want you all to know I have no intention of giving this baby up.

With me, a promise made is a promise kept."

"Well, we'll just see about that," Douglas Harper muttered.

~

Matt stood in the doorway of the sheriff's office and stared at the town council building down the street. The lights in the windows told him the meeting was still in progress.

He agreed with the council members that Emma shouldn't be raising Mandy, but that was only because he knew how hard it would be on her. He'd watched her closely these past few weeks. She'd been a wonderful mother to that baby.

She'd appeared so vulnerable when she walked in with Mandy. He was glad Cal and Liddy had accompanied her. But he was angry at the way Harper had treated her. He'd wanted to come to her defense, but the memories of his own mother struggling to raise him and his brothers kept him quiet.

Matt had left the room in the middle of the meeting. Sheriff Haynes and Deputy Carmichael would let him know if any problems came up. Besides, even though he didn't think Emma should raise the baby alone, he couldn't stand there and watch Harper try to take Mandy away.

He watched from the office until he saw Emma leave the building, with Mandy held close. Cal and Liddy were right behind her. From the smiles on their faces, he guessed things hadn't gone quite the way Harper had planned. And at that moment. . .he was glad.

~

Emma shook like a leaf as she scurried down the boardwalk. She couldn't wait to get Mandy back to the café.

Cal called to her. "Emma, slow down."

She stopped and turned. "I'm sorry. I—"

"It's all right, Em," Liddy said as they continued walking together.

"I think I'm going to have to run for councilman next time a position opens up," Cal said. "I thought our council was made of stronger stuff."

"So did I," Liddy said. "I'm sure the mayor would never let this happen."

"I don't understand why Harper is so set on taking Mandy away from me." Emma rubbed the child's back. "No one will take better care of her than I will. I'm not going to let it happen. I won't allow anyone to take Mandy away from me—especially not that snake, Douglas Harper!"

Chapter 4

Matt scrambled to catch up to Emma as she hurried toward the café, Liddy and Cal keeping pace beside her. Just before he reached them, Emma whirled around, almost smacking into him. Anger reddened her cheeks.

"Well, Deputy, I noticed you didn't stay to hear the outcome of the meeting."

"I can see you still have Mandy, so—"

"I hope you're prepared to arrest me," Emma interrupted, "because you might have to before this is all over."

"Em—" He touched her arm, but she jerked away, still holding the baby tight. "I'm sure it won't come to that."

"I'm not," Emma huffed. "Harper means to take Mandy away from me, but I'll go to jail before I'll give her up."

Liddy put her arm around Emma. "You're not going to jail. Now, let's get a cup of coffee and a piece of that pecan pie I brought in earlier, all right?"

Emma took a deep breath. "You're right. I do need to calm down so I can figure out my next move."

The ladies continued on down the boardwalk, and the men followed. Cal filled Matt in on what had happened after he left the meeting.

When Emma stopped at the door of the café, Matt was sure she was going to tell him to go away. Instead, her expression was soft and remorseful.

"I'm sorry, Deputy. My tirade was uncalled for. You're welcome to join us for coffee and pie if you like."

When she looked at him with those beautiful blue eyes, Matt wanted nothing more than to take her up on her offer. But she still seemed to think he was against her. "Thank you for the invitation, but I'm on duty. If you're all still here when I get through making my rounds, I might stop in."

Cal slapped him on the shoulder. "See you later, then. Hope your night is uneventful."

"So do I." Matt tipped his hat to the women. "Evening, ladies."

"Night, Matt," Liddy said.

"Good night, Deputy." Emma swept up her skirts and entered the café.

Emma couldn't decide if she was relieved or disappointed that Matt hadn't come in. She chided herself for wanting him around even though he disapproved of her keeping Mandy. She shouldn't care one fig what the deputy did or said. Of course, she'd been telling herself that for months, to no avail. She did care—too much.

Hallie came out of the kitchen just as they walked in. Emma let her take Mandy to the kitchen to play awhile before bedtime. Since no customers were in the café, Emma decided to close early. Liddy poured coffee and brought plates of pie to the table.

Cal handed Emma a piece of paper with a name printed on it. "I don't know if you'll be needing a lawyer, but I know an honest one. If you go see him, tell him we sent you."

"Thank you." Emma slipped the piece of paper into her skirt pocket. "Cal, do you think Matt is in cahoots with Douglas Harper?"

Cal shook his head. "I'm sure he doesn't like the man any better than we do."

"But Matt agrees that I shouldn't be raising Mandy."

"I don't think that's the case," Liddy said. "He's just concerned about you trying to raise Mandy on your own. But I told him that if anyone could do it, you could."

"Thank you. I don't imagine you changed his mind."

"I'm not sure. But I can't believe he'd be working with Harper."

"I hope not," Emma said. "You know, the town council should have more important things to do than try to take an orphan away from someone who wants to raise her."

Liddy patted Emma's hand. "Everything will be all right."

"I pray it is. I'll leave town before I'll let them take her."

"It's not going to get to that point. You have a lot of friends here. Give them a chance to act on your behalf."

Emma chuckled, remembering the expression on Alma Burton's face when her husband tried to get her to raise her hand. She already had eleven young ones at home. "I'll have to thank those women."

"A lot of them will be at the quilting bee on Saturday," Liddy said. "You could do it then. And bring Mandy along."

"I'd like that. Whose hope chest are we working to fill this time?"

"Beth Morgan is getting married next spring."

Emma took a drink of her coffee as she tried to put a face to the name. "Oh, she's an operator for the telephone company, isn't she?"

"That's right," Liddy confirmed.

"I don't remember seeing her with anyone. Who is she marrying?"

"She's going to Arkansas to marry a widower with two children," Liddy said.

"She answered an advertisement in the paper."

"Really?" Mail-order brides weren't uncommon in the West, but Emma had never met anyone who actually was one. She'd seen the ads in the newspapers and been curious as to what kind of women answered them. She'd have to pay close attention on Saturday.

Over the next week, Emma was able to express her appreciation to Nelda Harrison and Alma Burton when they came into her café. They both assured her that they would stand beside her. But the women who'd crossed the street rather than have any contact with Annie did the same thing now to Emma.

Emma thanked the Lord for women like Nelda and Alma. The others she prayed for—prayed that their hearts would change.

She was looking forward to the quilting bee on Saturday. She wasn't the best with a needle, and she was getting tired of making quilts for every engaged woman in town, but she did enjoy the chance to visit with women from her church. And she was curious to find out more about why Beth Morgan would agree to marry a man she'd never met.

The ladies at the quilting bee assured Emma that she would be a wonderful mother to Mandy. Their words encouraged her.

Mandy gleefully soaked in all the attention she received. Since the women taking turns holding the baby had much more experience raising children than she did, Emma began to relax and enjoy herself.

Beth Morgan was as sweet as she was pretty. Emma was glad when someone else had the nerve to ask her how she came to be engaged to a man she'd never met.

Beth smiled as she cut out a square of colorful fabric. "I told my friends I wondered what it would be like to correspond with one of those men who advertised in the paper, and they dared me to write to one. So I did. I never planned on falling in love with him."

The young woman giggled as she pulled a photograph out of her apron pocket. "This is a picture of him and his children. Aren't they lovely?" She handed the photo to the lady next to her to pass around. When it made its way to Emma, she was relieved to see that the man was clean-shaven and neatly groomed. His children appeared to be well taken care of.

"He appears to be nice, Beth," she said before handing the picture to Liddy. "I hope you'll be very happy."

"Thank you," Beth said.

"It occurs to me, Emma," said Harriet Howard, one of the older women in the group, "that might be the answer for you."

Emma scrunched her brow. "Answer to what?"

"Didn't Douglas Harper say that if you had a husband, there would be no problem with you keeping Annie's child?"

"Yes, but—"

"You could advertise for a mail-order groom!"

Emma chuckled along with the other women. "Why, Miss Harriet, I never heard of such an idea."

"If I were thirty years younger," Harriet said without glancing up from her stitching, "I might just put an advertisement in the paper myself."

Emma's amusement tapered off as she thought about the town council. "I can give Mandy a loving home all by myself. I don't need a man."

"Oh, I agree, dear," Harriet said. "But it's a splendid idea, even if I do say so myself."

"Don't seem quite fair, does it?" Alma Burton said from the other side of the quilting frame. "That a man can order a bride, but a woman can't do the same for a groom."

"Fair or not, that's the way it is," Nelda Harrison said.

Emma sighed as she threaded a needle. Yes, that's the way it was.

Matt hadn't seen Emma since the night of the town council meeting. He'd stopped by the café every night as usual. But yesterday she'd been shopping, and the day before that she was running errands. Now, according to Hallie and Ben, she was at some kind of ladies' meeting at church. Matt wondered if Emma was trying to avoid him.

He couldn't help but worry about her. He'd tried to talk to Sheriff Haynes about the situation with Harper. While the sheriff admitted he disagreed with what the town leaders were doing, they had to uphold the law. And if the town council voted to take the baby to Santa Fe, they would have to see that it was done.

Matt had heard plenty of grumbling around town. The men all liked gathering for coffee at Emma's. They were afraid raising a baby would be too much for her and she'd have to close down the café. There weren't many places in town where a man could get a decent meal and a cup of coffee, and none were as nice as Emma's, with the homey gingham tablecloths with matching curtains. The dining room in the Roswell Hotel was kind of uppity, and the hole-in-the-wall place next to the saloon down the street would get the men in mighty deep trouble if their womenfolk ever caught them there.

Not that there wasn't trouble now. Most of the wives, sisters, and mothers in town were hounding their men to pressure the council members into letting Emma keep the child. But together, those council members owned half the town. Harper himself had bought every spare parcel of land and property in Roswell, and it was difficult putting pressure on a man you owed money to.

Matt was beginning to question his own belief that Emma shouldn't have custody of Mandy. She wouldn't have to struggle to make a living like his mother had. Emma had a steady income, and she could hire people to help out. She loved the baby and would raise her well. Still, she'd been looking awful tired lately.

After finishing his afternoon rounds, he trudged back to the sheriff's office. He poured himself a cup of thick coffee, then took a seat outside, facing Emma's café. He propped his feet up on the horse rail and leaned back. He'd just watch her place until she got back.

Matt took a drink of the coffee and forced it down. He poured the rest out on the ground, then pulled his hat down to shade his eyes. It was getting near suppertime. Surely Emma would be back soon.

When he saw her emerge from the church on the corner and head toward the café, Matt was overwhelmed by a sense of relief. Hallie had told him the truth. She really was out.

When a loose board stopped the baby carriage, Emma fought to push the wheels over the uneven section. Matt rushed across the street to help. He lifted the carriage, baby and all, and set it down on the other side of the warped board. He tipped his hat. "Afternoon, Emma."

"Thank you for helping, Deputy," she responded with polite coolness.

"You're welcome." Matt pushed the carriage down the boardwalk. "She certainly seems to have enjoyed your outing."

Emma strolled beside him. "Yes, she did. We both did."

"You look good," Matt found himself saying. She seemed more rested than the last time he'd seen her. More relaxed.

"Thank you. I've been turning this whole situation over to the Lord. I'm also going to talk to a lawyer about legally adopting her."

Matt hoped the Lord would help Emma cope with whatever happened. He'd seen her church family reach out to her and believed they would support her, but he wasn't sure there was a lawyer in the county willing to go up against the town council.

"I can take it from here," Emma said.

Matt suddenly realized he'd pushed the baby carriage all the way to the café. "Let me help you over that hump in the threshold."

"Thank you," Emma said, opening the door and moving out of his way.

Once inside, she thanked him again and proceeded into the kitchen with Mandy.

"You're welcome," he called to her back. Matt strode out the door. Would he ever feel comfortable in Emma's presence again?

Chapter 5

Mandy fell asleep early that evening. Emma kissed her forehead as she laid her on the bed. How precious this child had become to her in such a short time. *Dear God, please let there be a way for me to keep Mandy. Don't let that windbag Harper have his way.*

That man should have been run out of town years ago. Emma couldn't help but wonder what his motives were in wanting to take Mandy away.

She called the lawyer Cal and Liddy had recommended, and he agreed to see her on Monday. She would ask him if he thought she could legally adopt Mandy, even though she had no husband.

Emma sent Ben and Hallie home, telling them she could handle the few remaining customers. As she tidied up the empty tables, Emma thought about how thankful she was that she at least had the means to take care of herself and Mandy. Since the railroad came in, Roswell had become a bustling little town, and Emma's business had thrived. She'd even tucked away a fair amount in a savings account over the last few years, enough that she could start over somewhere else if worse came to worst. But Roswell was her home. She had no relatives elsewhere. All of her friends and her church family were here. This was where she wanted to raise Mandy.

After the last customer left, Emma poured herself a cup of coffee. She wished Liddy and Cal had a telephone so she could call her friend. She was feeling quite lonesome. Matt hadn't come in after his rounds for several days, at least not when she was there. Of course she shouldn't miss him. But she did.

Emma rose to start closing up when the bell above the door signaled a late customer. Her heart skittered as Matt walked in.

"Any coffee left?" he asked.

"Sure." Emma poured him a cup. "You finished with your rounds?"

Matt sat at the table she'd just vacated and put his hat on one of the extra chairs. "Yes. It's quiet tonight."

Emma brought the coffeepot to Matt's table and poured herself a second cup. "That's good, I guess."

"Hopefully, it'll stay that way awhile. Sheriff Haynes took the train to Eddy this morning to testify in a trial there." He blew on the hot liquid in his cup. "Said he'd probably be gone the better part of a week."

A Promise Made

Emma sat across from Matt. But she didn't feel nearly as comfortable with him as she had a few weeks ago, and she found herself at a loss for what to say.

"Mandy asleep?"

"Yes." Emma smiled. "She had a very busy day. I took her to a quilting bee at church, and that little darlin' went from one woman's arms to another the whole time. Loved every minute of it, too."

"I bet she did. She's a charmer, that one."

Emma's heart warmed. "Yes, she is."

Matt cleared his throat. "How's your night going? Anything out of the ordinary?"

"No. Why?"

He rubbed his chin. "A few of the men in town are at odds with their wives over your decision to keep Mandy."

"I see." Emma set her cup down so hard the coffee sloshed over the side. "And you've come to talk me into giving her up?"

"No, Emma. I just want to try to protect you."

"From what? A few husbands who aren't man enough to stand up to Harper?"

"Some of them are really angry, Emma. Their wives aren't even talking to them. But they owe Harper money, and they can't afford to make him mad."

"Well, I don't owe Harper anything. And I don't care if I make him mad." Emma rose from the table and picked up the two cups, even though his was still half full. "I'm not going to change my mind, Deputy. You can go tell *that* to all those complaining men, *including Councilman Harper!*"

Matt stood and settled his hat onto his head. "Emma, I—"

"Good night, Deputy. I need to close up."

"Emma Hanson!" The front door was flung wide by Jed Brewster. Emma knew little about the man, except that he owned a small farm outside of town. But she'd heard rumors that he drank too much. From the way he was weaving as he stood in the doorway, Emma suspected he'd spent far too long in one of the saloons down the street.

"I hope you're happy," he bellowed, pointing a wavering finger at Emma. "You've caused a lot of trouble between my missus and me."

He wobbled toward the center of the room, but Matt put a hand against his chest. "Stop right there, Jed. You have no right to come into Miss Emma's establishment carrying on like that."

Jed stopped, but his belligerent hollering continued. "She's cashing—I mean cooshing—*causing* problems for half the couples in town. Just 'cause she won't let a married couple have that baby."

"I don't recall any couples in town volunteering to take the baby," Matt said.

"Now, you go on home, Jed."

The inebriated man glared at Emma. "Yes, well, I'd be taking that kid myself if I had anything to say about it."

Matt took Jed's arm. "Come on, it's time to go home. You need to sleep it off."

Jed jerked away. "No. I don't wanna go home. Laura's mad at me."

"I don't blame her. You smell like a still. How about I let you sleep in one of the cells tonight."

"I don't wanna go to jail."

"Well, you can come peaceable, or I can arrest you for causing a disturbance," Matt said, his hand hovering over the gun in his holster. "Your choice."

All the fight seemed to go out of Jed. His shoulders slumped, and he let the deputy lead him to the door.

Matt glanced back at Emma. "Be sure and lock up behind us. And if you have any problems, just put through a call to me, you hear?"

"I will," Emma said as Matt nudged Jed out the door.

Much as she hated to admit it, Emma was awfully glad Matt had been there when Jed came in. She wasn't sure how she'd have handled things if she'd been alone.

Jed's wife, Laura, was a sweet lady, and Emma sure hated to think that she and Jed were having trouble because of her. She didn't want to cause problems for any of the couples in town. But she couldn't let Mandy go. She just couldn't.

Emma climbed the stairs and checked on the baby. How precious she was with her eyes closed, breathing so peacefully. Emma twisted a little curl around her finger and felt its softness. *Oh, Annie. How beautiful she is. I wish you were still here for her. But I promised you I'd take her, and I'll do my best to keep that promise. With God's help she'll become the woman you would wish her to be.*

After church and then dinner at Cal and Liddy's, Emma spent some time resting and playing with Mandy.

The café was busier the next morning than it had ever been on a Monday. It seemed half the town showed up for breakfast or brunch. And not just her regular customers. Complete strangers came in, too. Gossip about the council meeting the week before must have spread to all the farms and ranches on the outskirts of town.

Emma couldn't break away from the rush to see Cal and Liddy's lawyer until midafternoon. When she did speak to him, he wasn't as reassuring as she'd hoped. He was going out of town the next day to represent a client at a trial, and he wasn't sure how long he would be gone. So he couldn't do anything right away, he said, even if there was anything that could be done. Still, he promised to check into the situation when he returned.

A Promise Made

Emma felt certain the town council would take things into their own hands before the lawyer got back. She left his office with a heavy heart, but as she walked back to the café, she reminded herself to leave the situation in God's hands. He would take care of everything.

When Emma opened the door to the café, she stopped in shock. The place was packed, every table occupied. But even stranger, all the men were seated on one side of the room, while their wives sat at tables on the opposite side. And each group was grumbling about the other.

The men barely glanced up when Emma entered, but the women surrounded her, gushing about how much they admired her for taking Mandy in. Emma was tempted to hightail it out of there, leaving the café in Ben and Hallie's hands.

"Afternoon, Emma."

She turned and saw Matt standing in the doorway. "Deputy."

He scanned the crowded room as the women resumed their seats and their mumbling. "I wondered why the streets seemed so deserted." He grinned. "Any problems?"

So far, none of the men looked like they were going to attack her. "Not yet."

Matt raised an eyebrow. "The air is a bit thick in here today, isn't it?"

Emma chuckled.

"That's a nice sound to hear again."

Emma shrugged. "Might as well laugh. Crying won't help anything."

"Deputy Carmichael is relieving me in about an hour. I'll come back then for supper."

"I'm sure I'll be fine, Deputy. No need for you to work overtime."

Matt raised an eyebrow and took his time looking around the room before heading to the door. "I'll be back."

After supper the crowd started to thin out. Emma breathed a sigh of relief. She felt utterly exhausted.

She padded into the kitchen, where Ben was finishing the dishes. Hallie came downstairs with a pajama-clad Mandy in her arms. When Emma took the baby, Mandy cuddled close. "Em-mama!"

Emma breathed in the fresh scents of lye soap and talcum powder. "You smell so sweet, Mandy baby. I haven't seen enough of you today."

"Sure was extra busy, wasn't it?" Ben said, putting away the roasting pan. "What's going on?"

Emma sat at the kitchen table, adjusted the baby on her lap, and took a sip of the hot tea Hallie set in front of her. "It seems the town is divided on whether I should keep Mandy or give her up. Mostly men against the women."

"Oh, that's not right," Hallie said, taking a seat across from Emma.

"No, it's not." Emma kissed Mandy on the top of the head. "But I don't know what to do about it."

"Not much you can do, Miss Emma," Ben said. "The way I see it, them husbands and wives are just gonna have to agree to disagree."

"Maybe once they get home, they'll talk it over." Emma rubbed her chin over the baby's soft hair.

The bell above the front door jingled, and Hallie peeked around the kitchen door. "I wouldn't count on that if I were you. A passel of men just came in. Want I should go take their orders?"

"No, thank you, Hallie." Emma rose, settled Mandy on her hip, and bustled out to the dining room.

"What can I get you fellows?" she asked the eight men who stood at the counter.

"We ain't here to eat," Homer Williams said. "We come here to try to talk some sense into you." He pointed at Mandy. "Why, just look at you. Trying to take care of a young'un and run a business at the same time. It's too much for one woman to do; can't you see that?"

"No, Homer, I can't. I'm taking care of everything just fine. And I do have help." She motioned for Hallie to come into the dining room. Then she handed Mandy to her and asked her to take the baby back to the kitchen.

"I refuse to discuss the subject of giving up Mandy," Emma said firmly. "Now, what can I get for you gentlemen? Mrs. McAllister brought in some real nice peach pies this morning."

"We're here for a meal," Harold Ferguson said. "Beatrice says she's not feeling up to cooking tonight."

"Nelda said the same thing," Jim Harrison said, glaring at Emma. "Said she wasn't much hungry. Well, no wonder, after all that tea and cake she ate here this afternoon."

The others started grumbling about their wives, too. Emma was tempted to tell them to take their business elsewhere, but these men were regulars, and she felt a little sorry for them. There wasn't much she could do, but she could at least feed them.

"The roast chicken is mighty tasty tonight. Any takers?"

Five of the men took seats at a couple of adjoining tables. The rest filed out the door, still grumbling.

Emma began to relax. "So that's five plates of roast chicken?"

"Make it six."

Emma spun around and saw Matt right behind her. He must have come in through the back door off the kitchen.

"You handled that very well," he whispered as he followed her to the kitchen.

Emma felt warmth creep into her cheeks. "Thank you." Her heart did its familiar somersault, and she wondered how long he'd been there. She tried not to show how glad she was that he'd come back like he said he would. With him in the café, maybe the rest of the night would pass calmly.

Emma dished out the plates of roast chicken, and the men ate their meals in relative quiet. Matt sat alone at the table next to theirs.

After the others left, he ordered dessert. Apparently, he intended to stay until she closed, and much as she hated to admit it, Emma felt safer with him there.

She poured Matt a second cup of coffee and sat across from him. "Thank you, Deputy."

"For what?"

He wasn't going to make it easy on her, and she couldn't really blame him. "For checking on me and Mandy, making sure we are all right, protecting us from the men of this town. . .even though you agree with them."

Matt set down his cup. "Emma, I'm not like those men."

"But you said yourself that Mandy would be better off with a married couple."

"And I still believe that."

Emma pushed herself away from the table and started clearing the one behind her. "You're off duty, aren't you? There's no reason for you to spend your time off making sure my night goes well. I'll just close early tonight."

"Emma, I don't mind—"

"I know." She shot him a withering glare. "But I do."

Matt stood. "I understand."

"Besides, I—" Emma caught herself before she told him she hadn't spent enough time with Mandy. That bit of knowledge certainly wouldn't make him change his mind about her situation. "I have a lot to do to get ready for tomorrow."

"I'll let you get to work, then." Matt paid for his meal, and Emma followed him to the door. "Tell Ben the food was delicious as always."

"I will."

"Good night, Emma."

Her heart twisted at the dejected expression in his eyes. She wondered if he felt as distressed as she did. He seemed about to say something more, but then he turned and walked out the door.

"Good night." She locked the door, flipped over the CLOSED sign, and pulled down the shade. This was one day she was glad to be done with.

Chapter 6

The next few days passed much the same for Emma. She was extremely busy with customers who were more than a little grumpy. . .all because she wanted to keep a promise.

When Liddy came in with her baked goods, she stared with raised eyebrows at the fifteen tables in Emma's café, all filled with people. "Appears you could use a little extra help."

Emma gladly accepted her offer. The two of them and Hallie had their hands full taking care of the crowd. Poor Ben worked triple-time to keep up with all the cooking.

Emma took orders with Mandy hoisted on her hip. The baby chortled at all the customers who talked to her and cooed at her.

At midafternoon, when the crowd finally left, Liddy let out a long sigh. "My goodness, Em! I should have brought more pies."

"If you had a telephone, I'd have called to ask you to bring more."

"Actually," Liddy said, "the telephone company has just started putting lines up out our way. As soon as they can hook us up, you'll be able to call me." She followed Emma into the kitchen with an armload of dirty dishes. "I wouldn't be surprised if every single person in town ate lunch here today."

"I think the only person I haven't seen lately is Harper," Emma said.

Liddy shivered. "Just the thought of that man makes my skin crawl."

Emma settled Mandy in her special corner of the kitchen. "I keep waiting for him to barge in here and take Mandy and deliver her to Santa Fe personally."

"Let him try," Ben said. "He'd have to get through me first."

"And me second," Hallie added. "We ain't gonna let him take this baby, Miss Emma."

"Bless you all," Emma said, grateful to God for such faithful friends. "But I think the sheriff's deputy is watching this place pretty closely. I sure am thankful we're right across the street from their office."

She looked at the new telephone on the wall. So far, she'd only used it for calls to the doctor. . .to check on Annie before she died. Still, she was glad she'd had it installed. "Even though my newfangled telephone doesn't get much use, it's comforting to know I can call the sheriff's office if I need to."

Hallie and Ben started on the dishes while Emma and Liddy straightened up out front. As Emma brought an armful of plates into the kitchen, she heard the distinctive peal of the telephone. It made one long and two short sounds to alert her that someone was trying to reach her. She set down the plates and crossed the room to the shiny wooden box hanging on the wall. She lifted the black earpiece from its hook and spoke into the cone-shaped mouthpiece. "Yes?" she said, both excited about receiving her first call and nervous about what the news might be.

"Miss Emma?" The woman's voice sounded soft and hesitant.

"Yes. Who is this?"

"It's Laura Brewster. I—I just wanted to apologize for my husband's outburst the other night. I hope you won't charge him with causing a disturbance in your café. When I got him out of jail, Deputy Johnson said you could, if you were of a mind to. But he's sobered up and he's real sorry."

Emma hadn't even thought about pressing charges against Jed. Matt had probably just said that to try to scare Jed into behaving himself. *He's not much of a man to let his wife apologize for him,* she thought as she heard Laura sobbing on the other end of the line.

"Don't cry, Laura. If Jed doesn't give me any more trouble, there's no need for me to charge him with anything."

"You mean it, Miss Hanson?" Laura sniffled. "Oh, thank you so much. I promise he'll act like a gentleman from now on."

Emma heard a jostling sound, then a sudden clunk. "Laura?"

"She's disconnected on her end, Emma," a familiar voice said.

"Beth? Is that you?"

"Yes, it is. Mrs. Brewster must have said all she wanted to."

"I guess so," Emma said, amazed at this new technology.

"Want I should ring her line?" Beth asked.

"No, thank you."

"All right. Have a good afternoon."

Emma placed the earpiece back on its hook and turned to the curious faces watching her from the table.

"What was that all about?" Liddy asked with a furrowed brow.

"Jed Brewster had too much to drink the other night, and he came in here to tell me I should give Mandy up."

"Manny up," the baby said from her corner. She grinned when the adults chuckled. "I hungy," she said, pulling herself up against the makeshift fence in the play area.

"I creamed her some potatoes just a few minutes ago, Miss Emma," Ben said. "She likes them that way."

Emma picked Mandy up and gave her a hug before settling her in her high chair. "Here you go, sweetie; let's get you some food."

"I'd better get on home and make sure my family has something to eat," Liddy said. She took her bonnet off the hook. "You be sure and lock up tight. Jed might not be the only one trying to cause problems for you. Wouldn't surprise me a bit if he was working for old Harper."

"That thought crossed my mind, too. Hopefully his wife has more influence on him than Harper does."

Liddy kissed the top of Mandy's head on her way out the back door. "I'm going to check with the telephone company to see when they think they'll be ready to install our telephone. It would be nice to be able to find out how you and Mandy are doing when I can't get to town."

"You just can't stand it because I have a telephone and you don't," Emma teased.

Liddy laughed. "Something like that. Actually, living out where we do, it'd be nice to know we could get hold of the sheriff's office or the doctor if we needed to. But what I'd *really* like is an icebox like you have."

"I am blessed, that's for sure," Emma said.

"So am I. But I do envy you sometimes."

"And I've envied you for your wonderful family."

"But now you have Mandy."

Emma choked back a sob. "I just hope I can keep her."

"Don't worry," Liddy said. "God will make sure everything comes out right."

"That's what I'm counting on."

That evening, Emma had Ben roast an extra cut of beef, preparing for the next rush. But dinnertime came and went, and almost no one showed up. It appeared the town was now staging a boycott of her place.

Emma sent Hallie home early and told Ben to put the meat in the icebox.

"It'll make a fine stew tomorrow." Ben took the beef out of the roasting pan, placed it on a wooden board, and cut it into stew-sized chunks.

Emma smiled. "It'll be our special of the day." As she started toward the front door to flip the OPEN sign around to CLOSED, Matt walked in.

"Anything left to eat?" he asked, hanging his Stetson on the hook.

"If you'd like roast beef, we have plenty."

"That'd be just fine." Matt took a seat at his regular table. "Slow night?"

"Very."

"You want I should fix a plate for the deputy, Miss Emma?" Ben asked from the kitchen door.

"Give the deputy a large portion, Ben. It'll be that much less to try to fit in the icebox."

Ben chuckled as he stepped back into the kitchen.

Emma poured Matt a cup of coffee. "I've only had a handful of customers this evening."

"Well, you had a lot in here for dinner. Maybe no one is hungry."

Emma shrugged. "Maybe."

Ben came in carrying a plate piled high with roast beef, carrots, potatoes, and gravy and set it in front of Matt. "Hope you enjoy it."

"I'm sure I will. Thank you."

Ben returned to the kitchen, and Matt looked up at Emma. "Why don't you sit a spell while I eat?"

"Might as well." Emma poured herself a cup of coffee and sat across from him. She took a sip. "I'm thinking of changing my hours."

"Oh?" Matt cut into the roast and forked a piece of meat into his mouth.

"I thought I might close for a few hours in the afternoon, then open back up for suppertime. That would give Ben and Hallie a break, too."

Matt swallowed his bite. "And it would give you more time with Mandy."

"Yes, it would."

"I think it's a great idea." Matt stabbed another piece of beef.

"I thought so, even before I started taking care of Mandy. But now I'm concerned that the town council could somehow use that against me, saying that raising a baby and running a business is too much for me."

Matt stared at her, his loaded fork in midair. "Is it?"

"No," Emma said sharply, tired of his incessant questioning of her ability to take care of Mandy and the café. "I guess I forgot who I was talking to. Why can't I remember that you're not on my side in this?"

"Emma, you're wrong about that. I just remember my mother trying to raise us alone—"

"And what if someone had decided to take you and your brothers away from your mother just because she was a widow?" Emma grabbed Matt's plate. "The meal is on me, Deputy. It's closing time."

She swung around and stormed into the kitchen.

Matt sat at the table with a forkful of beef partway to his mouth. He took the bite, but somehow it didn't taste near as good as the rest of the meal had.

Ben came though the kitchen door. "You need anything else, Deputy? Miss Emma took Mandy upstairs for the night and asked me to close up for her."

Matt took a last swallow from his cup. "No, thanks, Ben. I seem to have lost my appetite." He paid Ben for his meal.

Ben put the cash in the moneybox. "Miss Emma's had a rough week."

"Yes, she has," Matt said, putting on his hat. "But I wish she hadn't flown off like that. I wanted to let her know I'm going to be out of town for several days. I've got to take a prisoner to Lincoln."

"I'll tell her, Deputy."

Matt thanked Ben and made his way to the door. Then he turned back. "You watch out for her, you hear?"

"Oh, I will."

Matt clapped Ben on the shoulder. "I'll sleep better knowing you'll be keeping an eye on things."

"You have a safe trip," Ben said.

Emma came back downstairs to help Ben close up as soon as she was sure Matt had left. She shouldn't have been so rude to him. The way she'd practically forced him out of the café certainly wasn't very Christlike. Emma felt even worse when Ben told her Matt was going out of town for a few days.

"Don't you worry none about anythin' while Deputy Matt is gone," Ben said. "I promised to look after you and the baby."

"Thank you, Ben. And the Lord is going to take care of us all."

"Yes'm, He is."

They quietly cleaned up the kitchen and made preparations for the next day. After Ben went home for the night, Emma locked up. But she wasn't quite ready to call it a night. She brewed herself a cup of tea and prayed for forgiveness in treating Matt so badly.

Deputy Carmichael began taking all his meals at the café. Emma figured Matt must have asked him to keep an eye on her while he was gone. The young deputy was handsome and charming, if a bit shy. Emma was sure most of the unattached gals in Chaves County were scheming to change his single status.

Business returned to normal, for which Emma was grateful. She'd learned in the last few days that there was indeed such a thing as being too busy.

She was still contemplating the possibility of closing between three and five in the afternoon. That was when some of the ladies came in for afternoon tea, and Emma did feel a certain loyalty to them. But they could just as easily meet at the Roswell Hotel's dining room at that time of day.

That afternoon Beth Morgan, Myrtle Bradshaw, and several other ladies from church came in for tea.

"How is that little darling doing?" the doctor's wife asked.

Like a proud mother, Emma answered, "Growing every day and beginning to get into things. Would you like to see her?"

"We'd love to." Beth grinned.

Emma carried Mandy out front, and the little girl flew straight into Myrtle's arms. After getting a big hug, she went to each of the others at the table, securing her place in everyone's hearts.

"You know," Myrtle said, "anytime you need to run an errand and want someone to watch this pretty little thing, you just let me know."

"Me, too," Beth added. "At least, until I get married."

"How are your wedding preparations going?" Emma asked as she set cream and sugar on the table.

"Just wonderful. As a matter of fact, there's been a change in plans. He's coming here! He decided he wants to come out West to settle down."

"That's terrific, Beth." Emma was truly happy for her.

Mandy lunged from Opal Barber's arms into Emma's and laid her head on Emma's shoulder.

"She's quite attached to you, isn't she?" Beth asked.

"And well she should be," Myrtle said. "She loved Emma even before Annie passed away. I'll never forget the night you came and got her, Emma. She went straight to you and settled right down. She'd been fussy for me up until then."

"It'll be a shame if Harper gets his way and takes her away from you," Mrs. Barber said. Then she clamped a hand over her mouth.

"That would be a shame," Emma said, trying to put Mrs. Barber's mind at ease. "But I'm trusting in the Lord for that not to happen. I know He'll make a way for me to keep her."

"I wouldn't count on that, Miss Emma," a deep voice said. Emma swung around and saw Douglas Harper standing right behind her. "At least not unless you follow Miss Morgan's example and answer one of those advertisements for a husband." He chuckled.

Emma shook from head to foot. She wanted to tell that horrible man to get out of her establishment immediately, but she knew that wouldn't help her cause. She tamped down her anger and frustration and tried to speak calmly. "Did you come for afternoon tea, Councilman?"

"No, thank you. I just came to let you know that the folks in Santa Fe will be calling in a week or so with their final decision." He tipped his hat to the ladies at the table and sauntered out the door.

Emma sank into the nearest chair.

Myrtle poured Emma a cup of tea from the pot on the table. "That man makes chills run down my spine."

"What is it about him that has half the men in this town afraid to stand up to him?" Opal asked.

"At least *our* husbands don't agree with him," Myrtle said. She patted Emma's hand. "You can rest assured of that."

Emma smiled at the doctor's wife. "It does my heart good to know that."

"And hardly any woman in town is on Harper's side in this," Beth added, "except for those few who look down on a child from an unknown background. Everyone in our ladies' group is praying about it."

"I appreciate that more than I can say. I know God is listening."

"Still and all," Opal said, "it's too bad you don't have a husband. If you did, none of this would be a problem."

Chapter 7

Emma tossed and turned most of the night. She tried to tell herself that the town council must have changed their minds about letting her keep Mandy. But from the snippets of conversation she'd overheard from her customers, Harper seemed more determined than ever to try to take the child away from her.

Lord, please show me what You want me to do. She needed to stop worrying and truly leave things in God's hands. He had a plan. She just didn't know what it was yet.

Unable to get back to sleep, Emma trudged downstairs, hoping the "peace of God, which passeth all understanding" would overtake her in the still of the morning. While she was stoking the stove, she thought about Beth Morgan and her mail-order husband.

Emma snorted. "I certainly wouldn't want to answer an advertisement from a man I don't even know," she said out loud. "He'd probably want me to leave my business and move to where he lived." Beth's man had apparently decided to join her, but that wasn't the norm.

Then she recalled Harriet Howard's amusing comment about advertising for a mail-order groom. Emma chuckled to herself. Why not? Just because it had never been done didn't mean it couldn't be. That way, the woman could choose which letters to answer and respond only to the men who seemed to suit her.

Emma shook her head. She could never do that. She'd be the laughingstock of the town.

She poured herself a cup of tea and sat at the table. With a smirk tugging at her lips, she wondered what steps she'd take if she were to place such an advertisement. Lincoln and Eddy both had local papers, as did several towns in between. If she only advertised locally, she wouldn't be asking anyone to move terribly far from where he lived. And she could meet the applicants in person before she committed to one of them. Emma began to tingle with excitement as she considered exactly how she would word such an advertisement. . .if she were to write one. After mulling it over for a few moments, she dug a pen and a pad of paper from the stationery box she kept on a shelf by the staircase and jotted down some ideas.

She scratched out and rewrote several times, then finally settled on a paragraph she was sure would attract the right kind of man. . .if there were such a thing. As she read it over and over, she imagined men of strong moral fiber and firm Christian faith seeing this advertisement, believing the Lord Himself had led them straight to her—Emma Hanson of Roswell, New Mexico.

"You know, this could work," she told herself. If it didn't, she had nothing to lose. But if it did. . .she would have a husband. Mandy would have a father. And Harper wouldn't have a leg to stand on!

Emma rewrote the advertisement on a fresh scrap of paper, then copied it several times for the various newspapers she'd put it in. If she could get to the bank and have them draw payment drafts that morning, she could get the envelopes on the afternoon train to Hagerman and Eddy, and by stage to Lincoln and the smaller towns.

After closing the last envelope, she heard Mandy calling for Em-mama. Emma scampered up the stairs. She took the little girl out of her bed and swung her around, eliciting peals of laughter from the child.

"Oh, sweet Mandy. We're going to find you a daddy!"

After dressing herself and the baby, she hurried back downstairs and stuffed the letters into her apron pocket. She'd mail them as soon as business slowed down after breakfast.

If Ben was surprised to find her humming as she mixed the bread dough and set it to rise, he didn't say anything. But when Liddy arrived with her pie delivery, she pulled Emma to the side right away. "What's up with you?"

"Why, whatever do you mean?" Emma asked playfully.

"You're in a terribly good mood today. Did Harper pull up stakes and move away?"

Emma laughed. "I wish." Then, feeling that she had to tell *someone,* she decided to confide in her best friend. "I may have found a way to thwart his plans, though."

"Really? What is it?"

"I'm going to take Harriet's advice."

"Harriet?" Liddy appeared puzzled for a few moments. Then her mouth fell open. "Don't tell me you're thinking about advertising for a husband!"

Emma grinned. "I'm only going to put ads in the Lincoln and Chaves County papers, not the Roswell papers." She patted her apron pocket. "I plan on mailing these as soon as the breakfast rush is over."

Liddy put her hand over her mouth. "Oh, Em. Are you sure you want to do this?"

"According to the town council, I need a husband." She grinned. "Can you see Harper's face when I tell him that I found one?"

Liddy laughed. "I'll watch the café while you go mail those if you like."

"I think I'll take you up on that offer."

Emma made sure the customers who'd already placed their orders were served, then put Mandy into her carriage and walked out the door.

She strolled down the boardwalk, enjoying the sunshine. Her first stop was the bank. After getting the appropriate payment drafts for the different newspapers, she tucked each draft into its corresponding envelope. When she arrived at the postmaster's office, she handed Mr. Marley her stack. She held her breath while he gave them a once-over.

"You putting an advertisement in these papers, Miss Emma?"

"Yes," Emma answered without offering more information.

Mr. Marley nodded. "I don't blame you. It's certainly the way to go these days."

Emma felt heat rise in her face. Surely he didn't know what she was advertising for. "I hope so."

"My sister owns a boardinghouse up in Amarillo, and since she started advertising in the papers, she's seen a big increase in her business."

Emma cleared her throat. "That's wonderful."

"Hopefully, that'll happen for you. Although your café seems to be doing real well. I guess it don't hurt none to make sure." He dropped her envelopes onto the various stacks of letters behind him. "You have a pleasant day, Miss Emma." He leaned over the counter and grinned at Mandy. "And you, too, little girl."

When Emma returned to the café, she found Liddy taking orders as if she'd been doing it all her life. When she noticed Cal there refilling coffee cups, she said, "I'm sorry, Liddy. Did it get so busy you needed extra help?"

Liddy laughed. "No. I just forgot I was supposed to meet Cal at the Joyce Pruit store today. When I didn't show up, he came to find me."

"I was afraid she'd run away from home," Cal teased.

"He did track mud on my clean floor last night." Liddy winked at Emma.

"I promise I'll make it up to you," Cal said.

"I know you will."

Emma thanked them for their help, then watched them head for Joyce Pruit. Cal cupped a hand on Liddy's elbow, helping her along the uneven boardwalk. His head dipped close to hers, listening to what she was saying. Emma hoped she would have that kind of relationship with a husband one day—no matter how they might meet.

Emma hugged her secret to herself for the rest of the day. When she heard the whistle of the afternoon train, her stomach fluttered in excitement. Her ads were on their way. How long would it take before they came out in the papers? And how long would it be before she received her first response?

Hopeful excitement carried her through the rest of the day, and as she put

Mandy to bed for the night, she felt satisfied that she was doing all she could do to keep her. Just before she dozed off, she wondered what Matt would have to say about her advertisement.

Emma opened her eyes the next morning with a smile, listening to Mandy's soft breathing. She stretched leisurely, then suddenly remembered the ads. She sat straight up in bed, a wave of panic washing over her, making her wonder if she was going to be sick to her stomach.

What had she done? What was she thinking? Oh, why hadn't Liddy stopped her? Struggling for breath, she threw off the covers and gathered her clothes for the day. Maybe the letters hadn't gone out yet. Perhaps there was some kind of remorse rule about mail—that the postmaster had to hold all letters for a day before sending them on. Emma snorted. And maybe a prince would answer her advertisement! She put her hand on her chest and forced herself to take a deep breath.

Emma pulled on her stockings and cinched herself into her corset. *What kind of man would answer an advertisement like that anyway?* She tucked her shirtwaist between her petticoat and her skirt. *And how desperate will he think I am?*

Emma fell to her knees beside the bed. *Oh, dear Lord, please forgive me. I took things into my own hands instead of waiting on You. I'm so sorry.*

Mandy cried out, and Emma went to her bed. As she picked up the child and cuddled her, she realized that now she *had* to trust in the Lord to make everything all right. She certainly didn't know how to. She just hoped He understood.

Emma felt quite meek for the next few days. She went from praying that no one would answer the advertisement to praying that the right man would. In church on Sunday, she felt even more humbled when the sermon was about trusting in God. She acknowledged to the Lord, and herself, that she hadn't trusted enough. She prayed for greater faith that God would cause everything to work out for His glory.

After Sunday dinner, Cal took the children outside to check on the livestock while Emma and Liddy cleaned up the kitchen.

"What's wrong, Em?" Liddy asked. "Are you having second thoughts about the ads?"

Emma shrugged. "Am I that transparent?"

"Well, you aren't exactly humming today." Liddy poured coffee and motioned for Emma to sit down.

Emma sank into the chair across from her friend. "How could I have thought that was the answer? What would make me do such a silly thing?"

"I don't think it was silly. If you find the right man for you and Mandy this way, it will have turned into a blessing."

A Promise Made

Emma took a sip of her coffee, then put her cup down, twirling it around on its saucer. "And what if I meet the wrong man?"

"You don't have to answer any of the letters, you know."

Emma peered up at Liddy and grinned. "You're right. I forgot about that."

"That's why you put the advertisement in the paper. . .so you could have a choice. Just leave it in God's hands."

"Oh, I know He's the only One who can make things come out right. I have to remind myself that He's in control and quit trying to take it back from Him."

"We all have to remind ourselves of that. But when we do hand it over to Him, He turns everything to good in a way we never could. Remember how the Lord got Cal and me together? He even used you to get us started. Why, if you hadn't been blabbing your mouth about me to Cal—"

"That's the thanks I get for helping you two get together?" The women enjoyed a welcome laugh.

By the time she and Mandy got back home, Emma felt at peace. She still didn't know what to do, but she was convinced that God did.

After a cold supper, Matt tied his prisoner's hands and feet to a tree for the night. Horse thief Jack Carlson wasn't escaping on his watch if he could help it.

Matt threw a pile of sticks on the fire. The air was cooler up here in the foothills than down in Roswell.

"You ain't gonna live 'til morning," Carlson snarled. "My brother'll be here before dawn, so you better say your prayers."

Matt tried to ignore the man's taunts. Although most of his prisoner's cronies were in various jails across the territory, Jack's brother, Hank, wasn't. Matt had been on the lookout for Carlson's brother all day.

But the trip had been uneventful thus far. Matt uttered a prayer of thankfulness under his breath. Still, he wasn't going to let his guard down.

Leaning back against a nearby tree where he had a good view of the campsite, Matt kept a close eye on his prisoner until the man seemed to fall asleep. Then his thoughts wandered to Emma.

He couldn't stop thinking about what she'd said the night before he left. What if someone had decided his mother shouldn't be raising him and his brothers and tried to send them away? She would have fought with everything in her to keep her children, just as Emma was fighting now.

Emma and Mandy belonged together. He wished they belonged to him—that he could be both a family man and a lawman. Perhaps it was possible. After all, his duties weren't terribly dangerous. Most of the time he simply wandered up and down the streets of Roswell, making sure everything was quiet. . .which it usually was. The worst scrapes he'd encountered on the job were an occasional drifter cheating at cards or a drunken cowboy starting a fistfight.

For the first time, Matt began to seriously consider what it would be like to be married to Emma Hanson, to help her raise little Mandy. His heart yearned to make those two his family.

His thoughts were disturbed by a soft shuffling sound. Matt squinted at Carlson. The prisoner appeared to still be asleep. Telling himself it was probably just an animal, Matt shifted his position to try to get comfortable on the hard ground. He'd sure be glad to have this trip over with and get back to Roswell.

He heard a snap, as if someone had stepped on a twig. Every muscle in Matt's body tensed. It might not be anything more than a deer, but he couldn't be sure. He allowed his head to slump down, pretending he'd fallen asleep, but kept his eyes slightly open. He faked a small snore. Then, as silently as he could, he slipped the Colt .44 out of his holster and eased back the hammer.

Matt heard a crackle that sounded like leaves being crushed. He stayed perfectly still, his forefinger on the trigger.

Through the slits of his half-shut eyes, Matt saw on the ground a shadow creeping up from behind the tree he leaned against. The prisoner's eyes opened. Jack glanced at Matt; then his gaze shifted to a spot over Matt's shoulder.

With muffled whispering, a lone figure came around the tree Matt was leaning against and crept over to Jack. Matt barely breathed. The figure knelt in front of Carlson and began to untie his feet.

Matt aimed his pistol at the two men. "I'd stop right there if I was you," he said in his most menacing voice.

The figure turned, pulled a gun, and fired in one smooth motion. Hearing the *zing* of a bullet fly by his ear, Matt scrambled behind the tree. He shot at the dark figure. With a scream, the man grabbed his right forearm with his left hand. His gun flew into the air and landed in the dirt. The figure fell over, moaning with pain.

"You killed my brother!" Jack yelled.

"No, he didn't," Hank cried, holding the bloody arm close to his body. "But he might as well have. He got my shooting hand!"

Matt crept out into the open, his gun raised. "You're lucky that's all I aimed for."

Never taking his eyes off the two men, Matt gathered Hank's gun from the dirt, pulled more rope out of his saddlebag, and marched his new prisoner to a tree a few feet away from the first one. Hank hollered like a wolf when Matt pressed his injured arm against the tree trunk and wrapped the rope around his wrists.

"You just gonna let him bleed to death?" Jack asked.

Matt tightened the rope. "He'll be taken care of soon enough."

A Promise Made

Once both of the men were secured, facing in opposite directions, Matt checked Hank's hand. The bullet had gone straight through the palm, and although there was a lot of bleeding, it seemed to be a clean wound. Matt dug through his saddlebag, but found nothing that could be used as a bandage. He grabbed a clean shirt. After ripping it into pieces, Matt wrapped the man's hand as best he could. It would do until they got to Lincoln.

Matt didn't sleep a wink all night. When he wasn't thinking about his sudden brush with death, his thoughts returned to Emma. How foolish he'd been to entertain the idea of marrying her. Why, just moments ago he could have been shot dead. His job might be uneventful most of the time, but it would only take one bullet to make Emma a widow and Mandy fatherless again.

At first light, Matt found Hank's horse grazing near his own and the one he'd used to transport Jack. He untied the two men and retied them to the saddles, stringing the horses together.

Matt emerged from the Lincoln County sheriff's office, twisting his neck to get the kinks out. He'd brought Jack Carlson in safe and sound.

Sheriff Miller was pleased as punch that Matt had Hank in custody, too. Together, the two brothers had four outstanding warrants for their arrest. Their futures would be in the hands of a judge and jury soon.

Matt swung back into the saddle and headed down the street to the Lincoln Hotel. It was a small establishment, but it did have a dining room. He'd wash some of the dust off himself, enjoy a good meal, then get some much-needed sleep.

The warm bath eased his aches somewhat, but down in the dining room, after chewing on the toughest piece of meat he'd ever eaten and tasting one bite of lumpy mashed potatoes, he determined that Emma and Ben could out-cook whoever was in this kitchen.

Taking a last swallow of bad coffee, Matt admitted to himself that he didn't just miss the cooking. He missed the company at the café. He sure hoped everything was quiet in Roswell, and that no one else had given Emma a hard time while he was gone.

Matt wondered why Harper was so determined to place Mandy in an orphanage. He promised himself to look into that when he got home, but at the moment he was too tired to figure it all out. He headed upstairs to his room, yawning with every step.

By Monday, Emma figured her advertisement had been placed in at least a few of the local papers, but she realized it would be several days before she received any replies. Still, she began checking her post office box on Tuesday and felt relieved when she found nothing there.

Although her café kept her busy, things seemed pretty quiet around town. The sheriff was back, and he and Deputy Carmichael seemed to take turns eating meals with Emma. She wondered when Matt would be back but didn't want to ask anyone. Although she missed him, she convinced herself it was better that he was gone. She needed to accept, once and for all, that there was no future for her and Matthew Johnson.

Still, she did feel the need to apologize to him for being so rude the night before he left. He couldn't help how he felt.

Over the next several days, Emma checked the post office after each stage and train delivery. No replies to her advertisement appeared, and she didn't know whether to be relieved or disappointed.

She prayed for patience as she pushed Mandy's baby carriage back to the café. If a husband was in God's plan for her, He would see to it that the right man answered her advertisement—or that she would meet him in a more conventional manner—in His way and in His time.

After sleeping most of the day, Matt was ready to head back to Roswell. He bounded down the stairs and paid his bill, then braved the dining room for breakfast. Surely no one could ruin bacon and eggs. He placed his order and picked up a newspaper off the unoccupied table beside him.

First he caught up on the local news of Lincoln, then he scanned the Help Wanted section. A local rancher was searching for more hands. The hotel needed a new cook. *That's an understatement.*

The rotund waitress plunked down a coffee cup in front of him. He took a sip as he scanned the Personals. A young boy was searching for his dog. A church social was planned for the following week. Matt choked on his coffee when he read the next advertisement.

Husband wanted. Good Christian woman who runs her own business is looking for an upright, sober, faithful Christian man. Must like children. Please reply to Emma Hanson, Box 789, Roswell, Chaves County, New Mexico Territory.

When he finally got his coughing spell under control, Matt read the advertisement again. Guilt washed over him. What had Harper forced her into? He knew Emma wouldn't give up Mandy without a fight, but this? She could have her pick of men. As Matt read the advertisement one more time, a cold fear gripped him. What was Emma letting herself in for? Any type of man could answer that advertisement. And there were all types out there.

He threw coins onto the table to pay for the breakfast he no longer wanted, then grabbed his saddlebags and headed for the livery stable. He had to get back to Roswell as soon as possible—to warn Emma. . .and *try* to talk some sense into her!

Chapter 8

Emma took the envelope from Mr. Marley with trembling fingers. She went outside to open it, then quickly read the first reply to her advertisement. She didn't know whether to laugh or cry. The letter didn't indicate how old the man was, but he wrote that he'd outlived two wives and had ten children and eight grandchildren. He assured her he was "good for at least ten more years" and that he was a God-fearing man. Emma's innate sense of humor rescued her from disappointment. She tore up the letter and stuffed the pieces into her pocket.

It could be worse, she told herself as she strolled back to the café. *The letter might have been from a criminal.* She shivered just thinking about that.

"Em-mama!" Mandy greeted her with uplifted arms when she entered the café. Emma lifted the baby as Mandy added, "I luz you."

Emma hugged the child close. "I love you, too, my Mandy." *So much.*

The sun was just beginning to set when Matt returned to Roswell. He'd had a lot of time to think on the ride home, and he became more frustrated with each mile he traveled. Emma was one of the most intelligent women he knew. Surely she'd thought of the risks involved in putting that advertisement in the paper. At the same time, he was angry with himself. Emma was fully capable of keeping the promise she'd made to Annie, and he knew it. He needed to talk her out of this ridiculous mail-order scheme.

After cleaning up in his room at the boardinghouse, Matt checked in with Sheriff Haynes. He considered talking to him about Emma's advertisement but decided to wait until after he spoke with her.

Matt walked to Emma's café with long, purposeful strides. How many replies had she received to her advertisement? Did any of them sound promising? Had she already answered some?

The café was crowded when he entered, and he realized he'd have to wait to confront Emma. That wouldn't be difficult, he decided as his stomach rumbled in response to the appetizing smells that surrounded him.

He sat at his regular table just as Emma swung out of the kitchen, her arms loaded with plates from wrist to elbow. She delivered the orders to the table behind him. When she turned around, she stopped and stared at him.

Matt wasn't prepared for the tightness in his chest at the sight of her. His breath caught in his throat, and his heart started hammering. She seemed to be almost as glad to see him as he was to see her.

"Welcome back," she said as she wiped his table. "How'd it go?"

"Interesting," he said, thinking mostly about the copy of her advertisement in his shirt pocket. "How's Mandy?"

"She's wonderful. Growing every day." Emma rubbed her hands on her apron. "How was your trip?"

"Long. But everything went well." Matt noticed Emma was looking everywhere but at him and wondered why she was so distracted. "And how have things been with you? No problems?"

"None. Are you hungry? Or did you just stop by for coffee?"

I stopped by to tell you how crazy you are. But he couldn't say that. Not yet. He'd wait until he could talk to her alone. "I'd like some of whatever smells so good."

Emma grinned. "That's my new special, chicken and dumplings. It's been going over quite well."

"I'll have that. And a piece of pie, too, if you have any left."

"You're in luck. Liddy brought in an extra apple pie today." She darted off to the kitchen.

"You all right, Miss Emma?" Ben asked as he ladled the chicken and dumplings onto a plate and added a hot biscuit. "You look a bit flushed."

"I'm fine." Emma did feel flushed. She tried to blame it on the heat in the kitchen and rushing around, but in truth, she knew it was from seeing Matt. She was glad he was back, but she wasn't happy that her pulse still raced at the sight of him. Would she ever get beyond that?

Well, she'd have to. If she was ever going to have a life with another man, she would have to stop pining over Deputy Matt Johnson.

She took the plate from Ben and headed back to the dining room. Matt was reading a torn piece of paper, but he quickly stuffed it into his shirt pocket as she approached with his meal.

"Here you go." Emma set the plate down. "I forgot to ask what you wanted to drink."

"Coffee would be nice."

Emma filled his cup, then took the pot around to her other customers. She kept as busy as she could and tried not to think of how right it seemed to have him taking supper at her café again.

When Matt was nearly through with his meal, Emma brought fresh coffee along with his pie.

"You could give lessons to the cook at the dining room I visited in Lincoln," he said. "The sign outside the hotel states they serve the best food in Lincoln County. If that's true, I'm glad I live here in Chaves County."

"Why, thank you, Matt. Ben is certainly an excellent cook. I'm surprised he hasn't opened his own restaurant by now."

She was called away by one of her other customers, then spent several minutes with people paying their bills. By the time everyone had cleared out, Matt was finishing up his pie. Emma flipped the CLOSED sign around to face the street.

She shook the coffeepot. "There's one more cup left. Would you like it?"

"No, I'm fine. Why don't you pour it for yourself and join me? There's something I need to talk to you about."

Emma wondered what Matt could possibly "need" to talk to her about. She poured herself the last of the coffee and sat across from him. When Matt pulled out the piece of paper he'd been looking at earlier, her heart slammed to a stop.

He slid the paper across the table so she could get a good look at it. Sure enough, it was a copy of her advertisement. When Emma's heart began to beat again, she held her breath, waiting for Matt to speak.

His voice was low and steely. "Have you lost your mind, Emma?"

Probably.

"Do you have any idea what kind of man might answer this?"

I've been mulling that over.

"What made you do something so crazy?"

Finally, Emma found her voice. "I will not let Douglas Harper take Mandy away from me. He said if I had a husband there would be no problem. Well, I'm going to find one."

"This way? Emma, you haven't thought this through—"

"What other way would you suggest?"

"You could have your pick of men in this town, Emma. You must know that."

Oh? How about you, Deputy? You've been my pick for years. Emma shook her head. "Do you see anyone beating down my door to propose? Besides, even if someone were inclined to offer marriage, Harper would probably pay him to get out of town."

"How long did you request for these ads to run?"

That's none of your business, she wanted to say. "One month."

Matt groaned. "And how many responses have you received so far?"

Emma wasn't about to tell him there'd been only one. "Does it matter?"

"You could wire the newspapers and have them pull the advertisement," he suggested.

Emma straightened her shoulders and lifted her chin. "I could. But I won't."

Matt took a deep breath. "All right. But if you insist on going through with this, at least let me or the sheriff check out the responses and see if any of these men are wanted for any crimes."

Emma prayed for calmness. How dare he interfere in her personal life. Why should she let him have a say in who she picked for a husband? She could choose someone by herself quite well, thank you very much!

Besides, there was nothing to check out at present, since she'd already decided not to reply to the one response she'd received. But she wasn't about to tell Deputy Matthew Johnson that.

"The whole point in putting in the advertisement was so I could do the choosing. I assure you I will not answer any responses that sound suspicious." Emma chewed her bottom lip. "There is something you could do for me, however."

Matt reached across the table and touched her hand. "Anything. What is it?"

"I decided not to put the advertisement in the Roswell papers, so I would appreciate it if you would keep this to yourself."

He leaned back in his chair and snorted. "I won't be talking to anyone about this—other than the sheriff."

"There's no need for him to know."

"Emma, you gave your name and city of residence in that advertisement. It wouldn't be hard for someone to come here and check *you* out."

Emma's heart sank to her stomach. Why hadn't she realized that? Well, that was one more detail she needed God to help her with.

"Just let us check out—"

"I appreciate your concern, Deputy, but I'm ready to close up now." Emma stood and picked up the pie plate and fork.

Matt stuffed the clipping back into his pocket and crammed his hat on his head. He tossed some coins onto the table to pay for his meal and marched toward the door. "I am going to talk to the sheriff about this, Emma. Maybe he can reason with you."

Emma locked the door behind him. She'd never seen Matt so angry, at least not at her. Well, she wasn't very happy with him, either.

Matt stomped across the street to the office. Sheriff Haynes glanced up as he entered.

"You have to talk some sense into that woman," Matt said as he plunked down into the chair beside the desk.

"Oh?" The sheriff grinned. "And what woman is that?"

Matt handed him the advertisement.

Sheriff Haynes scanned the paper with a crinkled brow. "Why would Emma Hanson need to advertise for a husband? And why would she put her name right out there like that? Most of the men who place these kinds of ads just use their initials."

Matt pushed his hat back and rubbed his eyes. "She was in a panic over this town council thing. She's determined to keep Mandy, and she seems to think this is her answer."

The sheriff rocked back and forth in his chair, his brow smoothing. "Maybe it is."

"Marrying a complete stranger?" Matt shouted.

The sheriff chuckled. "You're worried about her, aren't you, son?"

"Of course I am. I'd be worried about any woman who did such a fool thing." Just not quite as concerned as he was about Emma, Matt admitted to himself.

"We could check up on those who respond."

"I already suggested that to her. But she doesn't want to hear anything I have to say on the subject."

Sheriff Haynes snickered. "I'll have a talk with her tomorrow."

"Thanks." Matt took a gulp of coffee. It tasted horrible, as usual. "I think I'm going to go home and get some rest."

"Good idea."

Matt turned back at the door. "Oh, and she seems to think that because she didn't put it in the Roswell papers, no one here will find out about it."

The sheriff nodded. "Well, the news won't come from me."

It didn't surprise Emma when Sheriff Haynes knocked on the kitchen door first thing the next morning, even before Ben arrived.

He tipped his hat. "Mornin', Miss Hanson. I was hoping to have a word with you before you opened up." He inhaled deeply. "That coffee sure smells good."

"Have a seat, Sheriff." She poured him a cup. "What can I do for you?"

"Well, with all due respect, I hope there's something I can do for you."

"Matt told you about the advertisement, didn't he?" Emma took a sip from her own up.

"He's right, you know. If you get any responses to that advertisement, you should let us check them out for you."

"Sheriff, did you offer to check out the advertisement Beth Morgan answered?"

"This is different."

"How so?"

The sheriff took a long drink of his coffee. "Beth chose to answer one person, and she might or might not regret it later. Maybe she should have come to us to check out that man first. But, Emma, by putting an advertisement in the paper yourself, you seem to be asking for trouble."

Emma motioned to the fenced-off area where Mandy was playing. "I'm determined to keep that child, Sheriff. And having a husband will make that possible."

"But, Emma, you want the best man to help raise her, don't you?"

"Of course I do. And I'm trusting that the Lord will send the right one."

"I believe God can do that. My problem is that you may think the wrong one is the right one. My job is to protect you. So just let me check out the letters before you read them. Men can be quite deceptive, and the Lord wouldn't want you to be misled."

Emma didn't want to tell him she'd destroyed the only response she'd received so far. But if other letters came in, she didn't want the sheriff, or his deputies, to inspect them before she had a chance to read them.

She watched Mandy playing with a rag doll Liddy had made her. *Lord, please help me know how to handle this.*

"So far there haven't been any letters I would consider answering," she said.

The sheriff drank his coffee in silence.

Certain she would never hear the end of it if she didn't agree, Emma finally said, "But if any interesting ones come in, I promise I'll show them to you."

Sheriff Haynes raised his cup. "Fair enough. And if you get any peculiar ones, you might think about bringing those over, too."

"I'll think about it."

He drained his cup and stood. "I trust you'll make the right decision. Deputy Johnson is certainly going to be relieved."

She saw the sheriff out, confident that she was doing the right thing. But she didn't like the idea that Matt might be gloating over her change of mind.

Chapter 9

"Mornin', Miss Emma," Ben said as he entered the kitchen. "Saw the sheriff leavin'. There ain't been no problem, has they?"

"No, Ben," Emma assured him, still mulling over her acquiescence to the sheriff's offer. "Everything's fine."

"That's good." He put the biscuits Emma had just cut into the oven. Then he started slicing bacon.

Emma took Mandy to the front and unlocked the door. She tickled the child on the way there and laughed at her giggles. No matter how gray the day seemed, all she had to do was cuddle Mandy close and the day suddenly brightened. How she loved this child!

She kept Mandy with her while she took her first few orders, but when business began to pick up, she settled the little girl in the kitchen with her toys. Hallie and Ben always gave her plenty of attention while they worked in the kitchen. No one could say Mandy wasn't well taken care of, even when she didn't have Emma's complete attention.

Matt entered the sheriff's office yawning.

"Morning, Deputy," Sheriff Haynes greeted him. "You don't look like you slept very well last night."

Matt took off his hat. "Kept worrying about that headstrong woman across the street."

"Well, I had a talk with her this morning."

Matt's heart jumped. "Did she agree to bring all the letters to us?"

Sheriff Haynes drummed his fingers on the desk. "Not exactly."

Matt slapped his hat against his thigh. "Stubborn woman," he muttered.

"Now hold on. No need to get riled up. She did agree to let us check the ones she might respond to."

"That's something, I guess." Matt knew he should feel better. But he didn't. "Did she give you any of the letters?"

"No. Said there hadn't been any she wanted to reply to."

Matt released the breath he'd been holding.

"I've been thinking, though," the sheriff said. "With her name and the town in the advertisement, anyone could come check her out."

Matt's stomach started to burn. That thought had kept him awake half the night—until he'd found himself praying about it. After he asked God to watch over Emma, he'd finally drifted off to sleep.

"I think maybe we'd better keep a closer eye on her place," the sheriff said.

"Good idea," Matt agreed.

"Shouldn't be too hard." Sheriff Haynes grinned. "She has the best food in town. Now I know why you spend so much time over there."

That's what I've always told myself. Deep down, Matt knew there was much more than good food that kept him going back to Emma's café. He'd been fighting his attraction to her for years. He just couldn't let himself act on his feelings.

But now she was determined to find a husband. And he was going to have to accept that fact, whether he liked it or not. At least he could try to make certain she didn't pick the wrong kind of man. Trouble was, he wasn't sure there would be a right kind for her. To his way of thinking, no man was good enough for Emma Hanson.

Matt noticed the sheriff smirking at him. What had they been discussing? Oh, yes. Food. "After tasting 'the best food in Lincoln,' it was nice to get back to Emma's café. I won't mind checking in a little more often."

Sheriff Haynes smiled. "I didn't think you would. It's just too bad the town council is being so narrow-minded about Annie's child."

"You know, we've both had a firsthand look at how well Emma's taking care of Mandy. At the next council meeting, we could assure the council members of how well they're both doing."

"We could do that. But I wouldn't count on it changing minds. Part of the problem is what they consider the baby's 'questionable background.' Just between you and me, I think some of those men might be wondering if they could be that child's father. They'd want to get her out of town before she grows up to look like them."

Matt had never thought of that.

"Truth is, Mandy looks just like her mama," Sheriff Haynes continued.

"Even if she did grow up to resemble someone, there's no way of knowing for sure who the father was. Can't they see that?"

"Fear doesn't reason, Matt. That's why we need to keep a watchful eye on Emma. She could be in as much danger from a councilman as she might be from an unknown suitor."

"I could use some breakfast. Mind if I take the first watch?"

"Go ahead. I'll go over at noontime."

Emma saw Matt crossing the street toward her café. Was he coming to gloat because she'd agreed to let the sheriff do some checking?

A Promise Made

He took off his hat when he entered the café. Since his usual table was taken, he chose a seat near the kitchen. "Good morning, Emma. Could I get some flapjacks and bacon, please?"

"Coming right up." Emma poured Matt's coffee, then left to give Ben the order.

When his food was ready, she brought it out with a tub of butter and a small pitcher of syrup. Setting it all down in front of him, she steeled herself for any remarks he might make.

"Thank you." He began to spread butter on his pancakes. Apparently, he wasn't going to rub it in.

Emma busied herself with filling the other customers' cups of coffee.

Matt finished his meal and paid for it. "Have a good day, Emma."

"You, too, Deputy." She breathed a sigh of relief when he walked out the door without saying a word about the advertisement.

The rest of the day went smoothly. At midmorning, when Liddy brought in her sweets, she coaxed Emma into taking a break. Since business had thinned out, Emma brought Mandy out and held her while she enjoyed a cup of tea with her friend.

"Oh, Em, she's growing so fast," Liddy said, watching the baby bounce on Emma's lap.

"She's going to be walking any day now. She pulls herself around the play area already."

Mandy bobbed her head and chortled as if she knew exactly what Emma was saying. Liddy's two-year-old son reached out and touched Mandy's foot.

"Your baby is growing up, too," Emma said.

"He certainly is." Liddy watched her toddler playing with Mandy's foot. Mandy giggled at the little boy's attention, and he laughed along with her.

"Oh, Liddy, wouldn't it be wonderful if they married each other when they grew up?"

Liddy gazed at the two children. "It'd be a blessing for us, that's for sure. Speaking of marriage, have you received any responses to your advertisement yet?"

"Just one. I tore it up." As Emma told about the letter, Liddy pursed her lips, obviously trying hard not to chuckle.

"Go ahead and laugh. It's what I deserve for doing such a silly thing."

"I'm sorry, Em. I'm sure you're going to get some wonderful answers soon."

Emma rubbed her temple. "Matt found my advertisement in a paper in Lincoln. He told the sheriff about it, and he came to see me. I promised to let him check out any letters I might consider answering. Assuming I get any more."

"That's a good idea." Liddy took a sip of tea. "What was Matt's reaction to the advertisement?"

"He seemed angry."

"That's interesting."

"Liddy, don't read anything into it. There's nothing there." Emma changed the subject. "How are Amy and Grace doing?"

"Really well. They're such good girls. They'll be a lot of help with the new—" Liddy clapped her hand over her mouth.

"Liddy? Are you expecting?"

She lowered her hand and whispered, "I haven't even told Cal. Don't tell a soul, promise?"

"Of course I won't. Oh, Liddy, I'm so happy for you!" Cal and Liddy had proven how much they could love each other's children, and Emma was thrilled they would now have one of their own to add to the mix.

"I guess I'd better plan a really nice meal tonight, so I can tell him and the children before I blurt it out to anyone else." She grinned at her little boy. "Come on, son, let's find your daddy so I can get home and start cooking."

After Liddy left, Emma asked Ben to watch the front so she could check her mail. Not bothering with the carriage, she carried Mandy the few blocks to the post office.

Her heart skittered when she was handed four letters. She'd wait until evening to read them. Who knew? Maybe one of these was from the man the Lord was sending into her and Mandy's life.

Sitting on the porch outside the sheriff's office, Matt watched Emma come out of the post office and cross the street with Mandy in her arms. She held envelopes in her hand. Were they answers to her advertisement? His chest tightened. He crossed the street and headed down the boardwalk toward her.

He tipped his hat. "Looks like you got some mail today."

Mandy grinned at him and giggled. She was an adorable baby; no doubt about it.

"A little."

That was it. Nothing more. He tipped his hat again. "Guess I'd better get back to work." He tweaked the little girl's nose. "Good-bye, Miss Mandy."

"Bye-bye." Mandy waved at him.

"See you for dinner, Emma." Matt crossed the street once more. If she'd received answers to her advertisement, Emma wasn't telling. He'd just have to wait and see if any of them were interesting enough to check out.

The rest of the day, Emma's spirits were high, and she often found herself patting the letters in her pocket. She would read them that night and see if any were promising enough to answer. She had to keep her thoughts on those letters.

Otherwise, they kept returning to the deputy who sat across the room eating his supper.

She knew he was curious about the letters, and she had expected him to ask if they were replies to her advertisement. But to Matt's credit, he hadn't mentioned them. And she hadn't volunteered any information.

As she was bustling around trying to get everyone waited on, she heard a loud cry from the kitchen. She and Matt got there at the same time. Hallie was holding a crying Mandy.

"I don't know what's wrong, Miss Emma. I was feeding her supper and she just puckered up and started crying."

"She did that earlier today, too." When Emma took Mandy, the baby's cries eased up for a moment. But when she tried to give the baby a spoonful of food, she started crying again. Emma stuck a finger in her mouth, being careful to miss the four front teeth. Before she could check out her back gums, Mandy jerked her head away and cried harder. "I think she may be cutting a new tooth." Emma wondered if Annie had gone through this same fussiness with Mandy when her first four teeth came in.

When Mandy saw Matt, she stopped crying, hiccupped, and reached out to him.

Matt appeared a little flustered as he took her, but he grinned broadly when she buried her head in his shoulder.

"Well, I'll be." Ben chuckled.

"I'll take her, Matt," Emma said, reaching for the baby. "You need to get back to work." But Mandy turned away from Emma and switched to Matt's other shoulder.

Matt's smile broadened. "I'm fine. Let me hold her awhile. I don't mind. Really."

Hallie reached into the icebox and chipped off a piece of ice. She wrapped it in a clean cloth and gave it to Matt. "See if she'll suck on this. It might ease her some."

Emma wasn't sure what to do. She wanted to be the one to comfort Mandy, but at that moment the little girl seemed to want Matt. As soon as the last few customers left, she would start closing up. On second thought, she could put the CLOSED sign out now. After all, it was her business. If her child needed her, she'd just lock the door.

Matt, Hallie, and Ben seemed to have things under control in the kitchen. "I'll close up as soon as those last two people leave."

Matt took a seat at the kitchen table and patted Mandy on the back. "She'll be fine, Emma. Go take care of your customers."

Mandy closed her eyes and smiled. Emma slipped out to the front. If she didn't know better, she'd think that child had staged the whole crying bit just to get into Matt's arms. She chuckled to herself. Maybe she should take some lessons from the baby.

She flipped the OPEN sign around and locked the door. She would let her last customers out when they were ready, but she wanted to make sure she didn't get any others. Before she could ask if they needed anything else, the Harrisons approached the counter, ready to pay.

"Is the baby all right?" Nelda asked.

"She's fine. Just teething. But I'm closing up early so I can try to ease her gums."

"It's time we were headed home anyway," Jim said, taking his change.

Emma saw them out, then locked the door and returned to the kitchen.

Mandy was fast asleep in Matt's arms. With his eyes closed, he rocked her back and forth. Ben and Hallie were quietly cleaning up the kitchen, with Hallie humming softly. Emma stopped in the doorway and soaked up the peacefulness of the scene. She hated to disturb it.

She touched Matt's shoulder gently. "It's all right," she whispered. "I can take her now."

His eyelids flew open and he cleared his throat. "She's fine for the moment. Do you want me to carry her upstairs?"

"It might be easier that way, Miss Emma," Hallie said. "She sure seems to be resting good."

Emma shrugged. "All right. Follow me. I'll get her bed ready."

She climbed the stairs ahead of Matt and turned down Mandy's covers. After he lowered Mandy into the crib, Emma covered her and bent to kiss her forehead.

She was almost surprised when she turned around and found Matt waiting for her. She'd expected him to hightail it downstairs, as he'd done the last time. Leaving the door to the apartment open so she could hear if Mandy cried out, she went back down the stairs, Matt close behind her.

As they reached the bottom step, Emma said, "Thank you, Matt."

"You're welcome. She's a sweetheart, isn't she?"

"I think so. Would you like a cup of coffee before you go?"

"No, thank you. I've been having trouble sleeping lately. I think I'll pass."

Matt told Ben and Hallie good night, then headed for the back door. Emma followed.

"See you tomorrow," he said. "I hope Mandy sleeps well."

"So do I. Thank you again."

"It was my pleasure. I've never put a baby to sleep before." He settled his hat on his head and tipped the brim to her. "Good night."

Ben and Hallie took off for home, and Emma headed back upstairs. She readied herself for bed, then opened the pack of letters and started reading. After a few minutes, she set them on her bedside table. It was hard to concentrate on what any of them said when her thoughts kept going back over the evening.

Emma couldn't get the picture of Matt holding Mandy out of her mind. Somehow she knew it would be with her for a very long time.

Chapter 10

Mandy slept fitfully that night. First thing the next morning, Emma placed a call to Doc Bradshaw. She was sure Mandy was probably just teething but wanted to make certain. He told her to come right over.

Emma left the café in Ben's care. The morning air felt cool; fall was coming soon. She'd have to buy warmer clothes for Mandy before long.

"Oh my, how she's growing," Myrtle exclaimed as she let Emma in. "You're doing an excellent job."

"Thank you. She's a precious baby. But she hasn't been feeling well lately, so I wanted to have Doc check her out."

"There's just one patient ahead of you. He should be finished shortly." Myrtle reached out to Mandy. "Do you think she'll let me hold her?"

Mandy answered by reaching out her hands to the woman.

"How sweet she is." Myrtle hugged her close.

Emma watched Mandy play with Myrtle's collar. "She's a wonderful baby. I'm honored that Annie trusted me to raise her."

Myrtle lowered her voice as if there were someone else in the room to overhear. "You did see the notice in the paper that there's another council meeting called for this Monday, didn't you?"

"No. I haven't had time to read the paper much lately. Surely they wouldn't hold a meeting about Mandy's future without officially notifying me." Emma's heart started beating hard.

"I don't know. But I wouldn't put it past Harper." Myrtle bustled into the parlor to get the newspaper and showed Emma the article. "If I hear anything about a change of agenda, I'll let you know."

"Thank you."

Mandy started fussing and reached for Emma. Emma took the child and jiggled her in her arms. "It's all right, baby. Doc will see you soon."

"I'll do that right now," Doc said as he came out of his office with his other patient. "Take her on into my office, Emma. I'll be right with you."

Emma had barely sat down before Doc came in. "Now, what seems to be the problem with this young'un?"

"I think she's cutting some teeth, but I'm new at this, so I wanted to check with you to make sure it's not something else."

"Well, let's find out."

Emma held Mandy while Doc checked her over. When he was finished, he confirmed that she was indeed teething, but otherwise she was fit as a fiddle. "She's flourishing in your care, Emma. Annie would be very pleased."

Tears sprang to Emma's eyes. "Thank you. That means a lot to me."

Doc Bradshaw cleared his throat. "You can try using a little vanilla extract on those gums." He went to his medicine cabinet and handed her a small vial. "If that doesn't ease her, try this. It's called paregoric. Put a tiny drop of it on a clean rag and try to rub it on her gums. It should ease her until the teeth cut all the way through. Don't be surprised if she sleeps a little more than usual."

"Thank you, Doc. What do I owe you?"

"Oh, I'll bring Myrtle over to the café for a meal one of these days; how's that?"

"That would be fine," Emma said, bundling Mandy back up. "I'll be expecting you."

She started back to the café, relieved that Mandy was all right except for the painful teething she was going through. Her thoughts were so focused on the baby, she didn't see Harper crossing the street until she almost bumped into him.

"Miss Hanson, I see you've come from the doctor. Is anything wrong with the child?"

Emma was sure he would latch on to any reason at all to think she wasn't taking care of Mandy. "She's doing beautifully. She's teething, and Doc gave me something to make her more comfortable."

"Oh? I'm sure that isn't pleasant." Harper reached out to cup Mandy's cheek with his hand. She must have thought he was handing her something to chew on because she turned and chomped down on his thumb.

"Ouch!" Harper howled. "You little minx."

Mandy started crying. Emma gathered her closer. "I told you she was teething, Mr. Harper. Now you've made her cry. If you'll excuse us, I need to get some medicine on her gums."

Emma rushed along the boardwalk, relieved to get away from the man. When she reached the café door, she looked back to see Harper, his meaty thumb in his mouth, marching toward Doc's place. Emma admonished herself for not feeling bad for the man. Hard as she tried, she couldn't work up any sympathy for him.

Matt walked out of the sheriff's office and looked down the street. He saw Emma run into Harper. The revulsion he felt at seeing the man standing so close to Emma and the baby made him start barreling down the boardwalk.

When he saw Harper touch the baby, a desire to protect Mandy and Emma hit him with such force he almost started running. But when Harper howled, it was quickly apparent who had the upper hand. Matt tried to contain the laughter that fought to burst forth as he realized Mandy had bit the man. When he saw the ugly expression on Harper's face as he yelled at Emma and Mandy, the urge to laugh changed quickly to an itch to grab that menace by the neck.

Matt lengthened his stride, but Emma seemed to have everything under control before he was halfway to them. She took off down the other side of the street as Harper headed in the opposite direction.

Emma was quite a woman. And it looked like Mandy was going to hold her own in this world, too. Matt chuckled as he entered the café for breakfast.

He caught the smell of vanilla when he peeked into the kitchen. Emma was trying to apply something on a cloth to Mandy's mouth. The baby smiled when she saw Matt standing in the doorway, which enabled Emma to get the cloth back to where it needed to be.

"There! That should make you feel better soon."

"Shouldn't you put some kind of disinfectant on her, too?" Matt tweaked Mandy on the nose.

"I beg your pardon?" Emma put the top back on the bottle of vanilla.

"Well, you never know what germs biting Harper might have exposed her to."

The corners of her mouth curled upward. "You saw that?"

Matt nodded. "And heard the yowl."

"Oh, wasn't that priceless?" Emma chuckled. Her laughter ignited Matt's, and soon they were holding their sides, with Mandy giggling right along with them, as if she knew what was so funny. Emma brought Ben and Hallie up-to-date between gasps.

When the door to the dining room opened and Beth Morgan peeked around it, they tried to get their laughter under control.

"Miss Emma?" Beth said hesitantly. "You have several customers out here. Would you like me to take their orders?"

"Oh, that's sweet of you, Beth." Emma handed Mandy to Hallie. "But no need; I'll be right there."

Matt slapped Ben on the shoulder. "I'll save Emma from having to take my order. How about some pancakes and bacon for me, Ben?"

"Comin' right up, Deputy." Ben began stirring the bowl of batter on the counter by the stove.

A few more giggles managed to escape as Matt followed Emma out the door and took a seat at his usual table. "That's some child you've got there."

"She's very intuitive, isn't she?" Emma grinned, then went to check on her other customers.

A Promise Made

Matt ate his breakfast, snickering every so often as he watched Emma go about her business.

Emma chuckled off and on all day, every time she remembered the look on Harper's face when Mandy took a chunk out of his thumb. She hoped the child didn't get sick. He'd probably make an issue about it at the meeting on Monday.

The vanilla made Mandy smell wonderful, but the poor little thing was still fussy, so Emma decided to use the paregoric and put her down for a nap.

It wasn't until the afternoon lull that Emma remembered her letters. She ran upstairs to get them. On the way she stopped to check on Mandy. The medicine seemed to have worked, as she was sleeping soundly, like Doc said she would.

Emma sat at a table in the dining room with a cup of tea and started reading the letters. Two of the respondents asked if she would be willing to relocate her business, and one wanted to know what kind of business she owned. The last one sounded sweet and sincere, but the sender wanted her to move to a ranch near Eddy to help him raise his five children. None of the letters struck a chord in her.

The sheriff came in just as she finished reading the letters. He sat across from her. "Anything there we need to check into for you?"

Emma shook her head. "There's one I'll reply to, but only because it seems the right thing to do. I won't be asking him to answer."

"Either way, it'd be best if you'd let us check our wanted files."

Why not let the sheriff's office do a check, even if it was on someone she didn't intend to continue a correspondence with? She picked up the letter she'd like best and slipped it out of the envelope, then handed the envelope to the sheriff. She tucked the letter, along with the other three, back into her apron pocket. "All right."

He studied the return address. "I'll get it back to you as soon as I can."

"That's fine." There was no rush as far as she was concerned, but Emma didn't tell the sheriff that. She left him to his coffee and went upstairs to check on Mandy.

The baby was still sleeping peacefully, and Emma was relieved that her pain had eased enough for her to sleep soundly. Leaving Ben and Hallie in charge, she slipped out the back door to make a quick trip to the post office. She was pleased to find four more responses waiting for her.

She entered the café and shuffled through the envelopes. There were two from the Lincoln area, one from Eddy, and one from Hondo. She stuck them in her skirt pocket and headed for the kitchen.

During the evening lull, she pulled the letters out of her pocket and tore open one of the envelopes. It was from a rancher near Hondo. He couldn't leave his ranch, but maybe she could get someone to run her business and join him. *"It sure is lonely out here."*

She'd felt lonely, too, before she started taking care of Mandy. But Emma didn't want to leave Roswell.

The next letter was from a man in Eddy. He ran a livery stable and wondered if Emma might want to merge her business into his. His stilted wording gave her the impression he wanted a career partner more than a wife.

One of the men from Lincoln asked all kinds of questions. Was she a good cook? How many children did she have? What kind of business did she run, and how many people would it support? She had to give him credit. He wanted to understand what he might be getting into, same as she did.

Emma blew the bangs off her forehead. None of the letters appealed to her enough to answer. But she'd keep them, just in case. They might be the best of the lot—or the last.

Matt knew Emma didn't see him walk in. She was too interested in the mail she was reading. She held several letters, and one seemed to interest her more than the others.

"Emma?"

She glanced up at him and then back down at the letter, folding it and sliding it back into its envelope. A delicate color spread across her cheekbones. "What can I get you, Deputy?"

"Whatever Ben has ready will be fine." He took a seat across from her and reached into his shirt pocket, pulling out the envelope the sheriff had asked him to bring back to her. "Sheriff Haynes said to tell you this one is all clear."

Emma took the envelope and added it to her stack. She slipped all of the letters into her apron pocket. "Thank you."

"He also said you should let us know whenever you need anyone else checked out."

"I'll do that."

Matt watched her go to the kitchen, wishing he knew what was in the letters she seemed to be guarding so closely. Had someone captured her interest?

The bell above the door jingled, and he looked up to see Douglas Harper enter, his thumb thickly wrapped in gauze. Anger welled up in Matt. If it weren't for Harper, Emma wouldn't have put that advertisement in the paper.

The councilman headed straight for the kitchen, but Matt stood to halt his progress. "Anything I can help you with?"

"I need to talk to Miss Hanson." He took another step toward the kitchen.

Matt stopped him again. "She'll be right out. She's bringing me dinner."

Harper kept walking. Matt moved to block the kitchen door just as Emma flung it open. She bumped into Matt and he lost his footing for a moment, knocking him into Harper. The banker held up his bandaged hand to ward Matt off. It didn't work. As Matt righted himself, his shoulder caught Harper's thumb and bent it back. Harper yelped in pain, then uttered a string of expletives.

"Mr. Harper!" Matt cried. "I realize you're hurting, but you need to apologize to Miss Hanson for using foul language in her presence and in her establishment."

"Apologize? To her? I got this injury because that brat she's raising bit me! She's the one who owes me an apology."

Emma set down the tray she'd managed not to drop. "I apologize for Mandy biting you, Mr. Harper. But I can assure you it wasn't intentional on her part. You did put your thumb in close proximity to her mouth, and teething babies like to chew."

Matt put his hand on the councilman's shoulder, desperate to get him out of Emma's café. "Come on, Harper. I'll walk you over to Doc's, and we'll have him check out that thumb."

Harper jerked away from Matt. "I've already seen Dr. Bradshaw about this injury." He pulled a piece of paper out of his pants pocket. "As a matter of fact, I came over to give Emma this bill. Since the child in her care bit me, it only seems fitting that she pay for my treatment. However, since I have to have my injury rechecked now, I will bring the total bill by later." He tossed the receipt on the counter, then lumbered out the door, holding his bandaged thumb.

"Why, that beats all." Matt shook his head. "He expects you to pay for him practically inviting Mandy to bite him?"

"Don't worry about it." Emma took his plate off the tray and set it on his table. "Eat your dinner while it's still hot."

"But—"

"It's all right. Mandy is my responsibility, and she did bite him. I'll pay Doc." She freshened the coffee in his half-empty cup. "Besides, the expression on his face will be worth every penny."

Matt chuckled. "You're right. In that case, I'll help pay the bill."

Emma's smile faded. "I don't think this will help my cause, though. Harper is going to be more determined than ever to take Mandy away."

She reached into her apron pocket and pulled out the letters. She slid each one out of its envelope and handed all the envelopes to Matt, except the one he'd brought back to her. "Could you have the sheriff check these out, please?"

Matt's heart seemed to dive into his stomach. This was what he'd wanted, wasn't it? To be able to check out the men who answered her advertisement? Actually, he'd been hoping no one would respond. Even though he knew some would, he wasn't the least bit happy about it. He took the envelopes. "Certainly."

Emma left him to wait on a couple of late customers. Matt peered down at his plate. Everything smelled delicious. But for some reason, his appetite had disappeared.

Chapter 11

Matt's appetite didn't improve much over the next few days. The stack of letters Emma brought back from the post office seemed to grow with each passing day, as did the number of envelopes she sent over to be checked out.

His stomach churned when he came in for an afternoon break and found her at a table writing a letter. She seemed distracted as she got up to serve him a piece of chocolate cake and a cup of coffee. When she went back to her letter writing after barely acknowledging him, Matt was sure she'd decided to reply to one of the men who'd answered her advertisement. He fought the jealousy he could no longer deny.

He kept telling himself he should be happy for her. Finding a husband would get the council off her back, and she wouldn't be raising Mandy alone. That had been his main concern, hadn't it? That raising the baby by herself would be too hard on Emma?

But that was before he'd watched her and seen that she could handle the challenge.

The thought of Emma marrying anyone who wasn't good enough for her or Mandy, who didn't realize how special they both were, had Matt's stomach burning and his temper on edge. He was almost as mad at himself as he was at the council. He should have stood up for her. He knew Emma's character. There'd been no doubt that she would do everything in her power to keep the promise she'd made to Annie.

The next council meeting was only a few days away. He'd be there, and this time he wasn't leaving in the middle. He couldn't let them take Mandy away from Emma or force her into marrying someone she didn't even know.

Until then, he'd make sure Harper didn't cause her any more problems. And he'd try to get his frustration under control.

He forced down a bite of pie, his stomach rumbling. Maybe he should see if Doc had anything to cure his awful heartache—that is, *heartburn*.

Emma's heart sank. None of these letters lit even a tiny spark of interest. Oh, some were nice, and she was sure the men who wrote them were, too. But there was nothing in the letters that made her want to answer them. Still, she needed to find one or two, at least to see if a correspondence might spur some interest that a single letter wouldn't. The council meeting was coming up soon. If she answered at least one letter, she could honestly say she was trying to find someone suitable.

Trouble was, the right person was sitting across the room, staring out the window with a frown on his face. Matt was so wonderful with Mandy, always asking how she was feeling, wanting to look in on her. He'd even fed her a few times over the last few days. He seemed to especially like it when she fell asleep in his arms.

Emma couldn't deny that her feelings were deepening for the lanky deputy, even though she knew they'd never be reciprocated. She pulled a piece of paper toward her. Dipping her pen in ink, she began to reply to the letter in front of her. Matt wasn't going to suddenly declare his undying love for her, and Harper wasn't going to let up on trying to take Mandy away. She had no choice but to make an effort to find someone. Time was running out.

"Emma, could I bother you for a cup of tea?" Matt interrupted her train of thought.

"Tea?"

"Yes, please. My stomach isn't taking well to coffee this afternoon."

"I'll be right out with it." Emma slipped the letter she'd been writing into her apron pocket and hurried to the kitchen. Ben was handing Mandy a wooden spoon and pan to play with. The little girl loved banging and making a racket. Each time she hit the pan, Ben held his hands over his ears.

"I peeked out, Miss Emma, and there weren't no customers, 'cept for the deputy. I figured he wouldn't mind a little noise."

"Not at all, Ben," Matt said from the doorway. "I did have to come check out who was making all that commotion, though."

Mandy grinned up at Matt and hit the pan extra hard. Emma poured Matt a cup of tea and handed it to him. "I'm sorry your stomach is feeling poorly. Maybe you ought to check with Doc about it."

"I'll be fine," he answered in a husky voice. "It's good to see her playing again. Did that tooth come through yet?"

"Yes," Emma replied. "I heard it clink against the spoon when I fed her some oatmeal this morning."

Matt patted Mandy on the head. "I sure am glad that old tooth decided to come through, Mandy baby."

The little girl stopped banging the pan and gazed up at Matt adoringly. Emma's heart twisted. What would it be like to be married to this man? To share her days and nights with him, to have him help her raise Mandy?

Whoa. I can't let myself think that way. Matt had no intentions of marrying.

Emma felt sorry for him. He might not realize it, but he needed someone to love him, someone to take care of him.

Matt glanced over his shoulder and raised an eyebrow at Emma. "Good thing Harper didn't pick today to put that thumb so close to Mandy's mouth."

Emma chuckled. "With five teeth instead of four, she might have just taken it clean off," she joked.

Matt drank a few sips of the tea, then handed the cup back to her. "I'd better get back to work."

Emma followed him to the front counter. "I hope you feel better soon."

He paid for his food, tipped his hat, and took his leave.

Emma watched him cross the street. Something about the way his shoulders slumped made her wonder if he was all right. Something certainly seemed to be bothering him. Perhaps he was lonely. Stubborn man. He needed someone as much as she and Mandy did. As she gazed out the window, she prayed the Lord would send the right person into Matt's life, to make him see he could keep his job and have love, too. At the moment it didn't even matter if it was her or someone else.

Emma sat at the kitchen table to finish her letter. She almost hoped she wouldn't get a reply, yet she prayed she'd get a letter from *someone* who would touch her heart and get her thoughts off the man who'd just left the café.

Doc assured Matt that he wasn't seriously ill but was probably just suffering from heartburn. He gave him some medicine and told him to cut down on his coffee intake.

"There's a substance in coffee called *caffeine,*" Doc explained, "that acts as a stimulant on the nervous system. When taken in small amounts, it's harmless for most people. In large amounts, however, it can cause nervousness and loss of sleep. It may also create headaches and digestive disturbances."

"I had no idea," Matt muttered. "Guess I'd better start drinking tea, huh?"

Doc smirked. "Tea contains a smaller percentage of caffeine than coffee, but it still has some. Your best bet is to start drinking milk."

Matt's eyes flew open. "Milk?"

Doc patted Matt's back. " 'Fraid so, Deputy."

Matt returned to the sheriff's office and took two of the pills Doc had given him, washing them down with a tall glass of water from the pump. He was sure it would alleviate the heartburn, but he didn't think anything could take away the heaviness in his heart. A lawman he was and a lawman he intended to stay, but he wasn't sure he could remain in Roswell and watch Emma make a life with some strange man. Yet he wasn't ready to consider leaving this place that had become home.

That afternoon Matt strolled to the end of Main Street, making his usual rounds. The saloons were quiet, not usually getting rowdy until evening.

The Gem served food in a dining room adjoining the bar. The cooking wasn't anything to brag about, and the clientele consisted mostly of saloon patrons who needed to sober up some before they went home. Usually, the place was quite busy. Customers from the Oasis Saloon, on the other side of the Gem, often came in for a bite to eat.

Matt sauntered into the dining area and was surprised to find it occupied by several of the town council members. Douglas Harper sat at a round table in the middle of the room, talking with Homer Williams and Ed Bagley.

"Afternoon, gentlemen," Matt said with a tip of his Stetson. "I thought your meeting was scheduled for Monday night."

"It is," Homer Williams said. "We're just discussing a few things aforehand." If Homer's wife knew where he was, she'd be dragging him out by the ear. The same thing could be said about several of the men gathered there.

Matt took a seat at a table across the room. He ordered a bowl of stew, then picked up a newspaper someone had left there and pretended to read. He didn't want to appear to be eavesdropping, but as deputy sheriff, that's what he did a lot of the time.

He only heard bits and pieces of conversation, but he couldn't move closer without raising suspicion. He heard something about the stretch of railroad up in Amarillo that'd be finished in a little over a year, and something about prime property. Matt recalled Harper bragging that he'd bought up a fair amount of land in and around Roswell over the past few years. Rumor was, it hadn't always been what the owners wanted. Matt wondered what property he was talking about now.

Matt's stew arrived, and after staring at the layer of grease on top, he pushed the bowl to the side.

As he turned the page of the newspaper he was pretending to read, Jed Brewster entered the room. . .not from the saloon entrance but from the street. The other councilmen rose to leave, but Harper remained seated at the table. When Jed took one of the vacated chairs, Harper welcomed him as if he'd been expecting him.

Harper glanced in Matt's direction, and the deputy pulled his stew close and pretended to take a spoonful. The banker said something to Jed, too quiet for Matt to hear. The younger man shook his head in response.

Harper slid an envelope across the table to Jed, who pushed it back and stood. "You'll have to find someone else," Jed said with disgust. "I'm not interested." He stomped out the door.

"You'll be sorry," Harper called to Jed's back. When the door slammed behind him, Harper lowered his head and tried to discreetly tuck the envelope into his inside jacket pocket. Then he glanced around the room. When his eyes met Matt's, he scowled, rose, and exited the saloon.

Matt threw some coins onto the table to pay for the stew he hadn't eaten, then headed outside. Harper hadn't made it very far—he'd stopped a few yards down the street to talk to Zeke Anderson. Zeke owned a small farm just outside of town. It was rumored that he gambled away most of his earnings.

Harper handed Zeke an envelope similar to the one he'd tried to give to Jed, then ambled down the street.

A few strides farther, Harper handed another envelope to Robert Morris, an older gentleman who dabbled in real estate in the area.

Matt hurried back to the office and told Sheriff Haynes what he'd seen.

"Perhaps he was just handing out invitations to the council meeting," the sheriff suggested.

"I don't think so," Matt argued. "The meeting's open to all townspeople. No invitations are required."

The sheriff rubbed a hand over the stubble on his chin. "Harper's up to something. And it sounds like it might involve some more real estate ventures. Course, there's not much land left around Roswell he hasn't already tried to purchase. I guess he could be starting to buy up more property in town. Nothing wrong with that, but I don't trust the man's ethics. We'll have to keep an eye on him."

"Yes, sir." Matt rubbed his chin. He figured it wouldn't hurt to pay a little visit to Jed Brewster. He'd just have to be real subtle about it.

Emma was delighted to see Cal and Liddy and their children enter the café that evening. She took them to the best table and winked at Liddy. "Celebrating anything special tonight?"

"We sure are." Cal was beaming. "My wife is expecting."

"That's wonderful news!" Emma acted surprised as she hugged Cal and Liddy.

"Thanks," Liddy whispered into Emma's ear.

"You're in luck tonight. We have a couple of choices. Fried chicken or pork chops, with panfried potatoes, green beans, biscuits, and corn bread. My treat."

Cal pulled a chair out for his wife. "Emma, we can't let you—"

"Oh, yes, you can. After all the Sundays I've had supper with you?"

"Well, I guess it'd be all right, then." Liddy arched an eyebrow at her. "Providing you eat with us again this Sunday."

Emma knew better than to argue with Liddy when she raised that eyebrow. "Mandy and I will be happy to have dinner with you after church."

After Emma took their orders, Liddy added, "If Mandy isn't asleep, bring her out. Grace and Amy will entertain her. And bring a plate for yourself so you can join us. I'm sure Hallie could wait on your other customers so you can have supper with us."

Emma brought out Mandy and her high chair. The baby loved Cal and Liddy's children and was quite happy with the extra attention. Emma headed back to the kitchen to help Ben dish up the plates. When she brought out the food, she found Matt sitting at the McAllisters' table next to Mandy's high chair.

"We asked Deputy Johnson to help us celebrate," Liddy said, barely holding back a grin.

Emma smiled at Matt as she distributed the meals. "Wonderful news, isn't it?"

"Sure is." He seemed to be feeling better than he had the last time he'd been in her café.

"What can I get for you?"

"I'll try the pork chops. . .and a glass of milk, please."

Maybe he wasn't feeling better. "Coming right up."

Emma fixed herself a plate and brought it out with Matt's, then sat on the other side of Mandy. Matt had already started feeding her some mashed-up fried potatoes.

Emma offered the little girl a piece of biscuit, but Mandy shook her curly little head. "No. Wan Matt."

Everyone at the table laughed. "Emma, I do believe that child of yours has a mind of her own," Liddy said.

"Just like her Em-mama," Matt said with a wink.

Emma swallowed around the lump in her throat. It almost felt as if she and Matt and Mandy were a family, like Liddy and Cal and their children. She knew it wasn't real, but how wonderful it felt to imagine it for just a moment.

"Have you received any good mail lately?" Liddy whispered.

Emma glanced at Matt, but he and Cal were carrying on their own conversation, so she felt safe in answering. "Nothing really."

"Oh, Em, I'm sorry. But don't give up hope. I know the Lord is going to send the perfect man for you and Mandy. Just hang on."

"I'm trying, Liddy. With that council meeting on Monday night—"

"Don't you worry about that, either. Cal and I will be going with you, and there's no way we're going to let them take Mandy from you."

"But Harper seems so determined—"

"That nasty man had better not mess with us or the people we care about."

Emma was grateful for her friends, and she knew they would stand beside her. But she'd need more than their help if she were to keep Mandy. She needed the Lord to intervene.

"Are you pretty ladies talking about Douglas Harper?" Cal asked.

Liddy patted Emma's arm. "She's worried about the meeting on Monday."

"That man has been acting suspicious lately," Matt said.

"What's that scoundrel doing now?" Cal asked.

Matt rested his elbows on the table and leaned in. "I overheard him mentioning something about prime property, but I didn't catch any details."

Cal snorted. "I'm surprised there's anything left. He's already bought up or foreclosed on just about everything in sight. What could he be wanting now?"

"Emma, what about your place?" Matt asked, raising an eyebrow. "It's in a prime location to the railway station."

"Maybe that's what he's after," Cal suggested.

"If that's the case," Emma said, "why threaten to take Mandy away? It doesn't make sense for him to get me angry if he plans to make me another offer on my property."

"That's true," Liddy said. "And you don't owe him money, so he can't threaten to foreclose on you, like he did me."

"I sure wish I knew what that man is up to," Matt growled.

"No good, I'm sure," Cal said.

Emma cleared off the last table and began to close up for the night. It had seemed natural to have Matt at the table with her and Mandy, enjoying a meal with their best friends, as if they were a family, too. It had been the most enjoyable evening she'd spent in a long time.

She carried a tray of dirty dishes to the kitchen and had just crossed the threshold when she heard a sudden cracking sound, as if a gun had gone off, followed by the shattering of glass.

"Get down, Miss Emma!" Ben yelled from the sink. He crouched, also, and they strained to listen. All was quiet. "Stay here. I'll get some help."

"I have to check on Mandy." Emma crawled to the stairs and crept up them while Ben rushed over to the telephone on the wall.

She heard him cranking it and yelling into the mouthpiece. "Operator? Are you there?"

"Get me the sheriff's office, quick," Emma heard Ben bellow as she tiptoed to the bedroom. "Sheriff? Oh, Deputy Johnson. You gotta get over here to Miss Emma's right away. Somebody shot a gun into the café!"

Emma found Mandy sleeping peacefully, a thumb in her mouth. After making sure everything was fine upstairs, she kissed the baby's head and hurried back downstairs just in time to hear Matt hollering from outside the café, "Emma! Ben! Are you all right?"

"Yes, sir, we is," Ben yelled back as he and Emma rushed to the front. One of the windowpanes in the door had been shattered, and bits of glass—large chunks, tiny shards, and everything in between—covered the floor and the tables under the window.

Matt burst through the door, his gun drawn, his boots crunching glass. After scrutinizing the room, he put the pistol back in his holster. "Is Mandy all right?"

Emma tried to sound calm. "She slept through it all."

"Was it gunfire, Deputy Matt?" Ben asked.

Matt's eyes searched the café. "I don't think so. I heard the crash from the office. It wasn't near as loud as a gunshot."

He motioned to the floor about halfway across the room. Under a chair sat a rock about the size of one of Emma's biscuits. A piece of paper was tied around it with string. Matt picked it up and released the paper. He eyed it quickly, then handed it to Emma.

The note was written on good stationery with bold handwriting. "If you know what's good for you and the town," she read aloud, "you'll give up that baby."

She blinked back tears.

"I sure don't understand some folks," Ben muttered as he began sweeping up the broken glass.

Emma was thankful the damage wasn't any worse. At least the big picture window with her café's name engraved on it remained intact.

Matt held out his hand toward Emma. "I need that note for evidence."

She handed it back to him. "I'll have to find something to put over that window until I can get the pane replaced."

"You can't stay here tonight, Emma. Whoever threw this might come back."

"I'm not going anywhere, Deputy. This is my home."

"Let me take you to Cal and Liddy's."

"No. I'm staying here. Besides, aren't you off duty?"

"I can bed down in the kitchen, Deputy," Ben said. "I'll telephone you if I hear a sound."

"I'm not leaving you here with only a telephone for protection." Matt sat at one of the tables and propped his feet up on the chair across from him. "Put on a pot of coffee, Emma. It could be a very long night."

Chapter 12

After several uneventful hours passed, Matt finally convinced Emma to go upstairs and get some sleep so she could take care of Mandy and her business the next day. Ben chose to stay and keep Matt company, dozing off and on. Matt managed a catnap here and there but jumped at every sound.

He'd never been so frightened in his life as when Ben called and said someone had shot into Emma's café. What if it had been a gun? Or what if the rock had hit Emma in the head? He felt sick at the thought.

He thanked God that Emma and Mandy were all right, and he promised himself he'd do everything in his power to make sure they stayed that way.

Emma insisted on treating Matt to breakfast before he left the next morning. She tried to give Ben the day off, but he wouldn't hear of it.

As soon as Jaffa-Prager opened, Emma sent Ben to buy a pane of glass and two door locks. She and Hallie took care of the cooking and waiting tables while Ben replaced the windowpane and installed the new locks on both the front and back doors. Emma sent up prayers of thanksgiving that God had not let anything happen to Mandy or her.

The sheriff showed up later that morning to ask questions. He assured Emma that he and his deputies would be watching her place extra closely until they found out who was responsible for throwing the rock.

Emma went through the motions of taking care of Mandy and her customers, trying not to think about the incident the night before. Matt was in and out the rest of the day. She knew it was all in the line of duty, but she did feel safer with him around.

She had to explain what happened over and over again as her customers asked about the window or begged for confirmation about the rumors they'd heard. The only other evidence left in the café was the scratched surface of her floor where the rock had skidded to a stop.

Knowing the sheriff and his deputies were right across the street, Emma slept fairly well that night.

She enjoyed the church service the next day, drawing strength from her church family. The singing raised her spirits, and the sermon reminded her that God watches over His children.

The rest of Sunday passed peacefully. Cal and Liddy repeatedly assured Emma of their faith that the Lord would not allow the town council to take Mandy away.

But when she awoke on Monday morning, Emma's heart was filled with dread. She dropped to her knees beside the bed and prayed for her faith to grow stronger, and for the Lord to give her courage to face whatever decision the council made.

Emma knew God would take care of everything. Still, she had to remind herself all day not to worry.

Business slowed down after supper, and Emma asked Hallie to close up so she could prepare for the meeting. She had just finished dressing Mandy and herself in their nicest clothes when Liddy and Cal showed up to walk with her.

She was relieved to have them at her side when they walked into the packed room. This time she saw many friendly faces in the crowd. Still, she felt intimidated as she took a seat at the front of the room and faced the councilmen seated at the table. The same men who were absent before were still out of town. Matt had taken up his post at the back of the room with the sheriff. Deputy Carmichael manned the side door.

Harper had to tap the gavel several times before the crowd quieted down enough for the meeting to get under way.

When the crowd was finally silenced, Harper explained, "for the benefit of those who weren't in attendance at the last meeting," that the council had decided to check with the orphanage in Santa Fe about taking custody of Annie's child, even though Miss Emma Hanson opposed that course of action.

"We have heard back from Santa Fe," he said, bringing them all up-to-date. "The orphanage director says they are willing to accept the child if we can get her there. They would prefer to have a couple from here adopt her, but no one has come forward. So the next step is to find someone willing to accompany the child to—"

"May I address the council, Mr. Harper?" Emma asked as sweetly as she could without choking.

Harper frowned at her. "After I finish, Miss Hanson."

"Let her talk," a man from the back of the room yelled.

"Yes, Harper," Doc Bradshaw said. "We want to hear what she has to say."

Color crept up the banker's neck. "Very well, Miss Hanson. You may speak your mind."

Emma faced the crowded room, holding Mandy close. "I would like to request that the council rethink this course of action, especially since I—"

"There is no reason for us to *rethink* anything."

Emma whirled around to face Harper. "But I've taken your suggestion, and

I need a little more time to pursue it."

Harper spread a pudgy hand over his chest. "My suggestion? I gave you no suggestion, Miss Hanson."

"Oh, but you did," Emma said. "And I decided to heed your advice."

Harper twisted the neck of his shirt collar. "My advice?"

"Yes. Remember that day in my café? You advised me to find a mail-order husband."

The room instantly filled with titters, guffaws, and murmurs.

Harper's cheeks flushed. "Why, I never said anything of the sort."

"Oh yes, you did," Myrtle chimed in. "I was there."

"Me, too," Opal added.

Harper turned even redder. "But I—I—"

"You didn't think I'd go through with it, did you? Well, I have. I just need some time to—"

"Did you really suggest that, Harper?" Homer Williams asked, his eyes wide.

"Well. . .uh, I might have mentioned it—"

"Then we must give Miss Hanson some time to try to carry out that plan," Homer said.

Harper looked like he might explode. "But—"

Cal stood. "If it was your suggestion, Harper, you don't have much choice other than to give her some time to follow up on it."

"Councilman," Homer Williams said, "I believe we need to talk."

Harper strode to the table. Homer and the other council members huddled around him, whispering and gesturing toward Emma for several moments. Then Homer addressed her. "You have two weeks to show us some progress in this endeavor. We will reevaluate the situation at that time."

Two weeks wasn't very long. But Emma was glad for even a temporary reprieve. "Thank you, Mr. Williams."

Matt stepped forward. "You shouldn't have to reevaluate the situation at all."

Emma's heart stopped. What was he doing?

"Mandy has been well taken care of. If any woman is capable of raising a child by herself, it's Emma Hanson. You need to drop this whole thing and let her keep the promise she made to Annie Drake."

Emma's heart began to beat again. In double time. Matt actually thought she could raise Mandy. He was taking her side! *Thank You, Lord.*

Harper glared at Matt. "Deputy, I don't believe this is in your line of duty."

"I'm off duty, Councilman. I speak as a private citizen who has closely observed Miss Hanson—"

"Mr. Johnson, the matter has been settled." Harper pounded the gavel on the podium. "Miss Hanson has two weeks. This meeting is dismissed!"

Mandy clapped. Liddy giggled and hugged them both. Emma blinked quickly. She wasn't going to let Harper see her cry. Two weeks! How was she ever going to find a suitable husband in two weeks?

The councilmen disappeared out the side door. Emma took a shaky breath as Doc and Myrtle came over to wish her well.

"It's going to be all right, dear," Myrtle said as Minister Turley and Caroline came over to give their support. It was wonderful to have their encouragement. But would this reprieve actually do any good?

As the crowd began to thin out, Emma, Liddy, and Cal started up the aisle. Emma searched the room for Matt but didn't see him anywhere.

"Emma, you have some time to work with," Liddy assured her. "God is going to take care of everything; just you wait and see."

"Maybe He's telling me to get out of town."

"What?"

Emma stopped in the middle of the aisle and faced her friend. "Liddy, if I can't find a husband in two weeks, I'll have no choice but to board up my business and leave town with Mandy."

"Oh, Em. You can't mean that."

"I know God wants me to keep my promise. And if it means starting over somewhere else, then I'll go."

"It won't come to that. You'll see." Liddy hugged her. "It's going to be real interesting to see how God takes care of this."

"Yes, it is," Emma said. In an attempt to lighten the somber mood, she tickled Mandy and made her giggle. "Let's go to the café and celebrate."

The café remained closed while the three friends enjoyed chocolate cake and milk together. After the McAllisters left and Mandy was safely tucked into bed, Emma brought out her packet of letters and went through them to see if there were any she could possibly reply to. She reread them all once more and put two to the side. She'd answer them and see where it led. But she didn't hold out much hope.

It seemed the Lord was leading her away from this town she loved so much. If that was His will, then that's what she'd do. Ben could run the café. He might even want to buy it.

Emma quickly penned two letters, identical except for the salutation, and stuffed them into envelopes. She retired early that night, thankful that she had some time to figure out what the Lord had in store for her. And grateful for her friends who supported her. Her heart soared as she remembered the way Matt had stood up for her. But the town council still did not believe she could raise Mandy alone.

Dear Lord, please show me what You would have me do.

A Promise Made

Matt paced the floor of his room at the boardinghouse. The tightness in his chest had returned, more painful than ever. It had started when he overheard Emma tell Liddy that she would leave Roswell with Mandy if she had no other options. Not that he blamed her. What choice had the council given her? To marry a complete stranger or give up the child she loved? To his way of thinking, neither was acceptable.

He went to the sheriff's office and talked to Deputy Carmichael for a while. When it came time for rounds, Matt asked him to take his shift so he could stay and keep an eye on Emma's place. After Carmichael left, Matt made himself comfortable in a chair near the open front door.

It was a quiet night, with a lot of time to think. And the longer he thought, the more clear everything became. There was no use denying it. Matt loved Emma Hanson and the baby she'd agreed to raise. Yes, he was in a dangerous business, and there was a chance he might leave her a widow. But he hated the idea of someone else marrying Emma and being a father to Mandy. And he couldn't stand the thought that she might leave the area forever. She couldn't continue living alone above the café with rock-throwing people out on the streets. Yet the thought of some other man protecting them was unacceptable.

There was only one thing to do. And he had to do it before she agreed to marry one of those letter writers! Matt stood, straightened his shoulders, pressed his Stetson onto his head, and strode out the door. He'd march over to the café that minute and ask Emma Hanson to marry him without delay.

But as he crossed the street, he noticed the lights were out, even upstairs. Matt stopped in the middle of the road and stared at the dark building. He yanked his hat off his head and ran his fingers through his hair. Then he slammed the hat back on and strode back to the sheriff's office. Morning couldn't come soon enough.

After a restless night, Emma rose just after dawn. She padded down to the kitchen to begin her preparations for the day. She'd just put on a fresh pot of coffee when a knock on the back door made her jump. Who would be calling at this hour?

She opened the door a crack and let out a gasp when she saw Matt there, his clothes wrinkled and his hair mussed.

"Emma, can we talk?" he said, his voice hoarse.

"Of course." She opened the door wider. "Is anything wrong?"

"No," he said, crossing to his usual table. "I just wanted to ask you something."

Emma poured two cups of coffee. "I've been wanting to thank you for standing up for me last night," she said as she sat across the table from him. "I tried to find you after the meeting, but you'd already gone."

Matt rubbed the sides of his coffee cup. "I overheard you tell Liddy you might leave town if you don't find. . ." His voice trailed off.

"A husband? Well, I have to do something. I won't let them take Mandy away from me. And you can't arrest me for thinking about leaving town."

"No." Matt stared at the steaming coffee. "Could I have some milk?"

"Of course," she said more softly, regretting her sharp tone. She took a small pitcher out of the icebox and poured him a glass.

He took a small sip. "Emma, I came to ask you. . .I mean, I came to tell you that. . .there's no need for you to try to find a husband. I'll marry you."

Emma's mouth dropped open. She tried to shut it, but it refused to cooperate. Surely she hadn't heard him right. She thought he'd just said he would marry her!

His weary gaze met hers as he waited for an answer.

"Matt, I—I don't know what to say."

"Say yes. There's no need for you to marry a stranger. At least you know me. And so does Mandy. I'd be good to you and the baby. I could keep you both safe."

Emma wanted to cry. Deputy Matthew Johnson had finally asked her to marry him! Oh, how she'd ached to hear those words. But she wanted him to propose out of love, not because he pitied her. He was offering her the one thing she'd dreamed about for two long years. Yet she heard herself whisper, "No."

He blinked at her. "No?"

The shock on his face caused anger to rise in her throat. Obviously, he had expected her to fall into his arms and accept his mercy offering without hesitation. "You heard me, Deputy," she said evenly. "You have never shown any romantic interest in me before. I refuse to marry a man out of pity."

Matt reached for her hand. "It's not pity I feel for you, Emma."

"No?" She pulled her hand away from his. "Then why didn't you ask me to marry you when the council first tried to take Mandy away?"

Matt took a deep breath. "I never intended to ask anyone to marry me. I didn't want to take the chance of leaving a widow behind, like my father did. I know how hard his death was on my mother, and I promised myself I'd never do that to a woman."

Emma's heart went out to him. "I'm sure your mother was glad for every moment she had with your father because she loved him. People in love take those kinds of chances." She would gladly have taken the chance with Matthew Johnson. Everything in her cried out for her to accept his offer of marriage. But she couldn't. He didn't love her.

"Emma, if you marry me, the town council—"

Her back stiffened. "If you'd asked me to marry you a year ago, or even several months ago, I would have said yes."

His eyes widened with hope. "Really?"

"But if you really cared for me, you would have shown it before now. I cannot marry a man who simply pities me." Emma rose and opened the back door. "I do appreciate your kind offer, Deputy."

"Emma—"

"But I need to go check on Mandy now."

Matt took a deep breath. "All right." He stood before her, close enough for her to see the hurt and confusion in his eyes. . .which almost made her melt into his arms. She steeled herself.

"If you change your mind—"

"I'll let you see yourself out." Emma scurried up the stairs. She couldn't let him see her cry.

Matt stood alone in the kitchen, wondering what he'd done wrong. Asking Emma to marry him had seemed the answer to her problem as well as his. But somehow he'd messed things up, and he had no idea how to fix it.

The thought had never crossed his mind that Emma might turn him down. She was willing to marry a complete stranger, but she wouldn't marry him? It made no sense!

As he stood there, gazing up the stairs, he vaguely heard a man's voice behind him. "Deputy Matt? Is ever'thin' all right with Miss Emma?"

Matt shook himself out of his stupor and saw Ben giving him a quizzical look. "What? Oh, yes. She's fine. She went to check on Mandy. I was just on my way out."

"Want me to fix you some flapjacks?"

"No, thanks. I'm not very hungry this morning." Matt wandered out the door, wondering if he'd ever be hungry again.

Emma was beautiful first thing in the morning. He'd never seen her hair long, the soft tresses curling around her face and down her back. His fingers had fairly itched to be able to run through those curls.

He walked down the boardwalk, with no particular destination in mind, finally ending up at the livery stable. This was certainly not the way he'd planned to spend his day off when he spent the night on the stoop outside the sheriff's office, waiting for the first sign of activity in the café.

Matt saddled his horse and headed out toward Cal and Liddy's. Maybe they could make some sense of this.

The McAllisters were just finishing breakfast when he reined up outside their house. The girls ran out to do their chores before school, and Liddy insisted on setting him a place and filling a plate with bacon and biscuits and gravy. He tried to eat, but the food just wasn't going down.

Cal let him sit in silence for a few minutes, then asked, "What's wrong, Matt? You look like you've lost your best friend."

Matt realized he might well have. "I asked Emma to marry me."

Liddy jumped up and hugged his neck. "I was hoping you would! When's the date?"

"She turned me down." His stomach felt like it was on fire.

Liddy sank back into her chair. "She did what?"

"She told me no. Said she didn't want my pity." Matt shook his head. "It's not pity I feel for her."

"Well, did you tell her that?" Cal asked.

"I tried to. She wouldn't listen. She said if I'd asked her a year ago. . .even a few months ago. . ."

"Well, she has been sweet on you for the longest time." Liddy rested her chin in her hand.

"That's not true."

"If you believe that, you haven't been paying attention. I'm her best friend. Believe me, I know. She's been interested in you since before Cal and I fell in love."

Matt slapped his hand on the table. "Then why didn't she ever show it?"

"Oh, she did." Liddy exchanged glances with Cal, then settled her attention back on Matt. "Remember right after you moved here? Didn't Emma bring you supper a few times when you were working?"

"Well, yes, but I—"

"But you insisted on paying her. Claimed you didn't want to be beholden to anyone."

"So?"

"So she took that to mean you weren't interested in her."

Matt groaned. "I never intended to marry anyone."

"What made you change your mind?" Cal asked.

Matt pushed his chair back and started pacing. "I can't stand the fact that she might marry a stranger, or that she might leave town. I love her." At that instant, Matt realized that he'd never said those words to Emma. No wonder she'd turned him down!

Cal grinned. "About time you figured that out. So what are you going to do now?"

"You aren't giving up, are you?" Liddy asked.

"I don't know what to do. She won't listen to me right now."

"Can you write?" Liddy cocked an eyebrow at him.

"Of course I can."

"And Emma can read. Matter of fact, she's been reading a lot lately." Liddy grinned at him. "Letters, mostly."

Cal laughed. "I think I know where you're going with this."

For the first time that day, Matt smiled. "I think I do, too."

Chapter 13

Emma managed to hold her tears at bay while she waited on her customers. But after the café closed, Ben went home, and Mandy fell asleep, she couldn't keep them in check any longer.

She sobbed into her pillow, hoping she wouldn't wake the baby. Her heart ached for what could have been. If only Matt had asked her to marry him earlier, even a couple of months ago, before the first town council meeting about Mandy.

She'd loved Matt for such a long time. She knew he'd make a wonderful husband and father. Even after waiting so long, this day could have ended joyfully. . .if only he'd said those three words she longed to hear.

But he hadn't. As difficult as it would be to marry a stranger, at least they'd be starting out with the intention of learning to love each other. The idea of marrying a man she loved, but who felt nothing for her but pity, was too painful to even think about. No. As much as she wanted to say yes, she couldn't marry Matt, knowing he didn't love her.

Emma's chest heaved with silent tears long into the night, until she finally gave it over to the Lord. She prayed He would guide her in choosing a husband from the letters she'd received. Then she asked God to help her get over Matt so she could learn to love another.

Early the next morning, Mandy's sweet voice woke her. "Em-mama, I hungy."

Emma felt drained but at peace. The Lord had given her this precious child to raise as her own. He would help her—whether by sending a good man to marry her or by enabling her to relocate. He was in control. She would leave everything in His hands.

Emma washed her face and peered into the mirror. Her eyes looked a little swollen from all the crying, but they weren't red. She dressed herself and Mandy and slipped downstairs.

All in all, she thought she was doing quite well. . .until Liddy came in with the pies and cakes. She took one look at Emma and said, "Matt doesn't look much better than you do."

Emma teared up again.

"I'm sorry, Em," Liddy said. "I didn't mean to make you cry." She gave

Emma a tight hug. Then she held her at arm's length and gazed into her bleary eyes. "Now, what is this I hear about you turning down that man's proposal? I thought it was what you've been waiting for."

"Liddy, I wanted him to love me." Emma wiped her eyes with a dish towel.

"And how do you know he doesn't?"

She sniffed. "I gave him plenty of opportunity to say so."

"Those words don't come easy for some men."

Emma began feeding Mandy her breakfast. "Liddy, I've got to trust the Lord to bring someone into my life who is at least willing to try to love me." She wished with all her heart that things could be different, but she couldn't daydream about Matt for the rest of her life. "Last night I wrote two letters of response to the men who answered my advertisement."

Liddy opened her mouth as if to say something, then shut it. "Would you like me to walk to the post office with you?"

"Thanks for understanding, Liddy. Would you mind putting Mandy in her carriage while I run upstairs and get those letters?"

"Not at all."

Liddy and Mandy were ready to go when Emma came back down, the two letters tucked into her skirt pocket. Emma asked Ben to watch the café for a while.

At the post office, Emma handed her letters to Mr. Marley, and he gave her another envelope. The return address showed no name, only a post office box right there in Roswell.

She had specifically decided not to place an ad in the local paper, and she'd asked Matt not to spread word around town. Yet somehow, someone had found out!

Emma glanced up at Mr. Marley, sorely tempted to ask him who owned the box marked on the envelope. But she knew he wouldn't be allowed to give out that information. So she kept the question to herself.

"Well?" Liddy asked, watching Emma stuff the unopened envelope in her skirt pocket. "Aren't you going to read it?"

Emma chuckled at her friend's impatience. "Later."

"Aw, Em, I have an interest in this, too. I don't want you moving away. Maybe I can help by giving you an impartial opinion on some of these men."

Emma handed her the letter. "All right. You read it first and tell me what you think."

Liddy gave it back. "No, no. I just want to read the ones you think you might want to answer."

Emma held the letter as they strolled back to the café. "I doubt there will be anything different in this letter than what I've read in all the others. But, like you said, maybe an objective eye will see more than I would."

When they returned to the café, Emma invited Liddy in for a cup of tea. As she settled Mandy in the play area, she watched Ben taking care of the cooking and waiting on customers. He didn't seem to have any problem handling both jobs. He ought to own his own place. Perhaps she really would sell him the café if she had to move.

Hallie came in for work, and Emma ran upstairs to get the packet of letters so Liddy could go over all of them.

When she came back down, she saw Liddy at the kitchen table, sipping tea. Emma dropped the packet on the table along with the new letter. "You might as well check them all out. Maybe you'll see something I missed."

Emma took out several orders and refilled coffee cups, then joined her friend in the kitchen. "Well?"

Liddy pushed several letters toward her. "I'd burn these. My goodness, Emma, I didn't realize there were so many men out there wanting a free meal ticket."

Emma laughed. "I'm glad I didn't let all their sweet-talking mislead me."

"Sweet-talking? One of these men asked right out if your business could support his family. Another one expects you to sign your business over to him before marriage. What nerve!"

Emma picked up one of the letters and waved it in the air. "What about the one who wants me to move to the top of a mountain, where there are no neighbors for miles around? You know I couldn't do that. I'm too used to having people around me every day."

Liddy took a sip of her tea. "Are you sure it was such a good idea refusing Matt's offer of marriage? It's not like you've received any wonderful responses to that advertisement."

Emma stood. "You don't have to read the rest." Emma reached for the letters. "You've confirmed that my instincts are accurate."

"Why don't I just read one more?" She held up the letter Emma had just picked up that morning.

Emma snatched it out of her hand. "I'll save this one for later," she said, deciding she'd rather be the first one to read it.

Liddy nodded. "All right. But don't give up hope. God is going to take care of all this."

"I know. I've already decided where I might go if I decide to leave."

"I don't want to hear about you moving." Liddy stood. "I'm not even going to discuss it with you."

Emma didn't want to talk about it, either. But she had to be prepared, and a plan was forming in the back of her mind. Matt had complained about the food at the restaurant in the Lincoln Hotel. If the council tried to take Mandy away, maybe Emma would set up business there. It wasn't far away, so she could easily come back to Roswell from time to time to visit her friends.

Liddy waved good-bye as Emma turned her attention to her customers.

During a lull in the early evening, Emma pulled the new envelope out of her skirt pocket. She opened the folded sheet of paper and read.

Dear Miss Hanson,

I put pen to paper not knowing quite what to say because I have never done this kind of thing before. But somehow I do not think you make a habit of advertising for a husband, either. I never thought much about getting married until recently. But lately I have been yearning for a home and a family of my own.

Emma's attention was caught. She sat in the nearest chair to give this intriguing letter her undivided attention.

Allow me to tell you a little about myself. I do like children, very much. How many children would you want?

Emma blushed. She realized she hadn't made it clear in the advertisement that there already was a child. She wondered why none of the other men had mentioned that.

I have a steady job, so I would not be needing your business to support us or any children we might have, although if you wished to keep your place of business, that would be all right with me.

Emma placed a hand over her heart. This was the first letter she'd received where the man had voiced a willingness to provide for her and any children involved. The paper shook as her hand began to tremble.

I do not drink, and I am a God-fearing man. . .although there have been times in my life when I did not lean on the Lord as I should have and forged ahead on my own. I am now trying to let Him lead me into the future.

Tears formed in Emma's eyes. It seemed she had something in common with this man right off the bat. Trying to be in charge, when they knew the only way things worked out was to seek God's will in the way they should go.

I would not expect you to make a decision on one letter alone. Therefore, I would like very much to correspond with you, should you be so inclined, so that we might get to know each other well enough to reach the decision the Lord would have us make.

I hope to hear from you in the near future.

Sincerely,
DMJ

She wondered why he signed only his initials. She thought of all the men she knew, but no names matched.

Emma reread the letter, her heart pounding with hope. Could this be the one she was to answer? Was this the man the Lord was sending to her and Mandy?

Matt stood across from Emma's café trying to summon up the courage to cross the street and go in. He hadn't seen her since she'd turned down his proposal, and he wasn't sure how she would react to him behaving as if nothing had happened between them. But that's exactly what he intended to do. He didn't want to give her any hint of what his plan of action was.

Thanks to Cal and Liddy, he wasn't giving up. Not yet. He'd thought about everything Liddy had told him about Emma's feelings for him.

Although Emma seemed convinced that all he felt for her was pity, she couldn't be further from the truth. But she wouldn't listen to what he had to say, and even if she did, Matt wasn't sure he could change her mind. Still, if she did care for him at one time, could she not care again? And if she was willing to consider a suitor by mail, why not see if she would consider him? It seemed to be his only chance.

He'd penned the letter at Cal and Liddy's house and put it in the mail that afternoon. He wondered if Emma would answer it. In the meantime, he couldn't stay away from her place. It was his job to make sure no one caused problems, especially after the council meeting. Harper and several of his cronies had been quite angry. They hadn't wanted to give her any extra time to find a husband. Matt was determined to make sure they gave Emma those two weeks as promised.

Matt had a job to do. He crossed the street and entered the café, taking a seat at his regular table. The place was busy, and he was glad for that. It would make things easier on both him and Emma.

She stopped by his table and set down a glass of water. "What can I get for you tonight, Deputy?"

"Whatever the special is will be fine, thank you." He gazed into her eyes for a brief moment before she blinked and headed for the kitchen.

Matt rubbed his hands on his pant legs and let out a deep breath. That hadn't been too bad. At least she hadn't told him to go away. He'd noticed dark circles under her eyes. Matt wished with all his heart that he could take her in his arms and assure her that everything would be all right. But he didn't have that right. If she didn't reply to his letter, he might never have it.

Matt also wanted to check on Mandy but figured he'd better bide his time.

He ate his meal in silence, missing the easy conversation he had once shared with Emma and now realized he'd taken for granted. He'd been content to see her several times a day, knowing there was no love interest in her life, assuring himself that she wouldn't be attracted to someone in his line of work and figuring he was doing her a favor by not pursuing her.

If she had cared about him, as Liddy indicated, he must have seemed callous and uncaring. Why should Emma have taken his proposal seriously? He had never given her a reason to believe that he felt anything but friendship for her.

No wonder she thought he felt only pity for her. He'd been too busy telling himself he was doing the proper thing by not acting on his attraction to her, by not showing her how much he cared.

Matt bowed his head over his food, and right there in Emma's café, he said a silent prayer. *Dear God, forgive me for my self-righteousness and arrogance. Please let Emma forgive me, Father. If I should be so blessed to persuade her to marry me, help me to spend the rest of my life making it up to her. In Jesus' name, amen.*

Emma breathed a sigh of relief when she let the last customer out and locked up for the night. She cleared off their table on her way back to the kitchen to help Ben with the cleanup, eager to reread the letter in her pocket.

She knew the only way she'd been able to handle waiting on Matt was thinking about that letter. That made it easier to face his pity.

She nearly pushed Ben out the door, assuring him she'd finish the preparations for the next day. Once alone, she brewed a pot of tea and sat at the kitchen table. She pulled out the letter and read it once more and then again. It was like a balm to her battered pride, and she knew she was going to answer this one. And she certainly wasn't going to hand it over to the sheriff to check out.

She gathered paper and pen and mulled over how to start. She dipped her pen in the ink and wrote.

Dear DMJ,

I must admit I am curious as to why you used initials instead of your full name. Might I ask the reason?

You are right; I do not make it a habit of advertising for a husband, and I feel awkward about doing it. But truthfully, I felt I did not have a choice. You have been straightforward with me, and now I feel you should know why I have done this, so that you can decide if you would like to continue corresponding with me.

You see, I have been given the opportunity to be a mother to the most wonderful child in the world. A woman who worked for me died, after extracting a promise that I would raise her daughter. Even if I had not fallen in love with this baby, I would have kept my promise to Annie. I feel honored that she trusted me enough to put her child in my care.

But the leaders of this town do not feel a single woman should be raising a child, and they have given me a deadline of two weeks to find a husband. If I do not find the right man by then, I will take my child and find a new place to live before they can take her away from me and place her in an orphanage.

If, after hearing all of this, you feel led to reply to me, I will answer in kind.

Sincerely,
Emma Hanson

Emma folded the paper and slid it into an envelope, addressing it to the post office box of the sender. She propped it against the lamp on the table and let out a shaky breath. It would go out in the mail first thing the next morning.

She felt an unexplainable peace about answering this man. She was certain it came from the Lord, and she was going to put her faith in Him. If she shouldn't feel that way, He would let her know. Until then, she would wait impatiently for a reply.

Chapter 14

Before he started his shift, Matt checked in at the post office. When Mr. Marley handed him a letter bearing Emma's return address, Matt tried not to show his excitement. His first thought was to tear into it immediately, but there were other people in the post office, and he wanted privacy when he read Emma's letter.

After work, he'd go home and read it. He folded it carefully and put it in his pants pocket. She'd actually replied to his letter. Whatever she wrote, it would be more than the cool remarks he'd received the last couple of days. Would Emma ever really talk to him again? He missed having conversations with her, missed her smile, missed feeling comfortable enough to walk into the kitchen and check on Mandy. If Emma's letter asked him not to write again, he didn't know what his next move would be. But he wasn't going to give up until he had the chance to convince her how much he cared about her and that little girl.

He loved them—plain and simple. He should have told Emma that the morning he proposed. But her refusal had made him realize how much he needed her and Mandy in his life, probably more than they needed him.

He walked out of the post office with a spring in his step. He knew it wasn't fair of him to write her anonymously and only include his post office box, but she probably wouldn't have read his letter if she'd known it was from him. He was hoping she might begin to care about him through their correspondence. At least he would have a chance to convince her that he loved her and truly did want to marry her.

It was all he could do to keep from tearing into the envelope while at work, and as soon as his shift was over, he hurried back to the boardinghouse and sat at the desk in his room.

Matt smoothed out the page and scanned the words. Emma had opened the door for him to correspond with her. He let out the breath he'd been holding and smiled. She was being honest with someone she thought was a complete stranger.

She asked about his initials, obviously wanting to know his name. He couldn't tell her yet—it would end it all immediately. He felt some guilt that he wasn't being completely honest with her. But he would be. Just as soon as he thought he could.

He immediately began composing an answer. With the town council's two-week deadline, there was no time to lose.

Dear Miss Hanson,

I am pleased that you have agreed to correspond with me. Thank you for letting me know why you thought you must advertise for a husband. I think your young charge is fortunate to be in the care of someone who cares so much about her well-being.

I am looking forward to meeting you both one day. I would consider it an honor to help you raise her for her mother.

I will be glad to meet with you in person whenever and wherever you say. I understand the time limit imposed on you by your town leaders, so I will leave it up to you on how to proceed. I confess to having admired you from afar for some time now, so I would not have to travel a long distance to meet with you. Just set the time and place, and I will be there.

Sincerely,
DMJ

Matt folded the paper and stuffed it in an envelope. He strolled over to the post office and dropped it in the after-hours door slot. He figured Emma would receive it the next day.

Emma felt giddy with excitement when she opened the letter she'd brought back from the post office. She scanned it quickly, as she had customers who needed her attention, but her stomach did flips at the knowledge that "DMJ" wanted to continue the correspondence. Since he lived in the area, she wondered if she'd met him before.

She knew she should be cautious in this correspondence with a stranger, but she felt peace about it, a peace she hadn't felt with any of the other letters. She was going to proceed and trust in the Lord to show her if she was wrong.

When Liddy came in that morning, Emma decided to tell her about this new man over a cup of coffee.

"Well, I finally answered one of the men who responded to my advertisement," she began.

"Oh?" Liddy's cup stalled midway to her lips.

"The last one I received was. . .different from the others." Emma twirled her cup in its saucer.

Liddy leaned in. "What did it say? Who was it from?"

Emma handed both envelopes to Liddy. She'd carried the first letter in her pocket from the first day and read it countless times. She knew she'd do the same with the one she'd received that morning.

Liddy quickly read both letters and grinned at Emma. "Oh, my. He sounds awfully nice. I think you did the right thing by replying to him."

"I do, too."

Liddy pursed her lips together. "When are you going to meet this man?"

Emma shrugged. "I haven't decided yet. Apparently he knows me, which puts me at a disadvantage."

"Did you give these envelopes to the sheriff or Matt to check out?"

"No. I don't want them knowing my business."

Liddy shrugged. "I guess I might feel the same way. Still. . ."

Emma grinned. "I'm trusting in the Lord, Liddy."

"Then it's bound to turn out right."

"That's what I think." Emma took a sip of coffee and sat back in her chair.

"Have you talked to Matt since he proposed?" Liddy asked, handing the letters back to Emma.

"He's been in a few times, but it's hard to go back to the way things were. I'll always care about him. But I have to get over him." She put the letters back in her pocket. "These are helping keep my mind off of him, and that's a good thing."

"If you say so." Liddy stood. "I'd better be going. I need to get some cocoa. The girls have been wanting hot chocolate."

"It is getting cooler. Especially at night." Emma cleared the table. "Hot chocolate sounds good to me. My customers will be asking for it before long. I'd better see about getting some cocoa for the café."

She hugged her friend good-bye, then patted her pocket as she returned to the kitchen. Maybe there'd be someone in her life to share a cup of cocoa with by wintertime. After Liddy's departure, there was no one else in the café, so Emma pulled out her writing supplies. She wanted to get her reply to the post office before she got too busy.

When Matt came in for an early supper that evening, he saw Emma standing at the counter, reading a letter. The bell above the door jingled when he entered, and she glanced up with a smile. But as soon as she saw him, the smile faded.

He caught a glimpse of the letter as she stuffed it into her pocket, and Matt almost chuckled as he recognized his own handwriting.

He knew Emma was going to be angry when she found out that he was the one writing those letters. And the day of reckoning was soon approaching. It was only a matter of time until they met in person.

Dear Lord, please let Emma care. Give me the words to convince her that I love her.

He didn't see her smile again that night. But he was comforted to see her slip her hand into the pocket holding his letter. His heart thudded with hope.

The next day, Matt sat two rows back from Emma and Mandy in church, trying to keep his mind on the service instead of the way Mandy grinned at him from over Emma's shoulder. *Oh, Lord, please let this work out. I want so much to be a good husband to Emma and father to Mandy. I don't want to even consider that any other man might fill those roles.*

The day passed slowly for Matt. Emma and Mandy went to Cal and Liddy's for Sunday dinner. He knew the couple was hoping for things to work out between him and Emma, but now wasn't the time for him to show up unexpectedly. Anxious for the day to end so he could pick up his mail the next morning, he offered to take Deputy Carmichael's shift so the young man could go visit a lady he'd been courting.

The sun was setting when Matt saw Emma and Mandy returned to town. Only then did he relax, knowing they were home safe. While he thought it was a good thing that Emma's café was closed on Sundays, he missed the opportunity to see her. If things worked out the way he hoped and prayed they would, he'd be seeing Emma and Mandy every day. He cast an eye heavenward and felt a sudden peace about it all. God was in control, and everything was going to be all right.

It had taken him a long time to come to that conclusion. For years he'd blamed the Lord for his father's death and his mother's hard life. But it was an outlaw who killed his father. His father had loved his job, and his mother had loved him. She never blamed God for her husband's death.

That night, as he started his last rounds, Matt saw the light still on in Emma's upstairs apartment. He wondered if she'd answered his letter yet. Would she agree to a time and place to meet? He wanted this charade to end as soon as possible.

He headed to the south end of Main Street, glad that it was a quiet night in Roswell. The saloons were closed on Sundays, for which Matt was grateful. He greeted several couples out for an evening stroll and hoped that one day he and Emma would be doing the same thing.

He sauntered back up the street, checking locks and peering into windows. When he neared the café, he noticed Emma's light was off. She must have gone to bed.

But as he came closer, he realized things weren't as peaceful as they seemed. His nostrils flared when they picked up the acrid smell of something burning. He couldn't see any smoke, but he started running toward Emma's. When he rounded the corner of her building, he saw flames. They seemed to be coming from a pile of rubbish outside her kitchen door.

A Promise Made

Matt banged on the door. "Emma! Wake up!"

He kicked dirt at the growing fire and yelled again. "Emma!"

The flames began licking the side of the wall. Matt backed up and ran toward the door, slamming against it with his shoulder. A piercing pain shot through his arm, but the door didn't budge. "Emma!"

He stepped back to try again just as Ben came running from around the front of the building. Matt heard the clang of the fire engine in the distance.

"Help is comin'," Ben said.

Matt rammed into the door with his other shoulder, and it gave way with a crack. Matt ran in and met Emma on the stairs, Mandy in her arms.

"What's burning? What's going on?"

Matt grabbed her and pulled her and the baby through the doorway. He rushed them out into the alley just as the firemen arrived and began to douse the flames. Two firemen manned the hand pumps on either side of the wagon, filling the hose from the water tank, while two others directed the hose at the fire.

Emma's hand came to her mouth. "How did this happen? I don't remember leaving anything on the stove."

"This is not your fault," Matt assured her. "The stove is nowhere near the fire. Those flames started on the outside wall, not inside."

"Who would do such a thing?"

Matt's arms encircled the two most important people in his life, and he sent up a prayer of thanksgiving that they were all right. Taking a deep breath, he fought for composure and shook his head. "I don't know. But I intend to find out who's behind this, no matter how long it takes."

Emma felt chilled when Matt released his hold on her and Mandy. He sent Ben to awaken the sheriff, then started scouring the alley for clues. When Ben returned with Sheriff Haynes, the two men assisted in the search.

Emma was grateful that the outside wall to the café was only scorched, thanks to Ben's quick action. Once the fire was out, the fire marshal brought everyone inside and began asking questions.

"I saw a man run off from here a few minutes ago," Ben said, "just before the flames started up. I ran to the fire station right away to get help, so I didn't get a good look at his face."

Mandy fell back to sleep amid all the chaos, and Emma put her down in her little corner in the kitchen. She put on some coffee for the men, listening attentively to their conversation.

Her hands shook as she poured several cups. First the rock and now this. Was someone trying to frighten her? If so, he was doing a very good job. Emma sent a prayer heavenward, thanking God for putting Ben and Matt in the right place at the right time, grateful that they had worked so quickly to send for help and to get her and Mandy out.

She asked Ben to start breakfast for the men, then went back outside to inspect the damage. Her mind filled with the memory of how comforting it had felt to be held snugly in Matt's arms as he pulled her and Mandy out of harm's way. Never in her life had she felt so safe and protected. She shook that thought out of her mind, sternly reminding herself that the deputy was only doing his duty. Besides, what was she doing daydreaming when she had such a huge mess to clean up?

Matt's heart still hammered in his chest hours after the fire was put out. Over and over again, he thanked the Lord that Emma and Mandy were all right. If anything had happened to Emma and the baby—

"Son, we're going to find out who did this." The sheriff slapped Matt's back as they walked to the office after eating the large breakfast Emma had served them.

"I know. I wish we'd found something in that alley to point to who did it. I have a few suspicions, though. I think we should start by having a talk with Jed Brewster."

"I had the same idea. I also think we should double the watch on her place."

"Sounds good to me," Matt said.

"Why don't you go on home and get some rest, son?" Sheriff Haynes suggested.

Matt went home, but he didn't rest. First thing in the morning, he got cleaned up and hurried over to the post office. His fatigue disappeared when he saw he had a letter from Emma.

Tearing open the envelope as soon as he got outside, he scanned the letter quickly. One line stood out.

> *Because time is of importance, would it be possible for us to meet this coming Wednesday, at my café, at 9:00 p.m.?"*

Matt almost let out a whoop of joy right there in the street. He sat down on a bench outside the post office and composed a response. It was time to tell her the truth. That he was the one writing the letters. And that he loved her with all his heart.

Chapter 15

Monday felt two days long. With so little sleep and so much going on, Emma had little time to wonder if "DMJ" had received her letter suggesting they meet on Wednesday evening.

Ben boarded up the back wall as best he could until a carpenter could get there to provide an estimate on fixing the charred wood. Once word about the fire got out, Emma's café was busier than ever with customers coming in to check on her. . .after they checked out the back of her building.

When Liddy and Cal came in and heard about the fire, they tried to convince Emma to move out to Liddy's old house.

"It's been empty since Annie passed away," Cal reminded her.

"Now what good would that do?" Emma said. "It would take the fire department twice as long to get there as here."

"You're right," Liddy said. "I just worry about you and Mandy here alone. Then again, maybe that won't be the case much longer?" Liddy asked, raising her eyebrows.

"We'll see." Emma had to admit that she would feel safer having a man around. She wanted a husband, and Mandy needed a father. While her first choice would have been Matt, he'd made no more mention of his proposal. If he really loved her, he wouldn't have taken no for an answer, would he?

She needed to keep her mind off the memory of being held by him when he rescued her and Mandy from the fire. Maybe her meeting with DMJ would put all thoughts of Matt out of her mind.

Emma thought she'd have a hard time sleeping that night, worrying if someone might come back to finish the job he'd started. But the sheriff had assured her that her place would be watched constantly until they found out who was behind the fire, and she was so exhausted she found herself drifting off to sleep almost before her head hit the pillow.

With all the work involved repairing the smoke and water damage, it was Wednesday before Emma had a chance to pick up her mail again. She brought the letter she picked up back to the café, and her fingers shook as she opened it.

He would be at the café *"promptly at nine o'clock in the evening. . .if not before."*

As she clutched the letter to her chest, Emma was certain God had sent this man into her and Mandy's life. But there was a niggling doubt about the fact that she still didn't know the man. How could this possibly work?

Then she reminded herself that there had been arranged marriages since Bible times. This wouldn't be much different, assuming DMJ actually did propose. . .would it?

The butterflies in her stomach multiplied as the day went on. Each time the bell above the door jingled, her heart skittered. She tried to keep her hair neat throughout the day, but there was no preventing the tendrils from escaping out of the bun at the top of her head and curling around her face. After supper she changed into one of her favorite dresses: a cream-and-rose-striped cotton with a deep lace yoke.

As nine o'clock drew near, Emma wondered if she should have had the sheriff check out the post office box number after all. Well, it was too late now.

A few minutes before nine, the bell jingled and Emma's heart jumped. She looked up quickly but saw only Matt. *Of course, he would pick now to show up!* She blew the escaping hairs up over her forehead and went to take his order.

"Evenin', Deputy." He did look nice, dressed in a new plaid shirt, his face freshly shaven.

"Evening, Emma." Matt sat at his table. "You and Mandy doing all right?"

"We're fine. Thanks again for helping the other night."

Matt's gaze caught hers. "You're welcome. I'm glad Ben and I were there."

The warmth in his expression reminded Emma of how it had felt to be held in his arms, and she gave herself an inward shake. She had no business thinking about Matt now. "What can I get you?"

"Just a piece of pie and glass of milk, please."

She hurried off toward the kitchen. Milk instead of coffee again, she noticed. He must still be having stomach problems. She hoped it wasn't anything more. Maybe she should suggest—

What was she thinking? Matt was a grown man. He could take care of himself. And she would do well to quit worrying about him. He wasn't in her future.

The sudden peal of the telephone interrupted her thoughts. She scrambled to answer it, wondering who would be calling her.

She'd no sooner pressed the receiver to her ear than she heard Liddy's excited voice on the other end. "We got our telephone today."

"That's wonderful."

"So, has *he* shown up yet?" Liddy asked.

"No. But naturally, Matt did. I don't want him here when—"

Emma thought she heard her friend chuckle, but it turned into a brief coughing spell. "I have to go," Liddy said when she regained her voice. "I'll talk to you later."

"All right." Emma placed the earpiece back on its hook. She grinned at Ben as she opened the icebox. "Think we'll ever get used to the telephone ringing?"

"Not me. That sound scared about ten years off my life."

Emma laughed as she poured Matt's milk and dished up his pie. She was still grinning when she set the food on his table. But when she glanced at his face, her humor died away. Matt was smiling at her, the expression in his eyes one she'd never seen before. Her heart began to beat ferociously, and she couldn't make herself turn away from the warmth of his gaze. She swallowed hard. A moment passed. Then two.

Matt cleared his throat. "Emma. . ."

She couldn't let Matt affect her like this. In just a few minutes, she was going to meet her future husband. She had to put her feelings for Matt in the past where they belonged.

Leaving him to check on her other customers, Emma saw that the last group who remained were ready to go. She took their money and cleared the table, trying to ignore Matt and calm herself down. The wall clock's hands were inching toward nine. She flipped the OPEN sign to CLOSED but didn't lock the door. She glanced up and down the street, hoping to catch a glimpse of her future husband.

When she turned around, she saw that Matt had finished his pie and milk. "Emma, could we talk a minute?" he asked softly.

She really didn't want him here. Not now. "Matt, I really have a lot to do."

Matt leaned back in his chair. "I know. You're waiting for someone, aren't you?"

Emma stopped breathing for a moment. "How did you know? Did Cal and Liddy—?"

"Emma, I. . ."

While she waited for him to finish his sentence, Emma decided there was no reason not to tell him the truth. He'd know soon enough, anyway. "I am waiting for someone, Matt. I don't mean to be rude, but I would appreciate it if you'd leave."

He shook his head. "I'm afraid I can't do that."

Why was he being so stubborn?

Emma's heart seemed to stop when she saw him pull a letter out of his pocket. The writing looked exactly like hers.

Emma sank into the chair across from him. "Where did you get that?"

"From my post office box. Your nine o'clock appointment is with me, Emma. I'm the man you're waiting on. I'm the one who's been writing the letters you've been answering." He shrugged. "I'm DMJ."

No. This couldn't be. Emma blinked back sudden tears. "I don't know what kind of joke you're trying to play, Matthew Johnson, but it's not funny."

He reached across the table and gathered her hand in his. "It's no joke, Emma. I came here to—"

Emma jerked her hand out of his. "No! You aren't—you can't be. . ."

"Deputy Matt Johnson. DMJ." He ran his fingers through his hair. "I'm sorry for misleading you, Emma. I hope you can forgive me. But I couldn't sign my name to those letters. You would never have answered me."

"I should have known." Emma fought tears of hurt and anger. How could he pull such a cruel trick on her? He'd always been her friend, or so she'd thought. This was a terrible thing to do to a person's emotions.

Emma jumped up and pointed to the door. "Get out of here, Deputy. This instant. And don't ever come back."

Matt didn't budge. "No," he said, calmly but firmly. "I'm not going anywhere until you hear me out. Emma, I meant every word I wrote in those letters. I would be honored to be your husband and be a father to Mandy."

"We've been through this before, Matt." Emma walked to the door and held it open. "We have nothing more to talk about."

Matt got up and walked toward her. "I believe we do." He gently shut the door. "And this time you're going to listen to me. If you don't like what I have to say, you can kick me out."

He cupped her cheek in his hand. "I'm not very good with words, Emma. I didn't say all I should have when I asked you to marry me last week. I'd never done that before, and I admit to not quite knowing how to do it properlike."

Emma's chin inched upward. She blinked rapidly and bit her bottom lip. She supposed she did owe him the courtesy of listening to him.

His hand moved to her shoulder, his gaze never leaving her face. "I seem to have left out the most important part of any proposal." Matt pulled her closer. "I love you, Emma Hanson. I've loved you for a very long time. And I love Mandy, too. I want to marry you; I want to help you raise that beautiful little girl. I want to spend the rest of my life showing you both how much I mean every word I'm saying. Just give me a chance. Please."

Emma couldn't stop the tears that flowed down her cheeks. "I don't want pity from you—"

"What I feel for you is *not* pity, Emma. You are the most amazing woman I've ever known. I love you. If the town council decided right this minute to give up the fight to take Mandy away from you, I would still be asking you to marry me. Please believe me."

It was everything she'd ever hoped to hear from Deputy Matt Johnson. . .and more. She nodded, slightly at first and then vigorously. Matt's head dipped, and his lips claimed hers in precisely the way she'd dreamed they would. She returned his kiss with all the love that was in her heart.

"Miss Emma?" Ben's voice ended the kiss as he pushed open the door from the kitchen. "Oh!" he said when he saw her in Matt's embrace. "Excuse me."

Emma and Matt chuckled as Ben headed back to the kitchen, muttering, " 'Bout time, that's what I say."

"That's what I say, too." Matt's lips found hers once more and lingered there for moments marked only by heartbeats. Finally, he broke off the kiss and led her back to the table. After she sat, he bent down on one knee and took her hand in his.

"Emma Hanson, I would be honored if you would accept my proposal of marriage. I love you with all that is in me. Will you be my wife?"

Emma's heart seemed to melt into a puddle. "I would be delighted to be your wife."

Matt pulled her face to his, settling his lips on hers again. When the kiss ended, he raised his head and gazed into her eyes. "I promise you, I will find some other kind of job so you don't have to worry about becoming a widow."

She brushed at her tears. "Oh, Matt, there's no need to change professions. The Lord willing, we'll grow old together. But if not, I'll be thankful for each moment we can share. . .just as I'm sure your mother was for her time with your father."

As Matt stood, he pulled her off the chair and into the circle of his arms for another kiss. Emma silently thanked the Lord for bringing Annie into her life. From the promise she made to raise Mandy had come her heart's desire—a family of her own. . .with the man she'd always loved.

Epilogue

Emma's heart sang with joy as she walked into the town council meeting the following Monday. But, at Matt and the sheriff's suggestion, she worked hard not to show it. She was doing just fine—until she glanced over to where Matt was standing, in his usual place at the back of the room. His almost imperceptible wink was nearly her undoing. Her heart pounded so hard she felt it would surely burst with all the love she felt for that man.

To keep her composure, she quickly glanced the other way and continued up the aisle with Mandy on her hip, Cal and Liddy following behind. They took their seats in the front row and waited for the meeting to come to order. The same men were seated at the table in the front of the room.

From the smirk on Harper's face as he sat at the table with the other councilmen, it was obvious he thought he'd won. Emma couldn't wait for him to find out what was in store for him.

He took out his pocket watch and examined it, then put it back and stood. "Ladies and gentlemen, it's time to call the meeting to order. The main issue of business tonight is finding a permanent home for the Drake child. The orphanage in Santa Fe is ready to take her as soon as we can arrange to get her there."

"Hold on, Harper," a deep voice from the back of the room called out. Everyone turned their heads to see Mayor Adams making his way up the aisle. "What's all this about?"

"Mayor!" Harper backed up a step and ran his finger around his collar. "We weren't expecting you back until next week."

"I finished my business back East earlier than expected," the mayor said, continuing up the aisle. "It would appear I returned in the nick of time. What's this about you trying to make Emma Hanson give up the child she promised to raise?"

Harper's smirk disappeared as the mayor joined him on the podium. A fine bead of perspiration formed on his upper lip. He pulled a handkerchief from his jacket pocket and mopped his face. "I—we—the council thought a single woman, particularly one trying to run a business—"

"From what I've heard since I got back into town," the mayor said with a nod at Emma, "Mandy Drake is in very capable hands."

Harper glared at Emma and cleared his throat. "I just thought that a married couple would be better able to—"

"That's not quite true." Sheriff Haynes traipsed up the aisle. "What you thought, Mr. Harper, was that you could run Miss Hanson out of town so you could buy her place of business."

The crowd began to murmur.

"I—I did no such thing!" Harper shrieked over the din.

"So that's what this was all about," Homer Williams said, rising from the table. He squinted at the mayor. "He's been going on and on about how valuable all the property close to the train station will be, once the line gets finished on into Amarillo in the next year or so. He must've had this plan in mind the whole time."

"That's preposterous!" Harper bellowed.

Jed Brewster stood and addressed the crowd. "No, it isn't." He glanced down at his wife, Laura, and she clasped his hand. He turned toward Emma. "Douglas Harper wanted to scare you out of town, Miss Emma. He paid me to come in drunk that night and cause a disturbance. Then he tried to pay me to throw a rock through your window. I turned him down."

Harper's face turned bright red. "No one is going to believe you, you drunk."

"Well, maybe they'll believe me," Zeke Anderson said. "I went in to the sheriff's office this afternoon and confessed to throwing that rock into the café and setting that fire, too. And I told them about you paying me to do them things." He turned toward Emma. "I'm real sorry, Miss Hanson. I promise I'll make full restitution for all the damage I done."

Harper turned suddenly and ran out the side door. He returned a moment later, backing up, Deputy Carmichael's gun held to his chest. Sheriff Haynes quickly slapped handcuffs on the banker and led him down the aisle through the tittering crowd.

"Sheriff, wait," Emma said.

The sheriff stopped and pulled Harper around to face her.

"Councilman Harper, there's something I'd like to know. What made you think you'd get my place if I left town?"

Harper shrugged. "It would have been easy to find someone to buy your property for me."

Robert Morris, the real estate dabbler, called out from the back of the room. "He paid me to make Miss Emma an offer on her place of business if she decided to sell. He didn't tell me he was trying to scare her into doing it."

"Well, Mr. Harper here isn't going to be doing much wheelin' and dealin' anymore." Sheriff Haynes led him out the door, amid cheers from the crowd.

The noise grew so loud, the mayor had to bang the gavel. "Before we call an end to this meeting," he said when the noise finally died down, "I'd like to apologize to Miss Hanson on behalf of the town council"—he gave the men at the table a wilting look—"for causing her so much misery these past few weeks."

"Thank you, sir," Emma said. "But all I'd really like is an end to all this. Since the council started this trouble, I'd like for them to formally proclaim that I have the legal right to keep Mandy Drake and raise her as my own child."

The other councilmen huddled together for a mere minute before Homer Williams stood. "Miss Emma, we're all agreed that's the least we can do for you. You have full and complete custody of Mandy Drake—and you don't have to have a husband to keep her."

"Too late for that, Councilman," Matt called out, making his way up the aisle to Emma's side. He put an arm around her waist and pulled her close. "She's already found one. Minister Turley married us this afternoon, and we invite you all back to the café right now to join in our celebration. Ben and Hallie have been busy all day, and they've prepared quite a spread."

Amid cheers and clapping, Matt kissed his bride. Emma returned the kiss, thanking the Lord above for making sure she kept a promise made.

A Place Called Home

To my Lord and Savior for showing me the way.
I thank Him for the family I was born into, for the family He's given me,
and for my parents, William B. (Red) and Thelma Heaton,
who faithfully instilled a deep abiding love of the Lord in us all
and who encouraged my love of reading and writing always.
What a blessing to know that one day I'll see them again
in their "place called home" in heaven.

Chapter 1

1898—Roswell, New Mexico Territory

Beth Morgan looked at the clock on the wall beside the switchboard. One thirty. She inserted the pin into Alma Burton's line's socket and pulled the lever for two rings. She pulled the lever again.

"Yes?" asked a sleepy-sounding Alma.

"Mrs. Alma, you wanted me to let you know when it was time to take your cake out of the oven," Beth reminded her. It wasn't unusual for her to serve as a kitchen timer a couple of times a day—especially for some of the older women in the community.

"Oh, thank you, dear. I would have plumb forgotten if you hadn't reminded me." Alma sounded more awake now.

"You are very welcome. You have a good day." Beth felt all but certain Mrs. Burton had been napping when she rang her. She pulled the pin out of the socket and chuckled. She still couldn't get over how very different being a telephone operator for the Roswell Telephone and Manufacturing Company was from the Bell Telephone Company where she'd received her training back East. There had been so many rules and regulations—the primary one being not to talk to the customers. Those rules never made it out to New Mexico Territory, and for that she was very thankful. Otherwise, she'd be in big trouble with the superintendent. Most of the telephone customers thought of the operators as their own personal message service.

The light over the sheriff's office line lit up. Beth connected the line pin. "Number, please."

"Beth? Is that you?"

Her heart skittered in her chest as she recognized Deputy Matt Johnson's voice. "Yes, it's me, Matt."

"We've heard from Jeb Winslow. He's on his way to Roswell."

Her heart sank. "When will he be here?"

"He was up in Colorado when he got the letter. He's on his way now. Sheriff and I figure he'll get to town sometime in the next week or so."

Beth nodded but couldn't speak.

"I'm sorry, Beth. I think we've all been hoping he wouldn't be found."

She swallowed around the knot of unshed tears in her throat. "Yes, well, thank you for letting me know, Matt."

Beth pulled the pin from the socket without waiting on a reply from the deputy. Her worst fear had just been realized. How was she going to let Cassie and Lucas go? They didn't even know their uncle. She was glad Jessica was busy at the other switchboard and hoped she couldn't tell how upset she was at the news she'd just heard.

Laura Brewster's light came on above her socket.

"Number, please?"

"Doc Bradshaw, please."

Beth connected the two lines and watched the light go out over both Doc's and Laura's sockets, letting her know she'd made a successful connection. She fought back the tears that threatened and glanced at the clock again. Her friend and coworker, Darcie Malone, would be relieving her soon, then she could leave. Most of the time she was thankful for her job as telephone operator at the Roswell Telephone and Manufacturing Company, but today she just wanted to get home. She needed to figure out what to say to Harland's children. She didn't quite know how to tell them their uncle had been found and was on his way to claim them.

It'd been only two months since their father and her fiancé had died in a cattle stampede, but she'd come to love Cassie and Lucas. And she didn't like the idea of giving them up to a man they didn't know, even if he was their uncle.

The lights came on again first over Laura's socket and then Doc's, alerting her that their conversation was over. She unplugged each socket. While Beth knew most of what went on in Roswell because of her job and the fact that everyone seemed to think she should or did know their business, she tried not to listen in on conversations—something the superintendent, Mr. McQuillen, was still working on with Darcie.

The light under the Roswell Hotel socket lit up, and she plugged the pin into it. "Number, please."

"Get me the sheriff's office, please, Beth," Morris Benson, the hotel clerk, requested.

Beth plugged the other pin into the socket of the sheriff's office and pulled the lever to ring their phone. She then made sure the lights went off before she answered the next call.

When Mr. Church, the general manager, and Mr. McQuillen had started the Roswell Telephone and Manufacturing Company in 1894, there were only thirty-five subscribers. Beth had been one of the first two operators hired, after her ailing aunt, whom she'd come out West to care for, had passed away. The company had grown considerably since it started, and now there were six regular operators and one relief. . .and about four installers who put up the lines and ran them into customers' homes. Nearby farms and ranches were being serviced now, and long distance to Eddy would be coming in the next year or so. No telling how many more employees there would be in the coming years.

She couldn't help but wonder if she'd still be here, if her life kept changing as much as it had in the past year. So much had happened. It was hard enough to believe she'd answered an advertisement for a mail-order bride as a dare, much less that she'd ended up accepting the proposal of the man who'd written back, even before he decided to join her out West in Roswell and start their life together.

He'd bought a piece of land, sight unseen, to start a small ranch and had planned on courting her proper while he got his herd started and refurbished the house on the land. Then they'd get married.

Barely a month after he arrived, Harland had been out working with the small herd of cattle he'd bought for the ranch when a dry lightning storm blew up. Evidently, from what one of the neighbors had said, a bolt struck close and frightened the cattle. Harland had been caught in the ensuing stampede. Just thinking about it made her shudder. She was so relieved the children had been staying in town with her until Harland was able to fix up the house and hadn't been there to see the death of their father.

Beth still couldn't quite believe it all. Feeling that it was her fault, she'd wished over and over again that she'd never answered that advertisement. . . believing that if Harland hadn't come out here, he'd still be alive. Now it seemed there was more heartache in store—if she had to give up the children she'd come to love.

Darcie showed up to relieve her, right on time, and Beth relinquished her spot in front of the switchboard quickly, as they'd been trained to do. Darcie immediately slipped into the chair right behind her and began connecting two lit-up sockets.

"Beth, what's wrong?" Darcie called as Beth pulled on the shawl she'd worn to work and started out the door.

"Oh, Darcie, I'm sorry." Beth turned back to her friend, realizing how rude she must have appeared, heading out the door without so much as a nod to her. She tried to keep her voice low so the whole office wouldn't know her business, but she knew it was only a matter of time until they did. "I'm not thinking straight. Harland's brother has been found, and Deputy Matt says he'll be here to collect the children in about a week. I just don't know how I'll be able to let them go."

Darcie jumped up and hugged her. "Oh, Beth, I'm so sorry I dared you to answer that advertisement for a mail-order bride. It's my fault you are so unhappy now."

Beth shook her head. "No, Darcie, it's not your fault. It's my own impulsiveness that caused my problem. I'd always wondered what it would be like to answer one of those advertisements. It was Harland's sweet letters that made me begin to care for him and accept his offer of marriage. And I feel to blame. If I hadn't accepted his proposal, and if he hadn't come out here and been caught in that stampede—"

"You'd be a happily married woman by now, instead of having two children to care for alone. Harland's death was not your fault, Beth." The switchboard lit up in several places, and Darcie slid back into the chair and hurriedly disconnected two parties and connected two others.

Beth sighed. Maybe it wasn't all her fault. . .but she wasn't sure Darcie's picture of the future would have been true. She'd been having second thoughts about marrying Harland and had been trying to figure out what to do about it before he died. Now she was just thankful that he hadn't known. She'd been terribly confused about so many things lately, but one thing was for certain, she didn't regret offering to keep his children. Not for one moment.

Lines unlit for the time being, Darcie turned back to her. "It might be for the best, you know, Beth."

Beth did know many in town would think that. All her friends thought she was a little daft for taking in Harland's children. Well, not Emma and Deputy Matt or Cal and Liddy McAllister. They had been very supportive of her, and she was thankful for that.

And she was blessed that she had a home to offer the children. Thankfully, they'd been living with her in the small house she'd inherited from her aunt Gertrude, so there was no need to uproot them after their father's death. She didn't make a lot of money, but the Lord would provide for them. Of that, Beth had no doubt. She'd taken them in, presumably, until Harland's brother could be found, but she didn't really think he would be, and she'd truly hoped he wouldn't. Now she had to face the fact that Lucas and Cassie's uncle at least cared enough to come and see his niece and nephew. She would continue to hope that Jeb Winslow would let her have custody of Harland's children. From what Harland had told her about his brother, he wasn't the settling-down kind. She was going to hold out hope that maybe, just maybe, he'd be glad to let them stay with her.

"It will all work out, Beth." Darcie tried to reassure her again.

Beth nodded. "Well, it's all in the Lord's hands now, but I sure hope Mr. Winslow doesn't take them far away. Maybe he'll decide to stay. Mr. Myers, Harland's lawyer, said he'd talked to him about making out a new will, but of course he hadn't had a chance to get to it with so much to do. His old will appointed Jeb Winslow as the children's guardian. They inherit the land, but he has the say so as to whether to sell it or keep it for them. I hope he'll settle here so at least I can keep watch over them."

The switchboard lit up again, and Beth was relieved not to have to keep talking about it. She waved good-bye and hurried out the door.

Jeb dismounted his horse and tied it at the hitching post just outside the cemetery gate, his heart still aching. He'd been riding for several weeks—ever since he received the letter telling him that his brother had died in a stampede, leaving two orphaned children behind. He'd come to take on the responsibility of raising them, even though the very thought of it scared him more than coming face-to-face with a mother bear. *Dear Lord, please help me to do it right. You know I know nothing about bringing up children, so I'm just going to look to You to help me.*

He thought about his niece and nephew. Last time he saw them, Cassie was about four or five, and Lucas was a toddler. Now they'd be about nine and six. . .ten and seven? He didn't know. Remorse flooded Jeb's soul. Why hadn't he visited them more often? But no. He'd always had other things to do, other places to go. Why, he hadn't even known Mary died or that Harland had decided to move out West until he got the letter telling him his brother had died. Jeb figured the Lord must have been guiding that letter through the mail for him to have gotten it at all. It had been to the last two places he'd worked before the post ever made it to him.

He'd only been working at this last ranch up in southern Colorado for little over a year—and that was long for him. His boss had been hinting about making him a foreman, and he was seriously thinking it might be time to settle down. He sure wasn't getting any younger; he still limped from the last time he'd been thrown trying to break a horse, and he didn't seem to be getting any better.

Dry grass crackled under his boots until he found the spot he was looking for. Taking off his hat, he knelt down and blinked through the sudden tears that formed on seeing the gravestone bearing his brother's name. Childhood memories came flooding back as he remembered the laughing, teasing, and fighting they'd done in their youth. His timing sure was bad. How he wished he'd gone home for one last visit. But all the wishing in the world couldn't undo the past.

He swallowed around the lump in his throat and stood. All he could do now for his brother was to raise his children the best he could. Taking a deep breath, Jeb set his hat on his head and took long strides back to his horse. He mounted and turned toward the main street of Roswell. He had to find his niece and nephew. They were the only family he had left.

On the outskirts of town, he noticed a cluster of nice new buildings on North Hill. He'd heard the New Mexico Military Institute had reopened in a new spot just this year, and sure enough, the sign outside the main building proved it hadn't been rumor after all. Funding had closed it down for several years, but he'd seen in a paper where it had been slated to open this very month.

As he rode into town and down Main Street, Jeb couldn't help but notice how much Roswell had grown since he'd last been through about three years ago. There were four or five large hotels, four mercantile houses, several drugstores, three blacksmith shops, two livery stables, three barbers, cafés, a bakery, a lumberyard, a telephone office—all kinds of new businesses that weren't here last time he'd been through. It was now a bustling, thriving town. He reined in and hitched his horse outside the sheriff's office and went inside.

A man about his age looked up from his desk and stood when Jeb walked toward him. "Howdy. I'm Deputy Matt Johnson. What can I do for you?"

Jeb nodded. "Afternoon, Deputy. I'm Jeb Winslow, and I need to know where my brother's children are."

"We've been expecting you, Mr. Winslow." The deputy stood up and extended his hand. He motioned to the chair in front of the desk. "Have a seat. I'm sure sorry about the loss of your brother. It was an awful accident."

Jeb shook the deputy's hand and lowered himself into the chair. He nodded and cleared his throat, suddenly finding it hard to speak.

The deputy crossed the room and poured a cup of coffee from the pot on the stove sitting in the middle of the room. He brought it over and handed it to him.

Jeb took a drink and swallowed. "Thank you. Road's been dry," he commented, but he had a feeling the deputy knew the dust had nothing to do with his hoarseness. "Can you tell me exactly what happened? How did my brother get caught up in a stampede?"

"Best we can figure, a bolt of lightning spooked his cattle, and he just got caught in the middle." He paused. "Did your brother have much experience ranching?"

Jeb shook his head. "Not that I know of. Harland was a farmer back home, but we hadn't seen each other in a long time. Still, I don't know that he ever owned a herd of cattle."

The deputy nodded. "Some of the neighbors said he seemed a little green."

"Might have been." Jeb had seen stampedes before, and the very thought of his brother dying in one still sickened him. He could barely think it, much less say it, but he had to ask. "Did the children see—"

"No, thank the Lord. They were in town."

Jeb sighed with relief and nodded. He gazed out the window a moment before speaking. "Can you tell me where they are now?"

"They're in very good hands. Harland's fiancée, Beth Morgan, has been taking real good care of them." The deputy ambled to the door and motioned to a building down a ways on the other side of the street. It bore a sign bearing the name, THE ROSWELL TELEPHONE AND MANUFACTURING COMPANY, and Jeb remembered passing it on the way there.

Deputy Johnson continued. "Beth works across the street as a telephone operator and lives in a house a few blocks away. She should be getting off work soon, but the children will be in school for another couple of hours."

Jeb let out a deep breath. "That'll give me time to clean up before I see them." He brushed at the travel dust on his pants. "I wouldn't want to scare them at first sight."

The deputy chuckled. "Probably wouldn't hurt to spruce up some. But, Lucas and Cassie are good children with nice manners. They'd never mention that thick layer of dust you've collected getting here to them."

"Thank you for your help, Deputy. I'm sure I'll be seeing you."

"The lawyer who handled your brother's will has an office over on Third Street, going west. It's about two blocks down. His name is John Myers," Matt informed him. "Harland got a good deal on the land. It's not a big ranch, but it's a prime location, just outside of town. But the house is in pretty bad shape. If you are going to stay, you'll want to do some repairs. You might consider leaving the children with Beth until it's livable."

Jeb hadn't even thought that far ahead. He just wanted his brother's children to know they had some kin left in the world. He needed to ride out to the ranch his brother owned and see how much work was needed to get the house habitable. . .and he'd better visit that lawyer and tie up any loose ends. But all that could wait. Right now he needed to board his horse at a livery stable and find a hotel room. After a bath, he'd go meet his niece and nephew. "Thanks, Deputy. I appreciate your advice. I'll think on it."

"Come on back when you're ready, and I'll take you to see the children."

Jeb nodded. "Thank you. I think I'll take you up on that offer."

Beth Morgan was on her way home from the telephone office. It'd been over a week since Matt had told her Jeb Winslow was on his way to Roswell. That was probably what drew her gaze to the sheriff's office across the street. But it was the sight of a tall, broad-shouldered cowboy coming out of the office that had her heart hammering in her chest. He walked with a slight limp and was larger than Harland, but there was something about him. . . .

He glanced her way and tipped his hat. For a minute she held her breath, wondering if he was Jeb Winslow, come to get the children. But when he headed down the other side of the street, she breathed a sigh of relief and hurried home.

Ever since Matt had told her Jeb was on his way back, she'd been meeting each day with a feeling of dread. She didn't want him to come after his niece and nephew, and she was aware she was being very selfish. She just couldn't help it. She wanted to raise them. From all she'd heard from Harland, Jeb Winslow was the last person who should have them. Harland had mentioned more than once how he wished his younger brother would settle down and how disappointed he was that he'd never been able to convince him to do so.

She went to the kitchen and put on the teakettle, disconcerted at how shaky she was at seeing the stranger coming out of the sheriff's office. Like it or not, Lucas and Cassie's uncle would be here before too long, and she was going to have to give them up. But however was she going to be able to do that? They didn't even know the man! Surely he wouldn't just come and get them and leave. She bowed her head.

Dear Lord, please help me to accept Your will in this. I know I'm not blood kin, but I love Cassie and Lucas, and they know me. I can't bear the thought of them moving away with a stranger, even if he is the only family they have left in the world. Please keep them here. In Jesus' name I pray, amen.

There was nothing more to do. She needed to leave it in the Lord's hands. The kettle began to whistle, and she made herself a cup of tea. Maybe it would soothe her frazzled nerves. She'd drink it, then go to meet the children at the Third Street School.

She'd taken to going to the school and walking home with them ever since Harland's death. Both children were still grieving. She knew they were. Yet they seldom let her see their tears, and that made her want to cry for them. Today, they seemed in good spirits when they came running out the door.

It was a crisp September day with brilliant blue skies and a light breeze that sent the cottonwood leaves swirling around their feet while they strolled home. Lucas kicked at the leaves as Cassie told Beth about their day, and both children were full of excitement about the upcoming fair at the beginning of October.

"Grace says they build a palace out of bales of alfalfa and have the exhibits in it. She says it is huge!" Lucas said excitedly.

Beth grinned at his little-boy enthusiasm. "It's called an alfalfa palace and, yes, they do have exhibits in it."

"I can't wait to see it." Lucas skipped a few paces ahead.

Cassie laughed. "That's all he's been talking about, Miss Beth."

"Well, we'll be sure to go, so he'll get to see it for real. The McAllisters are sure to have some exhibits. I wouldn't mind entering a few things. Aunt Gertrude's receipt for apple pie is hard to beat."

"Oh, that would be great fun!" Cassie exclaimed. "May we help?"

"Of course you can help. Maybe we'll make some jam, too." They were near home, and Beth watched Lucas run around a tree and dart ahead before coming to a sudden stop. She glanced past him to the front stoop of her home. Deputy

Matt stood there with the man she'd seen coming out of his office earlier. Her heart plummeted to her stomach as she grabbed Cassie's hand, then felt Lucas slip his smaller one into her other hand as he'd run back to her and his sister.

"Good afternoon, Beth," Matt greeted her as they came closer. He motioned to the dark-haired man beside him. "This is Jeb Winslow—Harland's brother. Jeb, this is Beth Morgan."

"Pleased to meet you, Miss Morgan." He tipped his hat to her and bent down to look at Cassie and Lucas. "I'm your uncle Jeb. . .your papa's brother."

Lucas scooted behind Beth and peeked out from behind her. Cassie held Beth's hand tight. Beth tried hard not to let the tension she felt show on her face, knowing that she had to take charge of the moment for the children's sake.

She tried to smile at Harland's brother. She could see the resemblance, but Jeb was younger, leaner. . .tougher looking. "How do you do, Mr. Winslow? I—we've been expecting you."

Jeb stood up straight and looked down into her eyes. Her heart leapt at the expression in them. He had the warmest brown eyes she'd even seen. He smiled and nodded. "The deputy told me. . .you were engaged to my brother?"

"Yes." *Although, I wasn't sure. . . . But, no—now isn't the time to be thinking about any of that.* "Yes, I was."

He nodded. "It seems we've all suffered a loss. I appreciate your taking in the children."

"I wanted to. Actually, they were already living with me. The house at the ranch isn't fit for them yet."

"So the deputy said—"

"They are more than welcome to stay with me—"

"But I—"

"I have an idea," Matt interrupted. "Why don't you all come over to the café and have dinner with Emma and me this evening around six o'clock? It's beginning to get a little chilly out, and it might be easier to talk things over after a warm meal."

Jeb glanced at Beth. "If Miss Morgan agrees, that would be fine by me."

"Oh, can we?" Cassie asked. Beth knew Cassie loved eating at Emma's Café. Most of all, she seemed to enjoy the opportunity to hold Mandy, Emma and Matt's two-year-old.

Beth sighed with relief. It would be so much easier to talk at Emma's. . .with friends there. Her smile felt almost genuine this time. "Thank you, Matt. We'd be glad to accept your offer."

Chapter 2

As Jeb walked back to the sheriff's office with Deputy Johnson, he had a feeling that Miss Beth Morgan was not the least bit happy to see him. Oh, she had been polite and smiled at him, but it never quite reached her eyes. She sure was pretty, though, with those eyes the color of fresh honey and that thick blond hair pulled up onto the top of her head.

"Beth has taken real good care of Lucas and Cassie." Deputy Matt broke into his thoughts.

Jeb agreed. "I could tell that right off. But she won't have to, now that I'm here."

"We didn't know if you would come for them. Beth cares about them. She'd be glad to keep them if you—"

"Oh, I couldn't let her do that, Deputy. They are my responsibility, and they're all the kin I have left."

They reached the office, and Matt stopped outside the door. He pointed to the café almost directly across the street with a sign that read EMMA'S CAFÉ. "That's my wife's restaurant. She serves the best food in town. I'll let her know you and Beth and the children will be having supper with us tonight."

"Thanks, Deputy. I appreciate the offer. I could tell Miss Morgan was a little uncomfortable talking to me. Maybe it will be easier over a meal, like you said."

"I hope so," Matt said. "We'll see you about six."

Jeb pulled his hat a little farther down on his head. "See you then. In the meantime, I have a few things I need to pick up at the mercantile, and I think I'll stop by the lawyer's office and make an appointment to see him tomorrow on my way there." He touched the brim of his Stetson and took off down the boardwalk.

Cassie and Lucas had all kinds of questions for Beth after Deputy Matt and Harland's brother had taken their leave. They continued as she helped them get ready to go to Emma's.

"How long do you think Uncle Jeb will stay, Miss Beth?" Lucas asked as she began to comb his hair.

"I don't know, Lucas." *But I hope it's not long.*

"Who was older, Papa or Uncle Jeb?" Cassie asked.

"I'm not sure, but I believe your papa was the oldest," Beth answered.

"Why does he limp, do you suppose?" Lucas's brow furrowed as he continued. "Do you think he might have been hurt in a stampede?"

"I don't know, dear. I'm sure that as a cowboy, he could be hurt in many kinds of ways." Beth tried to smooth down the cowlick in the young boy's hair, only to watch it immediately spring back up. She smiled and gave up. Turning him toward her, she straightened his collar and looked him over. "You look real fine, Lucas."

"Thank you, Miss Beth."

"How do I look, Miss Beth?" Cassie twirled around in her Sunday best.

"You look lovely, Cassie."

"Thank you." She turned to her brother. "We must be on our best behavior, Lucas. I would want Papa to be proud of us."

"I will, Cassie. Don't worry." Lucas slipped his hand into his sister's.

Beth turned to gather up their wraps, fighting back the tears that formed behind her eyes. He was being so brave. So was Cassie. She could tell they were both nervous. So was she. She handed them their jackets and helped Lucas on with his. "Your papa would be very proud of you both. . .and so am I."

She pulled her shawl around her shoulders and tried to lighten the mood. "Let's head on over to Emma's. I wonder what her special is tonight."

"Oh, I hope it's chicken and dumplings," Cassie said, pulling on her own shawl. "I surely do love Miss Emma's dumplings. They're almost as good as yours, Miss Beth."

"Why, thank you, Cassie. That's a wonderful compliment, because I think Emma makes them best."

"I hope she has some apple pie, too. Do you think she will, Miss Beth?"

Relieved that their worries seemed eased for the moment, Beth chuckled. "I certainly hope so, Lucas. Liddy McAllister furnishes pies for her. Hopefully, she made a delivery today. Let's hurry and find out."

Even though it had turned a little cooler with the setting sun, the breeze had died down and the short walk to Main Street and Emma's Café was a comfortable one. The children's questions had ceased, and Beth wondered if their hearts pounded in their chests as fast as hers did at the prospect of meeting Jeb Winslow again.

Beth took a deep breath on entering the café. Jeb hadn't arrived yet, and she was a little relieved. It gave her time to compose herself. She certainly did not want him to see how uneasy she was about his arrival in town.

Emma came out of the kitchen just as Beth finished hanging Lucas's jacket on a hook by the door.

"Beth! It's so good to see you!" She gave Beth a hug and whispered, "I know this isn't easy for you. Matt told me that Jeb seems like a good man, though."

Beth only nodded. What could she say? It didn't matter if he was a good man or not; she didn't want him taking Lucas and Cassie away.

Emma patted Lucas on the head. "It's great to see you two also, Cassie and Lucas. Mandy has been asking about you ever since I told her she would get to see you tonight."

Cassie's face lit up in a bright smile. "Is she in the kitchen?"

Emma nodded. "She's upstairs with her papa. He'll be bringing her down any minute now. I've set one of the large round tables for us."

Just then Matt came through the kitchen door holding Mandy in his arms. The toddler clapped her hands when she saw Cassie and Lucas. "Cazzie! Luc!"

The children hurried over to her, and she immediately held out her arms for Cassie to take her. The bell over the door jingled, and Beth and Emma glanced up to see Jeb entering. He smiled and immediately crossed the room to greet his niece and nephew.

Beth was pleased with the children's manners when they shyly greeted their uncle, but she was a little unsettled that they seemed so glad to see him again. She chastised herself. He was their uncle after all. Their father's brother. She should be ashamed of herself.

Matt welcomed Jeb and brought him over to introduce him to Emma. "Emma, this is Jeb Winslow, Harland's brother. Jeb, this is my wife and the owner of the best restaurant in Roswell."

Jeb tipped his hat. "How do you do, Mrs. Johnson? I have no doubt what your husband says is true. My mouth started watering a block away."

"Why, thank you, Mr. Winslow. That is the best compliment you could give me. I'd like to offer my condolences over the death of your brother. We didn't have a chance to get to know him very well, but from what we could tell and all that Beth has told us, we know he was a good man."

"He was that." Jeb nodded and turned to Beth. "And a good brother, too. He would have made you a good husband."

Beth forced herself to smile. "Yes, he would have." *I'm just not sure I would have made him a good wife.* She sighed. She certainly couldn't voice her thoughts. She motioned to the children instead. "He was an excellent father."

Emma motioned to the table she had set for them all. "Please, come sit down. I'll just go tell Ben and Hallie that we're ready to eat."

The children needed no coaxing to come to the table. Mandy was happy in her high chair, as long as she was seated between Lucas and Cassie. Beth sat down next to Lucas and held her breath until Jeb seated himself beside Cassie. She let out a small sigh and didn't know if it was one of relief or disappointment. For some reason, her heart had been pumping hard, as she wondered where he was going to sit.

"Hope you don't mind if your uncle sits by you, Cassie?" Jeb asked as he took his seat.

"I'd be glad for you to sit here, Uncle Jeb."

"You look a lot like your mother, Cassie. Mary was a beautiful woman."

The shy smile Cassie gave Jeb warmed Beth's heart.

"Did you know my mama well, Uncle Jeb?" Cassie asked. The wistfulness in her voice plucked at Beth's heartstrings. Harland's wife had only been gone a couple of years. Now the children had to come to grips with both parents being gone.

"I did. Mary was a wonderful woman. And she loved you and Lucas with all her heart."

Jeb's stature went up a notch as she saw the joyful expressions on the children's faces. At least he was sensitive enough to recognize that they needed to be assured of how much their parents had loved them.

Emma came back to the table and took a seat beside her husband. "Hallie will be right out with our meal. It is somewhat slow tonight, but I'm glad. I hope that I won't have to interrupt our meal to help out."

"It sure smells good in here, Mrs. Johnson. Smells kind of like chicken and dumplings."

Emma smiled at Cassie. "That's exactly what I made for us. I know it's one of your favorites."

"Is Mrs. Johnson right? Is that your favorite meal?"

Cassie nodded at her uncle.

"I'm kind of partial to it, too. But I don't think I've had that dish since the last time your mother made it for one of my visits. She was a real good cook."

Lucas propped his elbows on the table and rested his head in his hands as he gazed over at his uncle. "Did she make apple pies?"

Jeb grinned. "She sure did."

"Well, I'm sure I could never compete with your mother's cooking, Lucas, but Mrs. McAllister makes some of the best pies in town, and I just happen to have a fresh apple pie she made for our dessert."

"Thank you, Mrs. Johnson. I don't hardly remember what my mama's tasted like, but I know I sure like the ones you serve."

Beth grinned at the young boy. "He was hoping you would have apple pie, Emma. If I didn't know better, I'd think a little bird flew over and told you what they were wishing for tonight."

Hallie and Ben brought their food out, and after Matt said a prayer, the talk quieted down for a bit while they ate.

"Mrs. Johnson, I have to tell you, this has been one of the best meals I've eaten in a real long time. I would hate to have to be a judge between yours and

Mary's dumplings, that's for sure. It would have to be a tie."

"Please, call me Emma. Thank you. I know that is praise, indeed—that I might cook as well as Cassie and Lucas's mother."

"Maybe that's why I like apple pie so good, do you think, Miss Beth? Because my mama made it?"

Beth smiled and patted Lucas's shoulder. "I think that might be it, Lucas. Now that you mention it, I'm quite sure it is."

"I think it's about time for that pie, too. Don't you, Lucas?" Emma asked.

"Oh yes, ma'am!"

Hallie was busy with several other tables, so Beth got up to help Emma clear the table and bring dessert plates and the pie back to their table.

Emma had warmed the pie up in the oven, and it came to the table smelling freshly baked. It was a hit with everyone, but it didn't settle too well on Beth's stomach. She knew that she and Jeb Winslow had to discuss the children. There was no way around it.

As if Emma read her mind, she suggested, "Cassie, how would you like to take Mandy and Lucas upstairs to our apartment and play awhile?"

Cassie grinned and bobbed her head. She looked at Beth. "May we, Miss Beth?"

"Yes, you may. For a little while."

Mandy clapped when Cassie lifted her from her high chair. "We go play, Cazzie?"

Cassie giggled. "Yes, we are going to play. Come on, Lucas."

Lucas took a last bite of pie and wiped his mouth with his napkin. "I'm coming."

Jeb chuckled, watching Lucas hurry to catch up with the girls. He seemed quite taken with his niece and nephew. Beth took a sip from the coffee cup Hallie had just refilled and tried to calm her nerves. She hoped no one at the table could tell how jittery she was about the conversation that was coming.

She saw Matt and Emma exchange a look before Emma stood up. "I know you two have things to discuss, so I'll clear the table and listen for the children. If you need more coffee or anything, just let Hallie or me know."

"I'll go up and check on the children." Matt pushed back from the table, taking a cue from his wife.

Jeb stood as the couple turned to leave the table. "Thank you both for getting me in touch with Miss Morgan and my niece and nephew. And Mrs.—I mean, Emma, thank you for the wonderful meal."

"You're very welcome. We'll be back down with the children in a little while. Take your time." Emma twirled around and headed toward the kitchen.

Jeb sat back down and took a drink of his coffee before giving Beth a smile.

"It's *you* whom I need to thank most, Miss Mor—"

"Please, call me Beth."

Jeb inclined his head in agreement. "Only if you call me Jeb."

"All right, Jeb. You don't need to thank me. Really. I care about Cassie and Lucas."

"I can see that you do. And I do need to thank you." Jeb gazed down into his coffee cup before looking back at Beth. "I don't know what they would have done if it hadn't been for you taking them in."

"There are some good people in this town. Emma and Matt, or Liddy and Cal McAllister would have taken them. I'm just glad that they were with me." Beth closed her eyes and shuddered as she remembered the day she'd had to tell them that their father had died. She shook her head to clear the vision of the sorrow she'd seen in their eyes that day.

Jeb cleared his throat and nodded. "I'm glad, too. I really appreciate that they had you to turn to." He took a sip of coffee before continuing. "But now that I'm here, you can get on with your life and—"

"What are your plans for the children, Mr. Winslow? Harland told me you liked to travel. . .go from job to job. That won't be easy to do with two children in tow."

"It's Jeb, remember?" He propped his forearms on the table and captured Beth's gaze with his own. "I realize that my life will be changing. I am ready to take on the responsibility."

Beth's pulse raced as his gaze never wavered. "Jeb, I will be more than glad to raise Cassie and Lucas as my own. They are comfortable with me—"

He shook his head. "I can't let you do that, Beth. They are my kin. I am the only living relative they have left, and I plan to take care of them. After I meet with the lawyer tomorrow and ride out to see the ranch, I will know better what to do. I would appreciate it, though, if they can stay with you for another night."

Beth's heart twisted in her chest at the thought it might be her last night with the children. *Dear Lord, please, if it be Your will, please let Jeb Winslow decide to let me keep the children.*

"Of course they can. They can stay with me as long as needed."

"Hopefully, we'll be able to get settled in a few days."

"Jeb, the house is still in horrible disrepair. That's why the children were with me from the beginning. Harland felt it was important to get his herd started before he fixed up the house. He wasn't even living in it. He lived in a small room in the barn. He told me it was in better shape than the house, and he certainly didn't want Cassie and Lucas staying there like it is. They are more than welcome to stay with me until you can make the repairs that are needed." Beth held her breath and sent up a silent prayer as she waited for his answer. *Oh, please, Father. Let him agree to allow them to stay with me.*

Jeb took a sip of his coffee and stared into the cup for a moment before meeting Beth's gaze. He nodded. "Thank you for your generosity, Beth. I will take you up on your offer. It will probably be easier on them if they get to know me a little at a time before they come live with me, anyway. I'll go out tomorrow and try to get a handle on how long the repairs will take."

The relief Beth felt was immense. From all Harland had told her about Jeb, she figured he probably would not stick around long enough to make the repairs to the house. He had been roaming place to place for most of his life. She just hoped it wouldn't take long for him to decide to take off and leave Cassie and Lucas with her. She prayed so. In the meantime, she would try to be pleasant and wait him out.

"I think it's a good idea for them to get used to you before you move them out to the ranch. You're welcome to come see them anytime, though."

"Thank you. I will be doing that for sure."

Matt and Emma came back into the dining room with the children just then, and Beth stood up. "I think it's time I got the children home. They have school tomorrow."

"I'll walk y'all home," Jeb offered, getting to his feet.

It was on the tip of her tongue to tell him he didn't need to, but Cassie and Lucas were his family, and it was his right to see that they got home safely. Beth and Jeb both thanked Emma and Matt for their hospitality amid the flurry of getting wraps and putting them on. She felt blessed to have such loyal friends. This evening would have been much harder on her if they hadn't been nearby.

Still in high spirits from an evening they enjoyed, the children alternately skipped, walked, and ran toward Beth's house. Jeb chuckled as he watched them, while he and Beth followed at a slower pace. But at the house, Jeb quickly told them good-bye and that he would see them the next day.

"You're welcome to stop by and tell us your plans tomorrow evening," Beth found herself saying as she gazed up into Jeb's warm eyes.

He smiled down at her. "Thank you. I will do that. I'll know more what needs to be done by then. You go on in and get warm. It's getting chilly out. And please tell the children I'll see them tomorrow evening."

"I will. Good night." Beth felt a little guilty for not asking him in as she peeked out the curtained window and watched him turn and pause a moment before stepping off the porch and heading toward the street. Still, she couldn't bring herself to utter the words.

The next day, Beth tried to keep her mind off of Harland's brother. It wasn't easy. Darcie was working the switchboard next to hers and had all kinds of questions once she found out he was in town and that Beth had met him the night before.

"Is he going to stay? What does he look like?" Darcie asked when there was a lull that afternoon.

"I don't know what he's going to do." Beth shrugged. "He looks a little like Harland." *Only he's much better looking and—*

"What do the children think of him?"

"They are happy to know they have family, I think. When they left for school this morning, they were looking forward to seeing him later today."

"You don't sound too happy about that, Beth. What do you think of him?"

"He seems to like the children, and he appears to want to take responsibility for them. . .but Darcie, what if they get attached to him and he decides to take off? Harland told me he never stayed in one place for long." Beth's switchboard lit up just then, and she gave her attention to her work for the next few minutes.

"Poor dears." Darcie shook her head.

Beth had no doubts that her friend was very sympathetic to Cassie and Lucas. Darcie's own father had passed away only a few years before.

"I can't imagine losing *both* parents in such a short amount of time," Darcie continued. "Maybe Mr. Winslow will settle down, knowing that they have no other living relatives."

Beth knew she should be hoping for just that, but she couldn't. She sighed. "I guess only time will tell. He did say the children could stay with me until he can fix up the house. That way they will have time to get to know him better."

"Maybe by then you won't feel so bad about giving them up."

"Maybe." But Beth was pretty sure she would never feel good about giving Harland's children up. . .to anyone.

That evening, Jeb showed up just as they were finishing supper. Cassie and Lucas were thrilled and quickly used the manners they'd been raised with to ask him if he would like a plate of the stew Beth had made.

"No, thank you. I ate at Emma's Café before I came over."

She supposed she should have issued an invitation for him to eat with them the night before, but the last thing she wanted was for the children to be any more eager to see him. She truly feared that they would get used to having him around just about the time he decided he would move on. She had to protect them the best she could.

Beth did offer him a cup of coffee and put a plate of cookies on the table for them all to enjoy.

"Thank you," Jeb said as she placed the cup in front of him and sat down across the table from him. "You know, I meant to ask about how you and Harland met."

"We got to know each other through correspondence."

"Oh?" His left eyebrow rose a little, and Beth could tell she'd probably given him more to question by her answer.

There was nothing to do but tell the truth. "I answered his advertisement for a mail-order bride."

"Oh." He took a sip from his cup.

She felt he was waiting for more information from her, but she wasn't about to tell him that she'd done it on a dare. That little bit of information wasn't any of his business. "We got to know each other through our letters, and after I accepted his proposal of marriage, he decided that he wanted to come out here and start a new life."

Jeb inclined his head and took another drink of his coffee. "I see."

No, I don't think you do. Beth didn't put her thoughts into words, and she was thoroughly relieved when Lucas changed the subject.

"Did you get to see the ranch today, Uncle Jeb?" Lucas then took a bite of the cookie he'd just grabbed from the plate.

"I did. Your father picked a nice spread, not too far out of town. It has a lot of promise. He left it to the two of you with me named as your guardian. I'm going to try to get it running the way your pa wanted it to be." Jeb took a sip of coffee and held it with both hands. He looked over the rim of the cup and into Beth's eyes. "You were right about the house. It is in real bad shape. It's going to take awhile to fix it up, what with having to take care of the herd."

Beth nodded in agreement. Her heart hoped that it would be too long for him to stay around. But that hoped dimmed at his next question.

"You mentioned the McAllisters last night. Do you know them well?"

"Liddy and Cal? Yes, they're good friends of mine. Cal was a lot of help to Harland."

Jeb leaned back in his chair. "Mr. Myers, Harland's lawyer, told me that they were taking care of the herd until I got here or the estate was settled one way or the other. I guess I'd better get out there and collect the cattle and pay them for taking care of them."

"I'm sure Cal won't expect payment. In fact, I'm confident that he would be glad to keep them for a while longer. . .until you decide if you're going to stay or not."

"Yes, well, we'll see. It was mighty nice of them to step in and help like that. I'll ride out to their place tomorrow. I need to do some more checking on the house. I do appreciate that you are willing to keep Cassie and Lucas until I can get it ready for them. Hopefully, it won't take more than a few months."

Beth's heart sank a little at the children's obvious excitement that their uncle seemed to want to make a home for them, and she immediately felt guilty for wishing they wouldn't like him quite so much.

"Can we come out sometime and help, Uncle Jeb?" Lucas asked.

"Why certainly. Maybe on some Saturday when you aren't in school." Jeb's gaze met Beth's from across the table. "As long as you finish any chores Miss Beth needs you to do. Is that all right with you, Beth?"

She forced herself to smile. What could she say? He was their uncle, after all. "That will be fine."

Jeb left Beth's house with mixed feelings. He sure was surprised that she'd answered his brother's advertisement for a wife. Surely she hadn't needed to do that. She was a lovely woman. What was wrong with the men in this town that she felt the need to become a mail-order bride? Jeb shook his head. Could they not see what a fine wife she would make?

Well, their loss would have been Harland's gain. And Jeb had no doubts that his brother would have been a good husband to Beth. It appeared that they'd learned to care about each other through their correspondence.

She was probably still grieving, and he felt sorry for her. However, for some reason, Jeb had the feeling that she would like nothing more than for him to get on his horse and hightail it out of town and leave her and the children here. She seemed to have taken a disliking to him, and he wasn't sure why.

He almost wished he could say he felt the same about her. But he couldn't. He liked the fact that when he got to see the children, he also was able to see her. She was a good woman. That was obvious to him. She'd been taking wonderful care of Harland's children, and they adored her. He could understand why. She was pretty and sweet, and she truly cared about them. . .so much so that she would be happy if he would leave and let her raise them as hers.

But he wasn't going to do that, no matter how overwhelmed he felt at the prospect of raising them by himself. They were his kin—the only relatives he had left. And Harland had trusted him enough to want him to take care of Cassie and Lucas. Jeb was determined to raise them the best he could. With the Lord's help. And he needed all of His help he could get.

He strolled the few blocks to the hotel, sending up prayers and asking for just that.

Chapter 3

During the next few days, Jeb visited the children as often as he could while trying to settle his brother's estate. He made sure to show up well after he figured they'd finished with supper so Beth wouldn't mind if he offered a stick of candy each to Cassie and Lucas.

Small, but homey, Beth's cottage reminded him of the house in which he'd grown up. It consisted of a parlor, a dining room, and the kitchen downstairs, with the bedrooms—the children told him there were three—upstairs. There was a kind of warmth to it he felt the moment he walked inside that had nothing to do with the heat coming from the stove. He wondered if it was just because it'd been so long since he'd spent time in a house, but he didn't think so. More likely, it was because his brother's children were here, and it had been way too long since he'd been around family.

He tried not to outstay his welcome, but he loved being around his niece and nephew. They were full of stories about school and what happened there, and they were getting more and more excited about the upcoming fair.

"Beth is going to enter a couple of pies, and I'm going to help her make them," Cassie informed him one evening as they sat around the kitchen table while Beth was doing the dishes.

"Maybe I should teach you to make one and let you enter it," Beth proposed, smiling at the young girl's enthusiasm.

"I would love to do that!"

"I wish there was something I could enter," Lucas mumbled around the stick of candy in his mouth.

"Maybe we could enter some of your pa's livestock," Jeb suggested to the boy. "Cal is going to help me get the herd back over to the ranch tomorrow. I'll look them over again and see what he thinks."

"Oh, I would like to do that, Uncle Jeb!" Lucas grinned at him.

"Well, don't get your hopes up too high. But I will check into it."

Jeb glanced up just then to see Beth, a half smile on her lips, gazing at him from across the room. She looked away quickly, but not before he saw a faint pink color steal across her cheeks. It was the first time her smile seemed truly genuine. For the most part, she still seemed a little uncomfortable around him, and Jeb hoped that would change before too long. She tried to make him feel welcome, but he could sense that she wasn't at ease in his presence. He liked coming to her house and seeing the children, but he didn't like making her feel uneasy in her own home.

"Would you like the last of the coffee?" Beth asked, holding the pot up and shaking it slightly.

"No, thank you," he answered, even though he really would have liked another cup. "I'd better get going." The children had school the next day, and he didn't want to mess up their routine. He'd have to ask Beth exactly what that was before he moved them out to the ranch. That would be awhile yet. And he wasn't in too big a hurry. He rather liked seeing Beth along with the children.

~

It wasn't until after Cassie and Lucas were asleep that Beth finally allowed herself to contemplate the confusion she felt. Her pulse raced each time Jeb showed up at the door, but she sighed with relief each time he left for the night.

Oh, why did he have to come to Roswell and complicate things so? The children were already getting attached to him. How was she ever going to be able to protect them from an uncle who may or may not stay around?

Jeb did seem quite taken with them, however. Maybe Harland had been wrong about his brother. Just because he had moved around from one ranch to another for most of his life didn't mean he couldn't settle down, did it? If not, she sure hoped he realized it soon and moved on. . .for Cassie's and Lucas's sake. They had suffered enough loss.

Besides, hard as she tried to get used to the idea that they would be moving out to the ranch, Beth riled against it. She wanted them to stay with her. And she owed it to Harland to make sure they received good care.

What could Jeb Winslow possibly know about caring for children? The only person he had ever taken care of was himself. The more Beth thought about it, the more frustrated she became. *Dear Lord, please help me with the resentment I feel that Harland's brother showed up. He is the children's uncle. I should be happy for them. Please, if he is going to have them, please help me to accept it and know that it is Your will. In Jesus' name, amen.*

Beth pulled her Bible close and opened it for study, hoping to steer her thoughts away from Jeb Winslow, for what truly bothered her most right now was that she looked forward to seeing Jeb almost as much as Cassie and Lucas did. And that would not do. No, that would not do at all.

~

There was a lot to do at the ranch, but Jeb was pleased with the land his brother had bought. It wasn't a big spread, but a family could live on it comfortably. At some point, one of the owners had planted apple trees, and a nice orchard sat at the back of the house. The trees were loaded with apples that needed picking now. Next spring he would get the children to help him plant a garden outside the kitchen, and between that and the livestock his brother had bought, they'd be able to live well.

Now he stood at the edge of his brother's pasture and gazed at the small herd of cattle Cal McAllister had helped him bring over from his place. Harland hadn't done half bad in selecting the livestock to start his ranch. And they sure hadn't suffered any under Cal's care.

Jeb turned to the other man and held out his hand. "I can't thank you enough for making sure this herd stayed together and in good health, McAllister. I wish you'd let me pay you for their keep."

Cal shook his head and Jeb's hand at the same time. "It was the least I could do. No one knew if you would be located or if you would come back here, and until things were settled for the children, it seemed the best plan."

"Well, I thank you. If there's anything I can ever do for you—"

"I'll remember your offer. In the meantime, if you need help getting the house in shape, just let me know. It's going to need a lot of work."

"Thanks. I appreciate the offer, but you have your own place to run, Cal. I'm hoping to have the house ready in a few months. Until then, I'll move into the room in the barn where Harland had been living. Beth was right. It is in a lot better shape than the house right now."

Cal agreed. "It is. One reason Harland got such a good price on this place was because the times had gotten bad for the people who owned it. The Nordstroms had planned on it being a real showplace, and they'd come out West with what they thought was plenty of money. But their plans were larger than their pocketbooks, and they ran low on cash before they could finish it completely. To try to finish it and keep the ranch going, they took out a loan with one of the banks in town and put their place up as collateral. The next year wasn't any better for them, and when they couldn't make the payment to his bank, Douglas Harper, the banker, had threatened to foreclose."

"He wouldn't give them an extension?" Jeb asked. Harper sure didn't sound like a banker with whom he wanted to do business.

Cal shook his head. "He wanted it for himself. There was no love lost between Harper and the people around Roswell, and rather than let Harper just have the ranch as he expected them to do, the Nordstroms put it up for sale. All they wanted was enough profit to get back home and pay Harper so that he couldn't have their land. Once Harland bought it, the owners paid Harper's bank off and moved back East."

"I think I'll steer clear of Harper's bank," Jeb said.

"You won't have to," Cal assured him. "Not long after Harland made the deal and the Nordstroms went back East, Douglas Harper ended up in prison for hiring someone to set fire to Emma's Café, trying to get her to leave town."

"He's still there?"

"Yep."

Jeb contemplated the house. The roof had a few old boards nailed over a spot or two that had obviously been burned. "How did it catch on fire?"

"Before Harland could get to Roswell, an electrical storm similar to the one that caused the stampede he'd died in sent a bolt of lightning through the roof of the house. This storm had rain in it, though, and it put the fire out fairly quickly but not before a lot of damage had been done. In the next few months, without anyone to care for it, the place deteriorated even more."

Jeb nodded. "Well, it can be repaired. . .and the land it's sitting on is prime. Barn is in real good shape. I'll be all right in there while I work on the house. Harland was staying in a small room in there. I guess he was going to use it to store tools and saddles and so on."

"Yep. That's what he planned. He worked on the barn first. The children were safe and dry in town with Beth, and he figured he needed the barn finished first to store winter feed for the cattle."

"She's offered to let them stay until I have the house ready."

"Beth is a good woman." Cal pushed his hat back on his forehead and looked him in the eye. "She would have made Harland a good wife."

"I don't doubt that for a moment. Have you known her long?"

"She's been here for about five years. She came out to help take care of her ailing aunt Gertrude. Beth liked it here, and after her aunt died and left the house to her, she decided to stay on. She's been working for the telephone company for the past few years."

"I can't help but wonder why she would have needed to answer my brother's advertisement for a bride, though. Are the men in this town blind?"

Cal chuckled and shook his head. "I don't have an answer for you, Winslow. Liddy and I have wondered the same thing. . . we surely have."

The only peace Beth had in the next few days was while she was at work. . .until word got around that Harland's brother had been found and was in town to take responsibility of the children.

Alma Burton was the first to mention it when her line lit up and Beth asked, "Number, please?"

"Beth? Is that you?" Alma asked.

"Yes, ma'am. What number do you need?"

"No number, dear. I just heard about Harland's brother getting to town and wanted to see what you think of him?"

Beth sighed. She wasn't supposed to carry on personal conversations while on duty, but there were no other lines lit up at the moment, and Mrs. Burton just seemed so lonely since her husband had passed away several months back. Beth just didn't have the heart to tell her that none of this was her business. "He seems nice enough, Mrs. Alma. But—"

"You want to keep the children with you, don't you, dear?"

"Well, I have come to care for them. . .but Harland didn't have time to make out a new will, and his brother was named as their guardian in the old one. I have no choice but to honor his wishes."

"Is Harland's brother married?"

"No, ma'am."

"Is he engaged to anyone?"

Beth caught her breath. She hadn't even considered the fact that he might be. "I don't know."

"Man needs a wife to raise children."

Beth hadn't even had a chance to get used to Jeb having the children. That he might marry and another woman would take her place in their affections didn't sit well with her. Several lines on the switchboard lit up just then. "Mrs. Alma, I have to go. The switchboard is lighting up."

"I'll talk to you later, dear," Alma responded before her light went out.

Beth breathed a quick sigh of relief as she connected the next few callers. The last person she wanted to talk about was Jeb. But her relief was short lived, because the next caller was Emma.

"Hi, Beth. Get me Matt, will you? But first, how are things going with you and Jeb?"

"All right, I guess. The children look forward to his visits."

"That's good, isn't it? He seems real nice. He's been taking some of his meals here, and Matt says he thinks he'll stick it out and make a home here for Cassie and Lucas."

Beth was sure Emma was only trying to assure her that the children would remain close by, but it didn't really help at the moment. It especially didn't help that her friends seemed to be welcoming Jeb Winslow with open arms.

"I guess time will tell" was all she said to Emma. "I'll get Matt for you."

She quickly connected the two lines and sighed. By the time she left for the day, at least six more people had asked about Jeb and if she thought he would stay. Seemed there was no longer any place she could avoid thinking of him. . .or talking about him.

Or seeing him. And she couldn't keep her pulse from racing at finding Jeb waiting outside the telephone office when her shift ended and she started home. Her heartbeat fluttered against her chest as he tipped his hat and smiled at her.

"Afternoon, Beth."

"Jeb, is something wrong?" He never showed up this time of day. "The children are still at school. . .they—"

"They're fine, Beth. I just had to come in for some supplies and thought I'd let you know I won't be coming back in tonight. I wanted to see if it would be all right for the children to come out to the ranch tomorrow, since it is Saturday. After they do their chores, of course."

Lucas had been hoping Jeb would take them out there, and so had Cassie. She couldn't say no. "Of course they may. I don't have that many chores they have to do. What time would you like me to bring them out?"

"Oh, I'll come fetch them. You are more than welcome to come, too. A woman's opinion on some of the things that need done to the house would be appreciated. Maybe we could have a picnic. The days are still warm."

She knew the children would love it. It sounded wonderful to her. . .even sharing it with Jeb. Or was it especially because of Jeb being there? She told herself it was because, if she went, she wouldn't spend the whole day wondering what Cassie and Lucas were doing and if they were having a good time with their uncle. And this way, she could see how Jeb took to having them around more than a couple of hours at a time.

"They would love it, Jeb. I could fry some chicken and make a cake."

"That would be nice. But I didn't mean that you would have to cook. I could pick up something from Emma's Café."

"No, that's all right. The children will be happy to help me make the cake tonight. And they'll hurry to do their chores, knowing there's a treat in store."

They'd been walking toward Beth's house all the while they were talking, and she turned to him as they reached her stoop. "What time would you like us to be ready?"

"I'll come get you about ten, will that be all right?"

"That will be fine."

Jeb pulled his Stetson a little lower on his forehead and touched the wide brim before turning to go. "See you all tomorrow then."

"See you then."

Lucas and Cassie's disappointment that they wouldn't be seeing their uncle that night had quickly changed to anticipation when Beth told them they'd be going out to the ranch the next day. They had talked excitedly about it while she made the cake and iced it for the picnic.

The children did hurry through their chores the next morning. Beth had fried the chicken while Lucas swept the floor and Cassie dusted. She'd made some escalloped potatoes according to the receipt in the *Fannie Farmer Cookbook* her mother had sent her for Christmas from back East this past year. It had only come out a few years before, and she'd been thrilled to get it.

She'd put some bread rolls out to rise and popped them into the oven right after she took the potatoes out. Everything would be ready just about the time Jeb came to pick them up.

When his knock came at the door half an hour later, she sent Lucas to open it for him and hurriedly tried to brush up the strands of hair that had escaped from the psyche knot she'd worked hard to get just right.

When Jeb entered the kitchen, she'd just finished loading the potato dish and rolls into a basket and was covering it with dish towels to keep everything warm.

"Mmm, it smells good in here."

"Thank you, Jeb. Everything is ready to load into the wagon, I believe. This basket has the food in it and might be warm." She handed it to him and picked up the other one. "This one has plates, napkins, and cutlery. Lucas, you can carry it. Cassie, will you get the cake, please?"

Beth took off her apron and grabbed her and the children's wraps from the hooks beside the back door before hurrying outside. Jeb was instructing Lucas on how to put the food on the floor of the wagon, and Cassie was already sitting on the end of the wagon.

Jeb came around and helped Beth up onto the seat. She felt a little breathless as she sat down and he came around to take his seat beside her. It was a beautiful day, and she tried to concentrate on the clear blue of the sky, the birds flying south, and the traffic on Main Street as they made their way out of town. With wagons, stagecoaches, and single horses moving up and down the street, there was plenty to look at, but none of it could fully take her attention away from the man at her side.

Cassie and Lucas were asking a myriad of questions, and Jeb patiently answered as many as he could. The ranch wasn't far out of town. In fact, it was closer than Cal and Liddy's place. It was a lovely piece of land, east of town, near the Hondo River, with cottonwood trees and rich pastures. As they got their first glimpse of the house, Beth could only think what a shame it was that it was in such disrepair. It was going to take a lot of work to get it livable again—much less to turn it into the show home it started out to be. She shook her head. It certainly wasn't that now.

But the children didn't seem to mind as Jeb pulled the wagon close to the barn. They scampered out of the wagon and asked their uncle if they could look around.

"You can check out the barn while we set up the picnic, but wait until Beth and I are with you to check out the house. I haven't even inspected it all. But I know there are a lot of loose boards, and I don't want you to get hurt."

While Beth spread out the quilt she'd thought to bring and Jeb brought the food basket over, they could hear excited chatter and laughter as Cassie and Lucas explored the barn.

"I suppose you are staying out in the barn?" Beth asked as she laid out napkins and cutlery.

"Yes. As you mentioned before, Harland had been staying there. There's a small room with a makeshift bed in it and a small stove. It's fine for now. I've certainly slept in worse places."

"Harland told me that you liked moving from one place to another."

"I've seen a lot of country." Jeb stared off in the distance before turning back to her. "But my wandering days are over. It's time I settled down." He grinned as Cassie and Lucas came running out of the barn. "More than time."

It was a perfect day for a picnic. The crisp, fresh air gave everyone an appetite, and by the time they'd finished eating, there was only half of the cake left for a midafternoon snack. Everyone pitched in and helped to put things up before they took off to look at the house.

It was of Queen Anne style, a two-story with the irregular roof pattern typical of the style, a corner tower, and wraparound porch. They mostly strolled around the outside of it, although Jeb did let them peek inside. But it was hard for the children to see past the ruin to what it could be.

On the other hand, Beth could picture it all refurbished. . .the parlor with gleaming wood floors and the fireplace at the center glowing with warmth. They went around the back, and she could see that it also had a back parlor. She caught a glimpse of a kitchen almost twice the size of her own.

"Oh my, it's big enough for one of the newest Sunshine ranges and a larger worktable in the center." She'd seen the new ranges in the Sears, Roebuck, and Company catalog and had thought to tell Harland about them when he got around to working on the house. They rounded the corner and found another fireplace on a side wall with windows on each side. "Oh, he didn't tell me it had a dining room, too! How lovely it would be with a sideboard and table and chairs."

Beth only now realized just how little Harland had told her about the house other than it needed work. She had no idea how big it was.

"How many rooms are upstairs, Uncle Jeb?" Cassie asked.

"There are three big bedrooms and a small one up there. I'd let you go look, but like I said, there are loose boards everywhere and I'm afraid you might fall through. It can be a nice house. I can see that now. Thank you for coming out, Beth. Had you seen the house before?"

She shook her head. "No. Harland was so busy with the herd and all. . . ."

"Well, I'm glad you came out today." He turned to the children. "Come on.

Let's get another piece of that cake, and I'll show you your papa's herd."

Cassie and Lucas needed no prodding. The house was interesting, but since they couldn't explore, they were ready to find another adventure. Picking apples was the highlight of the day, and Beth knew she'd soon be busy baking pies and making apple butter and still have apples to send in the children's lunches.

By the time Jeb took them back to Beth's, they were tuckered out. But they were happy, and Beth was glad to see the smiles on their faces as she sent them to wash up while she warmed some stew from the day before.

She surprised herself by asking "Would you like to take supper with us, Jeb?"

"Are you sure you have enough?"

"I do." She always had plenty. She should have been asking him to eat with them instead of him spending money at Emma's or some other place in town. He didn't exactly have a place to prepare a meal at the ranch. And he shouldn't be having to spend all that money eating out when it was going to cost so much to get the house in working order.

"Thank you, then. I'd be happy to stay."

Jeb was glad he had stayed for supper. Beth was a wonderful cook, and sharing a meal with her and Cassie and Lucas served as the end of a near-perfect day as far as he was concerned. He couldn't remember the last time he'd had such a good one—only that it had been a very long time. Still, this was different. He was continually surprised at how content he felt when he was around the children and Beth, and he found that he didn't want the day to end.

As she told Cassie and Lucas it was time to get ready for bed, he knew it was time for him to go back to his barn. But that wouldn't be home forever. He had all kinds of ideas about the house after today and seeing Beth's enthusiasm about it. The children took their plates to the sink, and Jeb was quite touched when Cassie came around the table and gave him a hug.

"Good night, Uncle Jeb. Thank you for taking us to the ranch."

"Yes, thank you!" Lucas chimed in. "I really like it out there. I'd like to sleep in the barn sometime."

Jeb chuckled. "Maybe one day you can. But I think you'll like staying in the house a lot better once I get it fixed up."

"Could I maybe help you?" Lucas sidled up to Jeb and leaned against him.

"Maybe. Once I get those loose floorboards fixed."

"Thanks, Uncle Jeb."

Jeb patted him on the back. "You're welcome."

"Come on, Lucas," Cassie said. "Good night, Uncle Jeb and Miss Beth."

"Good night," Jeb and Beth responded at the same time.

Jeb watched as his niece and nephew went upstairs, then turned to Beth, who was refilling his cup. "Thank you for supper. . .and for the picnic today." He grinned and added, "And for leaving the last of the cake for me."

"You're welcome. It was a nice day. The children really enjoyed it."

"It was a great day. I have an idea what to do with the house now."

"What to do with it?"

Jeb nodded. "It needs a lot of work, and I didn't really know where to start. It took you coming out today to make me see the possibilities of it."

"It's going to take a lot of work. . .and money to repair it. It may not be worth it."

Jeb was silent for a moment.

Beth continued. "Jeb, Harland told me you liked the life you live. The going from one place to another. My house isn't very big, but it's big enough for me and the children. As I told you before, they are more than welcome to stay with me. You could come visit—"

"I realize I don't know much about raising children, Beth. But they are my family. They're my responsibility, and I want to make the ranch a home for them."

"But they need a woman's influence in their lives, too."

"I know they do." He took a sip of coffee before looking into Beth's eyes. "You could marry me, and they would have us both."

Had he just asked her to marry him? Jeb's heartbeat pounded like thunder in his ears. He could see the shock in Beth's eyes. It appeared that he had. He took a deep breath and waited for her answer.

She found her voice. "I—you can't mean that. I. . .you. . .that is a crazy idea." She plucked his cup out of his hand and took it to the sink. Then she spun back around to stare at him, her hands on her hips. "I can't believe you are serious."

Jeb couldn't either, didn't have any idea how those words popped out of his mouth, and he thought maybe he should take them back. Still, it rankled him that Beth found the idea of marrying him *crazy*. "Well, it isn't any crazier than answering a mail-order bride advertisement in the mail! You were ready to marry my brother sight unseen. Why not me?"

Chapter 4

Beth stared across the table at Jeb, at a momentary loss for words. She'd had a feeling he didn't approve of her answering his brother's advertisement for a mail-order bride, and she was certain of it now. And why not Jeb? She could see how he might be a little confused.

How could she tell him? She had barely admitted it to herself. But in the days before Harland died, she'd begun to have second thoughts about marrying him. There was something lacking in their relationship, and Beth had come to the realization that she'd acted foolishly in answering the advertisement. While she'd come to care about him, she hadn't been sure she could ever come to really love him. . .not the way she felt she should, and she hadn't been sure she could marry him.

But she hadn't told him. She'd been waiting for the right time, and it had never come. And, now that he was gone, she was glad she hadn't had to say the words to him. But one thing she knew for certain. She would never agree to marry another man she didn't know.

Still, it would be the perfect answer for keeping the children with her, and something deep inside wished that what Jeb was proposing could become a reality. But it couldn't—no matter how many somersaults her heart did or how fast her pulse raced each time he came near. After all Harland had told her about Jeb, she just couldn't believe he could commit himself to her and the children. It was only a matter of time until he took off. . .in spite of how good his intentions seemed to be.

Now, she tried hard not to let Jeb see how deeply his proposal had affected her. "Jeb, your brother and I corresponded for months before he moved out here. Enough to get to know each other a little." *But not well enough.* "You and I have only known each other a few days." *And you cause my heart to race in a way your brother never did.* "Besides, Harland told me you would never settle down. . .that you were used to going wherever you wanted to, whenever you wanted to. You aren't used to staying in one place."

"That doesn't mean I can't or won't."

Could he? Would he? Her heart thudded against her chest. If he did, might this be an answer to her prayers as a way to keep the children? Dare she allow herself to hope that he would stay? No. She couldn't. She would only be setting herself up for disappointment and heartache.

Beth just couldn't see him staying for long, and she had a feeling the only way she could deal with his proposal was to treat it lightly. "Well, I tell you what. If you stay around long enough to finish the house. . .maybe I'll just agree to marry you."

"Lady, I'm going to accept your challenge. I'll have it finished by Christmas. And when I finish it, you are going to have a decision to make."

Beth tried to ignore the warm wave of elation flowing through her at his words. She forced herself to laugh off his acceptance, praying he couldn't tell how flustered she felt. "By Christmas?"

"Yes."

"We'll see." Christmas was over three months away. He'd probably be long gone by then.

"Yes, we will." Jeb grinned at her as he stood to go. He sauntered over to the back door and took his hat off the hook beside the door. "We sure enough will. Good night, Beth."

Beth shut the door behind him and locked it with trembling fingers. Leaning her forehead against the curtained window, she took a deep breath and tried to will her rapidly beating heart to slow down. Had she really said she *might* marry him if he finished the house by Christmas? She thought back over the conversation. It appeared she had. And he had accepted her challenge.

She shook her head and pushed away from the door, trying to put it all out of her mind as she busied herself cleaning up the kitchen. But she couldn't get Jeb Winslow out of her mind. Part of her was sure he hadn't meant what he'd said. . .and another part was afraid to hope that he did.

Jeb made his way back to the ranch, but his mind was not on the road in front of him. It was back in Roswell, at Beth's. Just the thought of having her for a wife to help him raise Cassie and Lucas had his heart beating nearly out of his chest. He still couldn't believe he'd asked her to marry him. . .but now that he had, he wondered why he hadn't thought of it before now. After all, she'd agreed to marry his brother sight unseen. She loved Cassie and Lucas; that was clear. If she'd been willing to marry Harland, surely he could convince her to marry him.

Beth thought he wouldn't stay, but he was going to prove her wrong. Oh, he'd thought about putting the ranch up for sale and taking the kids back to Colorado with him. But that was before he'd thought the whole thing through and he'd seen the land Harland had left them. Roswell had become home to Cassie and Lucas, and they'd had enough to adjust to without having to move to a new town, knowing no one but him.

The ranch was prime land that would provide them with an inheritance from their father. And staying here, making a home for them on the ranch, might be his only chance to put roots down in a town he was coming to like a lot. That Beth might be part of all that. . .well. . .that was just the icing on the cake as far as he was concerned. Of course, he was going to have a job convincing her of that.

After taking care of the horses and settling down for the night, Jeb found the writing paper he'd bought in town earlier and sat down to write his boss. John Biglow was a good man, and he'd told Jeb to take what time he needed to get everything settled, but Jeb felt he owed it to John to let him know he wouldn't be coming back. He'd mail it on Monday when he went in to see the children. He needed to go to the bank and have his funds transferred from the bank in Colorado.

Tomorrow he was going to make a list of what he needed to get started on the house. It had suddenly become very important to him to get it ready for the children as soon as possible. Very important. Because he was going to prove Beth wrong. . .and he was going to try to win her heart in the process. He wasn't sure how to go about courting a woman, but he was going to do the best he could to do it right.

All day Sunday, Beth looked for Jeb to show up. Having Cassie and Lucas ask about him off and on all day hadn't helped. She'd watched for him at church and had been both relieved and disappointed that he hadn't shown up—relieved that she didn't have to pretend that his proposal hadn't had an effect on her and disappointment that he didn't appear to be a Christian.

It did feel good to be there, though, especially with all the confusion going on in her life. Minister Turley had a good message about waiting on the Lord, and Beth acknowledged that she needed to trust the Lord to help her sort it all out. . .in His time.

The children wanted to ride out to the ranch and check on their uncle, but Beth managed to get out of that by telling them that he was probably busy or he would have been in church.

"But what if something happened to him?" The fear in Lucas's voice was hard to ignore.

"I'm sure he's all right, Lucas. Besides, Cal and Liddy go right by there. . .I'm sure they will check in on him." She hoped. *Dear Lord, please let Jeb be fine. I don't think the children could take losing another family member.*

Beth searched her mind for something to do to get their thoughts. . .and hers. . .off their uncle Jeb. "You know, we could try our hand at making those apple pies we want to enter in the fair. Practicing sure won't hurt any, and we have plenty of apples since we picked so many at the ranch yesterday."

"Oh, yes! Let's do that," Cassie agreed.

The rest of the afternoon was spent peeling apples and making piecrusts. Beth used a combination of her aunt's recipe and one from the cookbook her mother had sent. She let the children mix the apples, sugar, nutmeg, and salt together. Miss Farmer's cookbook called for lemon juice, too, but Beth didn't have any, and her aunt had never used it in her pies, so they didn't worry much about it. She did add just a scant teaspoon of flour to thicken the juices, just as Aunt Gertrude had.

She set the mixture aside while she showed Cassie how to cut the lard into a flour and salt mixture. Then they slowly added enough water until the dough formed a ball of sorts. Beth divided it into four separate balls and let each child take turns rolling out two of the balls of pastry dough into nice big circles.

They each put their circle into a pie dish, and Beth helped them add some of the apple mixture to each. She let them dot the apples with butter while she rolled out the remaining dough balls.

One pie was covered completely with the dough, but she cut the other piece of dough into strips and let Cassie and Lucas make a lattice pattern on the top of the other. Lucas thought it was great fun.

She showed them how to seal the edges and quickly slid the pies into the oven. "Now we wait until the kitchen is filled with the smell of baked apples and the crusts are golden brown. I think we may have some winners here. The fair is in a few weeks. . .so we can have a couple more practice sessions before then."

Beth didn't even have to ask Cassie or Lucas to help clean up. They pitched right in. Cassie wiped down the table and washed the utensils they'd used, while Beth started a stew from the leftover meat and vegetables they'd had for Sunday dinner. She'd made enough for Jeb, just in case he came into town. But he didn't. Maybe if she'd asked him before he left last night. . .

She put the pot on the back of the stove and adjusted the heat.

"Mmm, those pies are beginning to smell delicious." Beth opened the oven door to check on them and sniffed deeply as she got a warm whiff of the baking apples and cinnamon.

Too bad Jeb isn't here to smell these, Beth thought. Maybe she could—

"Can we give Uncle Jeb one of the pies to take home when he comes back into town?" Lucas asked as he swept the flour up under the table. "He sure don't have much food out there."

So much for keeping Jeb out of their thoughts. Beth chuckled. She'd been thinking the same thing. "I imagine we can."

She was pleased that the children had been observant enough to know Jeb's living arrangements weren't nearly as comfortable as theirs were.

"It will be good when he can get the house fixed up so he can stay in it instead of the barn," Cassie commented.

"I'd like to stay in the barn. Do you think I might be able to one day, Miss Beth?" Lucas asked.

"We'll see." Beth could fight it all she wanted, but Cassie and Lucas already cared a great deal for their uncle Jeb. All she could do was hope and pray that if he was going to up and leave them, it would be sooner rather than later. But what if he took them with him? What would she do then?

Suddenly tired, she poured herself a cup of coffee and sat down at the table. *Dear Lord, please help me to accept Your will in all of this.*

After Beth's reaction to his proposal on Saturday night, Jeb decided he'd give her a day to calm down. He certainly didn't want to get her more riled up. Although she'd told him if he stayed, she might consider marrying him, he was pretty sure that she hadn't really meant it. He chuckled, thinking back on the look of surprise that had come over her face when he accepted her challenge anyway.

Sunday morning, he saddled his horse and went to check on the herd. He'd been a lot of places, seen some nice spreads, but this piece of land his brother had bought sight unseen was one of the prettiest he'd ever laid eyes on. Oh, the house was in bad shape, but it could be repaired. And it would be a real showplace when it was. The land alone was worth much more than Harland paid for it. Evidently, he had just been looking for land at just the right time, and the Lord had been looking out for him. If Jeb ever had to sell the property for the children, they'd be able to get much more than their papa paid for it.

For now, he just wanted to make it a home for them. No matter what Harland had thought about his ability to stay in one place, he'd trusted Jeb enough to make him guardian of his children, and Jeb planned to see that his brother's trust wasn't misplaced.

That afternoon, he began making a list of materials he was going to need. He started taking up the rotted and damaged floorboards and was pleasantly surprised to find that there weren't quite as many as he'd first thought. But there were problems with the roof. Leaks were abundant and the main cause of the rotted boards. He needed to patch the roof as soon as possible, but that would have to wait until he could get the supplies from town. The fireplaces were in decent shape, but they needed cleaning. The staircase would need to be almost completely redone, too.

By the time Monday rolled around, he was thankful that Harland had left enough money to run the ranch and to make a start on repairing the house. But it wouldn't be enough to fix it up the way Jeb pictured it after hearing Beth's ideas. He sure was glad he'd set aside a nest egg through the years. . .and he could think of nothing he'd rather spend it on than making a home for Cassie and Lucas.

First off, he mailed the letter he'd written to his boss. Then he went to the

Bank of Roswell and made arrangements to have his money transferred from his bank in Colorado. There were several banks in town—not counting the closed Harper Bank—but Cal had recommended this bank to him.

After his banking business was completed, he went to see about getting the lumber and the rest of the supplies he was going to need from the Jaffa-Prager Company. The huge mercantile sold just about everything on his list, and what they didn't have, they would order for him or he could order from the Sears and Roebuck catalog. He loaded his wagon with what he could and made arrangements for everything else he'd bought to be delivered to the ranch the next day.

He made a run out to the ranch and unloaded lumber, nails, and roofing material into the barn, glad that it, at least, was in good shape and he didn't have to worry about leaks. He checked on the herd, then came back to the house to take up more floorboards. He planned to go back into town when he knew the children were out of school and Beth would be home.

He was eager to see Cassie and Lucas. It surprised him how much he'd missed seeing them the day before. They'd quickly found a place in his heart, and he was determined to do the best he could to take care of them. All those years he'd been going from one place to another, he hadn't truly realized how much his family meant to him. . .until the only family he had left were his brother's children.

Now, as he worked in the house that would have been home to his brother, the joy he found in being around family again had a bittersweet quality to it. Jeb had taken off after both their parents had died, wanting to see the West, but his brother had tried to talk him out of it and had been trying to get him to move back to Arkansas for years. Jeb had stubbornly refused. Harland would have been so happy if Jeb had settled down nearby, but Jeb had no desire to do so. Until now—now that he realized how very much he'd missed in his absence.

Dear Lord, please forgive me for not being there for Harland when Mary died or not being nearby for Cassie and Lucas when Harland died. Please help me to raise them the best I can. I don't know much about raising children, but I know You will show me the way. And if it be Your will, please let me convince Beth that I will stay here and put the well-being of the children first. In Jesus' name I pray, amen.

With the Lord's help, he would raise the children the way Harland would want him to. And if it was the Lord's will, he'd have Beth at his side to help him.

On Monday, work was the only thing that kept Beth from stewing over Jeb and his proposal. She wondered if he would show up today. Cassie and Lucas had been wondering the same thing when they left for school. For their sake, Beth hoped he would. For hers. . .she hoped he'd already decided to go back to Colorado. If he stayed much longer, she was afraid she was going to begin to care far too much for him.

"How is everything going with Harland's brother, Beth?" Darcie asked during a quiet moment.

"The children are getting used to having him around. We went out to the ranch for a picnic on Saturday, and they love it out there. They had a wonderful time."

"What about you?"

"What do you mean?"

"Are you getting used to having him around?"

Beth shrugged and tried to evade the question. "I don't have much choice if he stays."

"He's awfully nice looking." Darcie grinned at Beth.

Beth sighed and shook her head at her friend.

"Well, he is," Darcie continued. "I had to go to Jaffa-Prager for Mama this morning, and he was there. It sounded like he was ordering all kinds of supplies to repair the house."

Beth's heart seemed to skip a couple of beats. It sounded like he planned to stay. She truly wasn't sure how she felt about it, but her heart seemed right glad. She ignored Darcie's first statement and tried to sound as if it didn't matter that much if Jeb left or stayed. "Oh?"

Darcie nodded. "Lumber, nails, all that kind of stuff."

Beth was sure Darcie knew what she was talking about. The younger woman just couldn't seem to help listening in on other people's conversations.

"Well, he's certainly got his work cut out for him, if he stays. The house is in pretty bad shape."

"It wasn't good when the Nordstroms lived out there."

"It sure has potential, though."

"Oh? You like it?"

Several lights lit up on the switchboard, saving Beth from answering right then. Yes, she liked it. . .and it would make a lovely home for Cassie and Lucas. . . but they had a good home with her, and the three of them were doing just fine. If Jeb left, they would be just fine. And she had to keep that thought first and foremost in her mind.

However, as she went up the walk to her house that afternoon and saw Jeb sitting on her porch, she had to admit that she wasn't being completely truthful with herself. The children would be heartbroken if he left. . .and she wasn't quite sure that her heart wouldn't break as well.

He stood and took his Stetson off as she approached. "Good afternoon, Beth. I hope it's all right that I came to see the children?"

"Of course. They watched for you all day yesterday."

He shrugged and grinned at her. "I thought maybe I outstayed my welcome Saturday night."

Beth's heart flipped against her ribs. Was he referring to her response about his proposal? She didn't know. She only knew that his very presence brought it all back to her. "Jeb, you are Cassie and Lucas's uncle," she said, struggling to keep her voice steady. "I wouldn't keep them from seeing you. Would you like to take supper with us? The children would be very happy if you would."

Jeb smiled down at her. "Thank you, yes. I'd like that. You're a good woman, Beth Morgan. My brother knew how to pick them, that's for sure."

Beth didn't know what to say. She felt she was living a lie by not telling Jeb that she'd decided she couldn't marry his brother, but she never got around to telling Harland, and she couldn't bring herself to tell Jeb now. She stayed silent.

"I have a few errands to run. When would be a good time for me to come back?"

"I'll be going to meet the children in about an hour. We'll eat about six, but you can come before then so you can visit with Cassie and Lucas."

"I'll be here about five or so, then. Is it all right if I bring them some candy for later?"

"As long as you don't give it to them until after supper. Otherwise, Lucas won't eat anything."

"I promise." Jeb put his hat back on and tipped the brim. "I'll see you in a little while."

Beth watched him go, her hand at her chest trying to still the crazy beating of her heart. Oh, yes, she'd been lying to herself. She did care whether Jeb stayed or left.

She managed to get her pulse under control before Jeb returned. But only until he returned. There was something about his slow smile that made her heart skip a beat or two. . .or three.

Hard as Beth tried to keep Jeb from knowing that she was glad he was there, Cassie and Lucas left their uncle with no doubt as to how happy there were to see him. They talked nonstop from the time he arrived until Beth told them to tell their uncle good night and sent them to get ready for bed.

By the time Jeb stood to leave with the apple pie the children had saved for him, it was apparent that he'd won the affections of his niece and nephew. Cassie and Lucas loved him already.

As Beth shut the door behind him, it struck her that she had to be very careful to guard her heart with all her might. . .for she suddenly knew that she was in serious danger of losing it to Jeb Winslow. He already seemed to be stealing his way into it.

Chapter 5

In the next few weeks, Jeb seemed to split his time between working on the house and taking care of the herd during the day and visiting the children as often as he could, usually coming over in the early evening. But he'd also taken them on another picnic and more apple picking at the ranch, too. It didn't seem to matter what they did, Cassie and Lucas loved seeing him anytime.

Telling herself that it was only to give Cassie and Lucas more time with their uncle, Beth continued to ask Jeb to have supper with them. The children looked forward to his visits, and he even began to help them with their schoolwork while Beth cooked supper.

He still hadn't attended church, and Beth knew that was one reason she had to try to ignore the rapid beat of her heart each time he smiled at her or when their hands accidentally met handing a dish across the supper table. There was no way she could yoke herself to someone who didn't put the Lord first.

The much anticipated Southeastern New Mexico and Pecos Valley Fair was coming during the next week, and they were all looking forward to it. For the past few weeks, the *Roswell Record* had been full of planning details. Everyone seemed to be getting exhibits ready to be judged. Beth and Cassie had practiced their pie-making skills, much to Jeb and Lucas's appreciation. So far they hadn't tasted a pie they didn't love.

"Did you find a calf or horse to enter in the fair, Uncle Jeb?" Lucas asked on Tuesday evening as he finished his alphabet writing practice.

"I think we have a heifer that will show well. We'll enter her and see what happens." He shrugged and ruffled his nephew's hair. "Who knows? Maybe we'll place somewhere in the judging."

Lucas practically bounced in his chair at the prospect of winning a ribbon. "Oh, boy! I wonder what the McAllisters are going to enter?"

"Cal has a couple of calves he's entering. Next year we'll have more to choose from."

"Liddy is entering several pies and some jelly and a few vegetables from her garden."

"Do you think we could plant a garden next year?" Cassie asked her uncle as she set the table.

"Sure we can. I don't know much about growing food, but we have some good soil and artesian water at the ranch. . .not to mention we're close to the Hondo River, too. I'm sure we can have a good garden. Cal says Liddy's is one of the best around, and they don't live far away."

Beth turned from the skillet of gravy she was stirring. "You know, you could enter the apples from your orchard this year. They are really good. I think our pies have a great chance of winning a ribbon, and it's your apples we'll be using."

"Oh, Miss Beth, that's a great idea!" Cassie said.

"It sure is," Jeb agreed. "They are sweet and crisp. And they surely do make a good pie."

"I can't wait until the fair!" Lucas could barely contain his excitement. "And I really want to see that alfalfa palace. Have you seen it, Uncle Jeb?"

As Beth began to bring dishes to the table, Jeb got up to help her. "I have seen the start of it. I rode out with Cal yesterday. He's taking some of his bales out and helping to put it up. I thought I might go over tomorrow and see if I can help."

"Ohh—"

No one could miss the longing in Lucas's voice. "Maybe we can take a ride out first thing tomorrow after school?" Jeb looked questioningly at Beth.

"I don't see why not." She took her seat at the table, and Jeb followed suit.

"May I go, too?" Cassie asked.

Beth nodded her approval as Jeb glanced at her once more. He didn't need her permission, but it was nice that he silently acknowledged that she was the one who'd been in charge of the children since Harland had died. "Of course."

Jeb waited for Beth to take a seat at the table before he sat back down. "I'll pick them up from school then, if that's all right."

"It will be fine." She waited for the children to settle down at the table, then asked, "Would you say the blessing, please?"

His prayers were usually short and to the point, and Beth wondered if he only said them because she asked and the children seemed to expect him to. They'd been used to Harland praying, and it probably never crossed their mind that their uncle wasn't as faithful a Christian as their papa had been.

"I wonder how tall they'll make that palace?" Lucas asked as soon as Jeb was finished praying. Obviously, his mind wasn't where it should have been any more than Beth's had been.

"I just can't imagine a palace made of alfalfa hay!" Cassie giggled.

"It should be something to see, that's for sure. I'd never even heard of an alfalfa palace until I moved out here. And with Aunt Gertrude not up to going. . . and working for others so they could, I've never been to the fair." Beth placed a fried chicken leg on Lucas's plate and passed the platter of chicken to Jeb.

"I hadn't thought a lot about it. I haven't lived many places where a fair like this was held. But it makes sense," Jeb commented, helping himself to the chicken. "With the hay harvested, tied into bales, and ready to store for the winter, it's handy to have it to put up shelter. It will protect the exhibits from possible rain, provide shade if it's hot and warmth if it turns cooler. . .and after it's over, it can still be used by the ranchers and farmers who've provided the bales."

"I have to admit, I am getting excited about it, too," Beth said. "We're going to make our pies on Friday evening."

Jeb slapped his forehead and appeared distressed. "Oh, no! That means you won't be practicing your pie making anymore!"

Cassie laughed. "Don't worry, Uncle Jeb. We have lots of apples. We'll probably be making pies for a long time, won't we, Miss Beth?"

"Oh, I imagine we will." She couldn't help but grin at Jeb's show of relief.

"Whew." He ran a hand across his brow and grinned at the children. "I was worried there for a minute."

"We just don't have dessert for tonight," Cassie continued.

Jeb patted his shirt pocket. "Never fear. I stopped at the mercantile on the way over. I brought some gumdrops."

"I love gumdrops." Lucas grinned at Jeb.

"I know. But you have to clean your plate first," his uncle insisted.

"I will, Uncle Jeb!"

Beth exchanged a smile with Jeb at the young boy's exuberance. It was contagious.

The rest of the meal was spent talking about the fair. . .who they knew that might be entering some of the exhibits. . .what had happened during the day.

Beth thoroughly enjoyed mealtimes with Jeb and the children. It had become the highlight of her day. This evening, as she listened to them talk so easily to their uncle, one thing became totally apparent.

They adored him. And how could they not? He was really trying to build a relationship with them. At first they'd been a little hesitant to talk much around him. But as he asked more and more questions about them and how their days went, listening closely to what they had to say, they began to really open up to him.

Harland had loved his children, but he'd been a bit sterner with them than their uncle was. Now, they seemed to feel confident that they could talk to their uncle Jeb about nearly anything. . .and it was comforting to Beth that she wasn't the only one they felt they could come to. But would it last? Harland had said Jeb would never settle down in one place. But Beth found herself now praying that he would. . .for the sake of the children.

The next afternoon, as Jeb left the fairgrounds and started into town to pick up Cassie and Lucas to take them to see the alfalfa palace, he couldn't help compare the anticipation of seeing them again with the loneliness he'd felt leaving Beth's the night before. Of late, he always felt that way going back to the ranch. He would be glad to have the house ready so that he and the children could move in.

He began his mornings looking forward to riding into town to see them later in the day. And he really enjoyed suppertime with them. It'd been a very long time since he'd sat around a kitchen table and felt part of a family. And he was part of one now. He was the head of a family that now only included himself and his brother's children. But he had a feeling they'd all be missing Beth's presence once he moved them out to the ranch. Someway, somehow, he had to convince her to marry him and become a permanent part of the family. He sent up a prayer asking the Lord to show him how to go about doing just that.

As he neared the schoolhouse, he couldn't help but wonder what the children would have to say about the alfalfa palace. He was sure they were going to love it. He'd been helping Cal and some of his neighbors for most of the afternoon, and it was really taking shape. He'd enjoyed feeling part of the community and was eager to see it finished.

Cassie and Lucas were raring to go when he pulled up in his wagon, and they clambered aboard almost before he could come to a stop. He had to chuckle at his nephew as he climbed into the wagon.

"I thought the day would never end," Lucas announced, taking a seat beside Jeb.

"He's been really excited, Uncle Jeb," Cassie said sitting down beside her brother.

"You have, too!" Lucas told his sister.

"It is exciting," Cassie admitted. "How big is the palace now, Uncle Jeb?"

"It's big. . .and getting bigger every hour," Jeb answered, thinking about what it would look like to Lucas. "Just wait."

Jeb grinned at his niece and nephew's exuberance as he turned the wagon around and headed for the fairgrounds. It was northwest of downtown, near the Spring River, on the opposite end of town from their ranch. As expected, Cassie and Lucas were very impressed by the castle of hay. Although he realized it was quite large, Jeb hadn't really appreciated it quite so much until he saw it from their eyes.

Now, as Lucas craned his neck and stared up at it, Jeb chuckled. At eighteen bales high, not counting the turrets, it did look majestic.

"That's the biggest thing I've ever seen," Lucas uttered with awe.

"Me, too," Cassie breathed. "Oh, I wish Miss Beth was here."

So did Jeb. "We'll tell her all about it tonight. In the meantime, let's go take a closer look. Sun will be going down before too long, and Beth will be looking for us."

He made sure to stay close to them as they explored the palace. The designer was actually one of the local building planners in town, Michael Snow. He was on the site this afternoon, and when Jeb was introduced to him, he asked if he might be willing to come out to the ranch and give him a little advice on some of the repairs he needed to make to the house.

Mr. Snow nodded. "I'd be glad to. I drew up the plans for that house, and every time I pass by, I think about what a shame it is that it never was properly finished."

Jeb had been thinking the same thing. . .especially since Beth had seemed to think it held so much potential. For the last week or so, about all he'd been able to get done was patching the roof until he could fix it proper and some minor repair work inside. There were several things he just wasn't sure how to go about repairing. . .some of the trim had been damaged.

Jeb couldn't believe Michael was the one who designed the house. He sure was glad he'd come out today. "Do you have a copy of the plans? I'd sure like to see them, if you do. And if you have the time, I'd like your advice on how best to restore it."

"Now's the time to do it. I'll come on out tomorrow morning with the plans, and we'll look the place over."

Jeb shook the other man's hand. "Thank you, Michael. I look forward to hearing your ideas."

By the time they started back into town, he wasn't sure who was the most excited. The children over seeing the alfalfa palace up close or him. . .contemplating what might be done to the house to make it the home of Beth's dreams.

Beth had watched the clock beside the switchboard for most of the afternoon. Since Jeb was picking up the children and she didn't need to be home, she'd agreed to work an hour longer for Martha, one of the other operators, so that she could run some errands for her mother before the stores closed. Darcie had just left for home, and the other operator, Jessica, was busy with the second switchboard.

Beth couldn't help but be a little jittery, even though she knew Jeb would take good care of Cassie and Lucas. She'd been the one responsible for them ever since Harland's death, and it was very hard to let someone else take over even partial care for them.

Alma Burton's socket lit up, and Beth put the line pin in the socket. "Number, please?"

"Beth? That you?"

"Yes, ma'am, Mrs. Alma. Who do you need to talk to?"

"Well, I thought Darcie would be there, and I wanted to ask her something," Alma answered.

"She went home a little while ago. I'm working a little late for one of the other girls today." Beth glimpsed at the clock once more. "But Darcie might be home by now. Do you want me to ring her house?"

"No, that's all right. She's probably helping her mother get supper on the table for those boarders. What about the children?" the older woman asked. "Where are they?"

"They went out to the fairgrounds with their uncle Jeb."

"I saw him the other day over to the mercantile. He's a right good-looking man."

Yes, he is. But she didn't say it out loud. She waited for Alma to continue, but she wasn't going to let Beth off the hook.

"Don't you think he's handsome, Beth?"

Beth sighed. "He's nice looking, Mrs. Alma."

"How do Cassie and Lucas take to him?"

"They think he's wonderful." She held her breath, waiting for Alma to ask her if she thought he was wonderful, too, but thankfully, she didn't.

"That's good. I'll try to get hold of Darcie later. I still want her opinion on a thing or two."

"Yes, ma'am. I'll tell her." Beth disconnected the line and breathed a sigh of relief. . .until it dawned on her that Alma was likely going to ask Darcie what *she* thought Beth thought about Jeb. So far, she'd been successful in avoiding telling her friend that she was beginning to care about the man. She only hoped she'd been successful in hiding just how attracted she was to him.

"Mrs. Burton trying to pry information out of you, Beth?" Jessica asked.

"Bless her heart, I guess she doesn't have much else to do," Beth commented as her switchboard lit up and kept her busy for the next few minutes.

But Jessica was waiting for a lull. "You know, Mrs. Alma isn't the only one in town who thinks you and Jeb should get married and make a home for those children."

"Jessica! Who else? Who has been talking. . ."

"Beth, we work in the telephone office. We talk to half the town every day."

"Well, we aren't supposed to be gossiping!"

"We don't control what some of our customers have to say when we ask, 'Number, please.' You know that."

She did know that. And Jessica wasn't one to gossip. "I know. I'm sorry. I just don't like having everyone talking about me and giving their opinion on what I should do."

Jessica nodded. "I understand. But I thought you ought to know."

Both switchboards lit up just then, and there was no more time to talk before Martha showed up to relieve her. Beth eased out of the chair in front of the switchboard, and the other woman slipped into it. Martha and Jessica would work until Jimmy Newland came in to work from eight o'clock in the evening until eight o'clock the next morning. Things slowed down quite a bit at night.

Since Beth had the children to take care of and was considered the head operator, she only had to work weekdays. Darcie, Martha, and Jessica's shifts changed each week, along with a couple of part-time operators. But it was considered unseemly for the women to work alone at night, and it was the young men who worked mostly nights and weekends.

"Thank you so much, Beth. I really appreciate you staying late for me today," Martha said once she was settled at the switchboard.

Beth took her shawl off the hook by the door. "You're welcome, Martha. The children were with their uncle so it wasn't a problem. But they should be showing up anytime now. I'd better get on home."

"I saw them coming into town on my way here. Harland's brother certainly is a nice-looking man."

Beth kept silent as she drew her shawl around her. To agree somehow seemed disloyal to Harland. He had been nice looking, but not near as handsome as Jeb. Or maybe it was that she wasn't as attracted to—

"Oh, I'm sorry, Beth. Of course, Harland was a good-looking man, too."

Beth smiled at the other woman, relieved that she'd broken into her thoughts. "Neither of the Winslow brothers had reason to cover their faces, that's for sure."

"You're right about that." Martha chuckled and waved as Beth opened the door and headed out of it.

"Good night, Martha. Good night, Jessica." Wondering if Jeb and the children would be at her house when she got there, Beth hurried home. She tried to think what she would fix for supper. There was some stew from the other night she could heat up. It would be good with a pan of corn bread.

Seeing Jeb's wagon outside her house set her heart to pounding, and she hurried her pace. She entered the kitchen to find him lighting a lamp and Cassie supervising Lucas as he pumped water into a jar from the kitchen sink.

"Miss Beth, were you at the telephone office?" Cassie asked. "We were thinking of ringing there to see. It felt strange that you weren't here when we came in."

"I worked a little late for one of the girls."

"Uncle Jeb told us that you would probably be tired and that we could all go to Emma's Café for supper," Lucas informed her.

Beth's gaze flew to Jeb. "Oh, that's not necessary—"

"After working late, I'm sure you don't feel up to making supper, Beth. Let me take us all to Emma's."

"No, it's all right. I have stew to heat up, and I can make some corn bread."

"Only if you let me treat on Friday or Saturday night, then. I eat here most nights, Beth. The least I can do is treat you to an evening free from cooking once in a while."

"Look, Miss Beth," Lucas said from behind her.

She turned to find him holding the jar he'd filled with wildflowers in water. "Oh, Lucas, they're lovely."

"We saw them on the way home, and Uncle Jeb thought you might like some."

Beth took the jar of flowers from Lucas's small hands and turned to Jeb. "That was very nice of you."

He shrugged and grinned. "We all thought they were pretty and agreed that you might think so, too."

"I do. They are beautiful, and I do love flowers of any kind. Thank you all." That they thought of her while they were out pleased her immensely. That they had stopped and picked them just for her touched her deeply. That Jeb was the one who suggested it had her heart fluttering against her ribs. Beth turned and busied herself by putting the jar in the middle of the kitchen table, hoping that Jeb couldn't see just how much she was affected by his actions.

Good to his word, Michael Snow came out to the ranch the next day with the original house plans and gave Jeb some advice on how to go about making repairs. He knew Beth would love Michael's suggestions. But, even if things didn't end up like he wanted them to with her, he and the children would have a wonderful house to call home. Jeb could hardly wait to get started.

"I'm glad this house will have someone who cares about it living in it," Michael said. "It's not quite as bad as it appears from the outside. I don't think it will take all that long to get it in good shape."

"That's good to hear. I would like to have it finished by Christmas."

Michael nodded. "I think that's possible. . .if we are spared any really bad weather. Refurbishing it and making it the home it was meant to be will definitely raise the value of the land if you ever decide to sell out."

Selling out wasn't in Jeb's plans, but knowing that he was doing the best he could to enhance the land Harland had left to his children gave him a good feeling.

"I'll see you later at the fairgrounds?" Michael asked as he mounted his horse.

Jeb nodded. "I'll be there."

He strode toward the barn, now excited about the house and the suggestions and advice Michael had given him. Due to the Nordstroms' depleted funds, the house lacked many of the decorative elements—the trim and finishing work.

He tried to remember some of the things Beth had mentioned when she'd looked around. Oh, he knew he might never convince her to marry him, but he wasn't going to give up without trying. She'd liked the flowers he and the children had brought her. Jeb had caught her looking at the bouquet several times throughout supper last night. He had been surprised at how good it made him feel to know he'd done something that really pleased her.

Up until last night, when they'd come into an empty house, Jeb hadn't realized just how much Beth did for his niece and nephew. She worked outside the home all day and still managed to take wonderful care of Cassie and Lucas. . . giving them the extra attention they needed, keeping their clothes clean, and feeding them well—not to mention that she even fed him most of the time now. And all of this because she'd been going to marry his brother. Jeb hoped Harland had appreciated her and realized how the Lord had blessed him with such a good woman. . .two great women, counting Mary.

Jeb was just hoping and praying for one good woman. He was pretty sure he'd found her in Beth. And if it was the good Lord's will, she'd be moving into the ranch house with him and the children come Christmas.

Jeb saddled up his horse and turned toward town. He was looking forward to the start of the fair and taking Cassie and Lucas. . .and Beth.

Chapter 6

The fair started on Tuesday, and Beth couldn't quite tell who was more excited—the children or Jeb. It was all any of them had talked about for the past week. But actually, the fair had been the talk of the whole town. On the first day, Mayor Adams had welcomed the governor, who'd made the trip down from Santa Fe to give an opening address.

There was much talk—both in the town newspaper, the *Roswell Record*, and all along the telephone lines—about the goings-on. Working at the telephone office, Beth had a good idea of who had entered the exhibits and what they'd entered. . .even who they were hoping to win over.

Liddy McAllister was entering her apple and peach pies. Beth didn't expect to win over Liddy, but Cassie was excited about entering something in the fair, and Jeb and Lucas had told them that their pies were excellent.

Jeb had decided to enter some of his apples, and although he didn't think he'd win, he entered a two-year-old Hereford in the cattle category. He promised Lucas that they would enter more livestock the next year, when he'd know more what to enter after this fair.

According to Darcie, Alma and several of her friends were entering quilts they'd made, and Alma was hoping to win first place. Of course, Myrtle Bradshaw, Doc's wife, and Nelda Harrison were both hoping for the same thing.

School was dismissed early each day, and Jeb came into town to pick up Cassie and Lucas each afternoon to take them to the fair, but it would be Saturday before Beth could go. Each night at the supper table, they entertained her with stories about what was going on.

There were horse races every day, and one of Cal McAllister's horses, Rusty's Son, won the first two days.

Cassie told about the ladies' textile exhibits with all kinds of needlework entered, and the cooking and baking exhibits. The cakes, pies, jellies, and preserves would be judged on Saturday. Beth could hardly wait until then. Not so much for the judging, but because everyone was having such fun and she would finally be able to join them.

On Thursday night, Lucas burst into the kitchen, laughing. "Miss Beth, you'll never guess what happened today!"

She turned from the stove and couldn't help but grin at him. "What happened, Lucas?"

"Well, we thought there was a fire in the palace!"

Beth placed a hand over her suddenly pounding heart. "Oh, that doesn't sound very funny, Lucas. No one was hurt, were they?"

Lucas shook his head. "No. 'Cause there wasn't a fire." He began to laugh again.

Jeb and Cassie chuckled as Lucas tried, but couldn't get more out for his spurts of laughter.

"You tell about it, Uncle Jeb," Cassie suggested.

"Well, like Lucas said, there wasn't a fire. Come to find out, Councilman. . . ?" Jeb looked at the children with question in his eyes.

"Bagley," Cassie reminded him.

"That's right. Councilman Bagley evidently lit up his pipe back in one of the exhibits, and with all that puffing, smoke was just a-billowing out around him. Someone yelled, 'Fire!' and I grabbed the children up and we rushed outside."

Jeb started chuckling then, and it took a moment for him to continue. "You should have seen the councilman's face when he came out of there with his wife a-yellin' at him, telling him what for with his pipe in her hand."

"Oh, dear." Beth put a hand to her mouth and began to chuckle.

"But that's not even as funny as what happened at the fair several years back," Cassie giggled. "Tell her Uncle Jeb."

"Well." He chuckled and paused a minute. "One of the old-timers told us about something that happened at the fair of 1893. And Cal said it really did happen. One of the bales of hay caught fire from a turned-over lantern, and even though they got it put out right away, everyone was rushed out of the palace. Most all of the people were outside when they turned to see one of the men carrying out a lady. Said they figured she just passed out from the smoke or something, but come to find out. . ." Jeb broke off and laughed as Cassie and Lucas burst into giggles again.

Beth waited. What could possibly be funny about a woman fainting or passing out? Finally, having to know, she said, "Well, come to find out what?"

"It weren't a woman at all, Miss Beth," Lucas shouted, bursting into laughter again.

"It was a"—Cassie stifled a giggle to get it out—"it was a dress form, all dressed up in one of the dresses entered in the ladies' textile exhibit." She couldn't contain the laughter any longer.

"Oh, dear." Beth chuckled. "I wonder what he said when he saw it wasn't a woman?"

"It was a cowboy from Lincoln County, is what I heard." Jeb was trying hard not to laugh as he continued, "He said, 'Well, I sure 'nough thought she was the lightest woman I'd ever carried.' Then he tipped his hat to the form and to everyone watching and skedaddled out of there."

Beth's chortle quickly turned into laughter that had her doubling over, as she pictured the sight. Oh my, oh my. She couldn't wait until Saturday.

When Saturday finally rolled around, Beth was up early, frying chicken and making a picnic lunch. Most everyone took food to the fairgrounds, and Liddy McAllister had told Beth not to worry about sending food during the week, because she would have plenty for Jeb and the children. Liddy was such a good woman and friend. Beth wanted to reciprocate and had told Liddy that she would help provide the food for today.

She and Cassie had made their pies the night before, and they were ready to go for the exhibit. But those were for the judges, so they'd made an extra one for their own lunch.

It was a beautiful day, warm and sunny, as it often was at the beginning of October. Knowing it would be dusty at the fairgrounds, Beth chose a tan skirt and beige shirtwaist with a wide collar and front ruffle.

Even though Cassie and Lucas had gone to the fair every day, they seemed almost as excited as Beth felt. Of course, part of that was because they wanted her to see everything. When Jeb showed up with his wagon and helped her load the food into it, he seemed in high spirits, too.

The children scampered up into the wagon bed, and Jeb held Beth's elbow to assist her in getting up onto the wagon seat. He took his place beside her and smiled. "Ready?"

"Oh yes, I am."

Wagons, buggies, and surreys filled the outskirts of the fairground; and lots of men, women, and children were making their way to the famous alfalfa palace. It was impressive, Beth thought as they started toward it. It was comfortable inside, not too warm or too cool. And although dim at first, once inside, Beth found each exhibit had lanterns hung from wooden rafters that had been layered between the bales of alfalfa.

Cassie knew right where to go to enter their pies for judging. Although Beth had supervised her, the young girl had done all the work on these pies, and they were entered in her name. They were placed on a table along with about twenty others, and Beth and Cassie were told that the judging would be finished by noon.

"Guess what, guess what?" Lucas asked excitedly as he came running up to them. He and Jeb had checked out the entries for the fresh fruit.

"We got first place for our apples!"

"Why, that's wonderful news, Lucas! Let's go see!"

Jeb was grinning ear-to-ear. "I know I didn't plant those trees in the orchard, but it sure makes me happy that whoever did certainly knew what they were doing."

"Well, I'm hoping that blue ribbon carries over to our pies!" Beth exclaimed as they walked over to the fresh fruit and vegetable display. There, right beside the basket of apples and the sign that read WINSLOW RANCH APPLE ORCHARD, was a big, first-prize ribbon.

Cassie hugged her uncle. "Papa would be so happy! Wouldn't he, Miss Beth?"

Beth's gaze met Jeb's. It was the first time either of the children had mentioned their father in a while. She hoped it meant their sorrow was easing a bit. "He certainly would, Cassie."

They browsed through the other displays. There were fruits and vegetables of all kinds—corn, wheat, oats, alfalfa, pumpkins, squashes, beets, carrots, cabbages, turnips, and parsnips. There were also sweet potatoes, Irish potatoes, watermelons, onions, and peaches.

They ran into the McAllisters, who were inspecting all of the entries, too. Liddy's and Cal's daughters, Grace and Amy, had entered a couple of watermelons they'd planted and tended on their own, and they were thrilled at the first-place win. The McAllisters' boys—Matthew, who was three, and baby Marcus—were a little young to enter anything, but they seemed to be enjoying everyone else's excitement.

"Those sure look like good melons," Lucas said. Everyone there knew he was a big fan of watermelons.

"We brought a couple to have when we eat," Cal assured him.

"But that won't be for another hour or so," Jeb reminded his nephew.

"Well then, let's go see the animals," Lucas suggested, changing the subject and jumping up and down in excitement. "Maybe we have a ribbon for the Hereford you entered, Uncle Jeb!"

Jeb swung him up onto his shoulders as they headed for the livestock exhibits. "I don't think we better count on that this year. But maybe next."

Beth's heart skipped several beats at his words. Would he be here next year? He talked so confidently about staying, but all she could remember was Harland saying his brother would never settle down. Never.

By noon, they'd inspected all of the livestock exhibits. Jeb was right. His Hereford didn't win anything, but they congratulated Cal on his first-place win. They ran into Matt and Emma, who had left the café in the capable hands of Ben and Hallie for the afternoon. They had Mandy with them, and she appeared to be having a great time.

It was time to find out who won the baking exhibit, and they all hurried over to the women's exhibition wing of the palace. The judges were just finishing tallying their score, so Beth and Cassie and Liddy and her girls, Grace and Amy, all held hands and waited.

There was no major announcement, only ribbons placed in front of the entries. Once the judges finished, the ladies hurried up to the table. Cassie gave a discreet little squeal when she saw the second-place ribbon gracing her pie. Beth enveloped her in a hug, while she congratulated Liddy for taking first place.

"Thank you," Liddy said. "But I think I've got major competition in the coming years if Cassie came in second at her age!" She hugged the young girl when Beth let go. "Great job, Cassie!"

Lucas grinned up at his sister. "I just knew you were going to win, Cassie! Mama and Papa would be proud of you!"

Jeb hugged his niece, too. "I knew when I had a bite of that pie you made the other night that you were going to win a prize."

"I'm gettin' hungry just looking at these," Cal admitted.

"Me, too," Matt added.

"Well, I guess it's time we feed these men, if they're going to have strength enough for the races this afternoon," Liddy said.

As they made their way out to the grounds and to their wagons to gather the food and quilts they'd brought, Beth couldn't help but notice how many people said hello to Jeb. Of course, he'd helped with building the alfalfa palace, but he seemed to have gotten to know a lot of people in the area in a very short period of time. Beth supposed that if one moved around as much as Jeb did and never stayed anywhere very long, one had to make an effort to get to know people quickly.

After sharing the food Beth, Liddy, and Emma had brought, they went to watch the horse races and cheered along with Matt and Jeb as Rusty's Son, Cal's horse, came in first place again. Then they split up, with the men and boys going to the other horse races and the women and girls checking out the ladies' textile exhibits. There were all kinds of entries in quilting, fine sewing, crocheting, knitting, and embroidering.

Alma's quilt did win first place, with Myrtle's coming in second. Beth and the others moved through the many samples of ruffles, tucks, puffs, edging, lacing, fluting, and openwork done with thread. The women of eastern New Mexico were quite skilled in all areas.

At midafternoon, Beth, Liddy, Emma, and the girls met up with Jeb, Cal, Matt, and the boys at one of the food vendors for tall glasses of lemonade or tea. After that, they all took in the other races. First were the bicycle races, followed by the fifty- and one-hundred-yard foot races.

When Jeb and Lucas signed up for the three-legged race, Matt and Cal did, too. Then Beth and Cassie, along with Emma and Liddy and their girls, as the men began the race on all fours. Beth laughed until her side hurt as she watched Jeb and Lucas take a tumble and try to get up. They finally righted themselves about the time Matt and Cal took a fall directly in front of them.

Seeing the four of them try to right themselves and get back into the race had tears of laughter streaming down the faces of Beth and the rest of her entourage. Still, Jeb and Lucas managed to come in third, while Matt and Cal came in fifth.

As the day came to a close, Beth truly hated for it to end.

In the days following the fair, Jeb couldn't remember when he'd had such a wonderful time. It had felt so right to share the day with Beth and his niece and nephew. He became more determined than ever to get the house finished by Christmas. He wanted the children in their own home, and he prayed the good Lord would see fit to help him win Beth's heart so that she'd be with them all.

The plans Michael Snow gave him were just what Jeb needed to envision the house as it should be. He was sure the children and Beth would love the house when it was finished.

After talking about the fair for months, all the planning for it, and then the actual preparations for it, there seemed to be a little letdown in town for the next few weeks. The mood at Beth's house was no different. But it didn't last too long after Jeb brought the Sears and Roebuck catalog over one evening.

For the next week or so, their evenings revolved around poring over all the items offered in the large book. . .with Jeb paying close attention to the items that particularly caught Beth's eye.

There were several ranges, and Beth gave much attention to each one, but it was a huge range called the Sterling Sunshine steel plate range that really caught her eye. There was also a large worktable called the Handy kitchen table she kept going back to. According to the advertisement, it had two large flour bins and two drawers for utensils and so on.

There were bed sets and parlor sets, dining room tables and sideboards. That catalog gave Jeb more insight into Beth's likes and dislikes in a house than several months of asking probably would have. He pored over it back at the ranch, too, making note of any new thing that Beth or the children had pointed out that he might be able to afford for the house.

During supper at Beth's on a Friday night, several weeks after the fair, the children began to talk about the next month and Thanksgiving. The days were flying by, and Jeb couldn't believe how fast November was approaching.

"What do you do for Thanksgiving, Miss Beth?" Lucas asked. "We've been learning about the first settlers. The other children were talking about what all their families do, but I don't remember what we used to do. . .do you, Cassie?"

Jeb's heart twisted at the thought that Lucas couldn't remember what they did for Thanksgiving. Of course, he'd been young when his mother passed away—

"Mama used to roast a turkey or bake a big ham. We had all kinds of good things to eat. But last year. . ." Cassie shook her head. "I don't remember what we did, Lucas."

Beth quickly took Jeb's cup of coffee to the stove to refill it, but not before he caught the gleam of a tear in her eyes. He'd had to bend his head and blink a couple of times himself to keep from giving his own emotions away to the children.

From across the room, Beth cleared her throat before speaking. "Well, my aunt and I always had a nice meal, and we usually spent the day with one of her friends. We'll plan for a wonderful day. We can have turkey or a ham—and, Cassie, you and I can pick out a few new pies to try our hand at. I've never made a pumpkin pie, but the pumpkins are really growing this year."

"Oh, I'd like that!" Cassie replied.

"Can we have apple pie, too?" Lucas asked.

Jeb had a feeling Lucas would always love apple pie. It seemed to be the only kind he could remember his mama making. His heart warmed when Beth answered his nephew.

"Of course, Lucas. I can't imagine having Thanksgiving without it." She set the fresh cup of coffee in front of Jeb.

"Thank you, Beth." He hoped she knew his gratitude was for more than the coffee. She was wonderful to his brother's children. No one could doubt that she cared deeply for them. And there was no denying that he'd come to care for *her* more each and every time he saw her. He thought about her first thing in the morning and last thing at night, and there was no denying the way his heart pounded in his chest when she welcomed him into her home of an evening.

"You're welcome. Anything special you'd like to have on the menu, Jeb?"

"Hmm. . .it's been a long time since I've had a big Thanksgiving dinner. Even longer since it's been with family. I seem to remember my mama"—he smiled at Lucas and Cassie, who gave him their undivided attention—"*your* grandmother, used to make some kind of pudding."

"Could it have been a rice pudding?" Beth asked, turning her head to the side as she thought.

He loved the way the lantern light shimmered on the golden strands of her hair. "Might have been."

"Or maybe a bread pudding?"

And the way her eyes sparkled in the light. "That could have been it."

"Did it have a sweet sauce served over it?"

"I think so." But he didn't know how it could be as sweet as her lips appeared to be in the lamplight. He was certain no sauce could be as sweet as a kiss from Beth might be. It suddenly occurred to him. He'd been thinking about doing that a lot lately—kissing Beth.

Beth nodded and smiled. "That sounds like a bread pudding. I'll see if I can find a receipt for it."

"That's not necessary. I'm thankful enough just to be taking dinner with family."

"Uncle Jeb?" Lucas stared at him from across the table, his chin propped in his hand.

"Yes, Lucas?"

"Why don't you go to church? You believe in God, don't you?"

There was silence at the table—as if everyone was waiting for his answer. "Why, of course I believe in God, Lucas. I can't imagine life without Him in it. Why, your papa and I were baptized in the Arkansas River on the very same day. I usually read my Bible every night and. . .on Sundays, I kind of get on my horse and ride and contemplate on what all the Lord has done for me. . .all kinds of things like that." Cassie and Lucas kept looking at him as if they expected more of an explanation. He could only tell the truth.

"I don't rightly know why I don't go to church. I've just never lived close enough to one to go every Sunday, and I guess I just didn't think about it now that I do." And now that he thought about it, Jeb wondered why it hadn't occurred to him to attend church with them.

"Well, will you come this Sunday?" Lucas asked right out.

"Yes, I will." Jeb glanced over at Beth and saw a half smile on her lips. She seemed pleased, and he wished he'd thought to accompany them on Sundays before now. He sure did wish that. "I will come to church on Sunday, I promise."

That seemed to be all that was needed. "Good," Lucas replied, grinning ear to ear.

Beth sat at the kitchen table long after Jeb left for the night and the children were fast asleep. Would he be at church on Sunday as he'd promised Lucas? So far, he'd kept his word to the children. But she was afraid to hope that he'd show up. . .she'd been praying that he would be there each Sunday, but so far he hadn't stepped foot in the door. She prayed that he was a Christian as he'd told the children he was. For his sake, for their sake, and for. . . Beth shook the next thought out of her head. She'd have to see what he did on Sunday.

She made herself a cup of tea and took it over into the connecting parlor. She sat in her favorite chair, a worn rocker of her aunt's, and took a sip from the cup. . .thinking back on the past month since Jeb had come into their lives.

Her opinion of him had changed so drastically since their first meeting. Beth had become accustomed to his company and enjoyed having him around. . .and she missed him when he wasn't. Which wasn't altogether a good thing. When he decided to leave, she would miss him even more. And so would the children. They loved him more each day. He was so good with them—and to them. What would they do if he decided the responsibility was too much and that he couldn't stay in one place?

Yet he seemed to be happy here—to love being around Cassie and Lucas as much as they loved being around him. Surely he would stay. But all she kept remembering was Harland telling her that he'd tried to get Jeb to settle down near him and Mary many times before she died, and Jeb would have none of it, saying there was just too much country to see, too many things he wanted to do.

She didn't want to see the children heartbroken. They'd been through so much as it was. Beth bent her head in prayer. *Oh, dear Lord, please let Jeb decide to stay for Cassie's and Lucas's sake. They need family, and they need stability in their lives. Please, please, let their love and the ranch be enough to make Jeb want to stay here. In Jesus' name I pray, amen.*

In another month it would be Thanksgiving. He seemed almost as excited as Cassie and Lucas about it—about spending it with them. But would he still be here then? A month after that would come Christmas. Would he stay to finish the house? And if he did, would he remember his proposal? He'd mentioned nothing more of it to her. Beth sighed deeply and took a long drink of her tea. Deep inside her heart, she was disappointed that he hadn't.

Chapter 7

Beth tried not to show the deep disappointment she felt that Jeb hadn't shown up to go to church with them. She'd had a hard time convincing the children that they couldn't wait any longer for him. In desperation, she'd kept their hope alive by suggesting that he might already be at church waiting for them. She tried to tamp down the anger she felt that he hadn't kept his word to Cassie and Lucas as they settled themselves in their usual pew, halfway up the aisle, on Sunday morning.

Still, Lucas kept craning his neck to watch for his uncle Jeb, and Beth didn't have the heart to tell him his uncle probably wouldn't show up. They were well into singing the second hymn of the morning when Lucas tugged at her skirt.

"He's here!" he whispered loudly.

Beth's head wasn't the only one that turned at his words. She peeked around Lucas to see Jeb Winslow, standing there in the door of the church, obviously looking for them. Her heart did a flip-flop down into her stomach and back up again as he spotted them and made his way down the aisle.

She and Cassie moved down to make room for him at the end of the pew, and Lucas handed him his hymnal. Beth quickly blinked back the tears that formed behind her eyes, telling herself that it was the look of joy on the faces of Cassie and Lucas that caused them. But she was totally aware that she was every bit as happy as they were.

When Jeb lifted his voice in song, her heart made music to match his beautiful tenor, and she began to sing "Amazing Grace" with a thankful heart.

Beth was totally aware of Jeb's bowed head as prayers were said, of the attention he gave to Minister Turley's sermon, flipping through the worn Bible he'd brought with him to find the verses the minister pointed out. Her heart soared with joy, and she sent up her own silent prayer of thanksgiving that Jeb had shown up and that she finally knew that he was a Christian.

But her joy was short-lived when she realized that didn't mean he would settle here for the rest of his life. Harland had been so convinced his brother could never stay in one spot for long. And even though he'd already claimed a large portion of her heart, she just couldn't allow herself to care more for him. How could she ever trust that he would stay? Jeb could still decide that staying in the Roswell area wasn't for him and feel the need to move on, leaving the children with her, all of them alone. Worse yet, he might take them with him, leaving her alone. And totally heartbroken. She could only pray that didn't happen.

When the service was over, Beth realized her thoughts had been anywhere but where they should have been—focused on Minister Turley's sermon. She sent up a silent prayer, asking forgiveness as she went down the aisle with Jeb and the children. It was slow going as first one person, then another stopped them to welcome Jeb.

The Johnsons and the McAllisters welcomed him like an old friend and waited patiently behind them as Mrs. Alma waited for an introduction.

" 'Bout time you made it to church, young man," she said to Jeb once Beth had introduced them.

"Yes, ma'am. I suppose it is," Jeb admitted with a smile.

"Well, we're glad to have you here."

"Thank you. It's good to be here, Mrs. Burton."

"See you come again," Alma instructed, with a short nod to emphasize her words.

"Yes, ma'am. I will," Jeb answered respectfully. Beth's heart warmed at the way he responded to the old woman.

Beth introduced him to Darcie and her mother, Molly Malone, to Jed and Laura Brewster, and to Miss Harriet Howard, one of Alma's friends, on their way to the door where Minister Turley waited to greet him.

The minister shook hands with Jeb. "Good to see you here, Mr. Winslow."

"Good to be here. Please, just call me Jeb, though."

Minister Turley nodded. "Jeb, I hope we'll see you again next week."

"Yes, sir, you will. I haven't always lived near enough to a church to hear many sermons, but I sure did enjoy yours today."

"Thank you. That's always a pleasure to hear."

"Uncle Jeb has been talking to God while he rides his horse," Lucas informed the minister from behind his uncle.

"Well, I'm of the opinion that we can talk to the Lord anyplace we are," the minister responded, with a smile. "Main thing is that we talk to Him."

Jeb nodded. "That's what I figure, too. And I'll keep right on doing that. But it's good to have a church close enough to enjoy the fellowship of others."

"It sure is," Matt agreed, giving Jeb a friendly slap on the back.

The group continued down the church steps and into the yard. "And speaking of fellowship," Matt continued, "Emma and I would like to ask you all to come over to the café for Sunday dinner. The McAllisters will be there, too."

"Whatever you want to do is fine with me," Jeb assured her.

She glanced at Cassie and Lucas and could tell they wanted her to say yes. She'd planned on roasting a hen, but she could do that the next night. At the moment, her emotions were in turmoil. . .thrilled that Jeb had come to church, that he trusted in Jesus as his Savior. . .just as she'd prayed about. And yet unable to trust that he would stay put, how could she ever give her heart to him?

It might be easier to spend the day with Jeb if mutual friends were around. She smiled and nodded at Matt and Emma. "That would be wonderful. Thank you for the invitation. What can I bring?"

"Just yourselves. Liddy brought some pies, and I have a very large ham baking. Just come on down whenever you want."

"We'll be there soon. At least I can help you finish it up and get it on the table."

"I'll take you all to Emma's. I brought the wagon," Jeb announced to Beth. "I'd meant to get into town early enough to bring you to church, but I never asked what time the service started."

He helped her up onto the seat while the children hurried to sit at the back of the wagon, and Beth saw the bouquet of wildflowers lying on the floorboard. Jeb handed them to her when he took his seat. "My excuse for being late. I passed a field of these on the way into town, and you liked the last ones we picked so well. . ."

Beth's heart melted, and she didn't know what to say except, "Thank you, Jeb."

"I'd meant to get them to you before church so you could put them in water. They're beginning to look a little limp."

"They are beautiful, Jeb." Hoping to hide just how very touched she was by his thoughtfulness, Beth brought them close to her face and inhaled the sweet scent of the blooms. No one had ever brought her flowers until Jeb did. Not even Harland. The fact that Jeb had been so thoughtful made her want to cry for some reason. Why did he have to be so thoughtful? She blinked quickly and chewed her bottom lip for a moment as she held the bouquet to her chest.

"If you don't mind, would you stop by the house so that I can put them in water?"

Jeb smiled. "I'd be glad to."

Beth noticed several couples watching them as Jeb turned the wagon out of the churchyard and started down the road, and she had a feeling they'd be the talk of the town very soon. She could just see the switchboard lighting up, with people hurrying to spread the word that Jeb had come to church and was taking them home. Oh, yes. If she didn't miss her guess, they would be the topic of conversation all afternoon.

Jeb wished he'd made it into town in time to pick Beth, Luke, and Cassie up for church. It had been a little embarrassing to stand there in the doorway looking for them, but the happiness on the children's faces had been worth more than any momentary discomfort he'd felt. And once the service was over, everyone had made him feel right at home. There were some really nice folks in this area. But the people responsible for making him want to think about settling down were sitting right here in the wagon with him.

Beth was lovely in a blue suit with gold-braided trim of some sort and a dainty hat of the same color atop her head. But she was truly beautiful on the inside, where it counted most.

He wanted to show her the plans Michael Snow had given him—to see if there were any suggestions she might have. But he wasn't sure how to go about it. He didn't want to risk having her think he felt assured that she would marry him when the house was finished. Nothing could be farther from the truth. He thought she was beginning to care about him, but it hadn't been that long since she'd been planning on walking down the aisle with his brother—even if she hadn't known him very well.

Jeb wasn't sure he could ever take his brother's place in her heart. It might well take more time than the few weeks left until Christmas to do that. He was determined to have the house finished by then. . .if the good Lord willed it so. And he was going to ask her to marry him again. But if she wasn't ready to commit to him then, he wasn't going to give up. Beth was a woman worth waiting for.

He pulled the wagon up to her door and helped her down from the wagon. He stood watching her hurry into the house, glad that he'd brought her the bouquet, sad as it was.

"She sure does like those flowers, doesn't she, Uncle Jeb?" Lucas asked.

"Yes, she sure does," Jeb agreed, grinning at his nephew. "Let that be a lesson for you, Lucas."

The young boy scratched his head. "What kind of lesson?"

"A life lesson in what a lady likes. It might come in handy one day when you are courting one."

"What does that mean?" Lucas asked.

Cassie giggled. "It means that you are trying to get her to like you enough to marry you, doesn't it, Uncle Jeb?"

"Something like that." Jeb grinned at his niece.

"Oh," Lucas squeaked. "Are you courting Miss Beth?"

"Well, I'm trying to. . .but don't tell her." Jeb figured he had already said more than his nephew needed to know.

"Why not?"

"It might not help my cause."

"What is your cause?" Lucas appeared really confused.

"Oh, Lucas! Never mind." Cassie rolled her eyes at him. "Just don't tell Miss

Beth that Uncle Jeb is trying to court her."

Lucas shrugged and shook his head. "I won't. I promise. I'm still not even sure what courting is."

"Neither am I. But thanks, Lucas." Jeb ruffled his hair and grinned at Cassie. "And thank you, Cassie."

"I sure hope it works, Uncle Jeb," she whispered, grinning back at him.

"So do I."

Beth came out of the house just then, and Lucas chuckled while Cassie nudged him and said, "Shhh."

Jeb helped Beth back up into the wagon, pleased at the smile she gave him.

"The flowers perked right up as soon as I put them in water. Thank you again."

"You're welcome." Jeb figured it might have been worth being late this morning, just to make her so happy. She sure did like flowers. He'd have to find a spot to plant some near the house so she could see them every day. . .should she ever consent to be his wife.

The McAllisters were at Emma's Café when they arrived, and Beth hurried to the kitchen to find Emma and Liddy dishing up the meal. Emma's Café was closed on Sundays, and Matt and Emma took advantage of it to have their friends over.

Several tables had been put together to accommodate everyone, with a table set for the children nearby, and Liddy had put her girls to work setting them. Beth didn't have to ask Cassie to help, as she offered as soon as they got there. She couldn't be prouder of Harland's children if they were her very own.

But all the children were well behaved, and they all bowed their heads as Matt said a prayer before the meal. Beth helped Cassie fix her plate and Jeb helped Lucas. . .she couldn't help but notice that they seemed like a family just as Cal and Liddy did, helping their children settle down with their food, or Matt and Emma, as they debated whether to seat Mandy beside them or let the girls help with her.

"Oh, please let her sit with us," Cassie begged Emma. "Lucas and I will help with her, Mrs. Johnson."

Grace and Amy added that they would help, too, and in the end, Mandy did end up at the children's table, having the time of her life with all the attention.

"How is the house coming?" Matt asked Jeb as he dished up a huge slice of ham onto a plate and handed it to him.

"It's going pretty good. If the good weather holds, I think I'll have it finished by Christmas."

Beth's pulse sped up as Jeb smiled and handed her a basket of rolls. Would he ask her to marry him again? Dare she hope that he would? As their hands brushed against each other and her heart skipped several beats, Beth knew that she already did.

"Harland would be proud of what you're doing to the place," Cal commented. "He really had big plans for the ranch and the future. I'm sure he'd like what you are doing to the house."

Harland. The man she'd been going to marry. Beth hadn't really thought about him in days. She'd been too busy thinking about Jeb. . .coming to care too much for him. Surely she wasn't trying to replace one brother with another?

"Thank you," Jeb answered Cal. "I don't know all the plans he had, but I know a lot about cattle, and I've even helped put up a ranch building or two. I'm trying to do what I think he would have done had he lived."

How could she care so much about Jeb now. . .when she couldn't learn to love his brother, whom she'd promised to marry? And had he lived, would she have told him she couldn't marry him? That she didn't love him?

Beth couldn't sleep that night. She tossed and turned, finally getting up an hour early to make a cup of tea, hoping it would take her mind off the guilt she felt that she couldn't get Jeb out of her mind long enough to think about his brother. The man she'd promised to wed.

She'd agreed to marry Harland, had been happy that he wanted to move to Roswell to start their life together. He was a good man. An honorable man. And yet. . .she had been thinking of breaking her promise to marry him.

Now here she was falling in love with his brother. . .and praying that he stayed around and asked her to marry him again. How could she be so disloyal to Harland's memory? No answers came to her, and she shook her head as she went to wake up the children and get ready for work.

By the time Beth got to the telephone office, her heart was heavy with the guilt she felt, and by the end of the day, she felt no better. Her switchboard had been lit up all day, but she'd made few connections. Most everyone wanted to talk to her. . .about Jeb.

Mrs. Alma was the first to comment. "That brother of Harland's seems a good man, Beth. You could do a lot worse than marry him."

"Why, Mrs. Alma! I—"

"It would solve all of your problems, Beth, dear. The children are his kin. You love them. The two of you could make a nice home for them."

"But, Mrs. Alma—"

"You just think about it. 'Nough said." With that, Alma hung up her receiver, and Beth disconnected her line.

Another one lit up. This time it was Doc Bradshaw's line.

"Number, please," Beth said.

It was Doc's wife, Myrtle. "Hello, Beth, dear. I just wanted to talk to you a minute. How are you today?"

"I'm just fine. And you?"

"Doin' good. And if I wasn't, Doc would set me to rights."

Beth chuckled. "That he would. What can I do for you?"

"Not a thing, dear. I just wanted to tell you what a nice-looking couple you and Mr. Winslow make."

"But we aren't a couple, Mrs. Doc." Myrtle refused to let anyone call her Mrs. Bradshaw. It was just too formal for her.

"Well, you should be, Beth."

Beth didn't know what to say. "I. . .well. . .I. . ."

Myrtle didn't seem to expect a reply. "I have to go, dear. It was nice talking to you."

Beth sighed and shook her head as she disconnected the line. Didn't these women have anything better to do than try to be matchmakers?

By afternoon, she was almost afraid to see her switchboard light up. She'd never had so many sweet busybodies telling her what to do. During a momentary lull, she leaned back in her chair and rubbed the back of her neck.

"No, Mrs. Howard, this isn't Beth. She's working the other switchboard this morning." Darcie grinned over at Beth.

Beth watched as her friend listened to the woman on the other end of the line for a moment, nodding her unspoken agreement.

"I'll be sure and tell her," Darcie said before disconnecting the line. She chuckled and turned to Beth. "Mrs. Howard wants me to let you know that she thinks that you and Jeb and the children make a beautiful family. . .and you'd better snatch him up fast. Of course, I think the same thing."

Sudden tears sprang to Beth's eyes. "Oh, Darcie. How can I? He may not even stay. And even if he did, how could I be so disloyal to Harland as to fall in love with his brother?"

Darcie jumped up and hurried over to Beth. "Oh, Beth. I'm sorry. I didn't mean to make you cry!" She pulled a clean handkerchief from her pocket and handed it to her.

Beth dabbed at her eyes and shook her head. "You didn't. It's me, don't you see?"

Darcie's switchboard lit up, and she rushed back to it, looking over at Beth. "It's not you. I think we need a cup of tea at Emma's after work. Don't you let everyone upset you so."

Her own switchboard lighting again, Beth composed herself the best she could and connected the line. "Number, please?"

"Get me the sheriff's office, will you?" Homer Williams, a barber and one of the town's councilmen, asked.

"Certainly, Mr. Williams." Beth breathed a sigh of relief that it wasn't someone else wanting to give her their advice and connected the lines.

The rest of the afternoon was busy enough that if a caller wanted to talk to Beth, she could honestly tell them she had another line to connect. Still she watched the clock and had never been more relieved than when Martha and Jessica came in to relieve her and Darcie.

"I called Emma and told her we were coming for tea," Darcie informed her as she closed the office door behind them.

"Oh, Darcie. I'm all right now. There's no need—"

"Yes, there is. I told Mother I would be a little late getting home, and Cassie and Lucas don't get out of school for another hour. It's been a long time since we've gone to tea."

Darcie rarely took time for herself, and she was trying to make her feel better. Beth couldn't turn her down. "All right. Let's go."

The day was cooling fast, and they hurried down the boardwalk toward Emma's. She met them at the door.

"I've been watching for you. It's really chilly out there," Emma said. "Hallie is going to watch the front for me. And we are going upstairs. Mandy is down for a nap, and we'll have more privacy up there." She led them through the kitchen and up the stairs to her and Matt's apartment. A small table had already been set for tea, and Emma motioned for them to sit down. "I'm so glad Darcie suggested this. We haven't had a chance to just sit and talk in a long while."

Beth took a seat and smiled at her friend. "No, we haven't. And I know you both mean well, but this really isn't necessary. I just. . .had too much advice this morning."

"Beth, we're your friends. And we aren't going to give you advice. But you seem to be upset, and we'd like to help you if we can." Emma sat down across from her and began to pour the tea.

Beth swallowed around the lump in her throat. She was blessed to have such caring friends. And she did need to talk. . .if for no other reason than to be honest with herself and them.

"I'm not sure I deserve your care."

"What makes you say that?" Emma asked.

"I'm just an awful person."

"Oh, Beth. That's the silliest thing I've ever heard you say," Darcie cried. "You are a wonderful person. . .look how you took in Harland's children, prepared to raise them as your own before Jeb was found."

Beth shook her head and stared into her cup. "I do love Cassie and Lucas.

But. . .I didn't love their father. . .not the way I needed to, to marry him. I was going to tell him. . .but then he died before I had a chance to. And, as sorry as I was that he died. . ." Beth began to cry, and there was no stopping the tears that spilled over. "I. . .I was relieved that I didn't have to hurt him." She laid her head on the table and sobbed.

"Oh, dear Beth." Emma jumped up and hugged her while Darcie patted her hand. "I'm so sorry I wasn't more perceptive. I think anyone feeling the way you did would feel the same way. I really do. You didn't want to hurt him."

"But why didn't I care enough? And why do I care so much for Jeb when I—" Beth took a deep breath and pulled out the handkerchief that Darcie had given her earlier. She wiped her eyes. "Do you think I'm trying to replace one brother with another?"

"Of course not," Emma assured her. "Maybe if you *had* loved Harland and were grieving deeply over your loss, I suppose one might think that. But you just said you didn't love Harland, but you do care for Jeb. How would that be replacing one with the other?"

"I don't know. I just—"

"What is different about how you feel about Jeb, Beth?" Darcie asked.

Beth sighed. Everything was different. Her pulse never raced at just a glance from Harland the way it did when Jeb looked at her and smiled. And her heart never hammered in her chest when Harland was around as it did each time Jeb came near. "I—he—my heart—"

Emma chuckled and sat back down. "You know, you and Harland really didn't have much time to get to know each other before he died in that stampede, Beth. He didn't even come into town every day like Jeb does, did he?"

"No." Beth had always wondered how he could go several days without seeing the children, but she never questioned him about it. "He was so busy trying to get the herd together and the ranch started, he didn't get into town as often as Jeb."

"So you've really spent more time with Jeb, getting to know him, than you ever did with Harland," Darcie added.

Beth thought of all the evenings they'd spent having supper together, the hours he'd helped the children with their schoolwork or watched her and Cassie make pies. The day at the fair and picnics at the ranch. . .and poring over the Sears and Roebuck catalog together, getting to know each other's likes and dislikes. "That's true."

"I think it's very simple, Beth. You couldn't make yourself love Harland any more than you can keep yourself from caring about Jeb."

"It's all my fault for daring you to answer that advertisement, Beth," Darcie exclaimed. "I am so sorry."

"It's not your fault, Darcie. I should never have taken the dare. But I thought we knew each other from our correspondence, and I truly thought it would all work out."

"You wanted to fall in love with Harland. I know you did," Emma said. "And I think you thought you loved him when he first arrived in Roswell. But it is hard to get to know someone just from a letter. And to tell you the truth, Beth, Matt and I never thought you and Harland made a very good match. He was a really good man, but he seemed too. . .too. . .stern, too serious. . .older than his years."

"I just feel so disloyal to him, the way I feel about Jeb." Beth expelled a deep breath. "It doesn't matter anyway. He may not stay. Harland was convinced that Jeb would never settle down, and I can't afford to let myself fall in love with him."

Emma glanced at Darcie, then back at Beth. Emma patted her hand. "Beth, dear. I think it's too late. I think you are already in love with the man."

Beth buried her head in her arms and cried in earnest.

Chapter 8

After her cry and the talk with Emma and Darcie, Beth felt decidedly better. Emma was right; it was too late. She did love Jeb, in spite of the fact that she was afraid he'd never stay in one spot. Even if he did stay, he'd never once mentioned his proposal again, and Beth wondered if he'd decided he didn't need her to help him raise the children.

Still, the children needed him in their lives, and she would pray that he stay and make a home for them, no matter how much she would miss them when they moved out to the ranch. They loved their uncle, and he obviously loved them. Surely he would stay for their sakes.

The next few weeks flew by, with Beth still receiving advice from just about everyone in town and trying not to think about it each time she saw Jeb.

One evening when he came for supper, he brought the plans for the house for them to see. While it was hard to tell just what it would look like when he finished, it was going to be very nice. Beth could tell that much.

Jeb tried to explain as he pointed to one of the upstairs rooms. "This will be Cassie's bedroom, overlooking the apple orchard and the barn, and Lucas, this will be yours. It looks out over the barn and corral."

Lucas pointed at a larger room. "Is this yours, Uncle Jeb?"

"Mine and. . ." Jeb paused midsentence and glanced at Beth with a slight nod and a smile. "Yes, it will be mine."

"And what is this?" Cassie asked, pointing to one of the main rooms downstairs.

"That will be the front parlor." Jeb pointed to the room in back of it. "And this will be the back parlor. This is the dining room and, of course, here is the kitchen. In the dining room, I think I'll put up a plate rail."

As he talked about the kind of trim work and other finishing touches he'd like to make, Beth noticed that he seemed to have taken some of her suggestions to heart, and she couldn't help but be pleased. Still it didn't mean that he'd propose again. . .it didn't mean that at all.

Cassie and Lucas were obviously looking forward to moving to the ranch, and Beth tried to be happy for them.

She refilled Jeb's coffee cup and her own. "Liddy telephoned me today. She'd like for us all to have Thanksgiving with them out at their place. She asked Matt and Emma, too. It sounded nice. I told her I would let her know. What would you all like to do?"

"Let's go!" Lucas shouted.

"I'd like to go. It will be fun to spend the day with Grace and Amy and Mandy," Cassie admitted.

"Anything is fine with me," Jeb assured her. "I like the McAllisters and the Johnsons."

Beth took a sip of coffee. "I'll accept the invitation, then, and ask her what I can bring."

Thanksgiving dawned sunny and cool. Beth was furnishing some of the desserts and was up early baking a three-layer chocolate cake, the apple pie she'd promised Lucas, and a pumpkin pie to go along with the cookies and bread pudding she'd made for Jeb the night before.

Cassie and Lucas could barely contain their excitement at spending the day out at Cal and Liddy's.

"When will Uncle Jeb be here?" Lucas asked, looking out the window once again.

"He'll be here, soon, I'm sure," Beth replied as she packed the desserts into picnic baskets to take to Liddy's.

"What all do you think we'll be having for dinner?" Cassie asked.

"Well, roast turkey, I know. Liddy is doing that. I think Emma may be bringing a ham. And mashed potatoes, of course, and other vegetables."

"I'm getting hungry just thinking about it," Lucas said.

Beth took off her apron and brushed at the skirt of her nicest dress. It was a burgundy and pink stripe with a deep lace yoke. She'd dressed with care today, wanting to look her best. Truth be told, she was excited about spending the whole day with Jeb and the children. And it was an added bonus that they would be with good friends of hers.

"Here he is!" Lucas said. He quickly drew on his coat, opened the back door, and ran out to meet his uncle. Beth could hear Jeb chuckling as Lucas told him to hurry.

"Good morning," Jeb said on entering the kitchen. "My, don't you two ladies look pretty."

Cassie giggled, and Beth could feel herself blush at the compliment she'd been hoping for. "Thank you."

"It sure smells good in here."

"It's the cake Miss Beth just made." Lucas lifted the lid of the basket that held the cake so Jeb could see. "She makes the best chocolate cake in the whole world!"

Jeb sniffed appreciatively. "Are we sure we want to share this with everyone else? Maybe we should just stay here and eat cake?"

Lucas laughed and shook his head. "Then we'd miss out on the turkey and everything else!"

Jeb ruffled his nephew's hair. "I guess we'd better be on our way then—before I give in to the temptation to cut this cake."

Beth grinned at him as she quickly grabbed the handle of the basket. It was probably a good thing he didn't know about the bread pudding. "I best take charge of this basket then." She nodded toward the other baskets on the table. "You can bring those."

"What's in them?"

"Cookies and pumpkin pie and—" Cassie stopped in midsentence.

"Good things." Beth grinned and finished for her as the child realized she had come close to giving Jeb's surprise dessert away. She grabbed the basket it was in and handed it to Cassie. "Here, you are in charge of this one, dear." She leaned down and whispered, "See your uncle doesn't go snooping, okay?"

Cassie giggled and nodded.

Jeb took a basket in each hand and headed out the door. "Well, now. If I need a snack before we get there, a cookie will be easier to get to than a piece of cake anyway."

"Jeb Winslow! You wouldn't dare!"

He laughed all the way to the street, and by the time Beth made sure the children had their wraps on and got out to the wagon, he was munching quite happily on one of the cookies. Beth couldn't help but smile as he grinned at her. "Hard for me to resist a dare, Beth."

Beth understood perfectly. Oh, yes. After all, she'd answered that advertisement of Harland's on a dare. She chuckled and shook her head, thinking she could probably teach Jeb a thing or two about taking a dare.

Still, she couldn't stop herself from blushing or her stomach from fluttering as if a hundred butterflies had been released when she saw the look in his eye before he flipped the reins and headed toward the McAllisters'. Had he been referring to the challenge she'd given him about the house? Or was that just wishful thinking on her part?

It was the best Thanksgiving Beth could remember in a long, long time. For several years after she moved to Roswell, it had been just her and Aunt Gertrude. Before that, her Thanksgivings were spent with just her and her parents and rarely anyone else.

But spending this one with Cassie, Lucas, Jeb, and her best friends was something she would never forget. Liddy and Emma kept bumping into each other while they finished preparing the meal, laughing all the while. They dodged the children. . .and the men as well. . .as they all ran in and out of the kitchen to ask when everything would be ready. Beth just couldn't imagine having a better time.

Liddy's dining room was filled to overflowing, but no one seemed to mind as Cal said the prayer.

"Dear Lord, we thank You for this day and for the many blessings You've given us. We thank You for providing for us always. For our loved ones, for old friends and new. For this meal we are about to eat. And most especially for Your Son and our Savior, Jesus Christ. It is in His name that we pray. Amen."

"Amen," Jeb and Matt added at the same time.

Joy flooded Beth's soul knowing that Jeb was a Christian. She would always be comforted knowing that, whether he stayed or went. But she sent up a silent prayer that he would stay.

The meal was delicious, consisting of the roast turkey with stuffing, baked ham, mashed potatoes, squash, and onions in cream, cranberry jelly, and breadsticks. There were nuts and cheese and crackers along with the desserts that Liddy and Beth had brought.

Beth would never forget the look on Jeb's face as she served him a portion of her bread pudding.

He gazed up at her with a grin. "You made it for me?"

She could feel the color creep up her neck, feeling everyone's gaze on them, but she only nodded and waited while he dipped his fork into it and took a bite.

Jeb closed his eyes as if to savor the taste, swallowed, then he gave her a huge smile. "It's even better than I remember my mother's being. Thank you, Beth."

"You're welcome." Her heart flooded with warmth when he asked for seconds a few minutes later. How good it felt to make him happy!

After eating so much, none of the adults had the energy to do much of anything except to play some checkers, watch the children at play, and visit for most of the afternoon.

For the next few days, Jeb smiled every time he thought of Thanksgiving. He had to have been young the last time he enjoyed a Thanksgiving quite so much. He'd forgotten how wonderful the day could be when shared with family and good friends. And hard as it was to know that his brother was gone, Jeb was thankful that he had family left in Cassie and Lucas.

They were the last of his kin, and he loved them. He'd come to love Harland's children more than he even imagined he could. . .and the woman who'd taken them in and cared for them as if they were hers.

For a little while Thanksgiving Day, it had felt as if he and Beth and Cassie and Lucas were a real family. And he hoped that they would be. Beth had captured his heart almost from the first minute he'd met her, that first day at her house, looking at him with apprehension while Lucas peeked out from behind her skirts. Getting to know Beth and how much she cared about Cassie and Lucas made him realize that her uneasiness that day had been due to worry that he might take the children away from Roswell. . .and her.

Well, he would be taking them out to the ranch, but he hoped with all his heart that she would agree to be his wife and come with them. In the meantime, he was working as hard as he could to get the house finished by Christmas.

It was too cool for Cassie and Lucas to come out and help on Saturdays. He was still living in the barn, and the fireplaces in the house weren't ready for a fire yet. He hoped to have that done soon, but he decided not to bring the children out until it was completely finished. He could hardly wait to see their reaction when they saw all the changes he'd been making.

He hitched up the wagon and headed to town. He had a few supplies to pick up and an order to place for some fixtures for the house. He'd been poring over the Sears, Roebuck, and Company catalog, trying to make a list. He'd check the different mercantiles in town, and if he couldn't find what he wanted there, he'd place an order to Sears and Roebuck.

As he headed into town, he was on the lookout for the few remaining patches of wildflowers. It'd been pretty cold lately and they were dying out fast, but he found a small clump just off the road and drove the wagon over to it. The pretty yellow flowers looked real cheery on the overcast day, and he was sure Beth would love them. He picked as many as were there and put them on the floor of the wagon.

He wondered if the seed catalog he'd ordered had come in. He'd check the post office while he was in town. He didn't know a thing about planting flowers, but he was sure that Liddy McAllister could tell him the best time to plant them so that they would be a surprise for Beth come spring.

He stopped at the post office on his way to the Jaffa-Prager Company. The catalog hadn't come in, but he did have a letter from his old boss, John Biglow. Figuring it was just an answer to the letter he'd sent the man, Jeb stuffed it in his jacket pocket to read later and went on to the mercantile. He put in his order, and Mr. Cormack promised he'd put a rush on it to see if they could get it here before Christmas.

Jeb loaded up the supplies he'd bought and put the bag of candy he'd picked up for Cassie and Lucas beside him on the wagon seat. He slapped the reins, and as if they knew right where they were supposed to go, his horses took off in the direction of Beth's place.

It was turning dark, and the light gray smoke curling up from Beth's stovepipe along with lights in her kitchen seemed to welcome him and put a glow in his heart. He gathered up the bouquet and hurried to the door, holding it behind him.

Cassie must have been looking for him, because she opened the door before he had a chance to knock. "Uncle Jeb. . .guess what we're having for supper?"

"What?" Jeb entered the kitchen and sniffed. The enticing aroma told him that Beth was making one of his favorite meals, but he let Cassie tell him.

"We're having pinto beans, fried potatoes, and corn bread," Cassie announced with a grin. It was one of her favorite meals, too.

Beth smiled from the stove. "Good evening, Jeb. We're having pork chops, too."

"Miss Beth spoils us, doesn't she?" Jeb asked, ruffling Lucas's hair.

"She sure does." Lucas motioned for Jeb to bend down so he could whisper to him. "We're having an apple pie, too."

"Apple pie?" Jeb whispered back. "I think Miss Beth deserves something special for that, don't you?"

Lucas and Cassie both nodded.

"Would you get a jar of water to put these in, Cassie?" Jeb asked, handing the flowers to Lucas.

It was warm in the kitchen, but Jeb couldn't miss the sudden profusion of color that flooded Beth's cheeks. He could tell she was pleased, and it made him happy that he'd taken the time to stop and pick the flowers for her.

"Thank you, Jeb. I thought all the flowers had died out by now."

"Most of them have. . .but I spotted these on the way in and thought you'd like them, even if they only last a day or two."

Beth stood on tiptoe and pulled a vase down from a shelf. "I found this the other day. It was one of Aunt Gertrude's. We rarely used it, and I'd forgotten about it."

"It looks a little fancy for wildflowers," Jeb commented.

"It's just right," Beth insisted, handing it to Cassie to fill with water.

Lucas placed the bouquet in the vase and handed it to Beth. She brought it to the table and set it in the center. "They are even more beautiful in the vase. I'm glad I found it."

Jeb was thankful that his brother had put a woodstove in the small room in the barn where he'd been staying. Otherwise, he wasn't sure he could have stayed out at the ranch until the house was finished. The nights were getting really cold.

He added a few sticks of wood to the fire he'd started when he got back from Beth's and poured himself a cup of warmed-over coffee from what he'd made that morning. He grimaced. It sure didn't taste like Beth's.

It was getting to where he was dreading coming back to the ranch at night. Oh, he loved the place and was eager to get the house finished. . .but it was awful lonely here in his room in a corner of the barn, with the only sounds a snort from the horses or the wind blowing outside.

He pulled his lone chair close to the stove and drew out the letter he'd picked up at the post office earlier in the day.

Dear Jeb, Got your letter. Been thinking on things. I sure hate to lose a good man like you. I wanted to see if you'd be interested in becoming a foreman for me? Your niece and nephew would be welcome company for my children, and I'd furnish you with a house. Job is open now. Let me know what you decide. John Biglow.

Jeb had been thinking about settling down even before he'd received the news about Harland. . .and a foreman job would have been exactly what he wanted. Especially one working for John Biglow. He was a good man to work for.

But now. . .he laid the letter down and shook his head. He'd found the place he wanted to settle down in. . .the place he wanted to call home. It was right here on this ranch with Beth and the children.

Even if Beth refused his proposal when the house was finished, he didn't think he could leave. That would mean taking the children away, because he couldn't imagine life without them now, and that was something he didn't think he could do. Not to Beth, not to Cassie and Lucas, and not to himself. But could he really stay if she said no? Would the pain of seeing her and not having her in his and the children's lives be too hard to bear? Jeb sighed. He really didn't know.

Still, he needed to answer John's letter. Jeb quickly penned an answer telling him that he couldn't give him a firm answer until after Christmas and that if he needed to fill the post, to go ahead. . .that he would understand.

Then Jeb turned to the only One who knew what the future held. He bowed his head and prayed.

"Dear Lord, I don't know what Beth will say when I ask her to marry me again. . .only You do. You know that I love her and that I want us to make a home for Cassie and Lucas. I pray that she feels the same way and will agree to marry me. But it's all in Your hands, Lord. I pray Your will be done. In Jesus' name. Amen."

Beth dressed with care on Saturday night. Jeb was taking them to Emma's Café for dinner as had become a habit in the last month or so. . .in spite of Beth's insistence that it wasn't necessary.

But Jeb felt it was. He told her that taking her and Cassie and Lucas to dinner once a week didn't seem much in the way of repaying her for the wonderful meals she managed to make for him and his niece and nephew after working at the telephone office all day.

Tired as she might be some days, Beth wouldn't have had it any other way. She'd come to love making dinner for them. The children were always appreciative, but Jeb even more so. She'd become so used to him being there, she knew she would be terribly lonesome once he moved the children to the ranch.

She always enjoyed the night out at Emma's, though. It had become a treat she looked forward to each week, and the children loved it. Sometimes, Matt and Emma and Mandy joined them, and sometimes it was just the four of them; but it didn't matter; it was an enjoyable evening either way. She was looking forward to this evening.

When she opened the door to Jeb, she was doubly glad she'd bought a new dress. It was black wool with a lace-trimmed bodice and a matching cape.

And from the way Jeb looked at her, she knew she'd made a good choice.

His gaze captured hers, and her breath caught in her throat as he commented, "You look lovely tonight, Beth."

"Thank you. So do you." And he did look quite nice in the new brown three-piece suit he'd worn to church last Sunday.

Cassie and Lucas came into the room right then, and Beth's heart warmed as Jeb made sure to tell them both how nice they looked, too.

"It's cold out. Be sure to wear your warmest wraps," Jeb instructed.

They bundled up and hurried out to the wagon, where Jeb's horses were stamping and snorting. It was a short trip to the café, but Beth was thankful for the warmth inside as they entered the establishment.

Emma and Matt did join them tonight as business was a little slow.

"When it gets this cold, most people stay in. I'm thankful to have friends like you. . .or I'd have to shut down," Emma said, as they all took a seat around the table.

Beth chuckled. "You know that's not true. I've heard many a person say that they'd rather come here than dine at either the Roswell Hotel or the Pauly."

"Still, I'm glad you all braved the cold and came in tonight. I have chicken and dumplings and an Irish stew to choose from. Either one will warm you up for the ride home."

The chicken and dumplings won out, and soon their food was dished up and served by Hallie. After Matt said the blessing, the table was quiet for a few minutes except for the clink of eating utensils against the dishes.

"This is wonderful, Emma," Beth said. "I wonder why someone else's cooking always tastes better than your own?"

"It does, doesn't it?" Emma agreed.

Beth thoroughly enjoyed the company as well as the break from her own cooking.

"Miss Beth, did you tell Mrs. Johnson about the Christmas program?" Cassie asked.

"No, dear. I was just getting ready to. Have you heard about the Christmas program at school, Emma?"

Emma smiled and nodded in Cassie's direction as she answered Beth. "Yes, Liddy told me that Grace and Amy are very excited about it. And she said everyone is welcome to come. I'm looking forward to it."

"That's right. They mentioned it last night, but I forgot to ask you about it, Beth. I've never been to a Christmas program at school—or anywhere else for that matter," Jeb admitted. "They never did such programs when I was in school."

"They didn't?" Lucas asked, his eyes big and round as he gazed at his uncle.

Jeb shook his head. "No. They didn't."

Lucas grinned. "I've never been to one, either. This is my first year in school, you know."

"Yes, I know."

"You'll come, won't you, Uncle Jeb?"

"Of course I will. But what do they do at a Christmas program?"

Beth chuckled. "Well, I'm not sure. I've never been to one, either. But between Cassie and Lucas, I've found out that it's held at the school. They say there will be a big Christmas tree set up, and the children will decorate it with things they bring from home. Lucas and Cassie want to make a garland from popped corn. Family and friends are invited and asked to bring desserts. Someone. . .Minister Turley or the school principal will read about the birth of Jesus from the Bible. I think they will sing some Christmas carols they've learned at school, then I think everyone else will join in to sing some favorites. I'm not sure what all else. But they are very excited about it."

"You know, it's been a long time since I spent Christmas with family or even in a town. I'm kind of looking forward to it," Jeb said.

"So am I. It's all the children have been talking about."

Once they were finished eating, Emma told Cassie and Lucas that they could take Mandy upstairs to play. They didn't need to be asked twice. Matt lifted Mandy out of her high chair, and she led the children through the kitchen.

"She isn't a baby any longer, Emma."

"I know." Emma sighed deeply, then she looked into Matt's eyes and smiled.

He smiled back.

Emma continued, "Maybe one day. . .next summer, she'll have a baby brother or sister to play with."

"That would be nice," Beth commented before she fully realized what Emma had said. Then she jumped up from her chair. "Emma, are you expecting?"

Matt's grin, which was ear to ear, told Beth before Emma did.

"I am."

Jeb congratulated Matt, while Beth rounded the table to hug her friend. "I'm so happy for you! Oh my! Oh my! What wonderful news."

"We are very happy about it, of course. Matt and I would like a large family."

"Will you still be able to run the café?" Beth asked.

"We'll see. It's been so much a part of my life, I'm not sure I can give it up. But I may need to. Matt and our children come first now."

Beth only nodded. She was happy for Emma and Matt. Truly she was.

Jeb took Beth and the children home, smiling at their chatter. They were so looking forward to Christmas. Once back at Beth's, she made some hot chocolate to warm up the children before bedtime and Jeb for his ride home in the cold.

Lucas and Cassie's excitement was contagious, and pretty soon they were all talking about what decorations they could make.

"I can get some cranberries from Jaffa-Prager. . .we could string some of them along with the popcorn," Beth suggested.

"Oh, that would be pretty. And even if some of the other children think of the same thing, a lot of garland will make the tree look pretty."

"I can help," Jeb volunteered. When Lucas seemed a little doubtful, he continued, "I can thread a needle and sew some. When you are out on the range by yourself, there are some things you have to learn to do."

"Well, we're going to have a lot to string, so we'll be more than glad to accept your help, Jeb," Beth said. "And maybe you can teach Lucas how to thread a needle. There are a few things boys need to learn to do."

Jeb grinned at Lucas and gave him a playful tap him under the chin. "I'll be glad to teach him a thing or two."

"Will you teach me to hunt? I'd like to learn to do that!"

"Yes. One of these days, I'll do that—if you learn to thread that needle."

Lucas giggled. "All right. I'll learn."

Jeb waited until the children had been sent off to bed before asking the question uppermost on his mind after all the talk about Christmas. . .well, the *second* uppermost question on his mind. He didn't think Beth was ready for his proposal just yet.

She poured him a second cup of hot chocolate and sat down across from him. "Thank you for dinner tonight. It was very enjoyable."

"I enjoyed it. . .and you deserved it." Jeb took a sip of the aromatic liquid before continuing. "I need to ask you something, Beth."

"Oh?" Beth paused and took a sip from her own cup. "What is it?"

"I don't know what to get the children for Christmas."

"Oh. . .well, I'm not sure, either."

"Have they mentioned anything?"

Beth shook her head. "Not really. There are some dolls at Jaffa-Prager that Cassie showed to me when we were in there, and Lucas mentioned something about an air rifle and a cap gun. I don't know what that is, but it seems to be one of the newest things. And I'm not sure he's old enough for either."

"Hmm. I'll have to think about that. I'll ask Cal and Matt what they think, too. All this is new to me. . .thinking about presents and such for children."

Beth smiled at him. "I know. For me, too. You know, Cal and Liddy can probably give us some ideas. They're old hands at this by now."

"That's a great idea. And by the time Emma and Matt need to know, we will be, too," Jeb said.

It was only after he'd taken his leave and was on his way to the ranch that he realized he'd implied they'd be a complete family by then. He didn't know whether he should be relieved or disappointed that Beth said nothing about his comment. She'd just ducked her head and took a sip of her chocolate—but not before he noticed she'd blushed once again.

He felt like she truly cared about him. . .and maybe he should be more obvious in his courting. Trouble was, he was afraid she would reject him outright, and he didn't want to chance it. But it wasn't long until Christmas, and that's when he'd told her he'd be through with the house and would ask her, again, to marry him. If the weather held, the house would be ready. And Jeb sure hoped Beth hadn't forgotten her challenge. He certainly hadn't.

Chapter 9

During the next week, Jeb finally moved into a corner of the house. The fireplaces had been cleaned, and he had plenty of wood chopped and stacked outside the door. It might not be finished, but it was a whole lot warmer than the barn, and he could put in an hour or two working on the house of an evening. With Christmas fast approaching, he was working as hard as he could to get everything finished.

He was still waiting for the last few items he'd ordered to come in, but everything was falling together nicely. Mr. Cormack had convinced him to put up that new tarpaper until the shingles came in, which he'd ordered to match those already on the roof. That had bought him time to get the inside of the house finished. The new shingles had arrived, and he'd picked them up today. He planned to start putting them up in the next few days. The house didn't even look the same as it had when Beth and the children first saw it, and he couldn't wait for them to see it.

The staircase was sturdy and beautiful. The damaged floorboards, upstairs and down, had been replaced or repaired and cleaned. As Jeb ambled across them now, they gleamed in the light of his lantern. He'd found he did need help installing the pocket doors in both parlors, and Cal had helped him. The wraparound porch had been shored up and, of a morning, he loved having coffee out there. He enjoyed walking around and looking out onto the orchard and the place he thought would make a good garden area.

There was a new sink in the kitchen, and he'd built a cupboard around it. He'd ordered the range Beth had pointed out as well as that nice worktable she wanted. He might be presuming too much, but even if she refused his proposal, he'd bought what the kitchen needed.

He still had some trim work to put up, but the house was near enough finished now that he was going to ask Beth to bring the children out for a picnic next Saturday. He wasn't sure whose reaction he was most eager to see. . .Lucas's and Cassie's. . .or Beth's.

He hadn't had time to get over to Cal and Liddy's to ask about their suggestions on what Cassie and Lucas might like for Christmas, but he'd ask Beth if she'd talked to them. Their excitement about Christmas and moving to the ranch was growing each and every day, and Jeb's was growing right along with them.

On Tuesday, he'd stopped by the post office before going to Beth's and found an answer to the letter he'd sent John Biglow. It was short and to the point.

Jeb,

Job awaits you whenever you decide to take me up on the offer. The children can be schooled with mine, here on the ranch. Just let me know.

Sincerely,
John Biglow

Jeb knew what he wanted his answer to be. He wanted to be able to tell John that he was going to settle down right here on this ranch with a new wife. But that was in Beth and the Lord's hands. Whether he could stay if she turned him down. . .well, that remained to be seen.

Jeb had taken them to church the past Sunday, and he was still coming in for supper, but he wasn't staying as long after dinner as usual, saying he needed to get back and do some work on the house.

Beth was beginning to be envious of the time he spent on that house! Of course, she wasn't that eager for him to have it finished. It would mean the children would move, and she was dreading being alone. She wanted to see what he'd been doing and how it was coming along, but he'd said he didn't want Cassie and Lucas out there until it was safe to do so.

She was trying hard to keep her mind off of Jeb and whether or not he would ask her to marry him again. But it was hard to do when she was bombarded by questions at work. Not only was she still getting advice about her relationship with Jeb, now she was being asked about what she thought of the house.

She kept telling everyone she hadn't seen it, but that wasn't good enough.

"Have you seen the house yet, Beth?" Alma Burton inquired.

"No, ma'am, I haven't."

"Well, when are you going to? I hear your young man is doing a wonderful job on it."

"He's not my young man, Mrs. Alma."

"Well, he should be."

"My switchboard is lighting up, Mrs. Alma. I have to go now." Beth disconnected the older woman's pin and connected with the Harrisons'.

"Number, please?"

"No number," Nelda Harrison said. "I just wanted to tell you that Jim and I drove past the Winslow place today, and we think the work Harland's brother is doing is wonderful."

"I haven't seen it yet."

"No? Well, you need to go out and see what he's done," Nelda advised. "You won't recognize the place."

Beth couldn't help but be curious about it. Even Liddy was impressed with what she could see from the road. When Beth called to ask for suggestions for Cassie and Lucas for Christmas, she mentioned it.

"Jeb is working really hard, Beth. It doesn't even look like the same place."

"I'm getting more and more curious, Liddy. Everyone is telling me that same thing. But. . .I guess I'll have to wait until Jeb is ready for us to see it."

"You could come to my place and pass by," Liddy suggested.

Beth giggled. "Now that's an idea. If he doesn't decide to ask us out soon, I may just take your suggestion."

It was getting a bit frustrating as more and more people asked what she thought about the house. She just couldn't tell them. She didn't know. Jeb hadn't offered to take them out, and she didn't feel quite right about just showing up with the children.

She was feeling a little testy when he came for supper that night. How could she tell him she wanted to see the house without reminding him of his proposal and the challenge she'd given him? Much as she wanted him to remember, she didn't want to be the one to bring it up, and she was beginning to think he'd forgotten all about it.

But she could be truthful. "The switchboard was lit up all day with people telling me how good the house is looking."

"Is it nearly finished, Uncle Jeb?" Cassie asked.

"Won't be long now." Jeb took a sip of coffee, and his gaze met Beth's over the rim of the cup. "I should have it finished right before Christmas."

"When are we going to get to see it?" Lucas asked.

"Well, I was thinking maybe you could come out and have a picnic on Saturday, if Beth doesn't mind bringing the food. The kitchen still isn't completely finished."

"Can we go, Miss Beth?" Cassie asked.

"Please!" Lucas added.

Well, finally. "Of course we can. I'll be glad to make a picnic lunch." At least when the next person asked her about the house, she'd be able to tell them she and the children would be seeing it on the weekend.

"I hope to be finishing the roof. Are you sure you don't mind bringing Cassie and Lucas out? I can come in and get you all."

"I know the way. We'll be fine. We'll be there around noon, if that's all right?"

"That sounds fine. I'm eager to see what you all think of it. And there are a few things I'd like to get your advice on."

All of the built-up irritation Beth had felt all day melted in a puddle at her feet. He wanted her advice about the house. Maybe that meant he was planning on asking her to marry him again. And maybe not. She couldn't let herself think about what it might mean. Beth jumped up to clear the table. She had to steer her thoughts into another direction. "I'm looking forward to seeing it."

"I'm glad I've had good weather," Jeb said. "Christmas will be here before we know it."

"It sure will be. And it will be time to decorate that tree at school. How about we string some popcorn and cranberries?"

"Sounds good to me." Jeb chuckled. "How about you, Lucas? You ready to learn how to thread a needle?"

Cassie ran to get Beth's sewing basket while Jeb and Lucas popped the corn. Then Beth brought out the cranberries she'd found at Jaffa-Prager, and they began making garland.

It took only a moment to teach Lucas what to do, and for the next few hours, they took turns stringing and eating the popped corn. By the time the popcorn was gone, they found that the cranberry garland was longer by at least half, but they had two beautiful contributions to the decorating of the school tree.

"Next time, I'll have to pop more," Beth commented as she began to clean up. "I think it's time for bed, children. You have school tomorrow."

Jeb got to his feet. "Guess I'd better get back to the ranch."

Cassie and Lucas gave him a hug, and Beth walked him to the door.

"Did you ever get a chance to talk to Liddy about Christmas?" Jeb whispered.

Beth nodded and pulled a piece of paper from her pocket. "I telephoned her. These are some things she suggested."

"Thank you. I haven't had a chance to get by their place. I guess I ought to see about getting one of those telephones installed. Can I get one out there?"

Beth nodded. "Yes, you're close to town, and there are lines out that way now. Cal and Liddy live farther out than you, and they have one. Would you like me to place your order tomorrow?"

"Would you, please? I've never had a use for one, but I suppose it would be good to have, once I move Cassie and Lucas out there."

"Well, naturally, I'm a big believer in having a telephone. Liddy and I can keep in touch much easier, instead of waiting to see each other on a Sunday or running into each other when she comes into town. Plus, if one of the children gets sick and you need a doctor to come out, it will make it easier and faster to get hold of him."

"I hadn't thought of all those things. Please, do put my order in tomorrow."

"I will."

Jeb stood looking at her for a moment. "You know. . .Christmas is almost here. The house is going to be finished soon."

Beth held her breath.

He reached out and touched a wayward curl of hair on her forehead. "You haven't forgotten your challenge to me, have you?"

She could only shake her head.

"Well, then. . .it appears you have some thinking to do. Because I haven't forgotten, either."

With that, he turned and ambled out the door, leaving Beth with her hand on her chest and a smile on her face.

Jeb came into town to have supper with them the next few nights, but he didn't mention anything else about the challenge or his proposal, and Beth was skittish as a newborn foal.

It appeared he really was going to stay in one spot, despite what Harland had said about him. He was a wonderful Christian man who loved Cassie and Lucas with all his heart. Beth knew he would raise them the way Harland would want them raised. And they loved him. . .as did she.

She could no longer deny that she'd fallen deeply, completely in love with the man. Deep down she felt he cared for her, too, and what she wanted most for Christmas was for him to ask her to marry him again. She knew what her answer would be.

By the time Saturday rolled around, Cassie and Lucas could barely contain their excitement about seeing the house. Beth kept them busy doing chores while she fried chicken and made the lunch they'd be taking out with them.

She'd made arrangements to rent a surrey from the livery, and it was delivered a little early, but Lucas thought that meant they should go ahead and go out to the ranch. Everything was ready, and Beth supposed Jeb wouldn't mind if they showed up a little earlier than planned. The children helped her load the picnic baskets, and they were on their way.

It was a beautiful, sunny day that had warmed up nicely. Still, it was cool enough for jackets. She was glad they'd be taking their picnic inside, but if the children were out moving around and playing, they'd be fine.

While Cassie and Lucas chattered to each other, Beth's thoughts were on Jeb and how wrong she'd been about him in the beginning. Maybe he had always moved from one ranch to another, and maybe he liked seeing other parts of the country, but what no one had taken into consideration was just how seriously Jeb took his responsibility or how much family meant to him, especially if they were now dependent on him.

"Oh, look how pretty it is," Cassie breathed as they rounded the bend in the road and the house came into view.

Beth reined in the horse so that they could get a good look. It truly didn't look like the same place. What had been a rundown and uncared-for house was now looking like a real home. And there, on top of the roof, with his back to the road, was Jeb, hammering the new shingles in place.

As Beth drove into the yard, Lucas yelled, "Uncle Jeb!"

Jeb turned and waved. "You're early."

"I'm sorry," Beth apologized. "The children couldn't wait any longer."

Jeb smiled. "No. It's all right. But I'd like to finish up this section. You can put the basket on the table in the kitchen. But wait for me to show you the upstairs, all right?"

"We'll wait," Beth agreed. He'd worked hard, and she could understand why he wanted to be with them when they saw the changes to the inside of the house for the first time. She and the children unloaded the baskets and took them inside.

Beth tried not to look too closely at anything as she headed for the kitchen. She couldn't help but notice that the stove had been removed, but there were new cupboards and a new sink. The trim work had been done, and with some curtains at the window and a nice worktable in the center, it would be a wonderful place to prepare meals. Beth slid the baskets onto the old table that Jeb had brought in from somewhere, and she hurried the children back outside, so as not to notice too many other changes until Jeb could point them out.

Lucas ran out into the yard and craned his neck to see his uncle. "Can I come up there and help, Uncle Jeb?" Lucas asked.

"I don't think that's a good idea, Lucas. It's pretty steep up here. But guess what's in the barn?"

"What?"

"Four new kittens. A tabby showed up a few nights ago and made herself right at home out there. This morning, I heard a tiny mewing sound and found she'd had babies during the night."

"Let's go, Cassie," Lucas shouted, taking off in a run.

"Don't pick them up. . .just look at them. I don't think the mama would take kindly to you holding her babies just yet."

"We'll only look, Uncle Jeb," Cassie promised, hurrying to catch up with her brother.

Jeb smiled down at Beth. "I only have a few more shingles that I brought up earlier. I'll be down soon. Don't you want to go see the kittens?"

I'd rather watch you. "No, I'm fine here on the porch. The house looks beautiful from the road, Jeb. Everyone is right. . .you've done a wonderful job on the house."

"Thank you. I hope you like the inside as well." He picked up a shingle. "I'll be down soon."

Beth watched as he knelt back down on the roof and began to hammer again. Her heart filled to overflowing with the love she felt. Not only had he developed a loving relationship with his niece and nephew, making time to see them nearly every day, he'd also put in long hours taking care of the ranch and making the house more than just livable again.

It was only a few minutes before Jeb came down from the roof, and Beth called the children from the barn.

"Let me show you the rest of the house before we eat," Jeb suggested. He led them up the porch steps and around to the back of the house.

"Oh, Jeb, this is nice. And the view of the orchards and the pasture is beautiful."

"It is pretty, isn't it?" He pointed to the side yard close to the kitchen. "I think that might make a good place for a kitchen garden. What do you think? Would you like that?"

Beth only nodded, not sure what to say. She'd always wanted a garden similar to Liddy's. . .one big enough to feed a family. Still, there was something about the way he'd looked at her that had her heart pumping in her chest, and she could feel the flush on her face as she let herself daydream about the future.

She suddenly realized she was alone on the porch, and, flustered, she hurried into the kitchen where Jeb and the children were already washing up with the water Jeb was pumping into the sink. "The stove didn't work, so I've ordered a new one. . .but I added a few cupboards and cleaned out the root cellar."

"It's going to be a wonderful kitchen, Jeb," Beth said. She could just picture it all finished. "You did a really wonderful job on the cupboards, too."

"Thanks. There is still a lot to do, but once the roof is finished, it will be almost livable."

"It looks pretty livable already," Beth commented. "It just needs some furnishings."

Jeb nodded. "I have some of those ordered."

He pointed out the new plate rails he'd put up as they went through the dining room. The front parlor was much the same, but the broken windows had been replaced. As they started up the stairs, Beth couldn't help but notice how beautiful they were, as well as sturdy.

Cassie and Lucas ran on ahead of them, finding the rooms Jeb had pointed out to them from the house plans.

"This is mine!" Cassie exclaimed. "It looks out onto the orchard. Oh, Uncle Jeb, I love it!"

"And here is mine." Lucas ran into the opposite room and over to the window. "I wonder if I can see the animals in the barn from here."

Jeb sauntered up behind him and placed his hands on the young boy's shoulders. "Probably not unless they come out of it."

"I like it, Uncle Jeb!" Lucas pointed outside. "And look, I can see a couple of horses in the corral."

"I thought you might like this view."

"When are we going to move out here?"

Beth felt a twinge in her chest. What if Jeb didn't ask her to marry him? It was going to be so lonesome. Yet, he'd told her he hadn't forgotten. Surely. . .

"Sometime around Christmas if all goes well and the weather cooperates," Jeb answered. "I've been praying it does."

"I will, too," Lucas said.

"May we see your room, Uncle Jeb?" Cassie asked.

Jeb's gaze met Beth's for a moment. "Of course."

This room was much larger than the others. . .with two windows. One looked toward town and the other had a view of the orchard.

"Oh, this is nice," Beth couldn't help commenting.

"Well, up here is where I need some advice—and in the dining room and parlor, too. At the mercantile, they told me wallpaper would make it look really nice, but I don't know a thing about wall coverings—what to choose or anything. I was wondering if you could help me pick out some."

Beth glanced around the room and nodded. "Oh, that would be a nice touch. I'd be glad to help."

"Oh, I like wallpaper. It's so pretty," Cassie said. "Miss Emma has some in her apartment above the café."

Jeb grinned. "I feel better already, knowing that decorating stuff is left in someone else's hands."

Lucas was getting restless. "Can we eat now? I'm hungry. And may we go see the kittens again after lunch?"

"We'll see," Jeb answered. "First things first. Let's go eat that nice picnic Beth made us."

The indoor picnic was a huge success. Jeb stirred to life the coals in the dining room fireplace and added a log. Beth laid the quilt she'd brought on the floor, and the children helped lay out the food and eating utensils.

"This room is so pretty, Jeb. With a nice table and sideboard, it will be a wonderful place to have meals in. I really like the plate rail, too." She could see the table set for company and almost hear the conversation. There was something about this room she just loved.

His gaze swept the room and he nodded. "It is nice. I think the Nordstroms had great plans for this house."

"And you've carried a lot of them out, I'm sure. It's gone from near ruin to a showplace in just a few months."

"Thank you," Jeb replied, finishing the large piece of pie Beth had cut for him. "I thought I'd follow you and the children back to town and we could go to Emma's tonight, but if it's all right with you, I'd like to get a few more shingles on this afternoon before we go in. Maybe, while the children are inspecting those kittens again and exploring the barn, you could go through the house and think about what kind of wallpaper might look good?"

"I'll be glad to do that. I'll clean up a bit; then I'll look around the house again and think about what you might like."

Jeb shrugged. "Anything you pick out will be fine with me."

He and the children went outside, and Beth began to clean up the picnic. After she'd packed everything to take back into town, she went back upstairs and surveyed the rooms. Cassie would probably like a wall covering with pink or lilac flowers in it, as those were her favorite colors. Beth wasn't sure about Lucas. Maybe a stripe of some kind would work. His favorite color was blue.

The small room would make a nice sewing room. . .or nursery. Beth shook off that thought for the moment, backing out into the hall and hurrying into the larger room. Although Jeb had hinted that he was going to ask her to marry him again, he hadn't brought it up since, and she needn't be thinking about nurseries until he did.

She walked over to the window of his room and looked out on the apple orchard. It was a wonderful room, sunny and bright. It would be hers, too, when and *if*—Jeb ever got around to proposing again. Was he ever going to? She just didn't know.

Beth shook her head and sighed as she headed back downstairs. Maybe the decisions on that room should wait until. . .well, they should just wait for now.

Beth decided to straighten and clean a bit until it was time to go back to town. There were little things she knew that Jeb might not think to get to right away. She swept the new floors, wiped down the windowsills, and cleaned the windows, polishing them until they shone. She dusted the fireplace mantels and was just finishing the last one when a folded piece of paper drifted to the floor. Beth picked it up, wondering if it had been here for long.

It hadn't. It was a short note. . .from Jeb's boss. . .telling him his job was open and the children were welcome. Beth's heart twisted in her chest. Was Harland right? Was Jeb fixing up the house only to sell out and go back North?

Well, there was only one way to find out. Beth ran though the house, down the porch steps, and around to the ladder leading to the roof. She clambered up it as fast as she could in her long skirts and holding the offending letter in her hand.

Jeb's back was to her when her head cleared the roof line. "Can you tell me the meaning of this, Jeb Winslow?"

"Beth?" Jeb whirled around. "The meaning of what? What's wrong?"

She waved the paper in her hand. "This is wrong! Have you been planning on taking this man up on his offer? Are you leaving here? Fixing up the house just to sell out? Are you taking the children with you?"

Jeb got to his feet and stared down at her. . .his mouth opening and shutting at first. Then he found his voice. "How could you think that? I just asked you to help me decorate this house! Why would I be working this hard. . .trying to get this roof finished before the first snow. . .the house ready before Christmas. . .if I didn't plan on making a home here?"

"You said that Mr. Snow thought it would add more value to the property!"

Jeb shut his eyes and shook his head before meeting her gaze again. "Beth Morgan—can't you see. . .I'm trying my best to get this house finished by Christmas to answer your challenge. And *why* would I be doing that?"

"I don't know. Why?"

"Because I—" Just as the words were out of his mouth, Jeb slipped and started sliding down the roof.

"Jeb!" Beth yelled, but there was nothing she could do except watch him fall. She didn't know if she heard or felt the thud as he hit the ground, but her heart seemed to stop beating as she saw him lying on the ground. Jeb didn't move. *No!* Tears streamed down her face. It was all her fault. Had she killed the only man she'd ever loved?

Chapter 10

Beth backed down the ladder as fast as she could, totally missing the last rung and jumping to the ground. She hurried to his side and knelt down, feeling for a pulse. "Jeb! Jeb!

"Oh, please, dear Lord—let him be all right. Please. Please. He's such a good man, and the children need him. I need him. Dear Lord, please let him come to."

She felt a faint pulse just as Jeb moaned, and Beth expelled the breath she didn't know she'd been holding. "Thank You, dear Lord. Thank You!"

Another moan assured her Jeb was alive but hurting. "Cassie! Lucas! Bring the wagon over here. Come quickly!"

The children came running. "Uncle Jeb! Is he going to be all right, Miss Beth?"

"I hope so, Cassie. We need to get him into town to the doctor."

Jeb opened his eyes and grimaced. "I'll be fine. Had the air knocked out of me. Just help me up from here."

"Lie still," Beth instructed as she noticed one arm seemed to twist at an odd angle. She gently touched it. He winced and groaned again. "Jeb, you're hurt. We need to get you to Doc's."

"Let me just. . ." Jeb put his other hand on the ground and tried to lift himself up, trying to get to his knees. "Arrgh!" Sweat broke out on his brow, but he managed a smile for Lucas, who was openly crying.

"I'm going to be fine, Lucas. Guess I should have had one of those telephones put in earlier."

"We'll get you some help," Beth promised. "Cassie, come get your arm up under your uncle Jeb's other arm. I'll try not to hurt this one any more than is necessary, Jeb."

He nodded, and Beth could tell he was gritting his teeth as they got him to his feet. Beth knew afterward that it was only with the Lord's help that they were able to get him into the wagon at all. He weighed more than she and Cassie together.

She lost no time getting him back to town. Thankfully, Doc Bradshaw's office was attached to his home, and before Beth got the wagon to a full stop, Lucas was up the walk and pounding on the door.

"What is it? What is it?" Doc asked, opening the door.

"Uncle Jeb fell off the roof of the house, and he's hurt real bad."

"Myrtle, call the sheriff's office and get someone over here to help me get Jeb in the office," Doc yelled back into the house. He hurried to the wagon to find Jeb had passed out.

"Is he all right?" Beth asked, wiping her eyes yet again.

"He's alive," Doc said. "All the jostling around most likely was just too much for him and he passed out. Tell me what happened."

"Well, we were. . ." How could she tell Doc that they were yelling at each other?

"Uncle Jeb was working on the roof of the house and he slipped off of it," Cassie informed Doc.

Beth sent up a silent prayer of thanksgiving that the children had been in the barn and hadn't heard her tirade. "I think his arm is hurt bad. . .and I'm not sure what else. I just know he's in a lot of pain."

Matt came running up just then. "What do you need, Doc?"

"Help me get Jeb into the office so I can examine him."

Matt took a look at Jeb, then back at Beth and the children. "Why don't you go over to the café and wait with Emma? I'll come get you soon as Doc has Jeb settled."

"But I—"

"It might be better for the children, Beth," Matt suggested, inclining his head in their direction.

Beth turned to Cassie and Lucas. The fear on their faces was obvious for anyone to see. Beth nodded. "Cassie, Lucas, let's go to see Emma. Your uncle is going to be fine. Doc will see to it."

Doc nodded. "I'll get word to you, soon as I examine him and get him comfortable."

When Lucas hung back, Doc bent down and looked him in the eye. "Lucas, I promise your uncle is going to be all right."

Only then did the young boy slip his hand into Beth's and let her lead him across the street to Emma's Café.

Emma met them at the door, Mandy in her arms. "Myrtle telephoned me and told me you were on your way here."

"Uncle Jeb is hurt real bad," Lucas told Emma. Cassie was unnaturally quiet.

Emma nodded. "But, you know, Doc is real good about helping people, and we're going to pray that your uncle Jeb gets well real soon."

"Can we pray now?" Cassie asked.

"Yes, we can," Beth answered.

And there, in the doorway of Emma's Café, huddled in a tight circle, they did just that.

Emma suggested they all go up to her apartment so that Mandy could help occupy the children's minds and she and Beth could talk. She brewed a pot of tea for her, and Beth then settled the children at the table with some molasses cookies and milk.

Mandy had Cassie and Lucas laughing in spite of their worry over their uncle, and Beth was glad Matt had suggested that she bring them here.

She and Emma took their tea to a small table in the parlor. Beth took a sip from her cup and let out a deep breath.

"He'll be all right, Beth," Emma tried to assure her.

"I pray so." Tears sprung to her eyes again. "It was all my fault, Em."

"What was?"

"Jeb's fall. We were yelling at each other—"

"Yelling? You and Jeb?"

Beth nodded and sniffed. "I found a letter, and I thought it meant he was going to leave. . .and I climbed the ladder and confronted him about it."

"What did he say?"

"Before he fell off the roof?"

Emma nodded.

Beth sniffed and tears began to fall again. "He. . .got angry and was trying to tell me I was wrong when he. . .when he slipped and fell off the roof!" With that, she began to sob.

Emma jumped up and came around to hug her. "Oh, Beth. It's going to be all right. Did you hear what you just said? Jeb was telling you that you were wrong. Probably was going to say he's staying. It's all going to work out for you, you'll see."

"Oh, Em. How can it? Because of me, he's hurt really bad. . .and could have died! How will he ever forgive me for that?"

"I'm sure he already has. Beth, he slipped. You didn't push him. He knows that."

Beth rocked herself back and forth. "It doesn't matter now. I just want him to be all right."

"He will be," Emma tried to reassure her.

Beth could only pray she was right as she watched the clock. The afternoon seemed much longer than the hour or so later when Matt finally telephoned Emma to let them know they could see Jeb. Beth and the children threw on their jackets and hurried back over to Doc Bradshaw's office as fast as they could.

"He's going to be fine, dear," Myrtle said as soon as she let them in. She led them to a room just down from Doc's examination room.

Doc came out of the room just then and smiled at Cassie and Lucas. "Your uncle is going to be just fine. He's awfully bruised and battered—may have a cracked rib, and he has a broken arm. He must have landed on it, and it's broke in several places. It will take awhile for it to heal." Doc patted Lucas on the head. "It *will* heal, but he isn't going to be able to climb up any ladders or pound any nails for a while to come. I'm going to keep him here for a few days to make sure that no infection develops, but you can come see him anytime."

"Can we see him now?" Lucas asked.

"Yes, you can. He's been asking to see you. But he'll be getting groggy from the medicine I gave him soon, so if he drifts off on you, don't worry."

"I won't," Lucas promised. He slipped his hand into Cassie's, and they waited for Beth.

"Thank you, Doc." Beth took Lucas's other hand and led the children in to see their uncle.

Although his broken arm was in a sling, Beth was tremendously relieved to see that he appeared decidedly better than the last time they'd seen him. There was a little color to his face, and he smiled and motioned the children closer with his good arm. "Come here and see that I'm alive and well."

He managed to hug each one as Beth watched from the doorway. She didn't know what any of them would have done if he. . .if he. . .

"Beth?" Jeb was looking closely at her. "Are you all right? You look a little pale."

"I'm not the one who just fell off a roof. I'm glad you're going to be all right, Jeb. I'm sorry—"

"It was my fault," Jeb insisted, as if trying to reassure her. "I knew better than to stand up."

Beth shook her head. "No, it was my—"

"Beth. It was an accident."

"A bad one, too," Lucas responded with a wobbly voice. "I—I thought you were dead at first."

"So did I," Cassie said with a sniff.

Beth's gaze met Jeb's. In silent agreement, Jeb changed the subject.

"Well, as you can see. . .I'm alive and almost well." Jeb reached out with his good hand and tickled Lucas.

The child's laughter was the best sound Beth had heard since Jeb fell off the roof.

Beth was exhausted by the time she got the children settled down for the night, but she was still too upset to sleep.

Jeb had drifted off just as Doc had told them he would, and Beth and the children had tiptoed out of the room. Matt was waiting for them to take them back to the café. Emma had insisted that they come back over to her place for supper before going home, and Beth had to admit she was glad for the company. She didn't want to be alone with her thoughts.

But now in the quiet of the night, she could no longer avoid them. *Dear Father, please forgive me for losing my temper today, for causing Jeb to fall. For accusing him wrongly. Thank You for letting him be all right. Please help him to heal completely. And please help him to forgive me, too. In Jesus' name, amen.*

Beth didn't know how he could. Not only had she caused him to fall off the roof, she'd judged him on the basis of a piece of paper. She wouldn't blame him if he never wanted to talk to her again after he moved the children back to the ranch, even though it would break her heart if that was the case.

He was probably only being nice to at her Doc's because he didn't want to upset Cassie and Lucas. He was such a wonderful person. He'd been more concerned about his niece and nephew's fears than his own pain, assuring Cassie and Lucas that he would recover before he'd drifted off to sleep.

Oh, how she loved that man! Not that it would do her any good now. How could he possibly want to marry a woman whose awful tirade had caused him all the pain he was now enduring?

After a restless night, Beth got ready for church, resolved to do what she could to help Jeb get the house finished so he could move the children out to the ranch by Christmas. She telephoned Doc Bradshaw's to get a report on Jeb for the children. Myrtle told her he'd slept all night and that she was making a breakfast for him now.

Beth was relieved that he'd been able to sleep, and she asked Myrtle to tell Jeb she would bring Cassie and Lucas to see him after church.

Myrtle promised to do just that, telling Beth that she was sure that would make Jeb feel much better.

Word had certainly gotten around about Jeb, which came as no surprise to Beth. Everyone she ran into asked her about him, and Minister Turley asked for prayers for his quick recovery. Cal and Liddy hurried up to her right after church, as did Emma and Matt, and Darcie and her mother.

"Emma called me last night and told me about Jeb, Beth," Liddy said. "Is there anything we can do?"

"Well, actually, I'm trying to figure out a way to get the roof finished for Jeb. He wanted to have it done by Christmas, but I don't see how he can do that now. Not with a broken arm and possible broken rib and being so bruised up. I was wondering—"

"Just leave it to Matt and me," Cal said. "We'll get a crew together and finish that roof in a day or two."

"I'll run over to the telephone office and have Jimmy Newland get the word out that you could use some help," Darcie suggested.

"That's a wonderful idea, Darcie," Matt commented. "How about asking any who are willing to meet us out at the Winslow place tomorrow morning?" He looked at Cal. "Will that work for you?"

Cal grinned and nodded. "I'll start asking around."

"Are we going to let Jeb in on this, or did you just want to surprise him?" Cal asked Beth.

"Well, I'm afraid that if he knows, he'll think he has to be out there, too."

"You're right, he would. Let's just keep it quiet for now, then."

"Thank you all—I don't know what to say."

"No need to say anything. Jeb would do the same for us."

The next day, Beth kept busy at work and hurried home to take Cassie and Lucas to see Jeb when they got out of school. Thinking that she was probably the last person Jeb wanted to see, she tried to stay in the background. . .talking to Myrtle while the children visited with their uncle. Although he was not happy about being laid up, he was always glad to see his niece and nephew.

Beth longed to tell him about all the men who'd shown up to finish putting the shingles on the roof, but Doc advised her not to when she asked him about it.

"I'm having enough trouble keeping him here as it is, Beth. If he found out there were people working out at his place, he'd be impossible to keep down."

"That's what I thought, too, but—"

"Don't worry. If he wants to know why you didn't tell him, I'll let him know I said not to."

"Thank you, Doc."

"You're welcome. Just be warned. . .he's a bit grouchy today."

Beth grinned and nodded. If he was grouchy to her. . .it was only what she deserved. She'd accept it. "I brought him some chicken and dumplings. Maybe that will perk him up."

"We can hope," Doc commented, heading back to his office.

"Where have you been?" Jeb asked as soon as she entered the room.

"I was talking to Doc. He says you are a bit. . .restless?"

Jeb shook his head. "I didn't mean just now. . .you haven't been—he said restless?"

Beth's heartbeat picked up in tempo. Had he missed her? "Well, his exact word might have been grouchy. . .but maybe it should have been both?"

"Well, how else would I be? I want to get that roof finished, and I'm not doing it in this bed."

"Jeb, I'm sorry—"

"Beth, we've been over that. I just want to get out of here and get back to the ranch."

"It won't be much longer."

"I keep thinking if I get ornery enough, Doc will kick me out of here," Jeb admitted.

"Uncle Jeb, you need to get well," Cassie responded.

Jeb sighed. "You're right, Cassie, love. I'm sorry. I'm not a very good patient, I'm afraid."

"Here." Beth handed him the bowl of dumplings and a spoon. "Emma sent you these. Maybe they'll make you feel better."

"They won't hurt none, that's for sure." Jeb grinned and dipped the spoon into the bowl. "Tell Emma thank you."

"I'll do that."

Chapter 11

By Tuesday, Jeb had been in bed just about as long as he could stand it. He'd had visitors and that helped. Matt and Emma had stopped by, and Cal had come by to tell him not to worry about his herd, he'd be watching out for it. But Beth seemed to be avoiding him, and it was time to get to the ranch. He wanted to get the house finished. . .if it was at all possible, by Christmas. Then she was going to have to face him.

Doc wasn't very happy about releasing him, but Jeb insisted. He was on his feet, his limp a little more prominent and his arm in a sling, but he was determined to go home—if he could find someone to take him.

"You are one stubborn man, Winslow." Doc Bradshaw shook his head. "You aren't going to be able to do much work out there. But there's no sign of infection in your arm, and it doesn't appear you broke any ribs. Your bruises seem to be healing well, so I guess I can't rightly keep you here forever."

"Doc, you can take me out, can't you? Or telephone Cal McAllister? I'm sure he'd come in and pick me up."

"I guess I'd be chomping at the bit to get back to my place, too, if I were you. I'll take you out there. You go on into the kitchen and have breakfast with Myrtle so she don't have to bring it to you, and I'll go get my surrey."

"Thanks, Doc. . .for patching me up and for puttin' up with my bad manners. I appreciate all you've done for me."

"Myrtle said you've been real nice to her. She thinks you are an exemplary patient." Doc rocked back on his heel as he motioned Jeb out of his room. "I guess you weren't too bad. Let's get you fed."

Doc followed him down the hall to the kitchen. "Look who's out of bed, Myrtle."

His wife turned from the stove where she was flipping pancakes. "Why, Jeb! Are you sure you feel well enough to be up and around?"

"He wouldn't tell you if he didn't, Myrtle. He's just determined to get back to the ranch. I'm going to get the surrey so's I can take him out there." He kissed his wife on the cheek before heading out the door. "Make sure he eats a good breakfast before I come back."

Myrtle did just that, piling Jeb's plate high with bacon, eggs, and the lightest pancakes he'd ever tasted. She poured his coffee and fussed over him until Doc came back. Jeb was going to miss all of her attention.

He kissed her on the cheek before he started toward the door. "Thank you for all the care you gave me, Mrs. Doc."

"You're welcome, Jeb. I wish all of Doc's patients were as good as you've been. You just try not to do too much, you hear?"

"Yes, ma'am, I do."

He limped out to the surrey, his body protesting with each step. It seemed to take forever, but he managed to get himself up onto the seat without bumping his bad arm. It appeared his battered body was going to hurt no matter what he did or didn't do.

"You sure about this?" Doc asked. "You ain't going to be able to do any work out there, you know."

"I've got a ranch to tend to, Doc. I can't just let it go."

Doc didn't say another word. He just shook his head, flicked the reins to his horse, and headed out of town.

Jeb was surprised at how badly he wanted to be home and even more surprised that he'd found a place he wanted to call home. But he had. He'd come to love the ranch. . .the house as he worked on it, the land, and the animals. He wanted to make it something Harland would have been proud of. And deep down, Jeb knew that his brother would be overjoyed that he wanted to settle here.

The day was beautiful, but Jeb was painfully aware that he wasn't in any shape to climb up on the roof to finish those shingles. And he realized that if he was honest with himself, he probably wasn't going to meet the deadline that Beth had given him, either. Still, there were things inside the house that needed his attention, and he'd get done what he could.

When they came to the bend in the road, Jeb felt as if he'd been away much longer than a few days. He waited in anticipation for his first glimpse of the house when they rounded the curve.

"What in the world—" There on the roof of his house were Matt and several other men. . .and it was almost completely shingled. Cal and some others were coming and going from inside the house, too. Most of them he recognized from church. . .some he'd met and some he hadn't. He shook his head and turned to the doctor for an answer, "Doc, what's going on here?"

"Appears to me that your roof is getting shingled." Doc chuckled. "We've had a hard time keeping quiet about this."

"But how. . .why—"

"One thing led to another. Beth knew you wanted the roof shingled before bad weather came and that you wouldn't be able to do it yourself. She voiced her concern, and Cal and Matt decided to get a group together. From what I heard, word spread pretty quickly from the telephone office, and it took off from there."

Doc pulled up into the yard.

"Jeb! Welcome home!" Matt yelled from the roof. He made his way down the ladder and started toward Jeb.

"Yeah, welcome home!" Cal added, crossing the yard toward them. "Doc, you let him go already?"

"I didn't have much choice. I think he would have walked, if he'd had to."

Jeb grinned and gingerly got out of the buggy. He turned to the men who'd come over to see how he was doing. "I don't know what to say 'cept thank you."

"Nothin' more needed," Cal said. "You'd do the same for us. We're 'bout through with the roof. But we've been busy inside, too. Mr. Cormack over at Jaffa-Prager heard you were down and that we were trying to help out. When your order came in, he telephoned me, and we told him to haul your stuff out here. We just got through setting your new range up. Come on and see if we did it right."

Jeb couldn't say anything. He was too busy swallowing around the lump in his throat. He'd never had people do anything like this for him. He'd be forever grateful to Matt and Cal. . .and all of these men who'd become his friends and accepted him as one of their own. He limped up the porch steps and went inside.

"That sure is some range you ordered." Cal cocked an eyebrow. "I didn't know you liked cooking that well."

Jeb laughed. "I was told it was a really great stove."

"Uh-huh. I wonder who might have mentioned it?"

"It's supposed to be new and improved." Jeb grinned and shrugged. "How does it look in the kitchen?"

"See for yourself. You barely had room on that wall for it. But we managed to get it in."

"Whoa," Jeb said when he saw it. "It is bigger than I realized." The Sterling Sunshine steel plate range was one of the largest he'd ever seen, with six holes and the water reservoir. But it sure did look pretty in the kitchen, and he couldn't wait for Beth to see it.

"Mr. Cormack says they come in different sizes, and this is about as big as it gets," Cal informed him.

"All I know is, Em is going to be jealous when she sees it." Matt leaned against the door facing. "I'll probably have to order her one."

"Yep. Same here," Cal agreed. "Probably ought to go ahead and do it."

Jeb just shrugged and laughed. Then he noticed the telephone. It was on the wall between the kitchen and the dining room. "When was this put up?"

"Yesterday afternoon. They said Beth told them someone would be here. We figured this would be the best place for it."

Jeb nodded. "Good. I guess I ought to let Beth know I'm back out here."

"Probably would be a good idea," Cal agreed.

"I don't know how to use it," Jeb admitted to his friends.

"It's easy," Matt assured him, walking over to the telephone. "Just pick up this black thing there on the hook and put it up to your ear. When someone from the telephone office says, 'Number, please,' you talk into this mouthpiece and tell them who you want to talk to."

"That's all there is to it?"

"That's it."

"I ought to be able to do that." Jeb wanted to telephone Beth, but he wasn't going to do it with all these men standing around. He would wait until they left the kitchen, then he'd try it. Maybe.

Matt and Cal exchanged a look and a grin. Matt nodded. "You'll figure it out."

"We're going to finish up those shingles while we have daylight."

"I really don't know how to thank you. . .all of you. If there is anything I can do—"

Cal laughed. "If you can figure out that fancy range, you could make us some coffee." He motioned to some crates on the worktable in the center of the kitchen. "There's some dishes and cooking things you ordered in those crates. We didn't know where to put them."

Jeb grinned. "Well, finally. . .something I should be able to handle. I'll call you when the coffee is made."

Beth heard about Jeb almost before he and Doc were out of town. Myrtle telephoned her to let her know that nothing would do for Jeb but to get back to the ranch.

"Doc took him out first thing this morning."

"How was he?" Beth chewed her bottom lip waiting for Myrtle to answer. He shouldn't be out there by himself. Surely he wouldn't try to—

"Well, not near as good as he'd like to be. But he'll be all right, dear. He's a sensible young man, and he's hurting more than he wants to admit. His body isn't going to let him do much. Besides, with all the men helping out there, he's not going to have to get back on that roof anytime soon."

"You're right, Myrtle." Beth prayed that she was. "I'm sure he will be fine out there." But her heart twisted at the thought that he was still in a lot of pain. And it was all her fault. . .and she knew it.

"Beth? Are you still there?"

"Yes, Myrtle, I am. Thanks for letting me know about Jeb."

"You're welcome, dear. Doc had a few stops he wanted to make on the way back in, but if there's any news I think you need to know, I'll get in touch with you."

"Thank you." Beth disconnected the line. Lucas and Cassie were going to be disappointed that they wouldn't see Jeb this evening. Maybe they could go out. . .no. It was getting dark early, and Jeb would think he had to see them back to town. She couldn't have him doing that. His telephone had been installed. Maybe she could ring him. . . . No, she couldn't do that. What if he was upstairs and had to hurry to answer it? He could fall or hurt himself worse.

Beth sighed in frustration. Maybe she would just ring Emma and find out from Cal how he was when he left Jeb's. At least she'd know how he was then.

In the meantime, she was still getting all kinds of advice for Jeb, for her. . . and for them as a couple.

"When are you two going to get married? If you already were, he wouldn't be out there by himself," Alma commented.

And the likelihood of that happening has become a lot more unlikely since I caused Jeb's accident. But Beth didn't voice that to Alma. Instead, she just said, "I'm sure he will be fine. Doc wouldn't have let him go home if he didn't think he would be all right. Sorry, Mrs. Alma, I have to get busy."

And busy she stayed for the rest of the day, telling everyone who inquired about Jeb that he had gone back to the ranch and must be on the mend. And, yes, she and the children would be checking on him. And agreeing that she was sure he was quite surprised at the help the men had been giving him. And on and on and on.

Beth was relieved when it was time to go home but dreaded telling the children that they wouldn't be seeing their uncle Jeb. And they were disappointed. However, they were very pleased that Jeb was well enough to go back to the ranch.

"When do you think we'll get to see him, Miss Beth?"

"Well, I'm not sure he'll feel like riding a horse for a while or how hard it will be for him to hitch up the wagon. But if we don't see him by Saturday, I'll take you out there."

That seemed to satisfy them, but it didn't help Beth. She fretted all the while she made supper, wondering how Jeb was doing. . .if he was hurting bad. . .if he was lonesome. . .until she could stand it no longer. She picked up the telephone.

"Number, please," Jessica said.

"Hi, Jess. Please get me the McAllisters' place."

"Right away, Beth."

Liddy answered. "McAllisters'."

"Liddy, I just called to see if Cal had mentioned how Jeb is doing?"

"Beth. It's good to talk to you. Cal said he was doing pretty well when he left there. And that Jeb was really appreciative of the work everyone had done. They finished up the roof today, but Cal is going back over tomorrow to help with the livestock, and Matt told him he'd be out to check on Jeb, too."

Beth breathed a sigh of relief. "Oh, good. I was worried that seeing to the livestock might be too much for Jeb."

"I understand. I'd be the same way. But he is going to mend, Beth." Liddy tried to assure her.

"I know." Suddenly, she felt like crying. "Thank you, Liddy. I'll let you go now." With that, she quickly put the earpiece back on the hook. She was sure Jeb was going to mend. . .but would he want her around when he did?

She tried to get her mind off of the guilt she still felt and suggested to the children that they make Jeb some cookies to send out with Matt the next day. She was sure Jeb and any of the men still working out there would appreciate them.

Cassie and Lucas helped, and before long they had a very messy kitchen and a whole crock full of sugar cookies for Jeb. Beth made a quick telephone call to Emma and asked if it would be all right for her to drop them by for Matt to take out to the ranch.

Emma made sure her husband was going out and came back on the line. "Matt said he will be glad to take them out, Beth. Things are pretty calm in town, and the sheriff has given him a lot of leeway to help out."

"That's really nice of him. And thank Matt for me. I'll bring the cookies by on my way to work. Did he say how Jeb was doing when he left?"

"He told me he thought he would be all right. He can't do too much with his arm in that sling, but at least it was his left one. He assured Matt and Cal that he would be just fine."

Beth breathed a sigh of relief as she told Emma good-bye and ended the call. Surely, if both Matt and Cal thought he'd be fine, she could stop worrying so.

She'd barely turned around when her telephone rang her ring. . .three short rings. . .a pause. . .and three more. She answered quickly, thinking it might be Darcie, as she'd already talked to Emma and Liddy, and those three were about the only people she talked to at home.

"Beth? Is that you?" Her heart dipped and dove down into her stomach at the sound of the masculine voice. It was Jeb. "Beth? Did I do this right?"

She finally found her voice. "Jeb. . .yes, it's me. You did fine."

"Good. I never used a telephone before. I wanted to thank you for getting it hooked up. . .and for—"

"You're welcome. Cassie and Lucas missed seeing you tonight."

"I missed them, too. I—"

"I know they would love to talk to you. . .let me get them."

It only took a minute for the children to get to the telephone. Not only were they excited to be hearing from Jeb, they'd never talked on the telephone before. Beth pulled a kitchen chair close for Lucas to climb onto so that he could reach the phone on the wall. He talked first, then Cassie.

"We made some cookies for you tonight, Uncle Jeb. Miss Beth thought they might make you feel better," Lucas said right off.

When it was her turn to talk, Cassie assured her uncle that they were both behaving for Beth. It was touching to hear each of them ask Jeb how he was feeling and when they would see him again.

From what Beth couldn't help but hear, Jeb asked about school and the upcoming Christmas program, and they each took a turn at telling him about their day. That they loved him was obvious. She knew they cared about her, but Jeb was family, a closer link to their papa, and they were looking forward to moving out to the ranch with him.

"Uncle Jeb wants to speak to you, Miss Beth," Cassie said, breaking into her thoughts.

"Thank you." Beth took the earpiece from her and held it to her ear. "I'm here, Jeb," she said into the mouthpiece. "How are you feeling?"

"Better since I talked to Cassie and Lucas. They're behaving for you?"

"Of course they are. They always do."

"Seems strange not to have seen them today," Jeb said.

"It did for them, too." *And for me.*

"I guess these telephones have their uses, don't they?"

"Yes, they do." Beth connected people every day in her work, but she'd never really appreciated the instrument at her fingertips until now.

Jeb chuckled. "Once you figure out how to use them. Took me a couple of tries 'til I got someone to say, 'Number, please.' And I did like Matt showed me and just told them who I wanted to talk to."

"You did just right."

"Well, thank you again for getting it hooked up for me while I was laid up."

"I'm glad they got to it before you got back out there." *I just wish you weren't there by yourself.* "You take care. Will you be able to make the Christmas program on Friday night? I'm sure Cal and Liddy would be glad to bring you in, if you're up to it. If not, I can bring the children out on Saturday, if you'd like me to."

"Oh, I'm planning on being there for that program. But I admit I didn't realize it was this week. I'll talk to Cal about it."

"Just let me know. And try not to overdo it, all right?"

"Don't worry 'bout me overdoing it. Not much I can do with this arm in splints and in this sling."

Beth was sure he'd be pushing himself as far as that arm would let him. "Liddy told me that Cal would be over to help you tomorrow. Try to let him, will you?"

"I'll try. Well, I guess I'd better let you go. You have to go to work tomorrow.

If I can't get to town, I'll telephone tomorrow evening."

"I'll tell Cassie and Lucas. I know they felt better just hearing your voice tonight." And so did she.

"Good night, Beth."

"Good night, Jeb." Beth replaced the earpiece into the hook. *Thank You, Lord, for letting us hear from him. Please watch over him tonight, please heal him, and keep him safe. In Jesus' name, amen.*

Jeb poured himself a cup of lukewarm coffee and eased himself into a chair at the table in the kitchen.

It had been so good to talk to Cassie and Lucas. . .and Beth. It wasn't anywhere near as good as talking to them in person, but it was better than nothing. He really missed them all tonight.

One thing the last few days had made crystal clear to him was that he was here to stay—no matter what happened between him and Beth.

He'd never been so touched in his life as he was when Doc pulled up in the yard today and he'd seen for himself just how this community had come together to help him in a way he'd never experienced before. He'd only briefly talked to some of these men at church, yet they'd shown their Christianity by caring enough to reach out a hand and help when he was in need. He wanted to be here to return the favor for any who might need him in the future, too.

It warmed his heart to know that it was Beth who first came up with the idea of getting help to finish the roof, as Cal and Matt told him. And they'd said they actually had to tell some people that they had enough help. This had become home.

He never really realized how lonely he'd been without family and close friends nearby. . .probably because he'd only been around other cowboys for so long. There were some good ones, but most were like him, moving place to place. It was hard to develop close friendships when no one stayed in the same place for long.

And John Biglow was a good man, but Jeb didn't really know him well enough to know if he was a Christian or not. Jeb had done the best he could to stay close to the Lord, reading his Bible and praying often, but he hadn't known what he'd been missing out on until he came to Roswell and became a part of a church family and a member of the community. He finally felt like he belonged somewhere.

Jeb took a sip from his cup. He should have heated it up. It had tasted better when it was fresh, but was still nowhere near as good as Beth's. Beth. What was he going to do about her? She'd sounded a little strained and distant tonight, but maybe it was just the way she sounded on the telephone. He'd wanted to thank her for her part in getting the roof finished and for all the help he had, but she kept changing the subject. He sighed and shook his head. He had a feeling she was still feeling bad and blaming herself for his fall. But it was his own fault. He knew better than to move quickly up on the roof. She'd just startled him with her accusations, and he hadn't watched what he was doing.

And she had looked so pretty while she was telling him off—even though she'd been so wrong about that letter and accused him of planning to leave. And to think, all he'd wanted was to get the house finished by that deadline she'd given him so he could ask her to marry him again!

He knew that the Lord led him here because of Harland's death, but Jeb believed that He had another purpose in bringing him to Roswell other than taking responsibility for Cassie and Lucas and making a home for them. He truly believed that the Lord had chosen Beth as his mate. Now, if he could just convince *her* of that fact.

He bowed his head and prayed for the Lord to show him the way.

Chapter 12

Beth didn't know who was more relieved after they talked to Jeb. . .she or the children. Lucas and Cassie seemed much happier for the rest of the evening and excited about the upcoming Christmas program now that they were hopeful their uncle would be able to attend. She sent them off to bed and finished cleaning up the kitchen, feeling much better herself. Just hearing Jeb's voice and knowing that he was all right had eased her mind a bit. . .at least about that. It also made her ever more aware of how quickly she'd become used to having him around and how very much she was missing him now.

It wasn't until Cassie and Lucas were fast asleep and Beth sat down at the kitchen table with a cup of tea that she considered how she was going to feel once the children moved out to the ranch. The roof was finished; the house was pretty much ready for them to move into.

She sighed deeply. It was going to be awfully lonely here without them. But, as much as she would miss Cassie and Lucas, she'd finally accepted that they needed to be with their uncle. And he needed them. He'd been without family for a long time, and, in the past few months, she'd witnessed a bonding between the three of them. She would be all right with their move to the ranch. Surely she would.

But she wasn't sure her heart would ever be all right again if Jeb couldn't forgive her for causing his fall. Oh, he'd said he was trying to finish the house to answer her challenge, but did that mean he cared enough to propose to her again? Besides, that had been before the fall. Beth shook her head. How could he want to marry her after the way she'd acted, climbing that ladder and yelling at him?

She could still see the confused look on his face as she'd accused him of planning on selling the ranch and the frustration as he'd yelled back telling her she was wrong—just before he'd fallen off the roof. Remembering the sound of Jeb hitting the ground, the sight of him lying there, not moving, Beth shuddered. She truly had thought he was dead.

Now all she really wanted was for him to forgive her for not believing in him the way she should have, believing what Harland had told her about him instead of what she was seeing with her own eyes, and causing him all kinds of pain and suffering. But she didn't deserve his forgiveness, and she certainly couldn't expect him to still care for her after the way she'd treated him.

Beth shook her head. She loved Jeb. Pure and simple. But she had to come to grips with the fact that, after the way she'd caused his fall, she would probably never have a life with him now.

Taking a sip of tea, Beth pulled her Bible close and began to read. It was only then that she realized what she needed to do was to go to the Lord in prayer. If He could forgive her, surely Jeb could, too—with the Lord's help.

She bowed her head and prayed. *Oh, dear Lord, thank You for letting Jeb be all right. Please watch over him through the night and ease his pain. Please forgive me for losing my temper and causing him to fall off the roof. And, please let Jeb forgive me, too, if it be Your will. In Jesus' name, amen.*

Finally, Beth felt some peace of mind as she sat in the quiet, knowing God heard her prayers. She got up and carried her cup to the sink. She would ask Jeb for his forgiveness when she could talk to him alone, then she would leave it all in the Lord's hands.

The next couple of days were a little tough for Jeb, but at least he could get around some. His limp was more pronounced from all the aches and pains he felt, but he continually thanked the Lord above that he hadn't been hurt worse. He figured he wasn't worth much otherwise, though. He hadn't been able to mount his horse to get into town to see the children, and, even though he'd talked to them on the telephone, it just wasn't as good as seeing them in person.

The beds he'd ordered had come in and were delivered on Thursday, and Jeb had set them up, with Cal's help. They'd dug through some of the boxes of the household items that Harland had brought with him in his move West and found some linens to put on them. He was thankful Beth had sent them out with him when he started work on the house so they would be there when he needed them. The worktable she'd pointed out to him that had the bins for flour had come in and fit just right in the kitchen. The place was beginning to feel like a home.

When Cal had suggested that the children move out after the Christmas program on Friday, Jeb quickly placed a telephone call to see if it would be all right with Beth.

"Of course it is, Jeb." She paused for a moment. "I'll have them ready to go. But it might take me a few days to get all of their things together."

Jeb could hear the sadness in her voice and knew that she was going to have a hard time giving Cassie and Lucas up, as he'd always known she would. The last thing he wanted to do was hurt Beth, and if he had anything to do with it, she wouldn't really be giving them up—at least not for long.

"That's fine. All they need right now is enough for the weekend. The house is ready. At least, near enough. I'd figured to move them out sometime next week, anyway. Maybe on Sunday I'll be up to bringing in the wagon and packing up the rest of their things."

"They're very excited about making the move out there."

Jeb had a feeling it took a lot for her to tell him as much. "I can't wait to have them here. I've missed them something terrible." He'd missed her, too. More than he truly realized he would. But now wasn't the time to tell her. . .not when she was in town and he was out here. No, that needed to be done in person, and he hoped to be able to see her very soon and convince her that he loved her.

"Jeb?"

"I'm here. I guess I was woolgathering." *About you. . .about us.*

"I'll have them ready to go after the Christmas program. They're going to be so excited that you'll be attending and that they'll be with you this weekend."

"Thank you, Beth."

"You're welcome."

Now here it was Friday afternoon, and Jeb couldn't wait until tonight, when he'd see them all at the Christmas program. Cal and Liddy were going to pick him up, and the children would be coming back with him. He'd see Beth and attempt to get a feel for how she would react to another proposal from him.

He remembered that he'd been about to tell her he loved her right before he fell. While he was laid up, he'd thought about her reaction to the letter from John Biglow over and over again. She'd been so upset about the possibility of him leaving, but had it only been because he would be taking the children with him or because she cared for him, too?

Jeb thought she felt something for him, the way her cheeks turned that pretty shade of pink when he sometimes caught her watching him with the children or when she glanced up to see him looking at her from across the table, the way she made his favorite meals and always made sure he had something to take back to the ranch with him. Maybe it was too soon to expect her to care. She might still be grieving over Harland.

So many little things she did for him made Jeb think she might really care for him. But did she? Or was it only wishful thinking on his part? He only hoped her acts of kindness were done for the same reason he brought her flowers and took her to Emma's on Saturday nights—because he loved her and wanted to make her happy.

Dear Lord, please help me to know. I love this woman with all my heart, and I want the two of us to make this house a home for Cassie and Lucas. Please guide me here, and let me know what to do. In Jesus' name, amen.

Beth found herself leaning on the Lord with all that was within her over the next few days. Her heart had dropped to her toes when Jeb called Thursday night, wanting the children to move out to the ranch. Oh, she'd known it was coming, and she'd told herself she would be all right, but deep down, she knew her house was going to feel awfully empty without Cassie and Lucas there or Jeb stopping by each day to see them.

She tried not to show them how sad she was just thinking about their move. They were so happy and excited that Jeb was coming in for the Christmas program and that they would finally be moving out to the ranch, she didn't want to put a damper on their joy.

After she'd talked to Jeb on Thursday evening, she had kept herself busy by making some sugar cookies for the program the next night, and she also baked a cake and more cookies to send out to the ranch with Jeb and the children.

Cassie had been reading her cookbook and helping with the cooking for some weeks now, and Beth knew that between her and Jeb, they wouldn't starve. But she sure was going to miss having suppers with them and sharing the evenings with them.

Now, as she sat at work on Friday, she tried not to dwell on how lonesome it was going to be at her house. But it wasn't easy to keep it off her mind.

Liddy telephoned while she was at work and apologized for Cal's part in speeding up the children's move. "I know Cal meant no harm, and he feels real bad that you might be upset with him, Beth. He just said Jeb seemed so lonely out there that the suggestion to go ahead and move the children just slipped out."

"It's all right, Liddy. They would have been moving soon anyway. I knew that."

"You know this isn't the end of—"

Beth didn't want to even think about endings. "Liddy, I'm sorry. . .my switchboard is lighting up. I'll see you this evening, all right?"

"Yes, of course—"

Beth disconnected the line and put the pin in for Emma's Café. "Beth?"

"Yes, it's me, Em."

"Oh, good. I never know who I'm going to get. Matt just told me that the children will be going back out to the ranch with Jeb tonight. Are you all right with that?"

"I don't have much choice in it, Emma. . .but I'll adjust."

"Oh, Beth. It's all going to work out. I just know it is."

"Thank you. It will. And Jeb needs them with him, too. Don't worry about me. I'll be all right. Cal and Liddy's wagon is going to be pretty full tonight. Would you and Matt mind picking me up?"

"Of course not. Are you sure—"

"I'll be fine, Em," Beth commented. And for the moment, she thought she would.

But by the time Cal and Liddy showed up with their children and Jeb to pick up Cassie and Lucas that evening, Beth wasn't so sure.

Everyone pitched in to help load the wagon with the food Beth had made for the ranch and the program and the personal items the children were taking to the ranch. By the time they all were settled back in the wagon, ready to leave, she was feeling pretty sad.

"I'll get the rest of their things packed up tomorrow so you can pick them up on Sunday," she said to Jeb.

"Thank you, Beth. You're going to the program with us, aren't you?"

"I'll be there. But I figured Cal's and Liddy's wagon would be plumb full, so I asked Matt and Emma to pick me up. They'll be here anytime now."

For the first time, the children showed a little hesitancy about leaving her.

"You are coming, aren't you, Miss Beth?" Lucas asked.

Beth forced herself to smile and nod. "Of course I am. I wouldn't miss it. You save me a seat, all right?"

"We have room for you now, Beth." Jeb patted the empty space beside him.

"That's all right. I already asked Em and Matt. I'll be there soon."

Beth pulled her overcoat closer around her and watched the wagon full of people she loved head toward the school. Her eyes filled with tears, and she blinked them away quickly as Matt and Emma showed up. Em watched her closely but didn't say anything as Beth stepped up into the wagon and greeted Mandy.

When they arrived at the school, it was to find that the children had been gathered behind a curtain that had been strung up in front of the platform stage some of the men had put up.

Liddy had put her dessert, along with Beth's, on a table in back of the room, and Emma hurried off to add hers to the rest.

Jeb and the McAllisters had indeed saved them all a seat. Beth's just happened to be between Jeb and Liddy, and Jeb stood to let her sit down. In order to accommodate his broken arm, she had to turn slightly toward him, and she was flooded with guilt all over again at seeing his arm in that sling.

Matt and Emma sat in the row behind them, and it took a few minutes for everyone to get settled before the program began. Once the curtain opened, the audience clapped wildly, letting their little ones know how proud of them they were.

A large Christmas tree had been put up at the back of the stage, and it was beautiful, decorated with things all the children had brought from home. The popcorn garland that Jeb had helped the children string had been added to several others and, intertwined with the cranberry ones, looked very pretty. Homemade ornaments cut from paper or made from lace and ribbon hung all over the tree.

Beth quickly spotted Cassie on the back row of steps, while Lucas stood on the first. They'd been a little nervous about performing in front of so many people, and she sent up a silent prayer, asking for the Lord to give them the confidence they needed.

And He did. As they began to sing, her heart expanded in love for them. Their sweet faces intent on remembering the words and their young voices harmonizing together, they sang "O Come All Ye Faithful" and then "Joy to the World."

She spotted Grace and Amy, too, and knew Liddy was feeling the same way about her girls. Trying not to be obvious, she glimpsed at Jeb out of the corner of her eye and found that he appeared every bit as proud as she felt. The audience was asked to join in singing several Christmas carols, and the sound of so many voices singing "It Came Upon a Midnight Clear" and "Silent Night" had Beth's spine tingling.

Minister Turley ended the program by reading the story of Christ's birth from the book of Luke. And a night that had started out on a down note for Beth ended on one of thankfulness for the Savior who'd come to earth.

Thunderous applause erupted when the curtain was closed and opened again. . .all the children taking a bow. Beth tried not to think of telling Cassie and Lucas good-bye; instead, she busied herself behind the dessert table giving out treats.

When it was time for the children to go, Beth swallowed around the clump of unshed tears in her throat and gave them each a hug, promising to see them on Sunday.

Sunday could come none too soon for Beth. By the time Saturday evening rolled around, she wished she'd been working. It didn't take anywhere near as long as she'd thought it would to pack up the rest of Lucas's and Cassie's things, and by that afternoon she was more than a little lonesome.

She kept busy, cleaning house and baking bread to send with Jeb and the children. Emma was thoughtful and invited her over for supper that night, and Beth was glad for the company but felt out of sorts that Jeb and the children weren't with her. It was going to take some getting used to, this being alone again.

After coming home to a house that seemed emptier than ever, Beth could stand it no longer, and she placed a call to the ranch. It took several rings before he picked up on his end.

"Winslow Ranch."

"Jeb? It's Beth." Now that she was talking to him, she felt a little silly.

"You sound a little funny. Is everything all right?"

"Yes, of course." *I just miss you all.* "I. . .I just wanted to see how Lucas and Cassie and you are all doing."

"We're making supper. I'm trying my hand at pancakes. Cassie told me I have to let them bubble up before turning them over. You should have seen the mess I made of the few I flipped too soon."

Beth chuckled just thinking about it, and she wished she had been there to witness him flipping those cakes.

"Cassie and Lucas helped me unpack some of those boxes of household things of Harland's that you sent out here," Jeb continued. "Cassie has this kitchen in good working order, and Lucas has been a big help outside in the barn."

They were such good children. "I'm glad they have been able to lend a hand to you."

"I'm just glad they're here. But I guess you're missing them, too."

"Yes, well, I'll get used to it." *Oh, dear Lord, please let me get used to it.* "I'll let you get back to your meal, and I'll see you all tomorrow at church." Beth didn't wait for Jeb to say anything else. She couldn't trust her voice to stay steady.

Sunday morning, Beth was up early. She put on a pot roast to cook while she was at church. She'd meant to ask Jeb and the children to come over for Sunday dinner when she'd talked to him the night before, but she'd been so flustered and emotional talking to him she'd forgotten. She would ask them at church, and if he declined her invitation, well then, she'd have her supper for several days.

She dressed in her best dress and took care with her hair. It was a beautiful day, with Christmas only a week away. She'd been knitting at night for some time now, making mufflers for both Cassie and Lucas, but she wanted to buy them something else. She needed to talk to Jeb and see if he'd decided what he was getting them.

With the prospect of seeing them all again, her heart felt a bit lighter than the day before. Beth chuckled and shook her head. She was pitiful. It had only been one whole day since she had seen them. She'd just put on her cloak and started out the door when Jeb pulled his wagon up.

"We were hoping we'd catch you. I'm still not used to having that telephone, or I would have placed a call to you to see if you wanted to ride to church with us." Jeb grinned at her. "It only dawned on me that I could have when we got to town."

"Yes, Miss Beth, we want you to come with us," Cassie said.

"We love it at the ranch, but we've missed you," Lucas added.

"I've missed you, too. And thank you. A ride would be nice." Beth climbed up onto the seat and sat down beside Jeb. He looked a little awkward holding the reins in only one hand, and guilt flooded her once more. "Would you like me to take the reins?"

"Thank you, but I'm fine. Got to handle it for the next month or so. Cassie and Lucas hitched up the wagon for me, and thankfully, my team is easy to handle."

Much as she would miss them, Beth was glad the children were able to help Jeb. When they arrived at church, Cassie and Lucas hurried out of the wagon and over to talk with the McAllisters' children. Beth didn't know when she might have the chance to talk to Jeb alone again.

Realizing it might be only for a minute, the words she'd been waiting to say tumbled out of her mouth. "Jeb, I am so sorry for causing you to fall. Can you ever forgive me?"

"Beth, I told you it wasn't your fault. There is nothing to forgive."

"Oh, yes, there is. I yelled at you. I was awful that day."

Jeb grinned at her and shook his head. "You had reasons. But if it will make you feel better, then I forgive you for yelling—but it still wasn't your fault that I fell."

"Thank you," Beth responded simply.

Jeb crooked his good arm and Beth took it, feeling as if a huge weight lifted off her shoulders. He might never ask her to marry him again, but he forgave her.

As they strolled into church together, the joy Beth felt in knowing that Jeb had forgiven her lasted well past the worship service and throughout the day, as Jeb and the children came back to the house and took dinner with her. She loved being in their company.

It was only when it was time for them to leave that Beth's joy turned bittersweet. She truly was glad they were happy at the ranch with Jeb. She just wished she was going back there with them, instead of staying in the emptiest house in town.

Jeb couldn't get the sight of Beth waving good-bye to them out of his mind. She'd seemed so alone and forlorn, and the children didn't look too happy about leaving her there, either. Maybe he should have waited until after Christmas to move them to the ranch.

When Liddy and Cal stopped by on their way back from town on Monday and asked if Cassie and Lucas could go home with them for the afternoon, Jeb realized he had the opportunity he'd been waiting for. He was determined that he wasn't going to wait any longer to tell Beth how he felt about her and that it was time to deal with the challenge she'd given him. He'd given her more than one chance to bring up the subject, and she hadn't done it. Well, he was going to bring it up himself. The house was finished, and he was about to propose to Miss Beth Morgan again, and this time it was for real.

"Sure. I need to go into town and pick up a few things. Cal, think you could help me get my wagon hitched up?"

"Sure can." It took only a few minutes, and Jeb was on the wagon seat ready to take off in the opposite direction. "I'll come by and get Cassie and Lucas when I return."

"Well, plan on staying for supper, you hear?" Liddy suggested.

Jeb grinned. "Thank you, Liddy. I'll look forward to it."

"Bye, Uncle Jeb," Lucas yelled from the back of the wagon.

"If you see Miss Beth, tell her we said hello," Cassie called to him.

Jeb nodded and waved back. He'd tell her. Because the main reason he was going into town was to see Beth. She'd given him a challenge, and he'd met it. It was time for her to make a decision.

Beth's switchboard had been busy all day. It seemed everyone in town wanted to know if the children were happy at the ranch or if she was missing them. Or when she would be seeing them again.

"Well, what are you going to do about Christmas, Beth?" Alma asked.

"I don't know just yet, Mrs. Alma. But I have plenty of friends. I'm sure I won't be alone."

"Well, if you want my opinion, you ought to. . ."

Beth's switchboard began to light up again. "Hold on, Mrs. Alma." She pulled the pin on the Pauly Hotel's socket. "Number, please?"

"Get me the sheriff's office, will you please, Beth?" Mr. Williams, the hotel manager, asked.

"Right away." As she reached to insert the hotel's pin into the sheriff's socket, she placed another pin into Doc Bradshaw's office socket. "Number, please?"

"Beth, it's Myrtle—"

"Beth?" It was Jeb's voice, but she hadn't connected his line, had she? "I need to talk to you."

She glanced at her switchboard, but his line wasn't lit up.

"Beth?"

Beth turned in her chair and saw him standing just inside the telephone office door. She jumped up, dropping the unconnected end of the lines she'd been holding onto the switchboard. "Jeb, what's wrong? Are the children all right?"

"They're fine. I came to talk to you."

Beth brought a hand to her chest. "Oh. . .I thought. . .but I'm working."

Jeb crossed the room quickly, his limp barely noticeable.

Her pulse began to race, and she placed a palm over her rapidly beating heart.

Jeb stood only inches away, looking deep into her eyes. "I told you I was going to ask you again once the house was done. Well, it's done and you need to make up your mind."

"Jeb, I—" Beth's heartbeat sounded like thunder in her ears, and she wondered if Darcie could hear it. She'd never felt so flustered in her life. She knew she needed to be doing something. . .she was at work. She turned around and found Darcie watching the two of them, several lines in her hand waiting to be plugged into sockets. "Can this wait? I'm working. I—"

"I've waited long enough." Jeb pulled her close with his good arm. "I need an answer now."

Now. He needed an answer.

Beth looked back to see her switchboard lighting up all over the place, and Darcie trying to take care of both switchboards while trying not to miss a thing going on in the office. For the first time since she'd come to work here, Beth decided some things were just more important than the Roswell Telephone and Manufacturing Company.

"An answer to what?"

"You told me that if I finished the house by Christmas, you just might marry me. Back then, when I asked you to marry me, we barely knew each other and it was for the children's sake. This time I'm asking simply because I love you. . . with all my heart, and I can't imagine not seeing you every day. I want you out at the ranch with me and Cassie and Lucas. I know you may never love me like you loved Harland, but, Beth, will you please marry me?"

It suddenly didn't matter if the whole town would soon know what went on here. She turned her undivided attention to the man she loved. "Oh, Jeb! I. . .you. . ."

Beth stopped and took a deep breath. She had to tell him everything. "I thought I could learn to love Harland. I truly did. But I'd been having second thoughts about marrying him for weeks before he died. I was going to tell him the next time he came into town, only I didn't have a chance before he was killed in the stampede. I promised myself that I would never marry a man I didn't know and didn't love after that. Then you came into my life, and I've felt so guilty over the growing feelings I've had for you. I—"

Jeb shushed her with a finger at her lips. "I understand. I've had my share of guilt over falling in love with you. But I have. Deeply and completely. And I want nothing more than to marry you, if you'll have me—"

Beth's heart seemed to have wings as it rapidly beat in her chest. "Oh, Jeb. You are the only man I've truly loved. . .and yes, oh yes, I *will* marry you."

Beth tried to be careful of his bad arm and sore ribs as Jeb pulled her closer and bent his head toward her. Their lips met and clung in a kiss that turned the challenge of a moment into a promise of a lifetime.

Epilogue

Christmas morning dawned bright and cold, but Jeb didn't feel it as he hurried downstairs to stir the coals in the fireplaces to life and add logs to them. The warmth he felt generated from the love in his heart. . .for his new wife and the niece and nephew they would raise together.

He had little time to think about it, however, as Cassie and Lucas rushed downstairs.

"Merry Christmas, Uncle Jeb!" Lucas shouted.

"Yes, Merry Christmas," Cassie called from behind him.

"Merry Christmas! I'm sorry we don't have a tree this Christmas," Jeb apologized. "Next year, I'll go with Cal to cut a great big one."

"It's all right, Uncle Jeb," Lucas assured him. "We have what we wanted."

"Yes, we do," Cassie agreed. "We've been praying that all that courting you were doing worked and that Miss—that *Aunt* Beth would agree to marry you so we could all live here on the ranch together."

Jeb laughed and nodded. "Well, I sure am glad the Lord heard those prayers. I surely am. Because that was my Christmas wish, also." He gave them each a one-armed hug. "I do believe, even though we don't have a tree up, there are a few other gifts for you in the back parlor. You go ahead, and I'll go get your aunt Beth."

The children rushed off, and he went to look for his new wife. He still couldn't believe that Beth had accepted his proposal and agreed to marry him on Christmas Eve. . .much less that they actually had been married the night before, with half the town as witnesses and a wonderful reception following at Emma's Café.

To thank their best friends for all they'd done to help them prepare for such a rushed wedding right on Christmas Eve, Beth had insisted that the McAllisters and the Johnsons come out to the ranch for Christmas dinner after church. It's what she wanted. . .and no one could tell her no, least of all him.

Beth had come down earlier, and now he found her in the kitchen, just closing the oven door on the huge turkey she'd put in to roast while they were at church. Jeb leaned against the door frame, thoroughly enjoying the chance to watch his new bride putter around, until she finally turned and spotted him.

The delicate color that stole up her cheeks and the sweet smile she gave him when she saw him were enough to warm him clear through.

"Jeb! I didn't hear you come downstairs. Coffee will be ready soon."

"I should have known you'd be down here with this stove. It's the real reason you accepted my proposal, isn't it?" he teased.

Beth giggled. "Well, I'll admit, my fingers have been itching to cook a meal on it ever since I found out you bought it. But it's certainly not the reason I married you."

Jeb crossed the room in two strides and pulled her close with his good arm. "No?"

She shook her head as she gazed into his eyes. "No. I married you because I do love you, Jeb. . .more than I ever thought possible."

Jeb's heart seemed to expand in his chest. He knew she loved him, as he did her. They'd told each other so over and over in the past few days. But he'd never tire of hearing it. . .nor of saying it. "I love you, Beth."

Jeb bent his head and captured her lips in a kiss meant to assure her completely that he was telling the truth. Cassie and Lucas yelled for them to hurry, and Beth quickly broke the kiss and pulled away.

"We're coming," Jeb answered. But he caught Beth's arm as she started out of the kitchen and pulled her back into his embrace. The children could wait another minute or two.

"Merry Christmas," he whispered right before his lips claimed Beth's once more in a lingering kiss.

"Uncle Jeb, Aunt Beth!" Lucas was getting impatient to open his presents.

Jeb chuckled as Beth broke the kiss and pulled him toward the parlor. He followed willingly, thanking the Lord above for leading him to Beth. . .and to a place called home.

Making Amends

To my Lord and Savior for showing me the way, the family I was born into, and the family the Lord has given me. I love you all.

Chapter 1

Late March 1899—Roswell, New Mexico Territory

The train pulled to a stop in Roswell, New Mexico Territory, and Attorney John Harper stood and stretched. It had been a long trip from Georgia, and he was glad it had come to an end. He dusted off the shoulders of his jacket, gathered his bags, and got in line to leave the passenger car. Stepping off the train, he was struck by how wide the cloudless blue sky seemed out here and how much closer than back home.

John started toward the train depot, more than a little surprised at the size of Roswell. From what his father had told him about the town, he hadn't expected it to be as large or as busy as it was. He'd thought he could get off the train and immediately find the office of the lawyer who had written to let him know he was his uncle's only heir. Instead he found a bustling town filled with people going about the day's business.

John did not even know his uncle, Douglas Harper. Moreover, from his father's account of his uncle, John could not understand why the man had left anything at all to him. The two brothers had not been on good terms for years. John had heard enough to know his uncle Douglas had been smitten with his mother, but she had not felt the same about him. According to John's grandmother, there was never a question of which brother would win the heart of her daughter, Margaret. Grandmother Smithfield had told John many times that his mother had fallen in love with James Harper the first moment she saw him.

Evidently Uncle Douglas had not taken her decision well. He'd left Georgia and traveled west to make his fortune, never to return. He refused to come back even when James had gone out to plead with him to return for the sake of their dying father.

John sighed deeply and shook his head. He did not know how his uncle had died, nor did he understand why Douglas Harper had named him in his will. He only knew he needed to find the lawyer who had written him, visit his uncle's grave site, and learn what had happened to him.

John crossed the boardwalk that led to the train depot, opened the door, and strolled up to the counter.

"May I help you?" the man behind the counter asked.

John smiled. "I hope you can. My name is John Harper, and I'm looking for my unclc's lawycr, a Mr. Elmer Griffin."

"You Douglas Harper's nephew?" The man behind the counter's right eyebrow crept up into his hairline.

"Yes, sir, I am. Did you know my uncle?" John could not help but notice an abrupt change in the man's demeanor.

"Not well. Elmer's office is over on Fifth Street, across from the courthouse." With that, the clerk leaned to the side and looked at the woman next in line. "May I help you, ma'am?"

"Would it be all right if I leave my valises here until I have a place to stay?" John asked, feeling as if he suddenly didn't exist.

"Here—give them to me," the clerk said gruffly and went to the end of the counter.

John handed his bags to the man. "Thank you."

The man grunted. John knew when he had been snubbed. He walked out of the office and blinked his eyes against the bright sunlight before realizing he hadn't asked which way Fifth Street was. But he certainly didn't want to go back in the depot and ask the clerk. An old-timer was sitting in a chair leaning up against the building. John approached him with a smile; he'd always had a soft spot for old people.

"How do, sir. I'm John Harper, and I'm looking for the office of Elmer Griffin. I was told it's on Fifth Street, but I'm new to the area and don't know where that is."

"Old Elmer don't do much business these days. 'Bout the only business he's handled lately is Douglas Harper's."

"Yes! That's who I'm looking for. Douglas Harper was my uncle."

"You don't say?"

"Yes. Did you know him?"

"I knew 'im." The older man sat up straight, plunking the chair down on its four legs, and pointed to the right. "Fifth Street is over that way a couple of blocks. Elmer has a sign out front—you won't miss it."

"Thank you." John tipped the brim of his hat to the man, but again he felt dismissed. The old man had already leaned back against the building and closed his eyes.

John started down the street in the direction the man had told him to go. The main street was full of surreys, farm wagons, and freight wagons, and people rushed in all directions. So far no one he'd met had been friendly. Neither of the two men had given him condolences about his uncle passing away; in fact, his very name seemed to put up a barrier of some kind.

He wondered why people would change as soon as they heard he was a relation of Douglas Harper. That seemed odd to John because, in his few letters home, his uncle had painted himself as one of the most important and influential men in Roswell.

The law office of Elmer Griffin was across from the courthouse, as he'd been told. It was a small office with a big sign outside. He opened the door and stepped inside to see a rotund man leaning back in a chair behind a massive desk, his feet propped up on it, his head resting on his chest. He emitted a snore so loud that John jumped back a step.

It was midmorning, and the man was asleep. Business must be slow. John cleared his throat from inside the door. The snoring only grew louder. He moved to the center of the room and cleared his throat again.

The rumbling snort stopped briefly, then started again. John walked closer to the desk and cleared his throat as loudly as he could. The large man stirred. John leaned toward him. "Excuse me, sir?"

This time he started. His eyes opened, and he jerked his feet off the desk. "Humph! Yes? Who are you? What can I do for you?"

"I'm John Harper." He pulled out a letter. "I believe you sent me this letter."

The man was on his feet in an instant. He reached across the desk and extended his hand. "Mr. Harper. Yes, I'm Elmer Griffin. I trust you had a good trip out?"

John shook his hand. "It was fine, all things considered. A little hot and dusty. Still, train travel is better than stagecoach or horseback."

"Yes, yes, I agree." Elmer Griffin motioned to the chair on the other side of the desk. "Please take a seat, Mr. Harper. As you know from my letter, your uncle named you as his only heir. His money has been placed in trust, and I am the trustee. Now that money belongs to you." He pushed his glasses up on his nose. "It is a sizable sum."

John's breath caught in his throat when Mr. Griffin named the amount.

"He was an astute businessman," he added as if in explanation.

"I'd say he was." His uncle had been a rich man.

"We can go to the Roswell Bank and transfer the funds to you as soon as you are ready. Other than that, I'm sure you have questions you would like answered."

"Well, yes, I do. First and foremost I'd like to know how my uncle died." John sat down in the chair and watched Elmer Griffin wipe his brow with a handkerchief he'd pulled from his coat pocket. The man seemed nervous to him.

"Well, he. . .ah. . .he died from the influenza. It swept through the prison, and before they could get a doctor in, five prisoners had died."

"My uncle was in prison? Why—and for how long?" This was news to him and would be to his family. He sat forward on the edge of the chair.

Elmer Griffin cleared his throat. "Yes, well, he died a couple of months ago. He was in the jail here—until his trial for arson. He was found guilty of hiring someone to set fire to Emma's Café. He was sentenced to five years in prison, but he had only served about a year and a half of that time when he fell ill."

John sat silent, trying to take in what his uncle's attorney was telling him. No wonder he had not been welcomed in the town with open arms. Apparently his uncle was not the fine upstanding man he had led the family to believe he was. On the rare occasion he had been in contact with them, he had indicated he was one of Roswell's leading citizens. And even though his father and his uncle hadn't been close, John wondered why his uncle Douglas hadn't contacted the family law firm when he got into trouble.

He looked at the older man. "You defended him?"

Elmer Griffin nodded. "Yes, I defended him—but only because the court ordered me to do so."

"Do you think he was guilty?"

The older man shrugged. "I don't know. Someone came forward and admitted he lit the fire—and said Harper hired him to do it. Your uncle did not have many people on his side, Mr. Harper. He treated some of the people in Roswell and in the surrounding area badly."

Suddenly John wasn't sure he wanted to find out how badly, and he had an urge to take the first train back to Georgia. But he knew he wouldn't do that. He wasn't that kind of man. He'd stay and get to the bottom of this—he had no choice, now that he'd been named his uncle's heir.

"I hope you are a better man than your uncle was, sir." The man let out a deep sigh. John had a feeling the lawyer had been dreading this meeting for a long time.

"I did not know my uncle, Mr. Griffin. But from what you've told me, it appears my family name is at stake here. I will do what I can to restore honor to it. I'm not sure, though, where to start."

Elmer Griffin looked at him closely before nodding. "If you mean that, I'll do what I can to help you, Mr. Harper."

"Please call me John."

"All right, John. And call me Elmer. You're taking on a large task. I hope you'll be able to stay and see it through."

"I'm a member of the family law firm. My father has told me to take as long as I need to settle my uncle's estate."

The older man looked in his desk drawer and pulled out a key. He stood up and handed it to John. "Your uncle's office at Harper Bank would probably be the best place to start. It has been closed down ever since he went to prison."

"What about the people who did business there? Were they able to get their money out?"

Elmer nodded. "The sheriff saw to it that they were able to do that before Harper went to trial. But I feel I must warn you—those who still owe money to your uncle probably won't be glad to see you. Just be sure you look over those papers with a fine-tooth comb. All may not be what it seems at first glance."

John took the key and slipped it into his pocket. "Can you tell me where the bank is?"

"I'll do better than that. I'll go with you. It'll be time to eat in a few hours. I'll treat you to a meal at the Roswell Hotel. It's not far from the bank."

"Thank you." Not looking forward to the task at hand, John was glad to have the company of the older man. "I appreciate your help."

Elmer showed John where his uncle's office was inside the bank and left with the promise of returning at noontime. After seeing him out, John walked back to the file cabinet behind his uncle's desk and pulled out several file folders. Plunking them down on the desk, he sat down and opened the top one.

After only a couple of hours, John realized how right Elmer was. A huge job was unfolding before him. It would take weeks to go over his uncle's papers.

True to his word, Elmer returned and treated him to dinner. John was impressed with the quality of food and service at the Roswell Hotel. But he wasn't sure he wanted to stay there. Leaning back in his chair, he smiled at Elmer. "Thank you. That was a wonderful meal."

"You're quite welcome. Are you going back to the office now? Have you decided on a place to stay? I've heard the accommodations here are very nice. It's where your uncle lived. Had the nicest suite in the place."

John briefly wondered why his uncle had chosen to live in a hotel instead of a home of his own, but he supposed it was fairly common for single men to do that, especially when they had no family around. He shook his head to Elmer's first question. "No, I'll go back to the office first thing in the morning. I guess the most important item of business for me now is to find a place to stay. I had thought to stay in a hotel, but it looks as though I'll be here awhile. Nice as this place seems to be, I think I might be more comfortable in a boardinghouse. Can you recommend any?"

"We have several in town, and they list their vacancies in the paper. Let me go find you a copy." He came back shortly with the morning paper in hand, turned to the inside, then handed John the advertisements.

John skimmed the page. "There's a room at the Roswell Inn, one at Malone's Boardinghouse, and another one at Brady's Boardinghouse."

"Oh, Molly Malone's is a great place to stay. She's a wonderful cook, and I've heard only good things about her establishment," Elmer said. "I'd try there first."

"I'll see if a room is still available. Can you tell me how to get there?"

After giving him directions to the boardinghouse, Elmer took his leave, assuring John once more that he would be glad to help in any way he could. They made plans to meet the next morning at the Harper Bank.

Darcie Malone shook hands with her supervisor, Mr. McQuillen, thrilled she'd just been given a promotion. She left his office with a grin on her face but let out a sigh as soon as she returned to her station. She had gone into his office thinking he was about to reprimand her for listening in on conversations again. Instead she'd come out as the head operator, in charge of training for the Roswell Telephone and Manufacturing Company. She suppressed the excited giggle that wanted release and took her seat at the switchboard.

She wasn't sure she believed it yet! Oh, she knew that with her best friend, Beth, now married and no longer working, she might be next in line for a promotion. But she'd been reprimanded so many times, she'd feared that would keep her from getting it. The few extra dollars she would make a month would certainly help her mother. They wouldn't be enough, though, for her to turn their house back into a private home instead of a boardinghouse. Darcie sighed. Maybe one day.

She plugged the line pin into her home socket and pulled the lever. She didn't want to wait until she got home to tell her good news. Her mother worked so hard; hearing a little more money would be coming in might make her tasks easier today.

Her mother picked up the receiver on the third ring. "Malone's Boardinghouse. How may I help you?"

"It's me, Mama. I have some good news to share with you."

"Oh? What is it, dear?"

Darcie could picture her mother's bright smile. "Well, as of tomorrow, I will be the head operator at Roswell Telephone and Manufacturing Company. It means a little more money coming in."

"Oh, you're right—that is very good news, Darcie! I'm so proud of you, dear."

"Thank you." Tears came to Darcie's eyes at her mother's words. She never held back on her praise for her daughter.

"I have some news of my own. We have a new boarder as of this afternoon."

"Wonderful!" Darcie could hear the excitement in her mother's voice, and she had to force herself to sound happy. It meant one more stranger to get used to in her home, not to mention more work for her mother. But the older woman wouldn't welcome her daughter's attitude, so Darcie tried to hide it the best she could.

"He seems like a nice young man. You'll meet him at dinner. I put a roast on earlier. I'm glad it's your favorite meal, since we must celebrate your promotion and a new boarder all in one day!"

Several lights on her switchboard lit up. "I must get back to work, Mama. I'll see you in a few hours." She pulled the pin from her home line, knowing her mother would understand the quick end to their conversation, and inserted a pin into the plug of one of the lighted lines. "Number, please."

"I need to talk to Emma, over at the café, Darcie."

Darcie recognized the voice of Matt Johnson, Emma's husband and a deputy sheriff. "Right away, Deputy."

She inserted his line pin into the line for Emma's Café and waited for an answer before turning her attention to the next lighted line. As she went about connecting and disconnecting telephone lines, her thoughts turned back to her promotion. She had only a few more hours to go on her shift—and tomorrow she would have a completely new job. More and more people were signing up for telephone service, and Mr. McQuillen had hired two new operators who were due to start the next day. It would be Darcie's job to train them. She sent up a silent prayer that she would do a good job and be a good example to them, as Beth had been to her.

Heading back to the train depot to pick up his bags, John left Malone's Boardinghouse with a spring in his step. Mrs. Malone's establishment was warm and inviting, and the smell coming from her kitchen reminded him of his mother's at home. The room she'd rented him was large and bright, overlooking the large cottonwood in the front yard. She was also the friendliest person he'd met in this town so far. He wasn't looking forward to his task of settling his uncle's estate, but for whatever time he was here, he would be comfortable.

Chapter 2

As soon as her shift was over and the evening operator showed up to relieve her, Darcie left for home. She hoped the friends she'd made at the telephone office would be happy about her promotion when they found out. She did not want to appear to be boasting about it and decided she would let Mr. McQuillen announce it the next morning as he planned.

As Darcie entered her home, she couldn't help but feel pride that it had become the best boardinghouse in town, even though she would have preferred it to remain a private home. Everyone who stayed there had commented on how warm and homey it was.

Of course she agreed. Her mother had decorated tastefully, from the downstairs to each room upstairs, and there wasn't a room Darcie didn't like.

The front parlor was done in gold and blue flowered wall coverings. It was furnished with a parlor set covered in gold silk damask, and burgundy silk draperies hung at the doorway and windows. The room was a favorite of the boarders. A chess set stood waiting for Mr. Mitchell and Mr. Carlton to continue their game later in the evening. The back parlor was finished in mostly deep rose with touches of gold and seemed to draw the women to sit and do needlework or read during the evenings.

Miss Olivia Waterford and Mr. Mitchell were in the front parlor, reading the newspaper, and Darcie waved at them before hurrying to the kitchen to see if her mother needed help putting dinner on the table. She marveled at how her mother managed to look fresh and energetic after spending a good portion of the day over a hot stove. In her midforties, she still had a trim figure and always dressed neatly, a crisp apron protecting her clothing. Although her red hair was beginning to fade a little, her blue eyes seemed brighter with age.

Her mother was taking the roast out of the oven when Darcie entered the kitchen. She looked up with a smile. "There you are. The new head operator—I am so proud of you, dear."

"Thank you, Mama. It smells wonderful in here. You must have been cooking all afternoon."

Her mother set the roast on the kitchen table and pointed to the cake beside it. "We have good reason to celebrate tonight, what with your promotion and all! I made that chocolate cake you like so much for dessert tonight, too."

Darcie walked over and gave her mother a hug. "Thank you. But you shouldn't have worked so hard."

"It's not work when it's for someone you love, dear. Did you see the new boarder when you came in?"

"No. Only Miss Olivia and Mr. Mitchell were talking in the parlor."

"He is probably settling in. He had to go back to the train station to pick up his valises after he rented the room. He seems to be a nice gentleman."

"That's good. I just wish we—"

"Darcie, dear, I do understand how you feel. Still, we need to be thankful we had this house to turn into a business and can earn a living from it. Besides, I really do enjoy it. I know that's hard for you to believe, but it would be very lonesome with only myself for company when you're at work."

It was hard for her to believe, but out of respect for her mother, she smiled and hugged her again. "I know you're right, Mama. I need to be more thankful for my blessings. I do thank the Lord for them—I really do." And she did—maybe not as often as she should, though. Darcie promised herself she would do better. "Now—what do you need me to do?"

"You can put vegetables on the table and the cake and dessert plates on the sideboard."

Darcie dished up the roasted potatoes, carrots, and onions into serving bowls and took them to the dining table. She loved this room. Scarlet upholstered chairs and scarlet draperies with gold trim enhanced the gold and scarlet printed wallpaper. The table was covered with an ivory lace tablecloth and set with her mother's best china. Darcie thought it was the most elegant room in the house.

She could hear more voices in the parlor as she put dessert plates on the sideboard and briefly wondered if the new boarder had come downstairs. Her mother carried out the meat dish and a gravy boat as Darcie went back for the cake. Just as she reentered the dining room, she could hear her mother calling the boarders to the table.

Darcie stood at her place at the opposite end of the table from where her mother would sit and smiled as the guests entered the room to take their seats.

"Darcie, dear, I'd like you to meet John Harper, our newest boarder. He's a lawyer and will be here for at least a month or so. Mr. Harper, this is my daughter, Darcie Marie."

Darcie looked up past the broadest shoulders she had ever seen and into the deep chocolate-colored eyes of the new boarder. *Oh. He's very handsome, his dark hair parted slightly to the left of center, his clean-shaven face nicely chiseled. . . .* Just looking at him left her breathless.

"How do you do, Miss Malone?"

Darcie could feel her cheeks growing warm as she stood there. She forced the air out of her lungs. "I—I'm fine, thank you. And you?"

"Very well, thank you." He smiled at her, then inclined his head in her mother's direction. "And I've become quite hungry smelling this food your mother has prepared for us."

Everyone else had taken his or her seat at the table. Three chairs had been empty at the table for eight, and her mother had hoped for new boarders to fill them. The one to Darcie's left had remained vacant since Mrs. Green had moved out. Darcie was pleased when she realized the new boarder would be sitting next to her. He pulled out her chair and waited for her to sit. She only hoped he could not hear the rapid beating of her heart—for it was quite loud to her own ears.

Darcie tried to will her heartbeat to slow its pace as she sat down. She was relieved when her mother spoke.

"Before I ask Mr. Mitchell to say the blessing, I have an announcement to make. Darcie has been promoted to head operator at the Roswell Telephone and Manufacturing Company."

"What wonderful news, Darcie!" Miss Olivia said. She'd lived at the boardinghouse for over a year. She had come out west to take care of her ailing sister and moved in after she passed away.

"They made a good decision in promoting you, Miss Darcie," Robert Mitchell added. He'd been living at the boardinghouse for about six months and was overseeing the railroad expansion.

"They certainly did." George Carlton nodded from his place to the right of her mother. Mr. Carlton taught school and had resided with them ever since he'd come to Roswell two years earlier.

"May I add my congratulations?" Mr. Harper asked.

"Thank you." Darcie had to force herself to look away from his warm gaze. "Thank you all. I'm a little nervous about it, but I'm very pleased, too."

"You'll do fine," her mother said, beaming at her. "Just fine. Now let's not let this meal get cold. Mr. Mitchell, please ask a blessing for us."

Darcie bowed her head and tried to keep her mind on his words.

"Dear Lord, thank You for this day and for Darcie's promotion. And thank You for the food we are about to eat. In Jesus' name, amen."

Her mother always complained about Mr. Mitchell's prayers being much too short, but he pouted if she didn't take turns asking him and Mr. Carlton. Hard as it was for Darcie to think about anything except the man at her left, she thought maybe it was just right tonight.

As the dishes were passed around the table, she tried to concentrate on the conversation.

"Ahh, beef with roasted potatoes and carrots. I think this is one of my favorite meals, Mrs. Malone," Mr. Carlton said.

"Thank you," her mother said.

Darcie glanced down at the table as she saw the wink her mother flashed her. She tried to hide her smile behind her napkin. Every meal her mother cooked was one of Mr. Carlton's favorites.

She looked up and found Mr. Harper watching her, a smile hovering around his lips as if he understood the unspoken conversation between the two women.

"Oh, dear," her mother said, her hand at her chest. "With the excitement of Darcie's promotion, I'm afraid I've forgotten my manners. Have you all met our new boarder, John Harper?"

"I have," Mr. Mitchell said.

Miss Olivia patted her graying fluff of hair and nodded. "Yes, I did—this afternoon. I was sitting in the parlor reading when he arrived. It's always nice to meet new lodgers."

"Pleased to meet you," Mr. Carlton said with a nod. "You'll find no better food in all of Roswell."

Mr. Harper smiled and nodded. "I've been told that. But even if I hadn't heard, I would have known when I came by to inquire about the vacancy. When I stepped inside and smelled the aroma coming from the kitchen, it reminded me of my mother's kitchen. I knew I'd come to the right place."

"Why, Mr. Harper, thank you," her mother said. "I'll take that as a high compliment."

He nodded in her direction. "As it was meant to be."

Darcie could tell her mother was pleased, and her opinion of the new boarder inched upward at the way he treated her—with respect and honor. She'd been through so much. Having her husband die from a sudden stroke, then losing all he'd worked so hard for—with the exception of the house in town, which they'd been able to turn into a way of making ends meet. Having to give up her privacy and the kind of life she'd become accustomed to through the years couldn't have been easy. Darcie gave herself a mental shake. No. She couldn't start thinking about the past. It never failed to bring tears to her eyes, and then her mother would tear up.

Mrs. Malone began to pass the dishes around so the boarders could help themselves, and quiet reigned at the table for a few minutes while they began to eat. John told himself to be sure to thank Elmer Griffin for suggesting the Malone boardinghouse. The food was excellent, and so far everyone seemed amiable. He would be comfortable here for his stay. Not to mention Mrs. Malone's daughter. He hadn't been prepared for the jolt of awareness he'd felt when he walked into the dining room and found her standing at the end of the table.

With her shining auburn hair and sparkling blue-green eyes, she was very lovely, and he'd found it hard to keep his eyes off her. To keep from gazing at her now, he tried to concentrate on the dinner conversation going on around him.

"I think being a telephone operator would be so interesting, Darcie. Don't you just love it?" Miss Waterford asked. She looked to be a little younger than Mrs. Malone. Perhaps in her late thirties, he thought.

"Yes, Miss Olivia, I do love working for the telephone company."

Miss Waterford nodded. "If I were younger, I'd apply for a position there. Isn't it amazing that one can talk to someone clear across town? That is so hard for me to believe."

"Oh, nowadays one can even talk to people outside town—even to Eddy and more," Darcie said with a smile for the older woman.

"You don't say?" Miss Waterford asked, holding her hand to her chest. She sighed. "So many new inventions to make life easier for us. What a wonderful time we live in."

John felt ashamed for thinking the pace of life wasn't moving fast enough. He'd wanted to place a call to his parents earlier and found that long distance in Roswell extended only a hundred miles or so.

"Why, some places make connections out farther than that. One of these days, I predict we'll be able to talk to people clear across the country," Mr. Mitchell said.

Miss Waterford gasped. "You don't say!"

"It's only a matter of time," Mr. Carlton agreed, handing John a basket of rolls. "Isn't that right, Miss Darcie?"

"Oh, yes, I'm sure it is," Darcie answered. "Lines are being strung daily, and they go farther out each week. In fact, the Roswell Telephone and Manufacturing Company hired two more linemen a week or so ago."

She was so animated while she talked about the company. When she caught his gaze on her, John felt flustered at the warmth in her eyes, and his heart pounded in his chest. He held out the bread basket. "Would you like a roll, Miss Darcie?"

"Thank you, yes."

Darcie took the basket from him, and their fingers brushed, sending a tingly sensation up her forearm.

"Pass the gravy, please, Darcie," Mr. Mitchell asked.

She picked up the gravy boat in front of her and handed it to the older man, silently sighing with relief that her hands didn't shake. Darcie had never felt so attracted to a man as she was to John Harper, and she was flustered by the way her pulse raced at his nearness. He was so handsome and seemed very nice. Just the kind of man she'd always dreamed of—

Making Amends

"How long did you say you'd be with us?" Mr. Carlton inquired of Mr. Harper, cutting into Darcie's thoughts. She listened closely to the answer.

"I'm not sure. Several weeks, a month or two—possibly longer. I don't know yet," he said.

Darcie's heart beat faster when she realized he might be here awhile, then promptly slowed as she reminded herself awhile was not forever. He had business here, and then he'd be gone. But what if—

"Harper, you say?" Mr. Mitchell asked.

"Yes, sir."

"Not any kin to Douglas Harper, are you?"

Harper, Harper. Why hadn't she made the connection? Darcie wondered, as she held her breath, waiting for the man's answer.

"Why, yes, I am. He was my uncle, and I came out here to settle his estate."

The dream Darcie was weaving crumbled as suddenly as her heart plunged to her feet. She felt as if the breath had been knocked plumb out of her. She should have known.

White-hot anger she hadn't been aware she still harbored welled up from deep within her. She looked down the length of the table. "Mama! How could you rent a room to any relative of Douglas Harper?"

"Darcie Malone. You'll not talk to me like that." Color flooded her mother's face.

Darcie couldn't keep the words from escaping her lips. "But how could you?"

Her mother pushed back her chair and stood. "I'll have a word with you in the kitchen. Now."

Darcie knew not to argue with that tone; she realized she'd gone too far. She pushed back her own chair and headed toward the kitchen.

Before leaving the room, her mother turned and spoke to those seated around the table. "Please excuse us and go on with your meal."

Darcie braced herself for the admonishment she knew she deserved and had no doubt was coming.

John Harper wasn't sure what to do as Mrs. Malone and her daughter left the table. What had his uncle done to the Malone family to cause such an outburst? And should he stay or go?

Mr. Carlton and Miss Waterford were both looking at him suspiciously. If only he knew why the people in this town reacted so negatively at the mere mention of Douglas Harper's name. At the same time, he dreaded finding out.

The other boarders made small talk among themselves, and he tried to concentrate on that instead of the rise and fall of voices coming from the kitchen.

Although he couldn't hear what was being said, John was certain he was the topic of conversation.

Mr. Mitchell cleared his throat and held out the platter of meat as if it were a peace offering. "Would you like more beef?"

John shook his head. He probably couldn't finish what was on his plate. "No, thank you."

He took a bite of roasted potatoes and found they didn't taste as good as they had only moments before. In fact, he had to struggle to swallow. He laid down his fork and took a drink of water. When he looked up, all eyes were focused on him. John put his napkin on the table and pushed away from the table.

"If you'll excuse me, I believe I'll call it a night."

"You aren't staying for some of Molly's chocolate cake?" Miss Waterford asked. "It's a favorite for all of us."

"No, ma'am. I'm a little tired from the travel. I won't wait for Mrs. Malone to come back, but please tell her I thought the meal was delicious."

"Yes, we will do that," Mr. Carlton said.

John turned and left the room, but before he was out of earshot, he could hear the whispers of the others. *Talking about me, no doubt.*

Chapter 3

Darcie could tell by the way her mother marched across the kitchen and looked out the back door that she was trying to compose herself. She tried to swallow around the huge lump in her throat. She felt awful, realizing she'd caused her mother to be so upset. But she still couldn't believe Douglas Harper's nephew had rented a room in their home.

Her mother turned to face her, unshed tears in her eyes. She shook her head. "I cannot believe you humiliated us both in such a way, Darcie. I—"

Darcie looked down, trying to keep her own tears at bay. "Mama, I'm sorry I spoke the way I did and that I didn't wait until we were alone." She glanced up. "But I can't believe you rented a room to the nephew of the man who put us through so much misery!"

"Darcie, dear, you must realize I didn't know he was Douglas Harper's nephew when I rented the room to him. But—"

"Of course you didn't!" Darcie sighed with relief that her mother hadn't knowingly rented to the enemy. "Then you must tell him to find another place to stay. There are plenty of hotels in town. Let him stay at one of them! I'll be glad to tell him for you, Mama."

Her mother shook her head. "No, we'll not do that, Darcie. He is not to blame for the sins of his uncle. And we need the money."

"Only because of his uncle."

"Darcie, John Harper has done us no harm. And until it becomes apparent he intends to, I will keep my agreement with him. He will be staying with us for as long as he is in town—unless you've insulted him so badly, he decides to seek other accommodations. I expect you to apologize to him and the other boarders for your rudeness just now."

"But, Mama—" Darcie paused. "He is still the nephew of the man who put Papa under so much stress that he had a stroke! How can we allow him to stay here?"

"Darcie, Douglas Harper is dead. He can't hurt us anymore. And his nephew is not responsible for his uncle's actions. You didn't see the look on his face at your outburst. I'm sure he doesn't even know why you are so upset, and he deserves an apology."

Darcie knew he did. Still, it would be one of the hardest things she'd ever done. She had no idea how she would stand having a relation of the man she held responsible for her father's death living under her mother's roof.

"Darcie—" Her mother paused, waiting for Darcie's response.

"Yes, ma'am. I will apologize for being rude. And I do truly apologize to you, Mama. I am sorry I hurt you in any way."

Her mother drew her toward her in a hug. "I know you are. And I understand your pain. But, Darcie, dear—you must learn to forgive. It's what I pray for daily."

The tears in Darcie's eyes threatened to spill over. Her mother was right. But so far she had not been able to forgive the man responsible for their present circumstances. And it hurt to think the only man she'd ever felt such an attraction to was related to him.

"Please keep praying for me, Mama, because I am still struggling with it." She took a deep breath to collect herself. "I'll go tell the boarders I'm sorry."

Her mother nodded and patted Darcie on the back. "Thank you. I love you, Darcie."

"I love you, too." Darcie returned her mother's hug, wishing she were more like her. With her gentle spirit, she had somehow forgiven the man who'd inflicted so much pain in their lives. Darcie wasn't sure she could ever forgive Douglas Harper the way her mother had.

She sighed and turned toward the dining room. She hoped she could make her apology to John Harper sound sincere. But when Darcie walked into the room, she discovered he had left the table. She wasn't sure if she felt relief or disappointment that she would have to wait until tomorrow to offer him her apology.

Apologizing to a sympathetic group of boarders presented no problem for her. She was sorry she'd ruined the nice meal her mother had planned for her. She grasped the back of the chair she'd vacated earlier and tried to smile at the three boarders still sitting at the table. "I am so sorry for my outburst earlier. I forgot my manners. I hope you will forgive me?"

"Oh, of course, Darcie, dear," Miss Olivia said.

"Think nothing of it," Mr. Mitchell added. "We understand." As her mother entered the dining room, he continued, "Mr. Harper was tired from his travels and asked us to tell you how delicious he found your meal, Mrs. Malone."

"Oh, I am sorry he didn't get a piece of cake. I'll be sure to save him a slice," she said.

Darcie knew from the look her mother shot her that she still expected her to apologize to John Harper; but, dear that she was, she said no more on the subject. Relieved for the moment, Darcie helped serve the cake. For the most part, the meal ended better than she deserved it to, considering how she'd disappointed her mother.

Feeling it was the very least she could do to show her mother she was truly sorry, Darcie insisted she leave the kitchen and dining room cleanup to her.

Her mother gave no protest. "Well, all right. I am a little tired tonight. Thank you, dear."

Determined the kitchen would be spotless when her mother came down the next morning, Darcie washed, dried, and swept, leaving no crumb behind. She even set the table for breakfast the next morning before she slipped up the back staircase to her room.

~

For more than an hour, John had paced the floor of the spacious room he'd rented earlier in the day. Finally he sat down at the writing desk to pen a letter to his parents. He couldn't telephone them long distance from here, and he didn't want to send a telegram. He didn't want people knowing any more about his business than was necessary. He wasn't sure what he was going to find out about his uncle, but from Darcie Malone's outburst earlier, he had a feeling it wouldn't be good.

He hadn't known what to do after Mrs. Malone and her daughter went into the kitchen. He'd felt uneasy sitting at the table with the other boarders and the silence that had suddenly fallen over the table. And he wasn't sure what to do now. Should he seek other accommodations or stay here?

Molly Malone was a wonderful cook. Her home was clean and comfortable, and he liked the woman. He shook his head. He'd sleep on it and decide tomorrow. Right now he needed to let his father know his only brother had died in prison.

John picked up his pen and started writing. He explained that his uncle had been in prison when he'd died and what he knew about it so far. He was honest with his father about not being sure how long the business of settling his uncle's estate would take.

How could he know how long he needed to uncover the depth of what he was just beginning to find out? And how could he voice his suspicions when that's all he had at the moment? Instead he promised he would stay as long as it took to settle everything—providing the people of Roswell didn't run him out of town before he could. But he didn't tell his father that part, either. It seemed enough for now that he had to tell him about his brother being incarcerated when he died. Perhaps by the time he had a reply from his father, he would have more of an idea of what settling his uncle's estate entailed. Slipping the letter into an envelope, he sealed and addressed it.

John stood up from the desk and stretched. It had been a long day, and he couldn't wait for the next one to arrive—just to get through his first day in Roswell. He didn't think he'd ever felt more unwelcome at any other time in his life.

He sauntered to the window and looked out before deciding to take a walk. Maybe the fresh night air would help him sleep soundly. He made sure he had the key to his room and the one Mrs. Malone had given him to the house, then put on his jacket and hat.

He heard murmurs coming from the back parlor; but no one was in the front parlor, and he was glad he didn't run into any of the boarders. He didn't want to feel he had to converse with anyone at the moment. He let himself out and turned in the direction of Main Street. The town was laid out well and the spring evening mild. He strolled up one side of the street and down the other. It appeared as if the dining rooms in several hotels were still open for business, but he was sure their fare couldn't hold a candle to Mrs. Malone's. Lights were out in the mercantile houses and other shops, but Emma's Café across from the sheriff's office appeared to be open.

He counted more than one drugstore in town and three blacksmith shops and two livery stables. The telephone office was still open, and he could see a young man working the switchboard through the window.

Several people were out and about and greeted him with a "Good evening."

By the time he turned back toward the Malone boardinghouse, he was feeling a little better. Maybe he'd been too quick to judge the people of Roswell. And besides, surely, the whole town hadn't known his uncle.

A plan had come to mind as Darcie was cleaning up. Once back in her room, she sat down at her desk and pulled out paper, pen, and ink. She quickly wrote a note of apology to John Harper.

Dear Mr. Harper,

Please accept my apology for my rude outburst at the dinner table this evening. I should not have taken my dislike for your uncle out on you. I disappointed my mother greatly tonight, and for that I am truly sorry. Please do not hold my bad manners against her. I can assure you she taught me much better than that.

Sincerely,
Darcie Malone

She was truly sorry about hurting her mother and could apologize sincerely for that. She folded the note and slipped it into an envelope and opened her door as quietly as she could. Making her way down the hall, she stopped outside John Harper's door and sent up a prayer that he wouldn't notice the note being slipped under his door—at least not until she was safely back in her own room.

The envelope slid under the door smoothly, and she let out a deep sigh of relief before turning and hurrying to her room. Darcie was aware she should have apologized in person and that her mother expected her to. But she hadn't been able to reconcile the way her pulse sped up at the thought of seeing him again with the anger she felt that anyone kin to Douglas Harper was sleeping in her home. She wasn't sure she could apologize to him any other way. At least not tonight.

After getting ready for bed, she picked up her Bible and settled in the window seat overlooking the front yard. The stars lighting the sky appeared close enough to reach out and touch. Darcie opened the Bible and tried to read her nightly devotional. But thoughts of the way she'd embarrassed her mother kept intruding. She tried to push them to the back of her mind, but the words on the page blurred through unshed tears. She slipped to her knees and bowed her head.

"Dear Father, please forgive me for upsetting Mama so. I am very sorry I hurt her. I was just shocked the nephew of that rat Douglas Harper had rented a room—"

Darcie bit her bottom lip and sighed as fresh tears formed and fell on her folded hands. "Father, I'm sorry," she whispered. "I know You would have me forgive my enemy. Mama seems to have. But I—I cannot get over the fact that Harper caused Papa's death. I'd pushed it to the back of my mind after finding out he died in prison. But now, with his nephew here—sleeping in this house—it's all come back, and I miss Papa so!"

She gave herself over to sobbing at the loss she felt anew. How could she ever forgive the man who'd caused her father's stroke? Because of him, her mother was working night and day! Yet her mother wanted her to forgive Harper and treat his nephew as she would any other boarder. Darcie wiped her eyes and sighed before continuing with her prayer.

"Father, I will try to be civil to John Harper, for Mama's sake. But please, please, if it be Your will—please let him decide to find another place to stay!"

How could she stand to have Douglas Harper's nephew—the last man she should ever be attracted to—staying in her home? Darcie shook her head. She didn't know. Only the Lord could help her. She finished her prayer. "Please help me to be more like Mama. In Jesus' name, amen."

John let himself into the boardinghouse, nodded to Mr. Carlton and Mr. Mitchell, who were playing a game of chess in the front parlor, and headed up the stairs to his room. He unlocked the door and stepped inside to find an envelope on the floor.

Slipping off his jacket, he hung it on the hook beside the door and laid his hat on the table before turning up the gas light so he could read the letter. He was surprised and pleased to discover it was from Miss Darcie and even more so to find it was an apology. He read it a second time.

In the morning he'd have to assure her he in no way blamed her lapse of manners on her mother and that he accepted her apology. A light knock on the door had him wondering if it might be Darcie coming back to see if he'd found the note.

He opened the door, expecting her to be there. Instead it was Mrs. Malone standing with a tray that held a huge slice of chocolate cake on a plate and a cup of coffee. His mouth watered just looking at it.

"Mr. Harper, I felt so bad that you missed dessert because of my daughter's outburst. I hope you won't mind if I try to make it up to you now—"

"Oh, Mrs. Malone, please don't worry yourself about it. There's no need to make it up, but I certainly thank you for bringing this to me." With the note still in his hand, he took the tray from her.

"I'll collect the tray in the morning, and please be assured that Darcie will issue you an apology in the morning."

John smiled at the older woman. "Oh, but she already has."

"She has?"

"Yes, I was just reading her note of apology."

"She gave you a note instead of apologizing in person? No. That is not good enough. I'll have another talk—"

"Mrs. Malone, please don't. I went out for a walk and just returned. She probably would have told me in person had I been here. The note was slipped under my door while I was out."

Darcie's mother shook her head. "Still—"

"It's a nice note, Mrs. Malone. And of course I accept her apology." John didn't want her to force her daughter into a face-to-face apology. After seeing her distress this evening at the table, he was surprised even to receive the note.

"Well, I—please accept mine, also. I'm afraid your first night here wasn't—"

"The meal was delicious. While I was out walking, I was thankful for such a nice place to stay while I'm here. I've never been particularly fond of hotels. And to come back to a piece of that delicious-looking cake—I'll have to thank Mr. Griffin for steering me in your direction."

He seemed to have assured Mrs. Malone to her satisfaction because she smiled and shook her head. "Thank you, Mr. Harper. I will let you enjoy your dessert. Thank you for letting me know Darcie did apologize, even if it wasn't in the way I would have liked."

"You are welcome." John inclined his head toward the tray in his hands. "And thank you."

Darcie's mother nodded and turned to leave. "Good night, Mr. Harper."

"Good night, Mrs. Malone."

She closed the door behind her, and John carried the tray over to the small table in front of the window. He pulled out one of the two chairs and sat down to enjoy the piece of cake. He closed his eyes as he took his first bite. It was as scrumptious as it looked and smelled. No wonder it was a favorite of the other boarders. He sipped the coffee, then leaned back in his chair. Maybe his stay here would turn out better than he first thought. He hoped it would. He prayed it would.

Chapter 4

Darcie was up bright and early the next morning, a little nervous about starting her new position. She dressed with care and chose a navy blue skirt and a crisp white blouse. She took extra time with her hair, pulling it into the fashionable psyche knot. When she was satisfied she looked professional, she hurried downstairs to help her mother get breakfast ready for the boarders.

The first meal of the day was not a formal one, but it was always large. Her mother prepared quite an array of items and set them out on the sideboard in the dining room so her boarders could help themselves whenever they came down.

Her mother greeted her with her usual cheery, "Good morning, dear."

"Good morning, Mama. I hope your day is an easy one." She kissed the cheek her mother turned to her as she was sliding flapjacks onto a plate.

"Thank you, Darcie. I hope for the same for you. And thank you for writing Mr. Harper that note of apology, though I wish you'd apologized to him in person—"

"He's been down already?"

"No, dear. Not that I know of. I felt bad that he'd missed dessert last night and took him a piece of cake—he told me then. He'd just come back from a walk and found your note."

"Oh. Well—"

"He appeared to be quite satisfied by it, and that is the main thing. He seems a nice young man and nothing like his uncle, Darcie." She added the last pancake to the pile and handed the plate to Darcie. "We need to—"

"I know. Get these to the dining room." Darcie took the platter from her mother, then glanced back on her way out of the kitchen and saw the look on her mother's face.

"Darcie, you know full well that is not what I was talking about."

"I know. I'm sorry, Mama. I will try." And she promised herself she would try to be civil to the man for her mother's sake.

"Thank you, dear. That is all I'm asking you to do."

Darcie breathed a sigh of relief as she entered the dining room and added the platter to the rest of the fare on the sideboard. Along with the pancakes were butter and warmed syrup, bacon and sausage, and scrambled eggs. A basket of sweet rolls and biscuits and an assortment of jellies completed the choices. As she fixed her own plate, she was sure no other boardinghouse in town put on the kind of spread her mother did. Darcie sighed and shook her head. If only her mother didn't have to work so hard.

She heard footsteps on the stairs and some of the boarders greeting each other, and she returned to the kitchen to eat her breakfast there as she did most mornings. She always tried to help her mother by washing up some of the cookware before heading off to work, but this morning she had the added incentive of not having to face John Harper.

"Have a good day, dear," her mother said as she took off her apron and prepared to join her guests.

"You, too, Mama. If you need anything from downtown, just telephone me."

Her mother nodded as she went through the door. Darcie heard her greet the boarders with her customary, "Good morning! I hope you all rested well?"

She could hear the murmur of voices assuring her mother they had indeed slept very well. But it was John Harper's voice that started her pulse racing and her temper rising as he told her mother he'd never slept better.

How dare he sleep so well under this roof? But of even more concern to her was how her heart could beat so fast at the sound of his voice from the other room! No longer hungry, she made quick work of washing her dishes and the cooking pans and utensils so her mother wouldn't have to, all the while trying desperately to get her mind off Douglas Harper's nephew.

Drying her hands on the dish towel, Darcie took a quick look in the mirror by the back door to make sure she looked presentable for her first day as head operator. Then she hurried out the door and around the side yard to the walk that would take her to Main Street. Relieved she hadn't run into any of the boarders—one in particular—she walked as fast as she could until she was out of sight of the house. She'd be glad to get to work.

John had dreaded coming downstairs and having breakfast with everyone after last night; but by the time he'd finished Mrs. Malone's delicious pancakes, he was even more thankful Elmer Griffin had told him about this place. The other boarders had warmed up to him after taking their cue from their landlady, who had gone out of her way to make him feel welcome. He knew that even though her daughter hadn't made an appearance at the table, he wasn't going to seek lodging anywhere else—notwithstanding the fact he was fairly sure Miss Darcie Malone would prefer it that way.

Surely she wouldn't decide to avoid meals altogether—and he doubted her mother would let her get away with that should she try. He was hoping to get a glimpse of her beautiful red hair and flashing blue-green eyes before the day was out.

He left the boardinghouse with Mr. Carlton and Mr. Mitchell and was glad for their company as they headed toward Main Street. He bid them goodbye and sauntered the few blocks to his uncle's bank, but he realized everyone still didn't welcome him. Several people slowed down their stroll past the bank, watching him unlock the door. When he tipped his hat toward them and wished them a good morning, they scattered, with frowns on their brows. Maybe some of them owed his uncle money, and as Elmer Griffin had warned him, they weren't going to be welcoming. Of course most of these people didn't even know who he was yet, but it didn't appear that any of them wanted to find out.

John's good mood of the morning suddenly dissipated as he realized the only place he might feel comfortable was at Molly Malone's—and probably only if Darcie wasn't around. He sighed and opened the dusty shutters over the windows. He sneezed then and realized he'd need to hire someone to come in to clean. He'd ask Mrs. Malone about that this evening.

As he entered his uncle's office, it occurred to him that Douglas Harper must have been a man who wanted to control his surroundings. The office was situated so he could see everything going on in the bank. Sitting in the massive chair, John pulled the pile of folders he'd left in the middle of the desk toward him.

By midmorning, he'd barely made a dent in the first batch of paperwork he'd chosen to review. At first it appeared his uncle kept detailed records, but on closer inspection many seemed incomplete. His uncle's handwriting was appalling and nearly impossible to decipher.

John was relieved to see Elmer Griffin when he showed up around eleven as promised. His uncle had apparently not been aboveboard in all his business dealings, and John realized he needed help in dealing with it.

He stood and shook Elmer's hand. "I'm glad you didn't change your mind about coming. I'm having trouble reading my uncle's handwriting."

"I'm fortunate I'm at a point in life where I can take only cases that interest me. Not many do. So I have nothing on my docket now, and you seem like a nice sort and nothing like your uncle. Let me see what you have." He reached for the pile of papers John pushed across the desk to him.

"I'd be glad of any help you give me, sir. I hope you can decipher my uncle's script better than I can."

Elmer pushed his spectacles up on his nose and peered at the top page. He shook his head. "We have our work cut out for us, son."

John nodded. "Yes, I'm afraid we do."

Mr. McQuillen introduced Darcie as the new head operator and supervisor first thing that morning. She was pleased no one seemed upset. In fact, her coworkers appeared genuinely happy for her. She accepted their congratulations and started her first day in her new position with the best intentions of being a wonderful example to the other operators, just as Beth had been to her.

But it didn't take long for those good intentions to fall by the wayside. Hard as she was trying not to think about John Harper when she arrived at work, it soon became obvious she wasn't succeeding.

When the Winslows' line lit up, she smiled as she put the line pin into the socket. She hadn't talked to her best friend in several days. It was always good to hear from her. "Good morning, Beth. Who can I connect you to?"

"Darcie, I want to talk to you! When were you going to tell me the news?"

Darcie's heart jumped in her chest. Who told Beth about Harper's nephew being in town? "Why, Beth, I didn't think word traveled that fast in this town. He only got here yesterday."

"He who?"

"John—" Darcie stopped midsentence. Did Beth not know? "What news are we talking about, Beth?"

Beth giggled on the other end of the line. "Right now we appear to be talking about John someone, and I can't wait to find out who he is. But I was talking about your promotion."

"Oh, I'm sorry. I meant to telephone you last night."

"It's all right. I couldn't wait to congratulate you! I put in a good word for you with Mr. McQuillen, and I was so hoping you would get the promotion."

"Thank you, Beth. I'll never be as good a supervisor as you, but I'll try."

"You'll do fine. Now—who is this John person?"

Beth took a deep breath. "He is John Harper. Mama's new boarder."

"Oh, I'm glad she has a new one—"

Darcie shook her head. "Not this one, Beth."

"Oh? Why not?"

"H-a-r-p-e-r. As in the nephew of Douglas Harper."

"Ohh. Darcie, I am so sorry. How did that happen? I can't believe your mother rented a—"

"She didn't know." Darcie was quick to take up for her mother. How could she have blamed her? She hadn't made the connection to Douglas Harper, either.

"What did your mother say when she found out who he was? And what is he like?" Beth shot off the questions. "And what did she do? Tell him to get out?"

I wish. Several lines lit up at the same time, and much as Darcie wanted to answer Beth's questions, she had to cut their conversation short. "Beth, it's getting busy. I—"

"I understand. I'm coming into town later. Ring me through to Emma's—

and plan to have afternoon tea at her place soon's you get off work, so you can fill us in."

"All right." Darcie connected Beth's line to Emma's Café. She was glad she didn't have to go into it here at work but would have a chance to talk to Beth later. She hurried to plug in another line. "Number, please?"

"Darcie, it's Alma Burton. Could you ring me through to Doc's, please? I need to talk to Myrtle."

"Right away, Mrs. Alma." Darcie plugged Alma Burton's line into Doc Bradshaw's socket. Alma Burton was a favorite of everyone who worked the switchboards. She hoped nothing was wrong with the older woman; her voice sounded odd. Alma had been lonesome since the death of her husband several years before, and she often rang through to the telephone office to catch up on news around town. Darcie was happy to oblige when she could, but now that she was head operator, she'd have to be more cautious.

The operators were supposed to be careful about carrying on personal conversations while at work, but everyone seemed to make an exception for Mrs. Burton. Besides, it was hard to keep everything on a professional level when most of the residents looked to the telephone operators to find out what was going on in town.

Of course if an emergency occurred, all rules were suspended. Then the operators were expected to get word out to the Roswell Telephone and Manufacturing Company's customers. According to Beth, hardly any rules existed out here in the West compared to the Bell Telephone Company back East where she'd been trained. Darcie had a feeling she would never have made head operator back East. She probably wouldn't have even made it as a regular operator.

She was trying hard not to start any gossip. So throughout the day, she managed to stop short of shouting to one and all that Douglas Harper's nephew was in town to settle the man's estate. What would that mean to so many in Roswell who'd done business with his bank? And shouldn't she be warning them?

Darcie finally convinced herself it was indeed her duty and mentioned it to Liddy McAllister when she rang in to put in a call to Emma's Café. Harper had been awful to Liddy when she was a young widow expecting her first child. She was thankful Cal McAllister had come along and taken care of Harper for her, but if he hadn't been around, the banker probably would have ended up with Liddy's land.

"Oh, Darcie. Do you suppose he's going to cause as many problems as Douglas did?"

"I certainly hope not, Liddy, but I don't know."

"I pray he is nothing like his uncle. How did he—?"

"Liddy, I have to go." Darcie watched as one line and then three more lit up. It was promising to be a busy day, which was probably for the best. "I'm going to meet Beth at Em's for tea about four o'clock," she said hurriedly. "If you can, try to come in then, too. I'll fill you in then."

"I'll be there," Liddy said right before the connection was broken.

It was half an hour later before they had a lull. Darcie glanced over at Jessica Landry, one of the other operators on duty, and blew out a deep breath.

Jessica smiled at her. "Darcie, I haven't meant to listen in, but did I hear you mention earlier that Douglas Harper's nephew is in town?"

"Yes, you did."

"Oh, dear. I hope that doesn't mean trouble."

"So do I. Especially as he is staying at my mother's boardinghouse." Darcie understood Jessica's sharp intake of breath. "Mother says we can't hold his uncle's sins against him. I know she's right, but—"

"That doesn't make things easy for you, does it?"

Red lights lit up on Darcie's switchboard once more. She saw the same thing happening on Jessica's board and only had time to shrug at the other woman before they both went back to work.

When she heard Jessica mention to several customers that Douglas Harper's nephew was in town, she couldn't bring herself to reprimand her. After all, the other girl had overheard Darcie mentioning it to Liddy. Besides, she truly felt deep down that people needed to know John Harper was in town and there to settle his uncle's estate.

By four o'clock, Darcie was more than ready for a cup of tea. Her three dear friends were waiting for her at a corner table at Emma's. Emma Johnson was the proprietor of the café and the wife of one of the town's deputies, Matt Johnson. She was expecting a child in a few months and had never looked prettier. Liddy and Emma had been friends for a long time, and in the last few years, they'd become good friends with newly married Beth Winslow and Darcie. They'd shared heartaches and joys with one another, and Darcie felt blessed to have each one in her life.

Now the other women barely waited for Darcie to take a seat before they began to quiz her.

"Is it true Harper's nephew is in town, Beth?" Emma asked as she poured her a cup of tea.

"Yes, it is true, Em."

Emma groaned. "I thought we'd heard the last of Douglas Harper when he died in prison."

"So did I." Darcie took a sip from her cup.

"What do you think his nephew is doing here?" Emma asked.

"I don't know, Em. He says he's here to settle his uncle's estate."

"Humph! I hope that doesn't mean more trouble for the citizens of Roswell," Emma said.

"So do I," Beth added.

Darcie had to tell them. "He's also staying at the boardinghouse."

"At your boardinghouse?" Emma questioned.

Darcie nodded. "Mother didn't know he was related to Douglas Harper when she rented a room to him, but she won't tell him to find another place."

"Oh, dear. How do you feel about that?"

Before or after I found out who he was? "Upset." *Especially as I can't quit thinking about how handsome he is or how nice he seems to be.*

"I can understand that. I feel that way just knowing he's in town," Emma said.

Darcie nodded. "I know. But Mother says we can't hold him accountable for his uncle's actions."

"She's right, you know," Liddy said. "But it's very hard, isn't it?"

"Very hard."

"What is he like, Darcie?" Beth asked.

"Well, he has nice manners and—" The bell over the café door jingled then, and Darcie looked up to see the topic of their conversation walk in the door with Elmer Griffin. When he spotted her, he smiled and tipped his hat in her direction before sitting down at a table on the other side of the room.

"And there he is," she whispered, hoping no one could see the slight tremble of her fingers as she picked up her teacup and took a sip to try to hide her reaction to the man.

"That's him?" Liddy whispered back.

Darcie nodded over the rim of her cup. He certainly did look handsome in his black Barrington worsted suit.

"Oh, dear," Beth said. "He doesn't look anything like his uncle."

"No. He doesn't, does he?" Liddy said. "Let's hope he's as different from the man as he looks."

Emma glanced at John Harper and nodded. "We can hope. And time will tell, I suppose."

Darcie looked up to find Beth's thoughtful gaze on her. She only hoped her best friend couldn't see what a turmoil her emotions were in.

Beth took a sip of tea and nodded. "Yes, only time will tell."

Chapter 5

John was glad Darcie was at the dinner table that night. He'd found it hard to get her out of his mind after running into her at the restaurant that afternoon. She'd left Emma's Café before he and Elmer had, and he'd hoped she wouldn't go into hiding once she got home. She looked lovely tonight. She'd changed into a pretty yellow dress that made her hair seem even brighter than usual.

Tonight's meal was much more pleasant than the previous night's had been. When he walked in the front door, he caught the aroma of the rich stew Mrs. Malone had made from the leftover beef, and his stomach started to growl. With it, she served corn bread and biscuits that melted in John's mouth.

But it wasn't the food that made the evening for John, good as it was. It was the fact that Darcie was civil to him, and everyone else at the table seemed amiable, too, as if taking their cue from her and her mother. He enjoyed listening to the conversation taking place around him.

"How did your first day as head operator go, Darcie?" Miss Waterford asked.

"I think I will have to grow into the job, Miss Olivia," Darcie answered. "I'm sure I'll never be as good a manager as Beth was, but I will try."

"How is Beth enjoying married life?" the other woman asked. "Have you seen her lately?"

Darcie smiled and nodded. "I saw her this afternoon. She is quite happy and not missing the telephone office at all."

"That's good," Miss Waterford replied.

"I think marriage agrees with her. She fairly glows from taking care of Jeb and the children. I'm so glad she and Jeb fell in love and can provide a family for his brother's children."

"I am so happy for them," Mrs. Malone said as she dished up apple cobbler for dessert. "The four of them make a beautiful family."

Mr. Carlton took a bite. "Mmm. This cobbler is delicious, Mrs. Malone."

"Thank you. The apples came from Beth and Jeb's orchard. The Winslow apples won first place at the fair last year. These are some of the last Beth brought us. I stored them in the cellar."

"Well, they deserved to win if they held up this long."

"Everything was wonderful, Mrs. Malone," John said.

"Thank you." She smiled. "I enjoy putting a good meal on the table."

"Well, that you do—each and every day," Mr. Mitchell said.

"Mama, have you talked to Alma Burton lately?"

John enjoyed the excuse to look at Darcie without appearing to be staring at her.

"Not in the last few days, dear. Why?"

"She rang through to talk to Doc today and didn't sound like herself. I hope she's all right."

Mrs. Malone's face clouded with concern. "So do I. I'll check on her tomorrow."

Darcie nodded. "Good. I worry about her."

"She needs to sell that house of hers and move in here. She's alone too much, and that isn't good for a body," Miss Waterford added.

"I think she hates to give up her home. She and her husband were very happy there, but I worry it's too much for her to keep up with, too." Mrs. Malone sighed.

"You know, she probably would enjoy living here if we could get her to try it," Darcie said. "I think she must get awful lonesome living by herself."

John was touched by their concern for their friend. As mother and daughter cleared the table and he excused himself from the room, he found himself wishing he could be included in the circle of people they cared about.

He returned from his nightly walk and went upstairs to his room; only then did he realize no one had asked about what he was doing in regard to his uncle's business. Was it because they didn't care or didn't want to know—or were afraid to find out?

The more he delved into his uncle's papers, the surer he was that it was one of the latter two possibilities. John sighed deeply. Well, they weren't alone in their fears. The more he found out about Douglas Harper's business practices, the more he feared what was to come. Soon he would have to talk to people in this town to find out if what he suspected about his uncle was true. He'd been praying he was wrong, but nothing he could find pointed in that direction. Nothing.

He couldn't change the past or what his uncle might have done to hurt the good people of Roswell. He could only hope to try to ease some of the pain, especially for the Malone family. Darcie must have had a reason for reacting so strongly that first night when she found out he was Douglas Harper's nephew. But he didn't know how to ask about it in a way that wouldn't upset her and her mother again.

John let out a deep breath and opened his Bible. He hoped that somehow, in researching his uncle's papers, he'd run across an explanation concerning Darcie's family. In the meantime, he'd gain strength from reading God's Word and go to Him in prayer for help in making things right. No matter how difficult that became or how long it took, he meant to keep looking to the Lord for guidance.

The next few days were a mixture of frustration and—something else Darcie couldn't quite name. Frustration because she couldn't stop her heart from beating faster each time she saw John Harper. Frustration because she found herself looking forward to seeing him each evening, then suddenly dreading it as she reminded herself he was the nephew of Douglas Harper—and the last person in the world she should be attracted to.

But charmed by him she was—and fighting it with every fiber of her being. Darcie entered the dining room and hurried toward the kitchen to help her mother. She tried to ignore her racing pulse as she recognized the deep timbre of his voice talking to one of the boarders in the front parlor. She released a deep breath when she stepped into the kitchen and placed her hand over her heart.

Her mother glanced up from the platter she was filling with fried chicken. "Darcie, dear, are you all right? You look a little flushed."

Darcie avoided meeting her mother's eyes. Instead she grabbed the bowls of mashed potatoes and cream gravy to carry to the dining room. "I'm fine, Mama. I've felt a bit rushed all day."

"Well, there's no hurry here, dear. I'm sure not one of our boarders will up and leave if supper is a little late getting to the table." She shed her apron and picked up the chicken platter.

"You're right about that." Darcie chuckled and shook her head. "They all know there isn't a better boardinghouse in town than Molly Malone's." She managed to give her mother a bright smile as they took the food to the dining room.

Her mother crossed to the hall and called her boarders to the table. Darcie greeted them as a group while they took their seats.

As he'd done each night since he'd come to her mother's establishment, John Harper held Darcie's chair for her and made sure she was comfortable before he took his seat. He had impeccable manners, which seemed to have a good influence on the other two gentlemen boarders. Darcie smiled as she watched Mr. Carlton extend the same courtesy to her mother while Mr. Mitchell did the same for Miss Olivia. The two men had been taking turns seating the two older women since Mr. Harper had started doing so his first night at the table.

After Mr. Carlton said the blessing, her mother passed the platters and bowls around the table while the others served themselves. When the dishes reached Darcie's end of the table, she handed them to John Harper. He always smiled when he thanked her, which made her catch her breath for a second, much to her exasperation. For then she sounded breathless as she answered, "You are welcome."

She was thankful for the temporary lull in conversation as everyone began to eat. She wondered if there was any way to persuade her mother to change the seating arrangements so she wasn't sitting so close to the man. Somehow she didn't think so. She was sure her mother would consider it rude, and Darcie knew it would be. But it was getting increasingly hard to ignore the way this man made her feel. He was so charming—so—

She took a sip of water and reminded herself his uncle had been engaging, too, when it suited his purpose. Perhaps that's what this man was doing. Her heart twisted in her chest at the thought he might be like his uncle.

"Darcie? Dear?"

Concern in her mother's voice brought Darcie out of her reverie. "I'm sorry, Mama. What were you saying?"

"I talked to Alma today. You were right to wonder about her health. She's not been feeling herself and went to Doc for a checkup." Her mother shook her head.

"What's wrong?" Darcie hoped it was nothing serious.

"It appears she's just getting over the influenza. Doc says she should have come to him earlier, and he doesn't want her to stay by herself until she's completely recovered."

"Oh, dear. What is she going to do?" Miss Olivia asked.

"I've convinced her to come stay here with us until she gets totally well."

"Influenza?" Mr. Carlton asked. "Isn't that contagious?"

"I talked to Doc about that, too. He says she weathered the worst of it by herself. She isn't contagious now," her mother reassured him. "We just feel it would be better for her to stay here so I can see she eats right and continues to recover."

"Well, I suppose that does make sense," Mr. Mitchell said.

"Of course it does," said Miss Olivia. "I'm sure it will do her good to be around other people, too. When will she be arriving?"

"Tomorrow. I'll prepare a room for her tonight—"

"If you need assistance getting her here, I'll be glad to help," John Harper said.

There he goes again, Darcie thought. *Being nice and sweet to my mother. Is it genuine, or is it an act?* She wished she knew.

"Why, Mr. Harper, how nice of you to offer. Thank you so much. But Doc said he would bring her over."

"I'll help get her room ready, Mama," Darcie said. "Do you think we can convince her to stay once she's better? I hate the thought of her being sick and alone. If she goes back, it could happen again."

"I know. And I'm hoping she'll decide to sell her house and stay with us."

Her mother smiled, then gazed around the table. "Mrs. Alma Burton is like family to Darcie and me. I hope you will help us make her feel at home here."

Darcie stifled a chuckle at her mother's directness. Put that way, they couldn't do much but agree.

"Of course, of course," Mr. Mitchell said, nodding.

"We'll do our best," Mr. Carlton said.

"Thank you," her mother said. "I feel much relieved that she'll be staying with us, and I intend to do all I can to convince her to stay."

"I'll strive to make her feel as welcome as you've made me feel, Molly," Miss Olivia assured her. "I'm sure it won't take long for her to decide to bask in your gentle care."

"Thank you for those kind words, Olivia. And thank you all for your support and loyalty," her mother added.

Once dinner was over, Darcie took over cleaning up the dining room and kitchen while her mother went upstairs to ready the room for Mrs. Alma. She suspected Miss Olivia would be keeping her mother company. She seemed glad they would have another woman boarder. Her mother had told her that sometimes Miss Olivia followed her around while she worked, talking the whole way. Darcie chuckled. She wondered how Mrs. Alma would take to Miss Olivia. And how they would all take to Mrs. Alma. She was a character and would liven up the dinner table once they got her on the road to recovery.

Mr. Carlton and Mr. Mitchell were already setting up their usual game of chess in the front parlor by the time she had cleared the table, and she supposed John had gone for his customary walk. As she plunged her hands in the hot water to wash the dishes, Darcie grudgingly admitted it had been nice of him to offer to help, and she could tell her mother had appreciated it. Could he be nothing like his uncle? Much as Darcie wished that to be true, she was afraid to hope it was. And what did it matter anyway? There was no way she could let herself care about someone related to the man she held accountable for her father's death. No way. No matter how fast her pulse raced at the sight of him.

After she'd dried the last dish and set the dining room table for the next morning, she went upstairs to see if she could help her mother. Much to Darcie's surprise, she found her mother directing John Harper on where to place a small settee that had been brought down from the attic.

"There—just center it in front of the window, please, John," her mother was saying.

"Oh, that looks very nice," Miss Olivia said from across the room.

John straightened the cream-colored settee and backed up. "It does look very nice there, Mrs. Malone. Much better than at the end of the bed, in my opinion."

Darcie noticed the bed had been moved, too. "Mama, I would have helped. Why didn't you call me?"

Her mother motioned her into the room. "I would have, dear. But Mr. Harper happened by before he went for a walk and kindly offered. His help has been invaluable, too."

Darcie looked around. Everything in the room seemed to be in a different spot. "I can see you've kept him busy."

Her mother chuckled and turned to John. "Yes, I have. Thank you so much."

"I was glad to help. Please feel free to call on me anytime. My mother loves to move furniture around, and my father hates to." He grinned. "Guess who gets to help her?"

"No wonder your suggestions were so helpful. Your mother sounds like a woman after my own heart."

"You do remind me of her. I think that's why I'm so happy to be staying here."

"Why, what a nice thing to say, John."

John nodded and grinned. "I meant it."

"I've taken up enough of your time tonight. You go on ahead with your walk."

"Are you sure everything is where you want it?"

"I think the room looks lovely, don't you, Darcie?"

Darcie had thought it was fine the way it was before, but it did look more inviting like this. The settee, a table, and a matching chair had been grouped closer to the fireplace to form a nice sitting area for Mrs. Alma. The four-poster bed had been turned to face the window. And another chair had been placed beside a bedside table. It seemed cozy, and she was sure Mrs. Alma would enjoy it. And she did appreciate John Harper's helping her mother, despite the fact she didn't want to feel beholden to him in any way.

"It looks wonderful, Mama. I'm sure Mrs. Alma is going to love it." She paused a moment before turning to John. "Thank you for helping my mother, Mr. Harper."

He smiled. "Glad to do it." He nodded to her mother. "Call on me anytime, Mrs. Malone. If the furniture is as you want it and you're sure you no longer need my help, I'll go for my walk now."

"You go on. I think Alma will be happy here. Thank you again."

"You're welcome." He paused at the door and turned back. "Good evening, ladies."

John looked in on the chess game for a few minutes before starting out. Mr. Carlton was winning at the moment, but Mr. Mitchell assured John he'd be ahead before long. Chuckling at the two men's banter, John bid them good evening, too, and headed toward Main Street.

All in all it had been a pretty good night. He was glad he'd been able to help Mrs. Malone, even though he could tell Darcie wasn't thrilled about it. She still wasn't happy about his staying in her home, but he was sure that, for her mother's sake, she would continue to try to make the best of it. John admired her greatly for putting her mother's wishes before her own.

He must find out the truth about what his uncle had done to hurt the Malones. Perhaps not yet. But soon he had to know.

Chapter 6

Mrs. Alma Burton moved to the boardinghouse the next day, and Darcie and her mother were much relieved to have her there. Although only in her sixties, her illness had taken a toll and seemed to have aged her, and they were determined to help her return to the feisty woman they loved.

Her mother seated her directly across from John and on Darcie's left side. It was Darcie's job to make sure the older woman ate enough. The other boarders tried to make her feel welcome, and Mrs. Alma perked up a little with their attention.

Her soft, graying hair was done up in a bun and her blue eyes were bright as she listened to the conversations at the table. Darcie knew her well enough to know Mrs. Alma loved people and little escaped her notice. She was acquainted with the older boarders as she'd taken a Sunday meal with the Malones from time to time, so it seemed natural for her to study John.

Darcie was sure she'd have something to say about him once he was out of earshot. Once the meal was over and the gentlemen left the room, Mrs. Alma scorned the suggestion that her mother help her upstairs; instead she insisted on staying downstairs.

~

Miss Olivia was delighted to have Alma Burton in the house and offered to show her the parlors and help her upstairs if she tired out.

"Thank you, Olivia, but I've been coming to the Malone home since before it was a boardinghouse. I know where the parlors are. And if I should need help getting upstairs, I'll be sure to ask," she said matter-of-factly.

Miss Olivia appeared about to cry. "Oh, I'm sorry, Mrs. Alma. I was just trying—"

"To be nice, I know. I understand, and I do thank you." Mrs. Alma nodded. "Guess I'm too independent at times. I didn't mean to hurt your feelings. I'll come sit a spell in the parlor with you."

Mollified, Miss Olivia quickly agreed.

"Would you like me to bring down your knitting, Alma?" Darcie's mother asked. Anyone acquainted with Alma Burton knew she liked to keep her hands busy with quilting, knitting, or tatting.

"I'll be glad to go get it for you," Miss Olivia offered.

This time Mrs. Alma agreed. "That would be good of you."

"I'll run upstairs and then meet you in the front parlor." Miss Olivia smiled sweetly at the older woman and hurried up the stairs.

"She's a nice woman, Alma. She just gets a little lonesome at times and needs some woman talk."

"I can see that, Molly. That's why you asked me to stay—to give your ear a break?" She smiled. Then, sure as Darcie had been expecting her to, she brought up John Harper. "Or are you trying to fix me up with that handsome new boarder of yours? He's a little young for me, you know. But he'd be just right for Darcie."

"Mrs. Alma!" Darcie could feel the heat rising in her cheeks and was thankful no other boarders were left at the table, especially John.

Her mother shook her head at her good friend. "Alma Burton, what are we going do with you?"

"Still and all, it's a thought," Mrs. Alma said, chuckling as she headed toward the front parlor.

And it was a thought so outrageous even Darcie had to chuckle as she began to clear the table. It might take awhile for the boarders to get used to the older woman, but she had a heart of gold and wouldn't intentionally hurt anyone. She just had a habit of saying what she thought. But she was way off in her thinking tonight. John Harper would be the last man her mother would try to fix her up with. The very last one.

~

The next day was Sunday, and John did as he would at home. After Mrs. Malone's self-serve breakfast on the sideboard—she had made it clear she felt her place was in the Lord's house on Sunday—he put on the coat to his best suit, then set out for church.

He'd asked Elmer about churches in town and was pleased to find one was located only a few blocks from the boardinghouse. He enjoyed the brisk walk to the small white building. The church was not as large as the one he attended at home, but it didn't matter. It felt good to sing God's praise and hear a message from His Word. Of course, several people turned their heads when they saw him, while others nudged the person they were sitting next to and whispered. He had no doubt he was the topic of conversation and that whatever was being said about him wasn't favorable.

Deep down he sensed they weren't reacting to him personally; they didn't even know him. But they'd known his uncle, and because of him and his actions, they didn't trust John.

He couldn't blame them. He just wished he didn't have to deal with it. But he did—not only for his sake, but also for the sake of his family's name. So he would do the best he could to bring honor back to his family name in the town.

John forced his attention back to the sermon and the message of 2 Timothy about fighting a good fight, staying the course, and keeping the faith. It was a lesson he needed to hear. Perhaps God was encouraging him to stay here and do what was needed. And he would—with His help.

Near the end of the service, he spotted Darcie, her mother, and Alma Burton in a pew a few rows in front of him. He couldn't explain the pleasure he felt seeing them there. Even though they were barely more than acquaintances, he suddenly felt as if he'd found long lost friends. Even if they were suspicious of his actions because of his uncle, at least they were civil to him.

Once the closing prayer was said, he stepped into the aisle. He planned to wait for the Malones and walk out with them. But he couldn't help hearing what people up the aisle from him were saying.

"Can you believe it? Douglas Harper's nephew is here in our church. How does he have the nerve?" one woman whispered loudly.

"Wonder what he's up to?" the woman at her side asked.

"Probably here to collect the debts owed to his uncle."

"Humph! Well, he'd better not come around my house. Harold will pull out his shotgun!"

With that, they swept past him and down the aisle.

John took a deep breath. It seemed each day, even on Sunday, he was to be reminded of how much the townspeople disliked Douglas Harper. He shook his head in bewilderment. How his uncle could have been so opposite from his father was beyond him. It was becoming obvious to him that no two brothers could be any more different.

He turned to go. He wasn't sure he was good company right now. Distracted, he almost missed the minister's greeting.

"Mr. Harper, isn't it?" The man held out his hand.

"Yes. John Harper," he said, shaking the older man's hand.

"I'm Minister Turley. Welcome to Roswell."

Taken aback by the sincerity in the minister's voice, John could only say, "Thank you." But he felt compelled to add, "I'm Douglas Harper's nephew."

Minister Turley nodded. "Yes, I thought so. I heard you were in town."

"Did he attend church here?"

The minister shook his head. "No. I don't know that Harper attended any church regularly."

John shrugged. "I didn't know my uncle well at all—and I—"

"I understand, son." Minister Turley clapped his hand to his shoulder. "I think you have a hard job ahead of you. But the fact you're here today tells me you know whom to turn to when life gets tough."

"I do." John smiled at the man and felt connected by their mutual faith in God.

"I look forward to seeing you next week," Minister Turley said.

"I'll be here." His faith strengthened by Minister Turley's lesson and welcome, John changed his mind about leaving right away. He walked down the church steps and stood under a huge cottonwood to wait for the Malone women and Mrs. Burton.

He watched the minister greet them. Darcie's smile was contagious as she responded to something the minister said to her, and John wished she'd smile at him that way, just once. Well, no. To be honest, he wished she'd smile at him like that all the time. But somehow the shine in her eyes seemed to dim when she caught sight of him, and he didn't know how to change it. For the first time in his life, he wished his last name was anything but Harper.

"John!" Mrs. Malone said as they strolled toward him. "If I'd known you were coming to church, we'd have waited and walked with you."

"I'd have been honored to escort you ladies to church. I hope you'll let me see you back home?"

"Of course," Mrs. Malone said, falling in step beside Mrs. Burton and leaving Darcie no choice but to walk beside him.

"How did you like Minister Turley's sermon today?" Mrs. Malone asked.

"He's a very good preacher. I look forward to hearing him again." *And, Lord, I'll try to keep my mind on the message instead of worrying about what everyone is saying about me.*

Darcie looked as fresh as the spring day in her green and white striped dress. In the sunlight, her eyes seemed even greener. Her auburn hair was pulled on top of her head and topped by a hat that matched her dress. John couldn't deny he was attracted to this woman—even though he was probably the last man on earth she'd ever let court her.

Court her? Now where did that come from? He was here to settle his uncle's estate. His family expected him home as soon as he'd finished. He had no business thinking of courting Miss Darcie Malone. None at all.

"Mr. Harper?"

"I'm sorry, Mrs. Malone. I must have been woolgathering—" John paused. No way could he tell her he was thinking about her daughter.

"You have spring fever," Mrs. Burton said all of a sudden, saving him from having to finish his sentence.

"Beg pardon?"

"You know, a young man's fancy turns to love in the spring."

"No, ma'am, I didn't know that." He felt his face grow warm, then glanced at Darcie to see a soft pink color rising on her cheeks.

"Alma!" Mrs. Malone chuckled and shook her head. "Don't mind Mrs. Burton, John. She's just teasing you. I was asking if you like ice cream."

"Oh yes, ma'am, I do."

"Good. I hope you won't mind taking a turn cranking our churn today. It's such a beautiful warm day—I think ice cream will make a good dessert. You men can take care of that while Darcie and I set out Sunday dinner."

"I'd be glad to help." He'd been debating whether or not to look through some of his uncle's papers he'd brought home the night before, but making ice cream sounded a lot more relaxing.

"I think I'd like some ice cream, too," Mrs. Burton said.

"I was hoping you'd say that, Alma. Doc says we need to fatten you up a little. I thought your favorite dessert might help."

As Darcie helped her mother set out the meal, she was keenly aware of the men outside the back door, cranking the ice cream freezer. Well, of John Harper in particular. He was always eager to lend a hand if asked. In truth, he seemed nothing like his uncle, but still Darcie didn't trust him. Couldn't let herself even begin to.

When the telephone rang four quick rings and one long one for their special ring, she hurried to answer it. They didn't get many calls this time of day on Sunday.

"Darcie?"

"Beth! How good to hear from you. Have you finished your dinner already?" She and Beth tried to talk every few days; if they were too busy during the week, however, they made a point to telephone late Sunday afternoon.

"No, Emma invited us to have dinner at her place. And since we were going to be in town later than usual, I thought I'd see if you'd like to come back to the ranch with us for a while. You should have time to finish helping your mother with everything."

"Oh, Beth, I'd love to, but—"

"Jeb said he'd bring you home in time to help with supper. You haven't been out in a long time, and I wanted to show you some of the things we've done to the house—"

"Who is it, dear?" her mother asked then.

"Excuse me a minute, Beth. Mama is talking to me," Darcie said into the mouthpiece and turned to answer her mother. "It's Beth. She and Jeb and the children are in town and want me to go back out to the ranch with—"

"Oh, how nice. You could use a break. You go right ahead, dear. I can manage here."

"Oh, I'll finish helping with dinner and be back in time to help with supper, Mother. But—"

Her mother surprised her by taking the earpiece out of her hand and nudging her away from the telephone. "Beth, what time are you going back to the ranch?"

She listened and nodded at whatever Beth was saying. "She'll be ready in an hour. I'll see to it. And thank you, dear. I think spending an afternoon with you and your family is just what she needs."

Darcie watched as her mother hung the earpiece back onto the telephone. It seemed the matter had been taken out of her hands. How nice it would be to go out to the ranch for the afternoon—rather than having to spend it trying not to run into or away from John Harper.

She and her mother finished setting the dinner dishes on the table and called in the boarders.

"Good timing, Mrs. Malone," Mr. Mitchell said. "That ice cream is frozen hard as a rock. By the time we finish eating, it should be just about right."

Darcie paid little attention to the dinner conversation. Her mind was on finishing the meal in time to freshen up before going out to the Winslow ranch. *What a luxury to go.* Normally she helped around the house in any way she could on the weekends, and she felt bad about leaving, even though her mother was always trying to persuade her to get out more. It didn't feel right to leave her. She glanced down the table, and her mother smiled at her, reassuring her she was happy her daughter was going out, so Darcie decided to feel good about it, too.

She passed on the ice cream so she could wash the major portion of the dishes before leaving. As she hurried up the back stairs, she heard her mother telling the boarders she was taking a much-needed break for the afternoon.

A few minutes later, she came back downstairs to tell her mother good-bye and go out onto the front porch to wait for the Winslows. She was surprised to find Miss Olivia helping with the dishes and Mrs. Alma having a second bowl of ice cream at the kitchen table.

"Why, how nice of you ladies to help Mama and keep her company in the kitchen!"

"I've told Molly I don't mind helping out around here. And I mean it. It's the least I can do when she's provided me a home."

"You pay me for room and board, Olivia. It's very nice of you to help out so Darcie won't feel guilty for spending an afternoon with friends."

"Molly, I've lived in other boardinghouses, but I've never felt I had a home until now. You can't put a price on that. As I said, I'm glad to help anytime," Miss Olivia said, drying an ice cream dish.

"What she says is true, Molly." Mrs. Alma added her two cents. "Besides, haven't you been telling me how I need to learn to accept help gracefully?"

Darcie's mother quirked an eyebrow in Mrs. Alma's direction before laughing. "Yes, I have. Guess I need to learn that same lesson, Alma. And, Olivia, thank you for helping me."

"Yes, thank you!" Darcie added. "I feel much better about going off for a few hours now."

"You are both welcome. Actually I think I should be thanking you. It makes me feel part of the family."

Darcie's mother laughed. "Well, I guess we'll have to see what more we can find for you to do around here. I sure like to have my boarders feel at home."

The women's laughter warmed Darcie's heart, and she felt easier about leaving. But then she looked out back and saw John putting the clean ice-cream freezer together and the other men setting out wickets for a game of croquet in the yard. She almost wished she were staying home. Almost.

Chapter 7

Darcie fully enjoyed her afternoon at Beth and Jeb's. It was a beautiful April day, warm enough and sunny, without a cloud in the sky. Cassie and Lucas, Jeb's niece and nephew whom he and Beth were raising, couldn't wait to show her the new litter of kittens out in the barn. And they were adorable. Playful calicos, they were hard to resist picking up and cuddling.

Next they visited the apple orchard that would soon be bursting with blooms and the new garden the children had helped Beth plant. They came up with so many things for Darcie to see and do until Jeb decided to take Cassie and Lucas to play with Cal and Liddy McAllister's four children, Grace, Amy, Matthew, and Marcus, at their nearby farm. That way Darcie and Beth could have a good visit by themselves.

Beth made them a pot of tea and brought out some cookies. Her kitchen was light, bright, and cozy, and she had a range that was big enough for the nicest of restaurants. Darcie's mother would have loved it, and she figured that even Emma would be envious of its size. When she commented on it, Beth giggled.

"It is much larger than it looked in the Sears and Roebuck catalogue. Cal and Matt installed it while Jeb's arm was broken. They said they nearly didn't get it in here. Emma has ordered one like it for the café. I'm sure she's going to like it as much as I do!"

Beth fairly glowed as she poured their tea. Marriage certainly seemed to agree with her. "I've never seen you this blissful, Beth. I'm so glad you accepted Jeb's proposal."

"Thank you. I've never been happier. But I didn't ask you to come out here to talk about me. I thought maybe you needed to get out of the house for a while—with John Harper there and all."

"Thank you, Beth. I think it's just what I needed."

"How are things going at home—with him being around all the time?"

Darcie knew Beth was truly concerned for her so she answered honestly. "It's—a little strained, but not quite as bad as I thought it might be. He's very considerate of Mama, and that helps somewhat."

"And makes it tougher in other ways?" Beth asked.

Her friend always had been able to figure out when Darcie wasn't telling everything. But she wasn't ready to get into how confused she was about the contradicting feelings she had for John Harper—at least not now. So all she said was, "Somewhat."

She was thankful when Beth didn't press her anymore and changed the subject. "Well, I'm glad you came out this afternoon. I've wanted you to see what we've done to the house since your last visit. Come on upstairs, and I'll show you the changes we've made there."

As they walked through the dining room and then the parlor on their way upstairs, Darcie was impressed with how beautiful the house had become with their hard work. When Jeb Winslow came to Roswell to raise his deceased brother's children, the house was in an awful state of disrepair. But he'd done a wonderful job of refurbishing it and making it into a showplace. Beth had added her homey touches, and now it was warm and welcoming.

"You know Jeb had finished the major work when we got married, but since he left most of the decorating to me, I let the children pick out the wallpaper for their rooms. We went through so many sample books that I thought they would never decide on anything." Beth led Darcie upstairs to the bedroom at the end of the hall. "But Jeb and I are pleased with their choices."

Darcie had to agree. For her room, Cassie had chosen a white background with pink roses climbing up green vines. A white coverlet and pink curtains at the windows complemented the paper.

In the room across the hall, Lucas had decided on blue and cream stripes, with a blue comforter and cream curtains.

"They have very good taste, Beth. Their rooms are lovely."

"I agree—I would have chosen the exact same papers for them." She motioned for Darcie to join her in the hall. "Come and see our room."

Darcie followed her down the hall to a larger room at the other end. It was papered in a burgundy and cream stripe, and Beth had made draperies out of burgundy and trimmed them in cream fringe. They were tied back with cream tassels.

The bedroom suite was of oak—all matching pieces. Darcie thought she recognized it as one of the newer styles from the Sears and Roebuck catalogue.

"Oh, this is very nice, Beth," she said. "And your matching dressing table is beautiful."

"Jeb ordered that for me for my birthday. It was too extravagant, but I do enjoy it so!"

Darcie tried not to feel envious, but the sudden longing she felt for a home and family of her own—a husband who cared that much for her—made it hard. And seeing the next room only made it worse.

The small room adjacent to Beth and Jeb's sparkled in sunny yellow. Beth's sewing machine occupied one corner, and across the room stood a beautiful crib.

White curtains hung at the windows, and a white and yellow patchwork quilt covered the feather mattress in the bed.

"Beth?" Darcie whirled to see a grin on her friend's face. "Are you expecting?"

Her friend's joyful laughter and nod answered her question, and Darcie couldn't help but be thrilled for her. "Oh, Beth, that is wonderful! When are you—?"

"In the fall. September, Doc says. Jeb and the children are so excited. And he takes such good care of me."

Darcie sighed. She'd love to be even half as happy one day as Beth looked, with an adoring husband and a baby on the way. Thoughts of a tall young man with brown hair and brown eyes crossed her mind, and he looked a lot like John Harper—Darcie jerked herself out of her reverie. What was she thinking?

She tried to concentrate on Beth's joy as she hugged her. "I am so happy for you! Let's go have another cup of tea and some cookies to celebrate your news!" She had to get out of this room and away from the longing for a home and family of her own. Her life was laid out for her at the moment, and the only man who came to mind was the last man she had any business thinking about.

The afternoon had passed pleasantly enough, but John kept watching for Darcie to return while trying not to be obvious about it. It was near suppertime, and the other women were in the kitchen helping Mrs. Malone put together the meal when she came back.

He'd just picked up the Sunday paper from the front parlor and was going to sit on the front porch and read it until Mrs. Malone called them to the table. Even though he'd been waiting for Darcie, he was taken aback at the sudden leap his heart took at the sight of her coming up the porch steps.

It was getting harder to dismiss the effect she had on him, and he wasn't sure what to do about it. For the moment, he chose to ignore it.

He opened the screen door. "Good evening, Miss Darcie."

"Good evening." She entered the foyer and seemed a little surprised he was opening the door for her.

"I trust you had a good afternoon." He hoped she wouldn't brush by him.

His unspoken prayer was answered as she paused and turned toward him. "It was a lovely afternoon. How was the croquet game?"

John chuckled. "Your mother beat the lot of us."

"She did?" Darcie chuckled and clasped her hands together.

"Twice. But she was very gracious at it."

Darcie smiled, and John wondered if she had any idea how beautiful she was. Somehow he didn't think so.

"Mama is the most gracious woman I know. I'm so glad she had a nice afternoon, too. I'd better go see if I can help her."

John watched her head for the kitchen and was bemused when she turned back. "Thank you for helping Mama have a pleasant afternoon, too."

"I—you're welcome." Surprised by her comment and that they'd almost carried on a conversation away from the dinner table, John wasn't sure what to say next. But Darcie disappeared into the dining room before he could think of a way to keep her talking.

Could she be changing? No. He'd better not read anything into her good manners. A few kind words from her did not mean she'd changed her initial opinion of him, and he'd do well to remember that fact. He found reason to remind himself of that thought several times in the next hour.

Mrs. Malone called everyone in for a supper of thick sandwiches made from the ham left over from their noon meal. They'd finished off the ice cream that afternoon, but she brought out some cookies she'd made the day before.

Everyone wanted to know how Darcie spent her afternoon, so she entertained them with stories of kittens, the orchard, and the changes Beth and Jeb had made to the house. Then she seemed to get a wistful look in her eyes.

"Beth is expecting a baby in the fall."

"Oh, how marvelous!" Miss Olivia exclaimed.

"Doesn't surprise me," Mrs. Alma added.

Mrs. Malone smiled from her place at the other end of the table. "I am so happy for the Winslows. And how nice that Emma's baby will have someone to play with, too."

Darcie nodded but didn't comment.

"It's 'bout time you found someone and married and had a family yourself, Darcie," Mrs. Alma said.

John heard Darcie's quick intake of breath before she answered the older woman.

"Mrs. Alma, I don't have time to find anyone right now. And besides—"

"Why, that's nonsense. You have plenty of opportunity right here—"

"Alma," Mrs. Malone interrupted. "I'm sure when the time is right, Darcie won't have to find anyone. He'll find her."

That seemed to satisfy Mrs. Burton. Or seeing the delicate shade of rose Darcie's cheeks had turned made her realize she might have caused the young woman discomfort with her remarks. "Of course he will," she quickly agreed, then popped a cookie in her mouth and nodded as if to reinforce her words.

"Wonder what the baby will be," Miss Olivia mused out loud.

"It won't matter once it gets here. Whatever it is—boy or girl—it will be exactly what they wanted, I expect," Mrs. Malone said. "I wish I'd had more children. I fear Darcie is too concerned about my welfare—"

"Mama, that is not the case. How could I be too concerned when you were left a widow and we lost near everything Papa worked so hard for—" Darcie clamped her mouth shut and sent a glance in John's direction that chilled him clear through.

There it was again—that thing in the past that caused her to dislike someone with Harper for a last name. He sighed inwardly. He had to find out what it was.

Darcie pushed back her chair and stood. "Would any of you like another cup of coffee?"

"No, thank you, I've had my limit." Mr. Carlton shook his head.

"None for me, either," Mr. Mitchell added.

The ladies shook their heads.

"I'll start cleaning the kitchen then, if you'll excuse me?"

"Of course," Mr. Carlton and Mr. Mitchell said at once.

"I'll be glad to help you," Miss Olivia said.

Darcie smiled at the other woman. "No, thank you. You helped in my absence. Thank you—and you, too, Mrs. Alma—for taking my place this afternoon."

With that, she grabbed several empty plates along with her own and hurried to the kitchen.

Earlier in the foyer, for a moment, John had let himself hope Darcie's opinion of him was changing or at least beginning to. But after the look she just shot him, he had a sinking feeling that if it had, it wasn't for the better.

Darcie couldn't get to the kitchen fast enough. All that talk at the table of her finding someone and starting a family of her own—when that's what she'd thought about all afternoon. Then to realize the only someone who came to mind was John Harper!

She plunged her hands into the dishwater and began to wash in earnest, shaking her head at the very thought. Well, she wouldn't let her heart go in that direction. Couldn't—

"Darcie, dear. I'm sorry. I didn't mean to upset you," her mother said upon entering the kitchen. "I shouldn't have voiced my thoughts out loud. Please forgive me for making you feel uncomfortable."

"It's all right, Mama. I know you didn't mean to. And I'm sorry if I embarrassed you again. But you must know I'm not looking for anyone. My life—our lives—are too busy to concern myself with—"

Her mother put her hands on Darcie's shoulders and turned her around. "We need to talk, dear." She took the dishrag from her hands and gave her a towel to dry them. "Come and sit down for a minute, Darcie."

From past experience Darcie knew when her mother said, "We need to talk," she meant just that, and she wouldn't let the subject rest until they did. She took a seat at the kitchen table.

Her mother poured them both a cup of coffee. It wouldn't matter if they didn't drink it; it was her custom to talk over a coffee cup. Darcie waited and watched while her mother added a dollop of cream and a teaspoon of sugar to each cup, a sure sign she was concerned or upset. She took her coffee black.

"Mama, you—"

"Please let me speak, Darcie. This has been bothering me for some time now, and I haven't been sure how to broach the subject with you. But tonight you've given me the perfect opportunity."

"But—"

"Darcie." Her mother's raised eyebrow told her to clamp her mouth shut for the moment. She sighed deeply before continuing. "Darcie, you are a wonderful daughter. I couldn't ask for a better one. But I do not expect you to put your life on hold for me. I never have. And it would break your papa's heart to know you are doing that."

She picked up her cup as if to take a drink but only held it with both hands, looking over the rim at Darcie as she kept talking. "You deserve to have the kind of life your friends have. A home and a family of your own to love. I want that for you. Your papa wanted that for you."

"But, Mama, I—"

"I'm not through." Her eyebrow arched again, and she returned her cup to her saucer without taking a sip. "What happened to your papa was awful. Not a day goes by that I don't miss him. I know you do, too. But he would want us to get on with our lives, and he'd be proud of how we've done it, Darcie. We count on the Lord to guide us through each day and aren't beholden to anyone but Him for our living."

Darcie briefly acknowledged she wasn't as good at leaving things in the Lord's hands as her mother was. She needed to do better.

"We can't undo the past," her mother continued. "We can only make the best of our future with the Lord's help. And I want your future to include time with your friends without worrying about me—and a family of your own. And I'd like my future to include grandchildren."

Tears sprang to Darcie's eyes. She wanted those same things. But just wanting them wouldn't bring them about.

"Mama, I know you want that for me, but there is no one—"

"Maybe not right now. But there will be. And when that time comes, I don't want you running away from it because you think you must take care of me. Promise me you won't do that, Darcie."

As any chance of that happening seemed remote, Darcie felt safe in answering her mother. "I promise."

Her mother sighed and leaned back in her chair. "Good. Because the best way you could take care of me would be to provide me with a son-in-law and a passel of grandchildren to love. Maybe one or two who look like your papa."

"Mama. What am I going to do with you!" Darcie could feel the heat steal up her face. She wanted those very same things—more with each passing year. But that was in the Lord's hands.

"You're going to take my advice to heart and quit feeling so responsible for me." As if that was her final word on the subject, her mother finally took a drink of coffee.

Darcie tried not to giggle at the look on her mother's face. But when she stared into her cup, as if trying to figure out how the sugar and cream got there, Darcie could no longer keep from laughing.

"You could have told me," her mother said.

Darcie raised her eyebrow. "I believe I tried to."

Her mother opened her mouth and closed it, then opened it again. "Oh. I guess you did."

She laughed, and Darcie joined her. Shortly their shared laughter filled the kitchen. Darcie was thankful it dissolved some of the earlier tension and ended a very touchy conversation—at least for that night.

Chapter 8

Darcie spent the next few days trying to ignore her growing interest in John Harper. But it wasn't easy to do. Ever since the Sunday night he'd greeted her at the door when she came home from the Winslows', her heart went into skittish little spasms each time she saw him.

She didn't know if it was because he was the one person who came to mind when she let herself think of a romantic future. Or if it was the dinner conversation that night when she'd looked at him and realized he'd been in her thoughts off and on all day. And he had rarely been out of them since.

Being at work didn't help, either. Word was getting around it was indeed Douglas Harper's nephew who was seen going in and out of his uncle's old bank. And he was staying at Malone's Boardinghouse.

If Darcie was asked one question a day, it seemed she was asked at least twenty.

From Doc Bradshaw's wife, Myrtle, "Wonder what he's doing here. Do you know, Darcie?"

"He says he's here to settle his uncle's estate, Mrs. Doc. All I know is he works over at the bank most of the day."

"Well, I sure hope he's not going to cause problems for folks around here."

"So do I."

From Nelda Harrison later that afternoon, "Why is he staying at your mother's boardinghouse of all places, Darcie?"

"I don't know why he picked it, Mrs. Harrison." *And I wish he never had.*

"Isn't it a little uncomfortable to have him there?"

That was an understatement if Darcie ever heard one. "A little."

"Well, dear, what in the world was your mother thinking when she rented a room to him?"

Loyalty to her mother had Darcie taking up for her. "She didn't know who he was. Lots of people have that last name, Mrs. Harrison. They aren't all related to Douglas Harper."

"Of course not. I'm sorry, dear. I know your mother couldn't have known who he was when she let him have a room."

And on and on it went, from first one and then another person.

Beatrice Ferguson asked, "Is he going to reopen the bank?"

"I don't have any idea, Mrs. Ferguson."

"Will he be trying to collect outstanding loans?" Iris McDonald wondered.

"I don't know, Mrs. McDonald." Darcie shook her head. She wished she did know. While she prayed she was wrong, that was exactly what she was afraid he might do.

The next day it would start over again, different people, same questions. The questions everyone raised served to keep her own doubts about him foremost in her thoughts. They reminded her this man she'd been dreaming about at night was Douglas Harper's nephew. And that was one fact she couldn't ignore. One she was determined not to let herself forget—no matter how much she might want to.

By Friday she was sick and tired of answering questions while trying not to voice her opinion about John Harper. When Emma called later in the day, it was as if she could tell Darcie was on edge.

"Darcie, are you having a rough day?"

"It'd be better if everyone in Roswell didn't keep asking questions about John Harper. Word has gotten out that he's here, and a lot of people are holding their breath, waiting to see what he's going to do. They seem to think I should know everything, and then I have to go home and—"

"Put up with him there. I'm so sorry."

"No, I'm sorry. I shouldn't be whining about it. Who can I connect you to, Em?"

"I'd like to talk to Liddy, but I'd like to see you, too. Why don't you stop by for some tea on your way home?"

Darcie hesitated only a minute. Her mother had made it plain she wanted her to have a life and spend time with her friends. And besides, she'd be home in plenty of time to help with dinner. "That sounds wonderful, Em—just what I need. I'll be there right after four."

"Good. See you then!"

Darcie connected Emma's line pin to the McAllisters' and sent up a quick prayer of thankfulness for her friends. After telephoning her mother to let her know she'd be a little late, she found herself looking forward to having that cup of tea with Emma.

John felt only frustration. He could find nothing pertaining to the Malones in his uncle's papers. Of course he wasn't halfway finished looking through the files. It could take days, weeks, or even longer to go through them.

Elmer was a great help; but he'd only represented his uncle at his trial, and that was because he'd had to. Then he had become trustee of Douglas Harper's money and written the will leaving everything to John. Other than that, Elmer knew no more than John did about his uncle's business dealings—except that he'd treated a lot of the citizens of Roswell and the surrounding area badly, and that was common knowledge.

But finding actual evidence of that was not easy. Douglas Harper had his own system for keeping track of his affairs, and it was more than a little confusing to the two men trying to figure it out. John had found records of several foreclosures that seemed legitimate. Then he ran across an entry that included a note not to extend credit anymore, but it seemed the person had been making all their payments on time. Trying to decipher his uncle's bookkeeping system, along with his handwriting, was proving to be a challenge.

By the time he'd put in a full day at the bank, he was ready to leave and go back to the boardinghouse. But, as the week progressed, being at the boardinghouse left him no less exasperated. Darcie was apparently going out of her way to steer clear of him except at the dinner table, and then she seemed to avoid talking directly to him. Yet she listened when he talked to the others. And every once in a while, he found her gaze on him. But the moment she realized he'd caught her looking his way, she would glance away, a delicate pink drifting up her cheeks.

He thought back to the first night before she found out he was related to Douglas Harper. He'd felt then that she'd been as interested in him as he had been in her. But connecting him to his uncle had put an end to any attraction she might have felt toward him. John wished it had done the same for his interest in her.

Instead it seemed to grow with each passing day. The way she came in from work and immediately began helping her mother, her tender concern for Mrs. Burton, and her consideration for her mother's boarders—even though he was sure she didn't like her home being let out to strangers—all of that made his opinion of her rise continuously.

She was even civil to him despite the fact he knew she wished he would find accommodations elsewhere. And perhaps he should. But he couldn't bring himself to look for another place to stay. He didn't want to.

He was probably as comfortable here as he would be anywhere in this town. Most likely more so. For the most part, the other boarders seemed to have accepted him—probably because of Mrs. Malone's example to them. And he'd learned the two gentlemen had not lived in the area when his uncle had been conducting business here, so they didn't seem to have a built-in resentment toward a relation of Douglas Harper. Still, they'd heard rumors, he was sure, and they were loyal to the Malones. One wrong move on his part, and Mitchell and Carlton would have no qualms about seeing him to the door. But as long as Molly Malone let him reside in her home, that was where he would stay.

And no telling how long that will be, no more progress than we've made, John thought, as he sat at his uncle's desk in the bank. He expelled a deep breath and pulled another pile of papers toward him.

Darcie was pleased to find that both Liddy and Beth had come into town to have tea with her and Emma again. They went up to Emma and Matt's apartment above the café, where the children could play and the customers wouldn't be disturbed. She was the first topic of conversation.

"You sounded so tired this afternoon, Darcie. Are you all right?" Emma asked.

She sighed and smiled at her dear friends. "I'm fine. It's just that I've been answering questions about John Harper all week. The whole town seems to know he's here, and they—"

"It doesn't take long for that kind of news to spread," Liddy said. "Why, I've even mentioned it to one or two people."

"So have I," Emma said. "Douglas Harper caused enough trouble in this town. If there is to be any more, they need to be warned."

Honest with herself, Darcie realized she probably had a bigger part than anyone in getting the word out. She'd mentioned it to several people the week before, and Jessica had mentioned it to even more. That was all it took to get the news spreading, especially with the telephone growing in use each day.

"And they all want to know why he's here, I'm sure," Liddy said.

"Well, he's only saying he's here to settle his uncle's estate." For a moment Darcie wondered if she'd have found out more if she hadn't thrown such a fit that first night.

"It would be nice if we knew what that meant," Emma said.

With no answers available, the other women nodded in agreement.

"Well, how are things going at home, Darcie?" Liddy asked.

"He's very considerate of Mama," she answered truthfully. Actually he was thoughtful of everyone, even her. No matter how cool she was to him or how hard she tried to ignore him, he was always pleasant to her.

Beth came to her aid. "It's still stressful for you having him there, isn't it?"

In more ways than one. Her confused feelings about the man were wearing her out. "Oh, yes, it is. I think I'll be glad when he settles things and is on his way home."

But once the words were out of her mouth, she realized they might not be true. More confusion. She sighed deeply and took a drink of tea.

Beth patted her hand while Liddy and Emma nodded.

Feeling the need to change the subject, Darcie prodded Beth to tell the others her news. Liddy and Emma jumped up to hug and congratulate the new mother-to-be, and the next few minutes were taken up discussing babies and growing families.

"At least you have a home large enough for your growing family," Emma said to Beth. "I don't know what Matt and I are going to do. We definitely need a bigger place."

"What will you do with the apartment?" Liddy asked.

"Well, as you might have noticed, Ben has taken on more and more of the management of the café. He's been my helper since I first opened the café, and Matt and I feel his loyalty deserves to be rewarded. We're going to offer it to him if we ever find a place." Emma sighed and shook her head.

"Mrs. Alma's place would be perfect for you if she'd sell it," Darcie said.

"Oh, that's right. She's staying at the boardinghouse, isn't she?" Beth asked.

"Until she recuperates from the influenza. We've been hoping she might decide to stay with us permanently. Her house is much too big for her to take care of now. But—"

"She does love that place. I don't know if she'd ever be willing to sell it." Emma shook her head and looked wistful. "But it would be perfect. I've always loved that place, and it's only a couple of blocks from here."

"Perhaps I can try to see how she'd feel about selling. We haven't actually broached the subject of her staying with us yet." It might well be the answer to keeping Mrs. Alma at the boardinghouse so they could look after her without her knowing that's what they were doing. She was such an independent woman that they didn't dare let her think she couldn't take care of herself.

"Maybe she would be willing to rent to us at first?" Emma asked, smiling.

"That's a wonderful idea, Emma," Liddy said. "That way she'd feel as if she was helping you and Matt while at the same time Darcie and her mother would be helping her."

"And maybe she'd decide to sell to you, Em," Beth added.

"I'll discuss it with Mama tonight and see what we can come up with."

They were all excited, Darcie most of all. Not only did it seem the perfect solution to two of her dear friends' problems, but it also gave her something else to think about besides John Harper.

By the time five o'clock rolled around, John was more than ready to leave his uncle's office and the papers piled high on the desk. He'd found nothing that gave him any insight into what his uncle might have done to the Malones. And Elmer Griffin didn't know.

"Let's call it a day, Elmer. I'll buy you a cup of coffee before we head home."

"I'll take you up on that offer. We sure haven't gotten anywhere today, have we?"

"No, we haven't. I think we need more help. Do you know any of the people who worked for Harper Bank who might be willing to help us out?"

"I'm not sure if your uncle's secretary still lives in the area. If we can find her, I'm sure she'd be able to help us; but it's doubtful any of the tellers could enlighten us very much."

John locked up, and the two men took off down the street toward Emma's Café. He let out a deep breath and shook his head. "I'm not sure anyone but you would be willing to help, even if they could. In case you haven't noticed, I'm not the most popular man in town."

"Don't lose heart, son." Elmer clapped him on the shoulder. "I'll see what I can find out."

"I'd appreciate it, Elmer." At least he seemed to have made one good friend here. John sent up a silent prayer of thankfulness.

He opened the door to Emma's Café as Darcie came hurrying out of it. "Miss Darcie! I wasn't expecting to see you here. Good afternoon."

He must have caught her off guard because her smile didn't suddenly disappear and she appeared to be in a very good mood.

"Nor was I expecting you, Mr. Harper. I'm on my way home to help Mama prepare dinner. Good afternoon to you"—she glanced over at Elmer—"and to you, too, Mr. Griffin."

"Thank you, Miss Malone." He looked from John to Darcie and back again.

Suddenly John knew what he needed to do. He had to talk to Darcie and her mother and find out what his uncle had done to their family.

"Miss Darcie, may I have a word with you before you leave?"

She hesitated for a moment before the manners her mother had taught her prodded her to say, "Of course."

Elmer cleared his throat. "John, I'll go on in and get us a table and order some coffee."

"Thank you, Elmer. I'll be there shortly."

Darcie watched as the older man entered the café, then turned back to John. "What is it, Mr. Harper?"

He felt he must hurry or Darcie might change her mind. "I wonder if you would ask your mother if I might talk with the two of you after dinner tonight."

"I'll ask her, but knowing my mother, I can assure you she'll agree."

"Good. I—thank you."

"You're welcome. I'd better get going now."

"Yes. Well, I'll see you in a little while then."

She nodded before turning away. "See you at dinner."

Darcie couldn't help but wonder what John wanted to talk to them about. But it didn't matter; she knew her mother would fulfill his request. Darcie didn't think she would refuse to talk to anyone who wished to discuss something with her.

When she arrived home and hurried to the kitchen, she felt a little guilty for taking time for herself, but her mother eased that away by greeting her with a smile.

"I'm glad you had tea with your friends, dear. You should do that more often."

"And what about you, Mama? How often do you get out?"

"Why, Darcie, dear, I get out and about. You're in the telephone office all day. I have the freedom to come and go as I please."

Darcie put on an apron and looked over her shoulder at her mother. "You may have the freedom, but that doesn't mean you use it."

"How was everyone?" Her mother changed the subject deftly. "How are Emma and Beth feeling?"

"They're fine." Darcie began stirring up some biscuits. "Emma is a little worried about the size of their apartment. She and Matt would like to find a larger place."

"Oh, I guess it is about time they found a house."

"You know—Mrs. Alma's place would be perfect."

Her mother stopped stirring the gravy she was making to go with the chicken she'd fried and looked at her daughter. "It would be. It's just the place to raise a family."

"We aren't sure Mrs. Alma would ever agree to sell, though."

"Maybe not right away. But if she thinks someone would love it the way she does—"

"That's what I thought. Maybe she'd agree to rent it to them at first." Darcie cut out the biscuits and dropped them on a pan.

"We'll have to see what we can do about it. I'll try to bring up the subject soon."

The two women grinned at one another as Darcie crossed the room and slid the pan of biscuits in the oven.

"Oh, I almost forgot. I ran into John Harper just outside Emma's. He wants to talk to the two of us after dinner. He wanted me to ask you if it would be all right."

"And you told him?"

"That I was sure you would agree."

Her mother nodded, and Darcie knew she was satisfied. "I wonder what he wants to talk about."

"Yes, so do I."

"Well, we must hear him out, whatever it is. He may have discovered what his uncle did to your papa, or it may be something entirely different."

"And if he has?"

"We'll listen to what he has to say. Darcie, John Harper is a nice young man. I'm convinced he isn't anything like Douglas Harper, and I won't blame him for his uncle's sins. I pray you won't, either."

Chapter 9

"Oh, you're back, Darcie." Alma Burton peeked into the room then, saving Darcie from answering her mother. Her gray hair pulled up in a bun and her cheeks taking on more color, she seemed to have a little more energy than when she first came to stay with them. "I was coming to see if I could give your mother a hand with dinner."

Mrs. Alma looked disappointed that Darcie had returned and she wouldn't be needed, but Darcie and her mother assured her they wanted her in the kitchen.

"We can always use an extra hand, Mrs. Alma." Darcie waved her into the room.

"And even if we didn't need help, we're glad to have your company. So come in and stir this gravy while Darcie and I dish up everything. You might taste it and tell me if it needs more salt or pepper, too."

"Well, I ought to be able to manage that. I've made a lot of gravy in my day. I used to love to cook, but it ain't much fun to cook for one."

"No, I don't imagine it is," Darcie's mother said, exchanging a glance with Darcie as Mrs. Alma took the wooden spoon from her and began to stir. "It's also easier to cook for more people, too."

Darcie thought about how lonesome it must be for Mrs. Alma to live alone with no one to care for but herself. For the first time she had a glimpse into why her mother might be happy cooking and caring for boarders and why she insisted she loved what she was doing.

Mrs. Alma sampled a spoonful of the gravy and nodded. "It's real tasty, Molly. But you make great gravy. It's always good and always tastes the same." She laughed. "My brother used to tell me that's what he liked about mine. He said his wife must have 365 recipes for gravy because it tasted different every day."

All three women laughed while they finished setting out the dinner. Darcie was glad her mother had found something for the older woman to do. She seemed to perk up even more from helping that little bit. It would be so good for her to stay here. Darcie wondered if they should broach the subject of selling her house yet, but she would let her mother do it. She had known Alma Burton for a long time and would bring up the subject in the right way and at the right time.

Darcie had almost managed to put the upcoming conversation with John Harper out of her mind, but it only lasted until they met in the dining room. He usually arrived before she did. He had Darcie's chair pulled out for her, but he'd taken to helping Mrs. Alma each night, drawing out her chair and sliding it back to the table for her. If she waited, she was sure he'd help her push her chair closer to the table, too; but there was no need, and she was pleased he saw to the older woman's comfort first. She could tell by the way Mrs. Alma accepted his help without grousing that she liked the young man's attention.

Now as he pulled out his own chair and sat down, Darcie couldn't help but be curious about why he wanted to talk to her and her mother. As the meal progressed from the main course to the buttermilk pie her mother had made, she both dreaded the conversation and almost looked forward to it. It seemed any feelings she had concerning John were consistently—confused.

When the telephone rang their special ring, she exchanged a glance with her mother before hurrying to answer it. It was highly unusual for the telephone to ring during dinnertime, unless she was being called in for work. Tonight proved to be no different.

"Miss Malone?" It was her employer, Mr. McQuillen. "A fire has broken out on South Main, and we need as many volunteers as we can to help fight it. Could you come in to work to help spread the word?"

"I'll be right there, Mr. McQuillen. How bad is it?"

"I can see the flames from here. Try to get here as soon as you can, please." His voice was terse, and Darcie knew it was a true emergency. The town had only one fire wagon.

"I'm on my way." She hung up the earpiece and rushed back into the dining room. "There's a fire downtown. I have to help get out word that they need volunteers."

John stood. "I'll go."

"Yes, so will I." Mr. Carlton wiped his mouth with a napkin.

"As will I." Mr. Mitchell pushed his chair back from the table and stood.

"What is on fire?" Her mother began to clear the table.

"I don't know, Mama. Mr. McQuillen said he could see the flames from the office. I'll let you know as soon as I can, though."

Her mother nodded as Darcie and the three men left the room.

"You men be careful," Miss Olivia called as they rushed out the front door.

In minutes Darcie and the three men were hurrying down the street to the middle of town. They could see the glow before they reached Main Street. Her chest tightened with apprehension. "Oh, dear. I hope it hasn't spread to more buildings!"

The townspeople always feared that. Roswell had grown so much in the last few years that buildings were constructed closer together.

"It's hard to tell from here," Mr. Carlton said.

Once on Main Street, the men dropped Darcie off at the telephone office and started toward the fire. Mr. McQuillen was right. She could see the flames from the office. It was hard to tell what it was—perhaps a hotel or one of the saloons on the south end of town. But it could also be a number of other businesses.

A sense of urgency hit the men, and they suddenly took off running. "Please be careful!" Darcie called out to them. She hurried into the office, praying no one would be injured.

Jessica was already there, along with Jimmie Newland, one of several young men who worked nights, and Mr. McQuillen. He'd divided their customers into four groups and handed Darcie a list of people to contact. She took her place at one of the switchboards and began connecting lines.

As she explained what had happened and asked for volunteers to help with the fire, she tried to fight the thought that kept demanding her attention.

But after Emma called in, she could resist it no longer. "Oh, Darcie, it's you. Good. Matt went down right away, but I haven't had any word since he left. It's been awhile since we've had a fire this size."

"I know. Are you and Mandy and everyone all right? Can you see anything from your apartment?"

"No—only the glow of flames." Darcie could hear her sigh. "I wish I'd get over this, but every time we have a fire of any kind in town, I remember when my place was set on fire. If it hadn't been for Matt—"

"I know, Em. I've been thinking about the same thing. I hope they can get this put out soon. And I pray it doesn't spread and no one is hurt."

"So do I. Let me know if there's any news, okay?"

"I will. Try not to worry about Matt. I'm sure he'll be fine."

"I'll try. We actually have customers in spite of the fire. I'll keep busy."

Darcie disconnected the line and continued to the next person on her list, but she could no longer avoid thinking about the fire. Talking to Emma had reminded her it was Douglas Harper who hired someone to set Emma's place on fire. She thanked the Lord that Matt had rescued Emma and Mandy and the fire had been put out quickly.

Even though Emma's fire had taken place several years before, it suddenly seemed like only yesterday and brought back memories of Harper's trial and how glad Darcie had been to see him finally put behind bars.

Now they had another fire and another Harper in town. Surely John hadn't had anything to do with this one. Of course not—he'd been right there in the dining room of her own home when word had come about it. Yet his uncle hadn't actually set the fire at Emma's, either. He'd hired someone else to do his dirty work for him. John could have done the same thing.

No. He might be Douglas Harper's nephew, but she couldn't believe he would do something so abominable. Her heart would not let her accept that idea.

The volunteer fire department was hard at work. Two of the men manned the hand pumps on either side of the fire wagon, filling the hose from the water tank, while two more men directed the spray at the burning saloon.

As the fire spread, John was certain it would take the fire department and the other men who were showing up to get it under control. He was glad he'd come with Mitchell and Carlton. He had the feeling he'd have been run out of town if he hadn't. He wondered why everyone was looking so suspiciously at him, until he remembered Elmer telling him why his uncle had gone to prison. He'd hired someone to set a fire. The very thought that a member of his family could do such a thing sickened him. And yet Douglas Harper had been convicted.

John joined the fire brigade and took his turn filling pails and handing them off to the man in front of him. He couldn't blame the people of this town for the way they felt about Douglas Harper. But he was tired of the fact that the good people of Roswell assumed he was like his uncle. Nothing was further from the truth, but he didn't know how to convince them.

More men showed up, and another line formed in front of a mercantile across the street. At least the artesian wells around Roswell were plentiful. Most businesses had a well and pump on the premises, and tonight they were all being put to good use. Water was drawn from every pump, watering trough, or well within running distance.

As one man threw water on the fire or helped to fill the tanks on the fire wagon, they'd go to the end of the line and the next person would move up. Just as John moved back to the end of the line, two more men showed up to help. They introduced themselves as Cal McAllister and Jeb Winslow and lined up behind John. He recognized them from church and had heard good things about both men at the Malone dinner table.

John filled another pail with water and handed it to Mr. Mitchell. The heat from the flames enveloping the saloon and the café attached to it flared up again. He wasn't worried much about the saloon, figuring the town would be better off with one less. But other businesses could be threatened if the fire wasn't put out soon.

When the second story of the saloon collapsed, burning embers and ashes flew everywhere. The saloon couldn't be saved, so the volunteers concentrated on saving the nearby buildings. It was hours later before the area was considered safe.

Finally John and Mr. Mitchell and Mr. Carlton started back to the boardinghouse. When they reached the telephone office, they looked through the window and saw Darcie still working. John paused. Since the fire was out, she might be leaving soon, and he didn't like the idea of her walking home alone at night.

He glanced at the other two men, who were older and appeared even wearier than he felt. "Why don't you two go on and let Mrs. Malone know that I'll see Darcie home?"

"That's nice of you, Harper," Mr. Carlton said.

Mr. Mitchell wiped his brow with his handkerchief. "Yes, it is. Molly will appreciate it, I'm sure. We'll tell her."

John sat on the bench outside the telephone office and watched the men walk down the street. Mrs. Malone might appreciate his seeing her daughter home, but he wasn't sure Darcie would be of the same mind. He wondered if he should pursue the conversation he'd intended to have with her and her mother. He yawned and shook his head. No. Darcie was probably tired, and he was exhausted. It could wait for another day or two.

Darcie stood and stretched. At last the fire was out, and she could go home. She was thankful no one had been hurt and the buildings around the saloon and its café had been saved.

She and Jessica were preparing to leave when Mr. McQuillen came out of his office. "Thank you for coming down, ladies. You've done an important service for the town tonight."

"I hate to think of what might have happened without the telephone in this area," Darcie said. "We could never have gotten out word to enough people in time to help."

"I imagine more than the saloon would have burned to the ground," a male voice said from the doorway.

Darcie's heart did a somersault when she saw John Harper standing there, even though he was covered in soot from fighting the fire.

"I thought I'd see you home, if you have no objection."

In spite of her doubts about his character, her mother was sure he could be trusted. And Darcie was sure she would want her to accept John's offer to walk her home. In truth, she'd had a few qualms about walking home alone at this time of night, too. "I—no—I mean, yes, thank you. That's nice of you. Jessica lives only a street over, so we can see her home, too."

They started down the street with John in the middle of the two women.

"Jessica," Darcie said, "this is John Harper, who is staying at my mother's boardinghouse. Mr. Harper, this is Jessica Landry, my coworker and friend."

Despite the gray ash, John was a very nice-looking man; and from the way Jessica was gazing at him, she didn't seem blind to that fact.

"It's nice to meet you, Mr. Harper. You look very tired. I'm sure it was hard down there fighting that fire."

He did look exhausted, and Darcie was aggravated she hadn't been the one to mention it. But what bothered her most was the stab of jealousy she felt when John smiled at Jessica and said, "It was pretty warm down there. But it felt good to be of help."

"It does feel good, doesn't it? We were talking about that at the telephone office."

"You both must have worked hard yourselves to round up volunteers. A lot of men showed up."

"Oh, we did." Jessica didn't give Darcie a chance to respond even though John was directing his comments to her. "I'd already contacted quite a few of our customers by the time Darcie got there, but she was such a big help. It took awhile to contact everyone and answer all the questions."

Darcie was glad it was dark because she was sure her jaw dropped an inch or two at Jessica's words. She was certainly trying to make a good impression on John.

"I imagine you were busy," John said.

"Very." Jessica smiled up at him. "But not nearly as busy as you men were."

Darcie wasn't sure what made her jump into the conversation, but she felt a sudden need to do so. "We could have gone home earlier, but by then the switchboard was lit up with people wanting to know what was happening and asking for updates. Mr. McQuillen had gone to his office, and we didn't want to leave Jimmie there to handle it by himself."

By the time they arrived at Jessica's home, Darcie was quite ready to part company with her friend.

"Well, thank you very much for seeing me home, Mr. Harper," Jessica said to John.

"You're welcome, Miss Jessica. It was no problem since it is on our way home."

Darcie's heart warmed at John's words. Jessica looked a little chagrined as she glanced at Darcie.

"Good night, Jessica." Darcie tried to sound pleasant, but it wasn't easy. She'd never felt so exasperated with the other woman as she was now.

"Yes, well, thank you both. Good night." Jessica ran up the walk to her house. She turned and waved before going inside.

Darcie and John continued down the street. Now that they were alone, she wasn't sure what to say.

"She seems like a nice woman," John commented.

"Mmm," was all Darcie could make herself say. Was he interested in Jessica? She was pretty, and she'd certainly made it clear she was attracted to him!

They walked on in silence as she contemplated why it even mattered to her. Yet it did. But how could she be jealous over a man she couldn't let herself care about and wasn't sure she could even trust?

Darcie had been wondering all evening if John might have had something to do with the fire. And now here he was, his face and hair, his clothes, dusted with ashes from the blaze he'd helped put out. His eyes showed his fatigue. Surely this man couldn't have had anything to do with setting the fire—

"It's been a long evening, hasn't it, Miss Darcie?"

"Yes, it has. I'm so glad no one was hurt in the fire."

John nodded. "It was frightening when the second story fell through. I think we were all afraid the flying embers would catch the nearby buildings on fire, and they almost did. But I'm thankful the Lord took care of that for us."

His faith in the Lord seemed so real and natural that it was becoming increasingly hard not to care about this man. In fact, she was afraid she was already falling in love with him. What was she to do?

Chapter 10

The weekend was full of talk about the fire. At the breakfast table on Saturday morning, the ladies wanted a full accounting of what had happened. John left the rehashing of it to Mr. Carlton and Mr. Mitchell. But before putting in time at the bank and going over yet more papers, he decided to inspect the fire damage by daylight. Nothing was left of the saloon and café, but he thanked the Lord the buildings on each side of it still stood. They'd suffered some smoke damage, but that could be taken care of easily enough. It felt good to know he'd helped to save them.

John had hoped that helping with the fire would show the people of Roswell he had their best interests at heart and was not like his uncle. But it didn't take long for him to realize he was wrong.

Returning to the bank, he found some people still shied away from him, crossing the street or ducking into a store. He became more determined than ever to find out why half the town feared him and the other half avoided him.

He'd been at his uncle's desk a half hour when the front door opened. A young couple came inside looking nervous. He quickly stood and walked over to greet them. "Good morning. May I help you with something?"

The young man took off his hat and twisted it in his hands. "My name is Edward Hollingsworth." He touched the shoulder of the woman at his side. "This is my wife, Eileen. I hear tell you're here to settle your uncle's accounts. We need to talk to you."

"Certainly. Come this way." He led them to the office and motioned them to take a seat. "What can I do for you?"

Edward Hollingsworth cleared his throat. "I—I owed your uncle, and I guess I owe you—now he's gone."

John vaguely remembered the name Hollingsworth in the bank's records. He thought they were among the ones his uncle had charged with too much interest. "You took a loan out with my uncle?"

"Yes. I didn't know who to pay after he went to jail, but now you're here, I guess we need to make arrangements to pay 'fore you decide to take our place away from us."

"Mr. Hollingsworth, I wouldn't do that. I don't even know what you owed my uncle yet. I'm trying to go over his papers, but I don't have a clear picture of anything now. Your account was under your name?"

"Yes, sir. I had to take a loan out several years ago to help pay for some feed and seed. I was late on a payment, and—"

"Your uncle threatened to take the farm." Eileen interrupted her husband. "Edward had to sell one of our work horses to make the payment; then old Harper got arrested before the next payment was due—and we—"

Probably thanked the good Lord for taking him out of business. John could tell she was trying not to cry. He had a feeling this young couple didn't have the money to pay him anything now. He finished the sentence for her. "You didn't know whom to pay. That's perfectly understandable."

The couple glanced at each other, then back at him, as if they couldn't believe his words and were at a loss for what to say next.

"I'm in the process of going over my uncle's papers now." John pointed to the pile of files on the desk. "I'll look up your account and get back to you as soon as I can grasp matters. But don't worry—you'll keep your place."

Edward stood and reached out his hand. "Thank you. We'll pay back what we owe, no matter how long it takes, Mr. Harper."

John shook hands with the man. "I'll be in contact with you once I have a chance to look over your account."

He'd no more than seen them to the door when another man entered with the same kind of story. Jim Benson owed Harper Bank money but didn't know whom to pay after Douglas's imprisonment. He wanted to set up some kind of payment schedule so he wouldn't lose his place. The Benson name sounded familiar also, and John figured he'd seen it among the papers he'd looked at. He'd have to take some of those papers home tonight and go over them again.

"Mr. Benson, I'm in the middle of putting my uncle's papers in order so that I know how to proceed. The only thing I can assure you of this minute is that I have no intention of foreclosing on you."

His words had an immediate effect on the man. John could see relief written on his face as he thanked him and left.

By the time he was ready to call it a day, five different people had paid him a visit, all of them nervous and expecting the worst from him. He tried to assure each of them he was not going to foreclose on their property; but he had the feeling that, much as they wanted to believe him, most were finding it hard to do so.

John felt relieved he could narrow his search for now with names of people who owed his uncle money instead of going painstakingly through the accounts of everyone who'd done business with Harper Bank. But the feeling didn't last long. He hunted for the Hollingsworth and Benson records but didn't see them in the files he was familiar with. What good would it do to have names if he couldn't find the records? He sighed and shook his head. These people had to be accounted for somewhere. First thing Monday morning, he had to see what he could do about getting some help. Maybe Elmer had been able to contact some of his uncle's former employees. He'd pray that at least one or two would agree to help them out.

Not long after the noon meal, Darcie's mother, Miss Olivia, and even Mrs. Alma determined they needed to make the trek downtown to see the damage from the fire. They'd never gone out together for an afternoon so they decided to enjoy tea at Emma's. Darcie's mother rented a surrey so Mrs. Alma wouldn't have to walk, and they headed downtown, along with Darcie.

Looking at it in the daylight, Darcie was even more amazed that nothing else had caught fire. While thankful no one was hurt in the blaze, none of the ladies was the least bit upset a saloon had been destroyed and not some other business. But, as Mrs. Alma pointed out, dampening their mood for the moment, the owner would probably rebuild and be up and running again in a few months.

It was a rare outing for the two Malone women, and Darcie enjoyed the afternoon immensely. Emma's teas had become popular several years earlier. The women of the town had wanted to show their husbands they supported Emma's determination to raise Mandy as her own. She'd made the baby's mother a promise and intended to stand behind it, even though she was unmarried at the time. Most of the men in town, stirred up by Douglas Harper, had fought it; for a while even husbands and wives were at odds. But it was settled to everyone's satisfaction when Emma and Matt married.

The women enjoyed the teas whenever they could take an hour or so out of their busy Saturdays. Today Darcie wasn't surprised to see many familiar faces there. Emma had joined their group when Liddy and Beth came in, so they made room at their table and pulled up two more chairs. After inspecting the damage, Liddy and Beth had left their children at Jaffa-Prager Mercantile with their husbands while they came to Emma's for tea.

With Mrs. Alma there, Darcie thought it was the perfect opportunity to bring up Emma and Matt's need for a bigger place to live.

"How are you feeling, Emma?" Darcie's mother asked.

Emma smiled. "Really well—Doc says about three more weeks."

"You're going to be kind of cramped in the apartment, aren't you?" Darcie prompted her.

"Well, yes. I wish we had a larger place to live in, but there's nothing right now. If I'd been thinking correctly, we'd have offered to buy Beth's home when she and Jeb married. But I didn't, and it was snapped up right away. Roswell is growing so fast, nothing is available now. I guess we could build, but. . ." Emma shook her head.

"Would you be willing to rent?" Darcie's mother asked.

"If the right property came available, I'm sure we would. But there's not much available there, either."

"Well, I'm sure something will turn up," Darcie assured her. "We'll all pray about it for you."

"Thank you. I'm confident the Lord will provide something. I just need to learn patience."

Darcie and her mother exchanged a look, and she knew they were both hoping Mrs. Alma would take the conversation to heart. She might not comment now, but she'd no doubt heard every word.

The conversation turned to the fire. Everyone wondered, was it set or was it an accident?

"Who would do something like that? And why?" Miss Olivia asked.

"A competitor possibly?" Darcie's mother suggested. "Someone who wanted to put the saloon out of business."

Mrs. Alma chuckled. "In that case, Molly, any one of us at this table could be the culprit."

They laughed at the truth in her words.

"Well," Mrs. Alma added, serious now, "at least we don't have to worry about Douglas Harper being behind it this time. He's gone."

Quiet suddenly descended on the table, and Darcie wondered if the others were remembering Douglas Harper had gone to prison for burning Emma's place. Had it not been for quick action by Matt and Ben and the fire department, Emma's Café might not be here now. She also wondered if they were questioning, as she had, whether his nephew might have had something to do with this one. It didn't take long for her to find out.

"Strange that his nephew is here, though, isn't it?" Liddy asked.

Emma nodded. "It does seem a little odd, doesn't it? I have to admit I've wondered if he could have had anything to do with setting this fire. I know it's because he's related to the man who was responsible for setting my café on fire, but still—"

Darcie took a sip of tea. Obviously she wasn't the only one a little suspicious, but somehow that didn't give her any comfort.

"Well, he was at my dinner table last night," her mother said with authority. "There's no way he could have had anything to do with it."

Liddy shook her head. "I don't think that would prove anything, Mrs. Malone. Douglas Harper didn't actually set Emma's Café on fire. He hired someone to do it."

It was very hard not to speculate if the man's nephew could have had anything to do with this one, Darcie thought. And yet hearing her friends voice the same suspicions she had suddenly made her want to take up for John. But what Liddy said was true, and how could they be certain? She wanted so badly to be sure he didn't have anything to do with it.

"That nice young man wouldn't do a thing like that," Mrs. Alma said.

"I agree," Darcie's mother said. "He wouldn't. And we can't judge him on the basis of who he's related to."

"I wouldn't count on everyone agreeing with you two ladies." Emma shook her head. "I've heard a lot of comments from my customers, and most are distrustful of anyone with the last name Harper."

"That's true," Liddy agreed. "But Cal told me he and Jeb worked side by side with John Harper last night and no one worked any harder."

"I know. Matt didn't work alongside him, but he said he saw him trying to put out that fire with as much energy as everyone else there," Emma added.

"It's hard not to remember what his uncle did."

"I've been a pretty good judge of character all my life," Mrs. Alma said. "And I tell you this—Douglas Harper was the worst kind of scoundrel, but his nephew is nothing like him. Quite the opposite, in fact."

Darcie found herself praying Mrs. Alma was right.

That night at supper, John was his usual considerate self, helping Mrs. Alma with her chair and complimenting her mother on the meal; but he was quiet, and his eyes looked sad.

"Are you all right, John?" her mother asked. Obviously Darcie wasn't the only one who seemed to think he wasn't himself.

"I'm fine, Mrs. Malone."

"You didn't breathe in too much of that smoke last night, did you?" Mrs. Alma asked.

"No. Really, I'm fine. I'm sorry if I appear rude tonight. I just have my mind on other things."

Darcie couldn't help but wonder what other things he was thinking about.

"That fire was something, wasn't it?" Mr. Carlton said.

"It certainly was," John said.

"I've never put out a fire before," Mr. Mitchell said. "It was very satisfying to be able to help."

"Made me feel ten years younger to keep up with the likes of John here and the deputy," Mr. Carlton added.

"You both certainly pulled your weight," John said.

The older men had been proud of themselves, and Darcie figured they had a right to be; but their smiles were looking a little smug to her. On the other hand, she wished John would smile, but he seemed miles away. What was he thinking about? The fire? His uncle's business? Jessica? That last thought didn't sit well with her, but then neither did the sudden pang of jealousy she felt.

John still seemed to be deep in thought when he asked, "Mrs. Malone, would you happen to know any of the people who worked at my uncle's bank? I could use some assistance in going over some of his records."

Darcie's mother thought for a moment. "I believe his secretary was a—Charlotte Mead? Does that sound right, Alma?"

Mrs. Alma nodded. "Yes, Charlotte worked for him."

"Does she still live around here?"

"I believe she does. Last I heard, she was living over on Sixth Street."

Suddenly John's mood lightened. "Thank you! I should have thought to ask you ladies that question long ago. I'll try to reach her on Monday if Elmer hasn't already. He was going to try to contact some of the former employees for me. My uncle treated some people in this town badly, and I need help in reading his special way of keeping records."

Darcie and her mother could tell him a few things about Douglas Harper's bad dealings. But he hadn't mentioned the talk he'd wanted to have with them on Friday again, and they still didn't know what he wanted to discuss. And much as Darcie wanted to find out some things herself, she knew her mother wouldn't bring up the subject of how his uncle had treated her family. She would leave it to John to bring it up.

The next morning Darcie's mother insisted they wait for John to accompany them to church, so she found herself lingering in the foyer with her mother and Mrs. Alma. Could he have meant what he said last night? Did he believe his uncle had treated people badly? And what did he intend to do about it if he found out it was true?

John came downstairs and smiled when he saw the three women had waited for him. "What an honor to be escorting three lovely ladies to church this morning!"

His gaze rested on Darcie, and she was glad she'd dressed in one of her favorite outfits, a blue and white linen suit with a big sailor collar. A blue hat with silk flowers and a white plume, along with a blue purse, completed the ensemble, leaving her feeling confident she looked her best.

John appeared to be in a much better mood. Maybe he'd just been exhausted from working the fire on Friday night and needed a good rest. Whatever it was, Darcie was relieved he didn't look as tired as he had the night before.

Once they'd entered the church building, she noticed some of the members glancing at John with a look of fear or even anger on their faces while a few whispered to each other. As they walked up the aisle to the pew she and her mother normally sat in, Darcie found herself feeling uncomfortable for John's sake.

But Minister Turley's sermon, based on Proverbs, chapter twenty-six, verse twenty, pricked her heart and gave her much to consider for the rest of the day: "Where no wood is, there the fire goeth out: so where there is no talebearer, the strife ceaseth."

She'd been so upset about John Harper living in her father's home that she had complained loud and often to those who would listen. But had she also become a talebearer, causing strife for John?

Chapter 11

By the time John arrived at the bank on Monday morning, two or three people had crossed the street to avoid him. He wondered if they'd been in debt to the bank. After Saturday, he knew many were afraid he would foreclose on their property, and it struck him that his uncle must have demanded collateral for a lot of the money he lent. Of course, that in itself wasn't wrong, but from some of the entries he'd seen, it appeared the man had demanded more than the norm.

He hoped Elmer Griffin had contacted some of his uncle Douglas's former employees over the weekend and that they would be willing to help out. If not, he would have to take out an advertisement in the local paper and pray that someone would answer it and apply to help them.

Elmer entered the bank around nine o'clock with someone following him. John was afraid yet another person had come to let him know he owed Douglas Harper money and wanted to find a way to pay it back.

This was a woman of about fifty, neatly dressed in a gray-striped skirt and matching jacket, her silver-gray hair pulled into a bun at the back of her neck. When she hesitated just inside the door, John's heart flared with hope that the older man had found some help.

"John, this is Charlotte Mead, your uncle's former secretary. She's here to help us out if you can convince her you mean no one harm." John crossed the room to where she stood as Elmer continued. "And Miss Mead, this is John Harper. As I mentioned earlier, he's here to settle his uncle's estate; but he's heard how Douglas treated the people in this area, and he wants to put things right—if he can."

"I know that's what you told me, Elmer. But after Douglas went to prison and I helped people get their money out of the bank, I said I'd never set foot in here again."

"I can understand how you might feel that way, Miss Mead," John said. She had such a sad look in her eyes, bright blue and large behind her glasses, that his heart went out to her. He took one of her hands in his and gazed directly into her eyes. "I need your help. I would like to bring honor back to my family name in this town, but I don't think I can do it without your assistance. I want to set things right."

Miss Mead's gaze met his and held it for several moments before she slowly nodded. "Elmer has assured me you are a good man—I hope he is right. What do you need me to do?"

John let out his breath. "Elmer and I have had an awful time trying to decipher my uncle Douglas's handwriting for one thing. And I'm having difficulty locating complete files on people who are coming to me and saying they owed my uncle money."

"I thought you said you wanted to help. Do you want me to help you foreclose on those people and collect the outstanding debts instead? Because I won't—"

"No, ma'am. I don't want to foreclose on anyone. But I would like to settle the accounts. I need to know what these people are talking about. I can find records on only a few, and I suspect my uncle's business practices left much to be desired. I need your help in sorting it all out. Will you do that for me—for the people of this town, Miss Mead?"

She tilted her head and gave him a long look. "All right," she said. "I'll be back this afternoon, and we can get started then. It's time someone 'sides me knows what Douglas Harper was really like."

Talk of the fire hadn't died down by Monday, and all morning people were ringing in to Roswell Telephone and Manufacturing Company specifically to talk to Darcie about it. Most voiced their opinions that it could have been John Harper.

"I tell you, Darcie—the sheriff needs to look at your mother's boarder—that nephew of Douglas Harper," Nora Hanson had said. "You know, it was setting Emma's place on fire that sent Douglas to prison."

Hearing it expressed like that made Darcie cringe. While she wasn't sure what John was going to do about settling his uncle's business, she'd become almost certain he had nothing to do with the fire.

"I don't think he had anything to do with it, Mrs. Hanson. Why, he was at our dinner table when we found out about the fire. He even helped put it out."

"Humph. That doesn't mean anything. He could have been trying to convince everyone he didn't when he did."

Nora wasn't the only one to voice her suspicions of John. All through the morning, when Darcie tried to take up for him, she was reminded she had been the one to express her distrust of the man when he first arrived in town.

"Darcie," Mrs. Waller said, "I know you are just as suspicious as the rest of us. How can you not be? He's Douglas Harper's nephew after all, and that man was probably the cause of your papa having that stroke. You told me you doubted him only a few weeks ago."

Once more she was reminded why she couldn't trust John Harper. It didn't matter that she was beginning to care way too much for him, whether she wanted to or not. Darcie couldn't deny what Amelia Waller was saying. She had voiced her distrust of the man to as many as would listen to her, especially in those first few days after people found out Douglas Harper's nephew was in town.

By that afternoon, Darcie had to face the fact it was indeed possible she had planted the seeds of suspicion in the minds of her friends and others she'd talked to since John Harper had arrived in town. And she'd even used her place of work to do it—something she'd been determined not to do after she was promoted.

Suddenly she realized that not only had she not been doing her job as she should, but even more important, she hadn't been acting in a Christian way. She had become a talebearer stirring up strife. And if John Harper intended to do the right thing, then she had wronged him horribly by churning up bad feelings. Tears sprang to her eyes as she closed them and said a silent prayer, asking the Lord for His forgiveness and to show her what to do to make things right.

John and Elmer were looking forward to working when Miss Mead returned and decided to have their noon meal at Emma's Café before then. While Emma was civil to John, most of her customers turned a cold shoulder to the two men.

After giving their order, John turned to the older man. "Elmer, I'm sorry that helping me out seems to be ruining your reputation around here."

Elmer shook his head. "Don't worry about it. The fire brought up old memories for a lot of these people. One of these days they'll discover you're nothing like Douglas."

John was beginning to think that would never happen. "Elmer, can you tell me what you know about my uncle's business association with the Malones?"

"No, son, I don't know anything about that. Maybe Miss Mead will."

John hoped so. Because of the fire, he'd had to delay talking with them, but it was time now. He had to find out why Darcie was determined to dislike him from the moment she found out who he was. He'd waited long enough.

When Charlotte Mead came back that afternoon, she was lugging two leather file cases. John and Elmer hurried to help her with them.

"What do we have here, Miss Mead?" Elmer asked.

"These are the records I took home with me when Douglas Harper went to jail. If you remember, I helped the sheriff's office make sure people got their money out of the bank." Miss Mead looked at Elmer. "You remember that, Mr. Griffin?"

Elmer nodded.

"But some owed money to the bank, and I didn't know what to do with those records. I didn't want those people to be hurt any more than they already had been, so I took 'em home with me. I prayed after I went home, and I'm trusting in the Lord and in you, John Harper, to do what is right by these people. It'll take awhile to explain it all to you. As you've already discovered, your uncle had his own bookkeeping system."

By midafternoon John had figured out his uncle's schemes were worse than he'd thought. He'd wanted to own as much of Roswell and the surrounding area as he could—and by any means necessary. And after reading the few records they were able to decipher with Charlotte Mead's help, he understood why anyone who had done business with Douglas Harper once wouldn't want to have anything else to do with another man named Harper.

John finally grasped why the Hollingsworths and Mr. Benson and the others feared he might foreclose on their property; his uncle made it a practice to foreclose after only one or two missed payments. And he had lent money at such high interest rates that it was almost impossible for the normal person to make every payment.

When Miss Mead pulled out the Malone file, John held his breath. His uncle Douglas had planned to foreclose on the family holdings shortly before Darcie's father died.

"What happened after Mr. Malone passed away, Miss Mead? Do you have any records of that?"

She thought for a minute and pulled the second file case toward her. "I believe Mrs. Malone signed over all the holdings except for the house in town and the cash on hand."

"And he let her?"

"Yes, he did. Your uncle—"

"Deserved to go to prison." John slammed shut the ledger he'd been reviewing and stood. He strode to the window and looked out on this town his uncle had planned on owning. It had been so hard for him to comprehend the kind of man his uncle was that at first he'd wanted to give him the benefit of the doubt. Maybe he had been accused wrongly—maybe he'd been misunderstood—maybe—maybe—maybe. Over and over again John had tried to understand a person he'd never even known. Now he knew he would never comprehend the mind of his father's brother. Nor did he want to.

But he did want to grasp the full story of what he'd done, and he knew the bank records alone couldn't tell him. It was time to pay a visit to the sheriff's office—to find out the truth, no matter how painful it might be.

"Let's call it a day," John said. "Miss Mead, I can't thank you enough for your help. You'll be here tomorrow?"

He held his breath for a moment as the older woman studied him, seeming to take his measure, deciding what kind of man she thought he was. Only when she smiled and nodded did he breathe.

"I can see you want to right the wrongs your uncle did, Mr. Harper. I'll be here first thing in the morning."

"I'll see Miss Mead home," Elmer offered.

"Why, thank you, Mr. Griffin," Miss Mead said.

John walked them both to the door and silently thanked the Lord for helping Elmer reach Charlotte Mead—and for her willingness to help. With her assistance, today had been more productive than all the days he and Elmer had put in trying to make sense of his uncle's handwriting. But today's revelations raised even more questions. John locked up and headed toward the sheriff's office. He had to have some answers.

The sheriff wasn't in, but a deputy was. He was pouring a cup of coffee when John entered the office.

"Afternoon, Mr. Harper. I'm Deputy Matt Johnson. What can I do for you?"

John was taken aback the deputy knew who he was. He didn't recall being introduced to him. But then nearly everyone knew who he was by now. Most didn't want to, though.

"I have some questions I'd like answered if you have a minute."

"I do. Want a cup of coffee?"

John shook his head. "No, thank you."

"Well, take a seat." The deputy motioned to the chair facing the desk. "What do you want to know?"

John leaned forward, his elbows on his knees, his hands laced together. He looked at the floor a moment before meeting the deputy's gaze. "I've been reviewing"—he paused, unable to say "my uncle"—"Douglas Harper's records. But they aren't telling me everything. I'm hoping you can tell me more."

"I won't have anything nice to say about him."

"I don't figure anyone in town will."

The deputy nodded. "You're right. A lot of people in this town came to despise the man."

"I realize that, and I'm sure they had good reason. But I'd like to know the facts that don't show up on paper."

"I see. All right. Where do you want me to start?"

"With whatever I need to know to try to undo some of the harm he did to this town."

"You sure you want to know it all?" The deputy leaned back in his chair.

"I have to. My family name is at stake here."

"You know he went to prison for hiring someone to set fire to my wife's café across the street?"

John nodded. "I'd heard that. But what I don't know is why he would do something like that. I mean, what possible reason—?"

"Douglas Harper knew the railroad here would extend all the way to Amarillo. He wanted to own as much of the town as he could. Emma's Café is on prime property, close to everything. But Emma never did business with him. He'd tried to get her to sell out to him several years before, to no avail. So he just decided to run her out of town. First he tried to take Mandy away from her."

"Your child?"

John shook his head. "No. We weren't married then. Mandy's mama was one of Emma's employees. She got sick, and before she died, she asked Em to take Mandy in and raise her as her own if she didn't make it. Of course Em agreed, and when Anna died, she took in Mandy."

"And Douglas wanted the child?"

"No. He just wanted to cause Em problems. He even convinced the town council to give her a deadline for finding a husband so she could keep Mandy. We figured he wanted to make it so hard on her to keep the child that she would sell out and move away." Matt chuckled. "He didn't know Em. She dug her feet in and stayed. She put in an advertisement for a husband, and, well, to make a long story short, I answered. It was at the town meeting where we told them we were married that the truth came out about your uncle. He'd hired someone to set fire to the café, then had another lined up to buy her out if need be so he'd get the property. When he was finally arrested, I think half this town breathed a collective sigh of relief. After all the things he'd done to people around here, finally he was going to pay."

It was so hard to take in. John stood. "I think I'd like that coffee now."

"Help yourself."

John poured a cup of the strong brew and sat back down. "What else can you tell me?"

"Well, let's see. He tried to blackmail Em's best friend, Liddy, into marrying him to pay off the debt her first husband owed after he died. She was expecting at the time. Cal McAllister helped her out by leasing some of her land so she could make payments. Once Cal finally convinced Liddy to marry him, he took great pleasure in paying Harper off for good."

It kept getting worse. John had no doubt that what the deputy was telling him was true, but it was so hard to believe anyone could be so repulsive. He had to ask the next question. "What about the Malone family? Did he have anything to do with Mr. Malone's death?"

Deputy Johnson leaned forward and propped his elbows on his desk. He sighed. "He didn't pull out a gun and shoot him, if that's what you mean. But most of us believe he put enough stress on the man to cause his death. Charles Malone was one of the most respected ranchers around these parts—didn't owe anyone a dime. In fact, most times he was helping others. Was doing real good—even bought the house in town a few years before.

"Then we had a year of drought, and he lost a lot of cattle. 'Bout the time he was pulling out of that, we had a real bad winter, and Charles lost most of his herd in one blizzard. He wanted to build his herd back up, so he went to Harper for a loan to buy more cattle."

"Why would he have gone to him if everyone knew how he did business?" John asked.

"He didn't know at the time. Keep in mind that at first no one had any idea what kind of man Harper was. He could be charming when it suited him, and obviously it suited him well enough to get a seat on the city council. No one knew his motive then was to acquire as much land around here as he could. That came out after Emma's place was set on fire."

So his uncle's claim to the family of being one of the most influential people in town hadn't been a total lie. He only neglected to say what kind of influence he wielded or that he'd also become one of the most hated men in town.

John took a drink of coffee, trying to grasp all that Deputy Johnson was telling him. "From the bank records I've just examined, I know Mr. Malone had trouble making the payments. Of course, at the rate of interest my uncle charged, most people would find it hard to make them."

The deputy nodded. "The winter after Charles took out the loan was almost as bad as the one before. He lost more cattle and was in trouble. Harper started demanding payment, and, well, I guess the stress of it all took its toll. Charles collapsed in his office at the ranch. Doc said he died of a stroke, but we don't know for sure what caused it. All I know is that the worry Harper put Charles through sure couldn't have helped his health any."

"No. I'm sure it didn't. And Douglas didn't let up on Mrs. Malone, did he?"

"No. And with no real way to pay him, Molly finally signed over the ranch and all other holdings to him. All except for the house in town and enough money to get her boardinghouse started. She did make sure he marked the loan paid in full."

John felt physically sick that a member of his family could have caused people so much pain. It was bad enough that his uncle's business practices with men were so corrupt, but the fact that he seemed to delight in making women miserable was appalling. No wonder no one in this town mourned the death of Douglas Harper.

Chapter 12

When Darcie left work for home on Monday and saw John entering the sheriff's office, she couldn't help but wonder what business he had there. Could he be trying to enlist the sheriff's help in collecting money owed the bank?

No. She shrugged off that thought. From what he'd told them on Saturday evening, he believed his uncle had not treated people right and wanted help in getting to the bottom of things. Maybe he was asking for the sheriff's help in that.

Or it could be—Darcie's heart seemed to stop beating for a moment. Feelings were running high against him in this town. She hoped he hadn't received some kind of threat. She hurried home, trying to put that thought out of her mind, too. If that were the case, she would have to bear the guilt for helping fuel the flame of anger at him.

"Dear Lord, please, I hope and pray John has not been threatened in any way, particularly not because of my words. But if he has, please keep him safe," she whispered as she ran up the front steps of her home. But her heart was heavy because she knew that, even if he hadn't been threatened, she had stoked the fire of resentment toward John Harper.

She rushed upstairs to change clothes and then back down to help her mother in the kitchen, happy to see that Mrs. Alma was there, also. She was stirring up some corn bread to go with the pinto beans simmering away on the back of the stove. Darcie set to work helping her mother peel the potatoes she'd fry to go with them. A simple meal, it was one of the boarders' favorites. She could smell the apple crisp her mother had in the oven for dessert.

"How was your day, dear?" her mother asked.

Enlightening. Much more so than Darcie would have liked. She had to face some distasteful facts about herself. But she didn't say that. "Busy."

"We've been busy here today, too," her mother said. "We had a slight emergency. Olivia fell down the stairs. We thought she broke an ankle. It was right after you left for work. We were thankful Mr. Carlton was still here. He telephoned Doc Bradshaw while Alma and I saw to Olivia."

"Oh, no! Is she all right?"

"Yes, she is. It's only a bad sprain, and nothing was broken. Alma helped me get her settled in the back parlor after Doc said the stairs would be hard on her for a few days." Darcie's mother set a big iron skillet on the range, added some bacon grease to it, and turned on the fire under it. "She's going to have to stay there for the time being. The gentlemen will have to keep to the front parlor until she can make it up and down the stairs again."

"I'm sure they won't mind." Darcie sliced the last potato, then chopped an onion for her mother to add right before the potatoes were finished cooking.

"No, they won't, I'm sure." Her mother took the bowl of potatoes over to the stove and carefully emptied the contents into the skillet. The sizzling sound confirmed that the grease was just right. "I gave her a little bell to let me know when she needed something, and she's—"

"About worn it out already," Mrs. Alma said. "She needed water; she needed her pillow fluffed; she wanted some company. And all that before the medicine Doc gave her made her drowsy enough to sleep."

Darcie's mother chuckled. "I don't know what I'd have done without Alma today. Olivia would have run me ragged, poor dear."

"I'm going to teach her to knit. I think she needs something to occupy her time."

"See?" Darcie's mother said. "I need Alma here. I've been trying to convince her to stay with us permanently. I so enjoy her company."

Darcie exchanged a glance with her mother before adding her own thoughts on the subject. "Oh, Mrs. Alma, it would be so nice if you stayed on with us."

"And I wouldn't want any rent from you, Alma. Just your company. You are like family."

Alma shook her head, but they could tell she was pleased they wanted to keep her there. "I'm thinking on it."

"You know, I never knew my grandparents that well with their being back East and all." Darcie crossed the room to the sink and pumped water out to wash the onion off her hands. "I've always thought of you sort of like a grandmother. I'd love for you to stay with us."

"I think that's the nicest thing anyone has said to me in a long, long time, Darcie," Mrs. Alma said. "Thank you."

"It's the truth." Darcie turned around and wondered if the sudden sheen she saw in the older woman's eyes was tears.

Just then Mrs. Alma wiped her eyes with the hem of her apron, but she didn't admit to sentimentality being the cause of them. She pushed the bowl of onions across the table. "Them are the hottest onions I've seen in a while. They're 'bout to make me cry."

Darcie and her mother agreed with their friend. Suddenly it seemed they were fighting tears right along with her.

"Those must be mighty strong onions," her mother said, wiping her eyes with the back of her sleeve.

By the time John left the sheriff's office, he felt emotionally drained. The thought that he was related to a man like Douglas Harper repulsed him. It had been hard enough to let his family know the man had died in prison. How would he tell them it was no less than he deserved?

The deputy had told him about others who had suffered from his uncle's greed. Jed Brewster, for one. Douglas had paid Jed to cause a disturbance at Emma's, then tried to blackmail him into scaring Emma by throwing a rock through one of her windows. He refused to do that and was a witness in Douglas's trial. When that hadn't worked, evidently his uncle hired a man called Zeke to throw the rock and later set the fire.

John's head was still reeling from what he'd found out. And while he was sure that what the deputy had told him was true about the Malones, he still felt the need to hear it from them—to hear firsthand how his uncle had impacted their lives. Somehow he had to find a way to bring up painful memories for them. But he wasn't looking forward to it.

He cared about those two women. Mrs. Malone reminded him of his mother, and Darcie—well, she had found a place in his heart whether she wanted to be there or not. After hearing their story from the deputy, though, he knew he would have to accept the fact that she wanted nothing to do with him. He couldn't blame her.

As he hurried up the porch steps to the boardinghouse, he knew none of that would stop his pulse from racing whenever she came into view. Even now, as he entered the house and heard female laughter issuing from the kitchen, he wished with his whole heart they'd met under different circumstances. He sensed she would be all he could ever want in a woman, and if things had been different—but they weren't. He had to be grateful the Malones hadn't turned him out on his ear.

Instead Mrs. Malone had let him stay when her daughter would have made him go. Even then Darcie had treated him as graciously as she could, for her mother's sake to be sure. Under the same circumstances, John wasn't sure he'd have been as civil.

As he climbed the stairs to his room to freshen up, the smell of dinner had his stomach growling. When he started back down, he thought he heard a faint jingle. And then another. Only when he reached the ground floor did he realize he was hearing a bell. The sound was coming from the back parlor. He watched Darcie and her mother disappear behind closed doors.

Darcie emerged a moment later. "Oh, good, you're home. I was going to the front parlor to look for one of the men. Mr. Harper, would you help us get Miss Olivia to the dining room?"

"Why, of course. Is something wrong with her?"

"Oh, I'm sorry. Of course you don't know. She fell and sprained her ankle badly this morning and for the time being will be staying here in the back parlor. Doc left her some crutches, but Mama thought it might be easier this first day if one of you could carry her into the dining room."

"Oh, certainly. I'll be glad to." John was more than happy to help. And he wished he could keep Darcie talking. This was the most conversation they'd had in a while.

"Thank you. Mother is helping her get presentable." Darcie smiled the way that always made his heart beat a little faster. "We're afraid it might be too painful for her to sit at the table, but she doesn't want to take dinner in here by herself."

"That's understandable."

Just then Mrs. Malone opened the doors. "Oh, good. Darcie found you, John. I believe Olivia is ready. Let me call our other boarders to dinner, and you can bring her in."

John was glad Darcie stayed with him as he entered the back parlor. Miss Olivia looked frail sitting on the settee with her feet propped up.

"Miss Olivia, I'm so sorry about your accident. Let me see if I can get you to the dining room without your suffering too much pain." John lifted her into his arms effortlessly and turned toward the hallway.

Darcie picked up a small footstool to take with them and made sure nothing was in his way before following him as he carried Olivia through the house. The other diners were already seated when he brought her in. John and Darcie helped Miss Olivia get as comfortable as possible amid the questions and concern about her ankle.

John set her gently in her chair, and Darcie scooted the stool under the table so she could prop her foot on it.

"Thank you so very much," Miss Olivia said as John and Darcie took their seats. "You all are so kind to me."

Dinner passed pleasantly enough, with a recounting for everyone about what exactly happened to Miss Olivia. John put talking to the Malones about Douglas Harper on hold again for the time being. Of course he wouldn't bring it up at the dinner table anyway, but he was determined to talk to them tonight. He couldn't delay it any longer.

Because the Malones had to help Miss Olivia settle down and had to do the dishes, John had to wait awhile before talking to them, so he went for a walk after dinner.

When he returned an hour later, he found Mr. Carlton and Mr. Mitchell deep in thought over their chess game in the front parlor. In the back parlor, Mrs. Alma was giving knitting instructions to Miss Olivia. He was pretty sure the murmur from the kitchen indicated Darcie and her mother were cleaning up. He might never have a better chance to talk to them than now.

He started whistling before he reached the kitchen so they wouldn't think he was eavesdropping on their conversation. By the time he stood in the open doorway, Mrs. Malone was welcoming him with a smile.

"Why, John, what can I do for you? Would you like a cup of coffee or something cool to drink?"

"No, thank you." He dreaded this, but at the same time he wanted to get it over with. "I–I'd like to talk to you and your daughter if I may."

Mrs. Malone glanced at her daughter. An unspoken question must have passed between them because Darcie gave her mother a slight nod.

"Come right in." Mrs. Malone motioned to him to take a seat at the table. "But I'm going to have a cup of coffee. Are you sure you don't want one, too?"

"Might as well—she'll end up pouring you one anyway," Darcie said, handing her own cup to her mother. "Mama thinks you have to have a cup to hold if you sit at the kitchen table for long."

Mrs. Malone chuckled, pouring the second cup for Darcie. "She's right. I do."

John nodded. "Then, yes, please, I'd like a cup." Maybe having a cup to hold would somehow make this conversation easier.

Mrs. Malone brought him a full cup and placed sugar and cream on the table before she and Darcie joined him there. She took a sip from her own cup, then looked him straight in the eyes. "What did you want to talk about, John?"

He grasped the cup in front of him and stared down into the warm, aromatic liquid. It was time. *Please, Lord, help me do this right and not cause these two women any more pain than they've already suffered from my uncle.*

He looked into Mrs. Malone's eyes. The expression in them was kind and caring, and John suddenly knew she didn't blame him for the pain in her past. It gave him the strength to go on. "I talked to my uncle's secretary today. And then I talked to Deputy Johnson. But I need to hear the truth from you." He paused, taking in a deep gulp of air and letting it out again, before asking the question he most needed answered. "Did my uncle cause your husband's death?"

For a moment it was as if no one breathed. It was so quiet in the kitchen, he could hear the sound of the pendulum swinging on the clock in the foyer and the soft murmur of voices elsewhere in the house. John looked from one woman to another, waiting for an answer he didn't want to hear.

"Yes," Darcie said thickly.

"He put my husband through a lot of stress." Her mother picked up her cup and held it close to her chest. "I believe all the worry became too much for him."

"Can you tell me what happened?"

Mrs. Malone bit her bottom lip, and tears welled up in her eyes.

John wanted to tell her "never mind," but he felt he must find out what he had to make right.

"Mama, you don't have to. I can tell him."

"No." Her mother shook her head. "I will. He needs to know. My husband was a very successful rancher. He started with a small herd and built it to one of the largest in these parts by the time we'd been married ten years. Charles worked hard to get to the point where people came to him for advice or a quick loan, and he never turned down anyone as far as I know. We prospered, and he built the house in town so we'd be closer to church and school and be more a part of the community." She smiled, a faraway look in her eyes. "And mostly because he knew I wanted to live in town."

She paused and took a sip of coffee. "Then we had a few bad weather years. We lost a lot of our herd in a drought. Then, 'bout the time we were pulling out of that, we had a real hard winter. Lost most of the herd in a blizzard that year. For the first time since we'd started, Charles needed help from outside. He went to your uncle."

John nodded. "A lot of help he was."

She reached over and patted his hand, and he had to blink to keep threatening tears at bay. How could she be so kind to him when his uncle had caused her so much pain?

"We didn't like putting up all our holdings as collateral, but we didn't feel we had any choice. Looking back, I've discovered a number of other decisions we could have made, but we didn't—and dwelling on them won't bring him back." She sighed. "Anyway, we put it all up with high hopes that we would pay Harper back early."

"And then another blizzard came." John felt he had to help her get through this. He'd heard enough to know that what the deputy had told him was true.

She nodded. "And we lost more cattle. Harper began pressuring Charles for payment and threatened to foreclose. Finally I believe it just got to be too much. I left Charles up with the books and. . ." She shook her head. She couldn't finish.

Darcie reached for her mother's hand. Tears were running down her face. John had to end it. He was putting them through too much. "I know. You found him the next morning."

Darcie let out a sob, and her mother shook her head. "No. Darcie did."

The breath left John's body as if it had been knocked out of him, and his heart felt as if it would break in two with the pain he felt for these women. He rubbed a hand over his face and pinched the bridge of his nose, trying to get his emotions under control. When he could speak again, all he could say was, "I'm sorry. I'm so sorry. Deputy Johnson told me what Douglas had done to your friends—his wife, Emma, and Liddy McAllister and others in town. Obviously he didn't make it up."

"No, he didn't," Mrs. Malone assured him. "Matt would tell you only the truth."

He took a deep breath and shook his head. "I promise you I will try to make things right if it takes the rest of my life."

Both women wiped their eyes, and Mrs. Malone pulled a handkerchief out of her pocket and blew her nose. "It's not your fault, John. You aren't responsible for the sins of your uncle, and you can't undo the bad he did."

"I have to do what I can to bring honor back to my family's name. I don't even know how to begin to tell my parents about this—the pain Douglas brought to this town. There are so many others—I've got to try to undo some of the harm. And with the Lord's help, I will."

There was no denying the remorse John must have felt at what his uncle had done. It was all over his face. The sorrow behind the mist of unshed tears in his eyes, the tension around his mouth. His determination to make things right.

He emptied his cup and stood. "I have a lot of work to do. So many records to go over. And I need to let my family know."

Mrs. Malone stood and patted him on the back. "I know that won't be easy for you."

"No. But it's nothing compared to what you've endured because of my father's brother. I—I think I'll go start that letter now."

He headed out the door, then stopped and looked back at them. "Thank you for letting me spend even one night in your home after finding out who I am."

He didn't wait for a reply but turned and hurried into the hallway.

Wiping her eyes again, Darcie's mother reached over and gave her a hug. "That wasn't easy on any of us. But I'm glad he knows the truth, and you finally see—"

"That you and Mrs. Alma were right." Darcie sniffed. "And you were. I was too judgmental, wasn't I?"

"You were. But you know the truth now and, I hope, have learned a valuable lesson about judging others. We can't hold a person responsible for someone else's actions."

Darcie could only nod. She had a lot of soul searching to do. She had been wrong.

Her mother gave her another hug. "I think I'd best go see if Alma needs a break and help Olivia get ready for bed."

Darcie began to clear the table. "You go on, Mama. I'll finish cleaning up in here."

She needed some time with the Lord. As soon as she was alone, she bowed her head and silently prayed, *Dear Lord, please forgive me for being so wrong. For judging John without even knowing him. I know I need to seek forgiveness from him, too. Please help me find the right way to go about it. And please help him forgive me, too, even though I don't deserve it. Please help me put the hurt in the past and forgive and forget. In Jesus' name, amen.*

It had been so hard to relive all the memories of those turbulent years when her parents were having such a rough time financially. Then finding her papa, collapsed in his office—

Darcie shook her head and plunged her hands into the hot water she'd prepared for washing the last of the dishes. She'd relived it once tonight, and that was enough.

As she washed the cups, she felt the urge to laugh and cry at the same time. Her emotions were nothing if not consistently at war with one another. She felt a bone-deep sorrow that she had judged John so wrongly. At the same time, her heart was soaring with relief that he truly was nothing like his uncle.

And while her mother and Mrs. Alma had been right about him, so it seemed had her heart. It had told her he could be trusted, that he was someone she could fall in love with. Darcie inhaled deeply as she realized she was already there—in love with John—and had been for some time.

She'd been fighting it for weeks now—by trying to convince herself and others he was not to be trusted. By being determined to think ill of him even as she saw with her own eyes that he was a truly good man and nothing like his uncle.

She could fight it no more—she was in love with John Harper. But as suddenly as that admission came to her, so did another thought. And the heart that had been soaring sank to her stomach like a rock. How could John ever love a woman who had made his time in Roswell so difficult by spreading ill will toward him?

Chapter 13

Darcie came downstairs after spending an almost sleepless night thinking about John and how much he wanted to make amends for his uncle's actions. And how hard she'd made it with her talk over the telephone lines. She'd misused her position at the telephone office and was seriously thinking of resigning as head operator. She didn't deserve the promotion.

But uppermost on her mind was whether or not she could ever right the wrong she'd done to John. Much as she wanted to see him, once she reached the landing, she was almost relieved to hear Olivia's bell tinkling in the back parlor. Her mother hurried out of the kitchen to answer the call, and Darcie waved her back in. "I'll see to Miss Olivia, Mama."

"Thank you, dear. I'm a little late getting things dished up this morning."

"I'll help you," Mrs. Alma said from the stairs. "I'm on my way now."

The bell jingled once more, and Mrs. Alma chuckled. "Your mama is going to rue the day she gave that woman a bell," she whispered to Darcie.

"I think you are right," Darcie whispered back. The bell jingled again. "I'm coming, Miss Olivia."

She hurried into the parlor and was relieved to see that Miss Olivia didn't appear quite as impatient as the bell had sounded. She hadn't slept very well on the settee, though. Her mother had helped her freshen up earlier, but she felt a little unkempt and wondered if Darcie would help her with her hair.

"Of course I will." She brushed Miss Olivia's hair, taking care to be easy with the tangles. "Will it be more comfortable for you down or in a braid? Or would you like me to put it up into a psyche knot?"

"Let's just go with a braid. I'm afraid the psyche knot would come down with my lounging around, and the braid will keep it neater."

Darcie had to smile. She'd be wanting to look her best, too. "I think that will work very well. If not, you can take it down later in the day."

It didn't take long to braid Miss Olivia's thick hair, and she seemed to feel better once it was done. "Thank you, Darcie. I think I might try to hobble to the dining room now."

"I'll be glad to help you, or if it's too much, I can get one of the men to carry you."

"Would you be a dear and do that? My ankle is still sore and a little stiff."

"I'll be right back." Darcie was disappointed to see that John had already left the table, but Mr. Carlton was still there. He only needed to be asked once. Although he didn't pick her up with the same ease John had, he managed and had her at the table in a few minutes.

"Thank you, sir," Miss Olivia said. "By this evening I hope I can get around myself with the help of those crutches Doc gave me."

Darcie's mother came into the dining room then. "I'll fix Olivia's plate, Darcie, dear. You'd better be getting to your breakfast, or you'll be late for work."

"I'll grab a biscuit and a cup of coffee in the kitchen; then I'll be on my way." Darcie had a feeling her mother would have an extra-busy day dealing with Miss Olivia and her bell. And she thought today Mrs. Alma would either agree to stay because she felt her mother needed her or run as fast as she could back to her own house.

Darcie hoped it was not the latter.

After mailing the letter he'd written to his family, John left the post office with new determination. A huge weight had lifted from his shoulders since finally talking with the Malones last night. But writing his parents after that about his uncle Douglas and how he'd mistreated the people in this town was one of the hardest things he'd ever done.

One of them. Having to see Darcie and her mother relive even a portion of the pain they'd gone through because of his uncle had been the hardest. No wonder Darcie had been so upset and wanted her mother to throw him out that first night and wished nothing to do with him. He'd have felt the same way. Now he could only pray she would realize he was different from his uncle and maybe someday would return the feelings he had for her. Maybe.

He wished he'd never heard of Douglas Harper or inherited this mess he'd left. But John was determined to make things right in this town. It didn't matter how long it would take or even if he had to use his own money to do it, though he was certain that wouldn't be necessary. His uncle had accumulated a mass of money through the years, and John was going to do his best to give most of it back.

At least now Miss Mead and Elmer were helping him sort through it all. And sort they did. It was a slow process, but Miss Mead filled in the blanks as best she could while Elmer made lists of the people he thought might still live in the vicinity.

John had decided to forgive the outstanding loans and wanted to notify those people so they could live without fear of being harassed for payment or losing their homes to foreclosure. Then there were those who had paid off their loans but had been charged too much interest for late payments. He wanted to pay them back that excess money.

And he truly wanted to find as many people as he could who'd had their land taken away after only one or two late payments and return it to them. He was aware it would take time to make a complete list, to decide what to do with each account, and to find those people still living in the area. He might have to enlist the aid of the sheriff's office or the town council to help, but he would do whatever he had to do to settle the affairs. He was more determined than ever to right the wrongs he could and restore honor to his family's name.

Elmer picked up their lunch from the Roswell Hotel, and they worked until quitting time. From Miss Mead's recollections and her personal notes, he was learning the stories to connect with the names.

There were the Hollingsworths. At first it seemed ridiculous to think his uncle Douglas would want their small ranch. Then Elmer and Miss Mead pointed out it was not far out of town when they'd bought it. Even though they hadn't realized the railroad would eventually run alongside their property, Douglas Harper had known. He figured the town would grow, as it had, and that one day their land would become prime property. If he hadn't gone to jail, he'd have foreclosed on them long ago.

Then there was Benson. He'd had some hard times. An electrical fire had set his place in flames, and he'd had no way to pay back his loan from Harper Bank. When he came to Douglas to ask him to lend him enough to start over and extend the life of the original loan, the man had flatly turned him down. It must have been a blessing to him when Douglas was put in prison.

"Another bank in town loaned him the money to start up again, but I don't know the particulars. He's kept his head above water, but I surely don't think he could pay back both banks," Miss Mead pointed out. "His wife has been sick, too."

"You know them well, Miss Mead?"

"They go to my church, and they've always been real nice to me, even knowing I worked for—"

"My uncle," John finished for her. "I hope you don't mind my asking, but what kept you working for him when you hated the way he did business?"

Miss Mead took off her glasses and rubbed her eyes. "I didn't realize what kind of man he was when I came to work here. He could be very charming, and I fell for that charm. I thought I'd fallen in love with him," she said softly. "He didn't return my feelings. As the years passed, I often wondered if a woman had hurt him at some point in his life. He held most with disregard, nor did it seem to bother him when he made their lives miserable. Of course he didn't single out women. He treated everyone about the same. Awful."

"Yet you kept working for him?"

She shrugged. "I gave him my notice once, but—"

"But what, Miss Mead? Did my uncle threaten you?"

Her slight nod filled him anew with revulsion for his uncle.

"My mother was very ill back East. Her care was costly, and I was paid well. But Douglas threatened to give me a bad recommendation—said I'd never work anywhere else in this town. The family counted on what I sent each month, so I kept working."

"I'm sorry."

"No. It was my fault. I should have left here and gone back East to help take care of her. I could have found a position there. But I still cared for him. I had some notion he would change one day. Hoped I might change him." She put her glasses back on and shook her head. "I made the wrong choice."

"Well, for what it's worth, I'm glad you are here now. I'd never be able to make things right if we hadn't found you."

"I'll take comfort in that, John. Thank you."

John hoped she would. Obviously she'd suffered pain because of his uncle, too.

Miss Mead pulled another stack of papers toward her, then glanced over at him. "I'm starting to believe the Lord kept me here so I could help you with this."

"You may be right. I've been so blessed you agreed to help."

John couldn't help but wonder if Douglas Harper had used the unrequited feelings he held for John's mother as an excuse for the kind of man he became. What a waste. He could have chosen to live a good life with a fine woman who loved him and would have done her best to make him happy. Instead he chose to become a bitter, hateful person determined to bring pain to almost everyone he encountered.

~

Darcie thought four o'clock would never arrive. It had been one of the longest days she could remember, and she couldn't wait to get out of the office and go home. She'd been fielding more questions about John all day. Hard as she tried to assure everyone he did not have anything to do with the fire and wasn't like his uncle, no one seemed to believe her.

Harriet Howard, one of Roswell's oldest residents, didn't. "What's gotten into you, Darcie? A couple of weeks ago, you wanted to have him thrown out of your mama's boardinghouse. What's changed your mind? I've seen him. He's a right handsome fella. Have you gone and lost your heart to Douglas Harper's kin?"

Darcie was taken aback by her question. And even more by her first thought. *Oh yes. I'm afraid I have.* Suddenly the irony of it hit her, and she had the urge to laugh. As a chuckle escaped her, she hoped Mrs. Howard took it as an answer.

"Well, I guess you think that's funny, do you?"

"I'm sorry, Mrs. Harriet. I"—*am at a loss for words.* Darcie was thankful when the light lit up over Emma's slot and she could honestly say, "I have to go now. The switchboard is lighting up."

She disconnected the Howard line and inserted a pin into Emma's slot. "Number, please?"

"Darcie, I'm glad I got you."

"What can I do for you, Em?"

"Well, I wanted to check on you. Matt said John Harper paid him a visit yesterday. He seems to think he might not be as bad as we first thought."

"He's right."

"Oh?"

"Mama and I had a long talk with him last night, Em. And she was right. He's not like his uncle. He wants to undo some of the harm Harper did. I was wrong about him and even more wrong to talk about him the way I have."

"Well, who could blame you, Darcie? I certainly understand."

"That doesn't make me right, Em."

"I know. But I was just as bad. I've been suspicious of him ever since I found out who he was. It wasn't just you thinking bad of him."

Darcie knew Emma was trying to make her feel better, but somehow she only felt worse. She changed the subject. "How are you feeling?"

She could hear Emma's sigh over the telephone line before she answered. "I'm excited, tired, and more than ready to have this baby. Doc says any day now."

"Oh! Well, Mama and I are working on Mrs. Alma. We're hoping she's almost ready to make a decision about staying with us."

Emma chuckled. "I sure wish she'd hurry up. But we'll be cozy up here in this apartment until we find something else. I walked past her house today, and it would be so perfect."

"I know. I'll let you know as soon as she makes a decision."

"Thank you. And, Darcie, I truly am glad John isn't like his uncle."

"So am I. I just wish I'd figured it out much earlier. You take care of yourself." She could hear Mandy in the background trying to get Emma's attention. "And give Mandy a hug. She's going to have a big adjustment, isn't she?"

"Yes, but I think she's excited she's going to be a big sister. We'll take special care to give her extra attention, too. Oops! I'd better go! She's trying to reach the cookies—'bye." The line went dead, and Darcie chuckled. Mandy was quite independent at three.

The clock struck four o'clock, and Darcie breathed a sigh of relief. Finally she could go home. She barely said good-bye to her coworkers before she was out the door and headed up the street.

Darcie scarcely felt the balmy May breeze against her skin. Nor did she notice the cloudless blue sky as she walked home. Uppermost on her mind was how to tell John she had played a major role in turning the people of this town against him. She didn't know what she would say, but she wouldn't rest until she told him the truth.

She peeked in on Miss Olivia before going upstairs to change clothes and found her napping, bell clasped tightly in her hand. After changing into a tan skirt and tan and white striped blouse a little more appropriate for helping prepare a meal, she took the back stairs that led to the kitchen.

The back door was open to let out some of the heat, and Mrs. Alma was shelling peas at the table while her mother was basting two plump chickens. She returned the roasting pan to the oven and took a seat at the table to help with the peas.

Darcie dropped a kiss on top of her mother's head. "What can I do to help? You two look exhausted."

Mrs. Alma chuckled. "You can see to that bell for the next few hours. I told you your mother would regret giving it to her."

"Oh, Miss Olivia has had you on the run today?" She smiled at her mother's sigh and nod.

"Oh, you could say that," her mother said. "If she's rung that bell one time, she's rung it thirty. She's thirsty—could she have some cool water? She's chilled—could she have a cover? And, oh, would it be too much trouble to make a cup of hot chocolate?"

"And at lunchtime she still felt too wobbly to get to the table—could she have her meal in the parlor?" Mrs. Alma added. "Once we had her settled and came back to our own lunch, that bell jangled again. She was quite lonesome eating by herself—could we join her?"

"I declare, if it wasn't one thing, it was another—all day long. But Olivia is just so sweet about it, you can't really get angry with her." Her mother glanced at the clock. "It's been quiet now for near an hour. I wonder what she's up to?"

"Well, she was napping when I came in. Maybe she'll—"

"No!" Her mother held up her hand and shook her head. "Don't say it. Don't even think it."

Mrs. Alma laughed outright. "She's right. About the time you think it and certainly by the time you get it out of your mouth—"

The bell rang. The two women burst out laughing, and Darcie hurried to see to Miss Olivia, thankful that at least they hadn't lost their sense of humor.

Darcie had wanted to ask John if she could talk to him after dinner, but the only exchange she'd had with him was when he helped bring Miss Olivia to the table. And the conversation at the table pretty much centered on the older woman and how she'd spent her day.

"Mostly I've been keeping Molly and Mrs. Alma on the run. I am so sorry to be so much trouble," Miss Olivia said sweetly.

"We threatened to take her bell away several times, but all in all it wasn't too bad," Mrs. Alma said. "I sat with her for a while and helped her with her knitting. I did decide one thing today."

"Oh?" Darcie's mother said. "What was that?"

"It feels good to be needed. And I was needed today. Olivia is right. It is very lonesome eating alone. I like having company around, too. I like the hustle and bustle here. Well"—she grinned at Olivia—"maybe not that bell, but I do like the other goings-on."

"So what was your decision?" Mr. Carlton prompted.

Mrs. Alma shook her head. "I've decided I don't want to live by myself any longer, so—if the offer to let me stay here is still good, I'll take you up on it."

Darcie's mother jumped to her feet and came around the table to hug her. "Alma, I am so glad! You are needed here. And I love having you around. I am so glad. So glad."

Then Darcie hugged Mrs. Alma. "I am thrilled. It will be so good to have you around all the time."

Mrs. Alma hugged her back. "Well, I must admit, your talk helped convince me. I'd love to be like a grandmother to you."

"Well, you already are. I truly feel that way," Darcie assured her.

"And I'm glad I didn't run you off with my bell," Miss Olivia added.

Mrs. Alma looked happier and healthier than she had in months. Darcie was sure she'd made the right decision.

"What do you want to do about your house?" her mother asked as she passed the bowl of peas. "You know Emma and Matt need a bigger place. Would you be willing to rent it to them for a while? I'm sure they would buy it, if you want to sell, but renting would give you time to be sure."

"Do you think they are still interested?" Mrs. Alma asked Darcie.

"Oh, I know they are—and the sooner the better. Doc says the baby could come anytime now."

"Well, then, I need to talk to them soon as I can."

"Oh, Emma is going to be so excited! She loves your place."

"So do I. But I like it here, too. And my home is too large for me. It was meant for a growing family." Mrs. Alma smiled and nodded. "I think I'd like knowing it was going to someone who loved it as much as I have."

"Would you like me to get Emma on the phone for you?"

"After supper or tomorrow morning will be good enough. She's probably busy right now."

"Well, no matter when you talk to her, you'll make her very happy."

"Just as you've made us," her mother said. "I think this arrangement will work out fine for the lot of us!"

Between answering Miss Olivia's bell after dinner, then helping settle her for the night in the back parlor, Darcie had a good idea what her mother and Mrs. Alma had been through that day. She scarcely had time to breathe. And now she wondered when she could talk to John.

When she got back to the kitchen, her mother and Mrs. Alma were finishing up. "I'm sorry. You should have left the cleanup for me."

"You helped plenty by seeing to Olivia for us." Her mother put up the last dish.

"That's for sure." Mrs. Alma chuckled. "I'm plumb tuckered out. I think I'll call it a day."

"Thank you for helping so much, Alma," her mother said. "I don't know what I would have done without you."

Mrs. Alma patted her on the shoulder on her way out of the kitchen. "I should be thanking you. I felt more needed today than I have in years, and I liked the feeling. See you both tomorrow." She turned back to Darcie. "You can telephone Emma and tell her the house is hers if you want to. Tell her we can go over the details tomorrow."

"Oh, Mrs. Alma, she will be so happy. Don't you want to talk to her yourself?"

"Tomorrow is soon enough." She yawned and gave a little wave on her way out the door. "Good night."

Darcie hurried to the telephone to give Emma and Matt the news. Her mother chuckled when she heard Emma's squeal of delight clear across the room. They talked for only a few minutes. Emma told Darcie to let Mrs. Alma know they'd be ready to talk details whenever she was.

"Thank you, my friend," Emma said. "I know you and your mother had a lot to do with this. Please thank her, too."

"I will. We're happy it turned out this way, too."

Darcie hung up the earpiece and grinned. "Needless to say, Emma and Matt are thrilled. They will be so happy in Mrs. Alma's house. And I'm so glad she decided to live here. I think it will be good for her."

"Well, it's certainly going to be good for me," her mother said, hanging up her dish towel.

"Mama, do you know if Mr. Harper has come in from his walk?"

"I don't think so. Why?"

"Last night he apologized to us for his uncle's actions. It's my turn to apologize to him."

Her mother put her arm around her shoulders. "For misjudging him?"

"Yes." And for causing more problems for him by talking about him to anyone who would listen. But she didn't tell her mother that.

"I see."

"I'd sure like to talk to him tonight."

Her mother untied her apron and hung it on a hook by the kitchen door. "You know, I tried all day to find time to sit in the swing on the front porch for a while and relax and smell the scent of the lilacs. How about we go sit a spell in that swing? John is bound to be back soon. When he gets here, I'll leave you to your talk."

Chapter 14

John was surprised to see both Molly and Darcie swaying back and forth on the front porch swing when he came up the walk. They'd been busy at dinner with Miss Olivia and their other duties, but they both had seemed more comfortable around him since their talk the previous night. Or maybe he was the one who felt more relaxed since he'd discovered the truth about his uncle and apologized.

"Good evening, ladies. It's a beautiful evening to be outside, isn't it?"

"It is. It was a mite stuffy in that kitchen," Mrs. Malone said. "We decided to come outside and relax a bit and enjoy the cool night air."

"It will only be getting warmer in the kitchen in the coming weeks," Darcie said.

Her mother nodded. "We'll be cranking that ice cream churn often."

John leaned against the porch railing and smiled at her. "Did you get Miss Olivia settled down for the night?"

"Well, for a while. I left her reading *Harper's Bazaar*. She enjoys that magazine so. I'm sure she'll be much more comfortable once she can sleep in her own bed again, but she isn't complaining too much."

"I'm sure she gets bored not being able to get around on her own," John said.

"Alma and I are going to work with her tomorrow and see if we can help her up the stairs. It'll be a start if we can just get her to hobble into another room." Mrs. Malone put her foot down and brought the swing to a stop.

"Be careful, Mama. We don't need you or Mrs. Alma getting hurt."

"I will. Much as I'd like to stay out here with you young people, I guess I'd better go see if Olivia needs anything before she goes to sleep."

"I can go, Mama."

"No, you helped earlier. And you worked all day, too. You deserve to sit awhile. Besides, Alma and I teased her a lot about the bell today. I need to make sure we didn't hurt her feelings."

Darcie watched as her mother went inside. For a moment John half expected Darcie to follow her mother in, but she didn't. She seemed tired tonight, and he hoped their talk of the night before and all the memories that had been dredged up hadn't given her bad dreams.

"Did you have a hard day, Miss Darcie?"

"It—was a long day." Darcie put the swing in motion again but only for a moment before she brought it to a stop. She looked over at him. "Mr. Harper. . .I—"

"Please—call me John. Right this moment I am not too fond of my last name."

"I'm sorry. I—"

She had no reason to be sorry for that. "It's certainly not your fault, Miss Darcie."

"No, not your last name, but—" She paused and took a deep breath before continuing. "Mr.—uh—John, I—would like to talk to you, if you have the time."

"Of course I have the time." Darcie seemed nervous, and he wanted to put her at ease. "What can I do for you?"

"Nothing. It's not what you can do for me. I need to—" She paused again and stood, then joined him at the porch rail. "I need to apologize to you."

"To me? Miss Darcie, what could you possibly need to apologize to me for?"

She looked down at the floor of the porch and exhaled before speaking. "I'm afraid I've had a hand in turning some of the people of Roswell against you. I couldn't stand that a relative of Douglas Harper was living under my mother's roof, and I used my position at the telephone company to—"

Disappointment settled deep inside him, but he couldn't be angry with her. "I understand."

And he did. As sorry as he was that she hadn't seen he was unlike his uncle, he could appreciate how she'd assumed he wasn't. And he couldn't blame her, not really. After all he'd found out about Douglas Harper, the horrible things he'd done, and now that he knew it was Darcie who had found her father—John could not blame her for feeling the way she did. He could only wish things were different as his hopes for the future suddenly seemed dim.

"You may understand," Darcie said, looking him in the eye. "But that doesn't make what I did right. I am truly sorry I've made your time here even more unpleasant than it needed to be. I—I don't know what else to say, except that one day I hope you can forgive me."

With those words, Darcie turned and ran back into the house, leaving him to ponder her words. It did pain him that she'd thought so little of him and told everyone so, but he admired her honesty now.

John turned and gazed up at the star-studded sky. He breathed deeply, and the scent of lilacs hit his nostrils—sweet and delicate, like Darcie. Except she wasn't that delicate. She'd been through a lot in her life and was stronger than she thought. She'd been determined to tell him the truth tonight and apologize.

Could she feel differently about him now? Could she finally be realizing he truly wanted to undo some of the harm his uncle had done?

A flicker of hope stirred in his heart. Maybe he could have a future in this town after all.

Darcie was glad she didn't run into anyone as she hurried back inside and up the stairs. Her heart had twisted in pain at the hurt she saw in John's eyes when she told him what she had done.

Fresh tears welled up as she entered her room and knelt at her window seat. How awful she must seem to him. He'd come here to settle his uncle's estate and had no idea of the corruption he would uncover. He was already hurting after finding out what his uncle had done. He wanted desperately to make amends to this town, and now it must seem she had gone out of her way to make trouble for him.

Darcie wept. In her own way, she was no better than John's uncle. She'd sinned, too—by judging John because he was related to Douglas Harper and then spreading ill will toward him. Whatever dreams she'd woven from that first night she met him, to the ones she'd only recently let herself dream again, had disappeared into the air because of her actions. She hadn't trusted him because of his uncle's deeds. But now how could John ever trust her—after her own? And how could she have the audacity to ask him to forgive her when she realized she must forgive his uncle?

Feeling as if her heart would break, Darcie prayed.

"Dear Father, please forgive me. I have been guilty of judging John so wrongly, and I've caused him pain because of it. I've made the work he's trying to do much harder. I've fought my feelings for him because of who he was related to, when I should have accepted him for who he is and recognized what my heart was telling me—what You were trying to get through to me. He is a good and honorable man, and I'll never find another like him. I pray that one day he will forgive me, too, even though I don't deserve it. I know I've destroyed any hope for a future with him. Father, please, please help me to find a way to make things right for him—to convince people I was wrong about him. Please help me, Father, to forgive Douglas Harper and put the past behind me. Your will be done. In Jesus' name, amen."

Darcie stood, wiped her eyes, and blew her nose. It was time to quit feeling sorry for herself. She may not have a future with John, but that didn't cancel the love she felt for him. She must find a way to undo some of her own wrongs. She had to find a way to convince the town John was trying to help them, not harm them.

She would sleep on it, knowing she would have an answer soon as to what to do. The Lord would help her, of that she had no doubt.

John hoped Darcie slept better than he did, but when he finally saw her, the dark circles under her eyes told him she probably hadn't. He wished he could assure her he harbored no ill will toward her and might have done the same under similar circumstances.

But he had no chance to talk to her this morning, what with her helping her mother with Miss Olivia first thing, then rushing off to work. He left for the bank, assuring himself he would make it a point to tell her he forgave her—before the day was out if he could.

Knowing what he was up against, after Darcie's confession to him, somehow made it easier to accept the people's reactions on seeing him. One person darted across the road while another ducked into the nearest business to avoid passing by him. Then others kept walking but didn't look at him or speak.

Instead of accommodating them by staying silent today, he tipped his hat, smiled, and said, "Good morning."

Several people looked a little surprised at his overture, but it didn't bother John. He finally understood why they'd treated him the way they had. Oh, Darcie thought it had a lot to do with her, and maybe she hadn't helped his cause, but they treated him the way they did because of his uncle's treatment of them and this town.

One of these days—soon, he hoped—they would see he meant them no harm. In the meantime he'd keep going through records and ledgers until he had as clear a picture as possible before he started contacting people. And he would keep praying he had the answers he needed soon, so he could make things right.

Elmer and Miss Mead could probably tell he was getting impatient because they worked as diligently as possible. They worked well together, and the new stack of records they were compiling began to overtake the old ones. The end might be in sight after all.

He prayed again that once he began making reparations, he could convince Darcie to give him a chance to win her heart. But that would have to wait until he could show the town a man couldn't and shouldn't be judged by his relatives.

Darcie called Emma, Liddy, and Beth and asked if they could meet for tea that afternoon. She was determined not to use her position at the telephone office to talk about this or anything else over the lines. If she messed up again—well, she would have to resign.

But when several people asked her about John, she took that opportunity to tell them she'd been wrong. That John Harper wasn't anything like his uncle and she should never have talked about him the way she did. And that she wasn't going to discuss him anymore. And she meant it.

But others in town had taken her words to their friends and neighbors, probably elaborating with each telling, as Darcie knew could happen. She wasn't sure how she'd ever reach them all when she didn't know who had been told.

But an idea was forming in her mind, and she wanted her friends' opinion about it. She watched the clock all afternoon, anxious to get to Emma's Café. While word would spread that she was now defending John, she didn't want him to have to wait. No. She needed to do more. And as quickly as possible.

When she arrived at the café, her friends were waiting for her upstairs in Emma's apartment. The children were playing happily together, and Darcie was pleased to have more privacy than the café would have offered.

Darcie had already told them she thought she'd been wrong about John and needed their help in finding a way to convince the town of the same.

"You're certain he isn't here to hurt the town, Darcie?" Liddy asked. "And what about the fire?"

"I'm certain. John had nothing to do with that fire. He only wants to make things right from his uncle. Mama and I talked to him the other night, and I'm certain he's being honest with us."

"I have to agree with Darcie," Emma said. "Matt told me they've determined the fire was an accident and that John had nothing to do with it. Matt thinks he is sincere in wanting to help the people of Roswell, and he's agreed to help John locate as many people as he can."

"Well, I am relieved and happy he is nothing like his uncle," Beth said. "Jeb said the way he helped with that fire told him a lot about the man, and he couldn't believe he was here to bring pain to anyone."

Just me. Darcie quickly chided herself for the thought. John hadn't been the one to bring her pain. She'd brought it on herself. If she'd followed her heart's lead that first night, she wouldn't be going through this heartache now. Instead she had to accept the fact there was probably no way they could ever have a future together.

Liddy sighed deeply. "Well, I'm just plain relieved. I found it a little hard to believe he was like his uncle. Douglas was the worst kind of man. I couldn't see that in John."

"If I hadn't spread the word about him, probably no one else would, either," Darcie said, shaking her head.

"Oh, I don't know about that, Darcie," Emma said. "Emotions run very high against Douglas Harper in this town. I think he'd probably have gotten the same reaction no matter how they found out who John was."

Darcie looked at Beth. "I'm sorry, Beth. I know you tried to drill into me not to spread gossip along the lines, and I truly intended to be like you when I got my promotion. I'm sorry I've disappointed you, too."

"Oh, Darcie, I do understand. I know all too well how easy it is for customers to draw one into talking about the things they want to know. Don't you remember when Jeb and I were at odds about the children and then falling in love? The whole town seemed to have an opinion on what we should do."

"But that doesn't excuse my actions. They were giving you their opinion, not the other way around."

"No, it doesn't. It was wrong, but you went through so much because of Douglas Harper—and then to have his nephew living under the same roof." Beth shook her head. "I'm not sure I could have done any better. And through all of this, I think you've learned a valuable lesson."

Oh, yes, she had. One she didn't think she would ever forget. Darcie was relieved her friends had come to the right conclusion about John, without her having to convince them, and she told them of her plan to get the town to accept him.

"I think that is a wonderful idea, Darcie," Beth said, smiling.

"I hope it will work. I have to do something."

"Well, it would certainly be a way to get the word out quickly and to as many as possible at one time," Emma said.

Darcie breathed a sigh of relief that they were willing to help her, and she silently thanked the Lord for the friends He'd given her. They were always so supportive.

"I don't know what I'd do without you all!"

"I'll telephone Matt now. Maybe he and the sheriff can help with this." Emma stood and hurried—as much as she could in her condition—into the kitchen to make her call.

Liddy's youngest let out a yelp just then, and she rushed to see to him, leaving Darcie and Beth at the table. Darcie had noticed Beth watching her closely as they all talked. Now she took advantage of the time they had alone to ask, "You're beginning to care about John, aren't you, Darcie?"

Beginning to? Hardly. But she wasn't ready to admit her feelings to her friend yet. "After the way I've tried to turn everyone against him, Beth, it wouldn't do me any good to care now, would it?"

"Oh, Darcie." Beth chuckled. "If Jeb could forgive me for misjudging him and causing him to fall off the roof and break his arm, I'm sure John can forgive you for any trouble you've caused him."

Beth's words caused hope to flare in Darcie's heart. But then she recalled the hurt she'd seen in his eyes and tamped it back down. She couldn't let herself think about that now. All she could concentrate on was getting out the truth.

With the sheriff's and Matt's help, she hoped she could do that soon.

The next few days were filled with frustration for John. Matters were going well at the bank, and he had almost all the information he needed to begin contacting people; but at the boardinghouse, Darcie seemed to be avoiding him. She stayed busy helping her mother in the kitchen and around the house and helping with Miss Olivia or working. On Thursday her chair was empty as they sat down for dinner.

"Where is Darcie?" Miss Olivia asked. "She's awfully late today."

"She'll be here soon," her mother said. "The city council has called a meeting for tomorrow night, and the telephone company has been asked to get out the word. It's open to the public. We'll be having an early dinner because I want to attend."

"What's the purpose of the meeting?" Mr. Carlton asked.

"I'm not sure, but it's been awhile since we've had an open council meeting. I think we all should try to go."

"Oh." Miss Olivia looked dismayed. "I'm not sure I—"

"Don't worry, Olivia," Mrs. Alma said. "We'll get you there."

John had never heard of a city council meeting being called like this. At home the newspapers carried a notice about a week in advance; this seemed like short notice to him. But then Roswell wasn't that large, and he supposed they had a different way of doing things out West.

Darcie breezed in then. "I'm so sorry I'm late. I'll wash up and join you." After a few minutes, she returned and hurried to take her seat at the table.

She looked tired to John but more at ease than he'd seen her. He couldn't help but wonder what had caused it. She even smiled at him when she thanked him for handing her the platter of fried chicken. He loved that smile and hoped he'd have a chance to tell her how much one day soon.

"Miss Darcie, can you tell us what the meeting is about?" Mr. Mitchell asked, drawing Darcie's attention to him.

She glanced at her mother before answering, and John wondered if she knew more about it than she'd be willing to tell.

"I think the council wants to address several things. We probably just need to be there to find out, Mr. Mitchell. I know I plan on going."

"Are you going, Mr. Harper?" Miss Olivia asked.

"Oh, I'm not sure. I'm not actually a citizen of Roswell—"

"It's open to everyone," Mrs. Alma put in. "You ought to come. Our city council meetings have always been interesting. I'm anxious to find out why they'd call a special meeting open to us all."

Darcie hurried through the meal, then excused herself. He had a strong feeling she was trying to avoid running into him, because he didn't glimpse that smile for the rest of the evening.

John didn't see Darcie the next morning, either, and he left for work with a heavy heart. Even though Darcie realized he was not the ogre she'd first thought him to be and despite the fact she'd apologized for expressing her opinion of him to many in town, she still evidently had no wish to know him better.

Elmer and Miss Mead were waiting at the bank for him, and they started to work right away. At the pace they were going since Charlotte Mead began helping them, John figured he'd have a complete set of records to work from by early the next week. And, odd as it sounded even to his ears, he couldn't wait to start giving away his inheritance. He hoped nothing was left of his uncle's money, and if anything was left after he settled accounts, he would find a good cause to support. He wanted none of it for himself.

Midmorning, Deputy Matt Johnson entered the bank, and John was pleased to see him. He'd offered to help locate as many people as he could, and John had a list almost ready to give to him.

"Mr. Harper, how's it going?"

"Please call me John. It's going well. We're making a list of people I might need help in finding. I should be able to have it to you by early next week."

The deputy nodded. "That's good. I'm sure you'll be glad to get all this behind you."

"More than I can say." He could never put his uncle's past behind him and get on with his life until it was settled.

"I thought I'd just check in and see if you needed anything, but I can see you have everything under control."

John chuckled. It sure didn't seem that way to him. "Looks can be deceiving, you know."

The deputy laughed on his way out the door. He waved good-bye to Elmer and Miss Mead. "See you all tonight."

John wasn't sure he'd be going. He didn't know what the meeting was about, and though he was curious, he didn't think he'd be welcome there. But when he got back to the boardinghouse that afternoon and checked his mail, he was surprised to find an invitation from the city council to attend tonight's meeting.

"Did you get a special invitation, Mrs. Malone?" he asked her when she called everyone to an early dinner.

"No, I didn't. Maybe you received one because you're working in your uncle's bank and they think you might be starting it up again."

"Hmm." *More likely they want to run me out of town.* A few weeks ago, he would have been relieved to go home. But now he had come to like Roswell and was seriously thinking of staying and setting up business. In spite of what his head told him, his heart was still hoping for a future with Darcie Malone.

"Will you attend?" Mrs. Malone asked.

"Well, how can I turn down a special invitation?"

She smiled at him. "I'd certainly find it hard to. I've rented a surrey to take Olivia there, and we'll have room for all of us. Darcie went to help Emma pack up some things so they can move over to Alma's this weekend. She'll stay in town and have supper with Emma and Matt and go to the meeting with them."

John's mind was made up. The only way he would probably see Darcie tonight was to go to that meeting.

Chapter 15

Darcie had met with several city council members over the last few days. Until then she hadn't realized how many residents of Roswell had been letting the councilmen know their feelings about Douglas Harper's nephew being there. After her meeting with them, they'd all expressed admiration for how she was trying to help settle some of the tension in their town.

When she arrived with Emma and Matt, Mayor Adams motioned for her to come to the front of the room and take a seat with the council. She was aware they expected much good to come from this town meeting. She took a seat and gazed out over the room; she hoped they were right.

Earlier her mother had telephoned Emma's to let her know John would be there. Darcie didn't think she'd ever been more nervous in her life as she waited for her mother and the rest of the boarders to show up. She just wanted to get through this night.

From her vantage point, she could see her mother, John, and the other boarders arriving. They found the seats Emma and Matt and her friends had saved for them and waved to Darcie as they sat down. Even with all the support she had in this room, Darcie turned to the One who would help her best. She sent up a silent prayer that she would be able to say what she needed to so the town would accept John for who he was.

The room had filled up fast. The mayor called the meeting to order, and Darcie took a deep breath as she waited for her introduction.

"We've called this meeting tonight because of an unusual request. After talking to one of our good citizens at length, it seemed the best way to put a bad period for this town to rest was to call an open town meeting. The board and I would like to welcome you all and especially Miss Darcie Malone to our meeting tonight. Without further discussion, I will yield the floor to Miss Malone."

Darcie rubbed her moist palms against her skirt and walked over to the lectern amid applause from the audience. Friends, neighbors, acquaintances, and others she'd never even seen before—she hoped they would all take to heart what she had to say.

Uncomfortable with the attention focused on her, she smiled and nodded her head at the councilmen before she began. "Thank you, Mayor and councilmen. I appreciate your quick response to my request."

She turned back to the room full of people. "I thank you all for coming tonight. I'm here to try to set a few misconceptions to rest—I hope for the good of us all."

She took a deep breath and looked out over the room. Her mother was giving her a heartening nod, while Beth encouraged her with a smile. Emma and Liddy were clapping and smiling. John seemed a bit confused, as did most of the others in the audience. But his gaze never left her as she began to talk.

"There aren't many in this room who do not know who Douglas Harper was, who weren't hurt in some way by him. And many of you know his nephew is here now, trying to—"

"Stir up trouble for us all again!" someone yelled from the back of the room.

"Or get money we don't have!" someone else called out from another direction.

"Or take our land!" another person shouted.

Darcie raised her hand and shook her head. "No, no! You have it all wrong. Please—listen to what I have to say." She sighed with relief when the room quieted.

"John Harper is not here to do anyone harm," she continued. "And I am afraid it is because of me that many of you think he might be. I was wrong to stir up trouble. From the first, I saw only that he was Douglas Harper's relative, and I assumed he was no better than his uncle. I've made no secret of how I felt about that man. But I was wrong to judge his nephew. John Harper is nothing like Douglas. All he wants to do is try to make things right—if we will let him."

Darcie looked out into the room. John was sitting forward in his seat beside her mother, his gaze steady on her. Her heart beating rapidly, she had to finish, had to get the words out. She looked into John's eyes and said the words the people of Roswell needed to hear. "Mr. Harper, I owe you and the whole town an apology for any hard feelings I stirred up. I am truly sorry for the trouble I've caused you. I've recently realized I need to forgive Douglas Harper and put all of that pain in the past, and I hope you will also forgive me."

She looked back toward the audience. "I hope you all will forgive me."

With that, Darcie turned back to the mayor and smiled, her palms spread wide. "I have no more to say."

Mayor Adams took her place as she hurried back to her seat. He cleared his throat. "Miss Malone, I think I speak for the whole council when I thank you for your honesty and for trying to bring good will back to our town.

"This city needs to put certain things in the past, also. I hope we can do that now." He looked into the audience. "I believe we should let Mr. Harper have a say, if he's a mind to."

MAKING AMENDS

John was stunned by Darcie's public apology. Now his heart slammed against his chest at the realization that this woman cared enough about him to stand up in front of these people and defend him. That she finally did realize he was totally different from his uncle.

His heart soared as he stood and nodded. While he strode to the front, he half expected some of the men to drag him away. Instead the room was quiet while he approached the mayor.

Mayor Adams shook his hand and motioned for him to address the crowd. Darcie gave him a sweet half smile, encouraging him enough to stand up in front of the room full of people. People who didn't want to have a thing to do with him but were willing to listen to him because of Darcie.

The tension in the room was thick while everyone waited for him to speak. John looked out at the crowd and back to Darcie. Seeing the sorrow in her eyes, he smiled at her. "Miss Darcie, there is nothing to forgive. After everything I've found out about Douglas Harper, I can understand why you would be suspicious of anyone with the same last name. Many times in the last few weeks I have wished my last name was not Harper."

He heard a twitter or two and maybe even a chuckle as he turned back to the room. "My—uncle—treated the people in this town abominably, and there is no way I can apologize to you all enough for his actions. But I want to make amends as best I can. I've been going over the bank records, and I'm to a point now where I think I can start to do that."

Several people in the room began to speak softly to one another as he continued. "I'd like to ask those of you who were affected by my uncle's business practices to come by the office as soon as it is convenient for you so I can begin to set things right. For those of you who feel you owed my uncle money, I plan on marking those debts paid."

A collective gasp went up over the room while John kept talking. "For those of you who feel Douglas Harper overcharged you or owed you money, I will strive to make things right—no matter how long it takes."

"And"—John spoke louder to be heard over the excited whispers that were spreading across the room in a wave—"if you had land and property taken away"—the murmuring stopped, and total quiet ensued—"I would like to see you get it back if possible. I want to make Roswell my home, but before I can do that, I must make amends to as many as I can and bring honor back to my family name."

With that, the room erupted with thundering applause, and for the first time since he had arrived in the town, John felt welcomed.

When the meeting was dismissed, Darcie watched the council members and more than a few from the audience approach John and either clap him on the shoulder, shake his hand, or say something with a smile. She felt an immense relief that things might change for him now.

She turned to greet Emma, Liddy, Beth, and their husbands as they came up and congratulated her on being so courageous and honest.

"Without your support, I don't think I could have done it. Thank you all," Darcie said. The friends the Lord had put into her life had truly blessed her.

They were just making plans to get together the next day when Emma gasped and held on to Matt.

"Another pain?" Matt asked. At her nod, he looked across the room. "I think it's time we find Doc Bradshaw. Emma's been having pains for the last few hours, but nothing would do her but to be here."

"Oh, Em! You go see about yourself now, you hear?" Darcie said.

"We'll see to her, Darcie," Liddy said as she and Cal took off behind Matt, who was leading Emma as gently and fast as he could over to the doctor.

Beth looked as if she wasn't sure whether to stay with Darcie or hurry after Emma. In her condition, Darcie could understand her wanting to go. She shooed her in that direction. "Go on. Just let me know when she has the baby, all right?"

Beth hugged her. "I will. This is so exciting!" She grabbed Jeb by the hand, and they took off across the room.

Darcie turned in the other direction and headed over to where her mother and the boarders were waiting for her. Her mother enveloped her in a hug. "That was a wonderful thing you did, dear. Your papa would have been so very proud of you, just as I am."

"Me, too, Darcie! I feel like a proud grandma tonight," Mrs. Alma added as she hugged Darcie.

"Thank you, Mama and Mrs. Alma. I wish it hadn't been necessary and that I hadn't—" She felt a touch on her shoulder and turned to find John looking at her. The expression in his eyes sent her heart dropping into her stomach and back up again to hammer against her ribs.

"Miss Darcie, I can't thank you enough for what you've done for me tonight." John touched his chest and smiled at her. "I feel I have a new start here because of what you did."

She shook her head. "I only did what I should have done from the very start. Had I not—"

"Tonight you made up for any harm you think you might have done," John said, looking deep into her eyes. "I—uh—I'd like to see you home, if I may?"

Darcie smiled and nodded.

John turned to her mother. "Mrs. Malone, would it be all right with you if

I saw your daughter home?"

Darcie's mother looked from one to the other before Mrs. Alma nudged her on the shoulder. "Oh, Molly, let the young man see Darcie home. You know he'll get her there safely," the older woman insisted.

"All right." Mrs. Malone smiled and nodded. "Yes, John. You may see Darcie home. But don't dawdle."

"Do you need help with Miss Olivia before we leave?" John asked politely.

"No. Mr. Carlton and Mr. Mitchell can help us get home. We'll see you there." Mrs. Malone started to lead her boarders to the door, then turned back. "I was proud of you both tonight."

Darcie could see how much those words meant to John by the look on his face. He cared about her mother; she prayed he cared about her, too. As he gripped her elbow and led her up the aisle, she had a feeling their relationship had changed in some imperceptible way. She prayed it was in the direction she'd been dreaming of but was afraid to hope too much.

As they walked out into the evening air, Darcie wished she'd thought to bring a shawl with her. It didn't seem to matter how warm it was during the day in New Mexico Territory, the night air turned cool. John looked at her then and smiled, pulling her hand through his arm as they left City Hall, and Darcie didn't notice the temperature quite so much.

Strolling down the street, John seemed surprised when several people leaving the meeting called out for them to have a good evening, some of the men tipping their hats to them.

"What a difference a day makes," John said. "I'd about given up hope of ever being greeted in a friendly manner in this town."

Darcie's heart felt near breaking at the way she—and the whole town—had treated him. But she was grateful for what had happened tonight. They turned the corner and headed down Fourth Street.

"Anyway, it feels good. And it's all due to you—"

She took a deep breath and shook her head. "No. All that pain was due to me, and I am so sorry for my part in—"

John stopped and turned toward her. Looking deep into her eyes, he said, "Shh. Let's leave that in the past where it belongs."

That's what Darcie wanted to do—with all her heart. But could John?

"I can't begin to tell you how it felt to walk into that room tonight." He chuckled. "For a moment I was pretty sure I was going to be run out of town. But then I saw you and—Darcie, you were so lovely up there and you spoke so eloquently that you took my breath away. You were wonderful, and suddenly I knew everything would be all right."

Darcie's heart almost melted as John gazed deep into her eyes. He'd forgiven her—she knew he had—yet she still needed to say more. "I—if I can do any more to help the people of this town accept you—"

"The only person I want to accept me right now is you." His voice was deep and husky. "But there is one thing more you could do for me, if you are of a mind to."

Darcie felt as if her heart would pound out of her chest as he pulled her into the circle of his arms. "What—what is that?"

He tipped her face up to his. "I love you, Miss Darcie Malone, with all my heart. And if you would consent to marry me, you would make me the happiest man in New Mexico Territory."

John loved her. Darcie felt it deep inside. And if that weren't enough, the love shining in his eyes was so strong and bright that it nearly took her breath away. But not before she uttered, "Yes, oh, yes, I will marry you, John Harper."

John's lips claimed hers with a kiss that promised he would cherish her all the days of their lives—and far surpassed any dreams she had woven when her heart told her the truth of how she felt.

Darcie wrapped her arms around John's neck and kissed him back, thanking the Lord for showing them both how to go about making amends.

Epilogue

June 1899

Darcie stopped at the landing and prepared to walk down the rest of the stairs in Malone's Boardinghouse for the last time as Darcie Malone. She still couldn't believe it was her wedding day. What was even more unbelievable to her was that in a few minutes she would be marrying the nephew of the man who had been responsible for giving her family and the whole town of Roswell a great deal of heartache.

Soon she would be Darcie Marie Harper—Mrs. John Harper—wife of the most wonderful man in the world. That she was marrying the nephew of Douglas Harper still had her shaking her head in amazement, and she had to stifle a giggle at the irony. The Lord had a wonderful sense of humor.

Darcie was sure old Douglas would turn over in his grave if he knew she was about to marry his nephew, John Harper. But there was not a doubt in her mind that marrying John was exactly what the Lord had intended when He brought him to Roswell—to marry her and set right in this town what his uncle had done wrong.

But Douglas Harper, who had done so much harm in Roswell, would not be happy or laughing right now. He would hate the fact that his nephew had used all the money he'd left him to pay back to the citizens of Roswell what Douglas had taken away. Nor would he be celebrating the fact that, because of everything John was doing, this town could finally get over the bitterness and hate they'd felt toward anyone with the Harper name.

In the past few weeks, land had been returned to some rightful owners, debts had been forgiven, and excess interest paid back. And Darcie was about to marry the love of her life.

Now, as her mother signaled to her to start the wedding march down the last short flight of stairs, Darcie's heart filled with so much love and thankfulness, she thought it surely would burst with joy.

She spotted her friends and neighbors waiting to witness her and John exchange their vows. She was struck once more at how true it was that all things work together for good to them that love God—and that vengeance was His. She could see God's work in her life and the way He'd brought her and John together.

And she had no doubt He had worked in the lives of her friends.

Liddy and Cal had a wonderful home and family they'd blended together. Had it not been for the Lord protecting Liddy from Douglas Harper's plans to take her land, they might never have met and fallen in love.

Had it not been for the Lord putting an end to Douglas's hateful plans to run Emma out of town and get her property, Emma and Matt Johnson might not have fallen in love and made a home for Mandy—and given her a new little sister.

Even Beth and Jeb Winslow had benefited from the Lord's condemnation of Douglas Harper's business practices. If it hadn't been for Him giving the Nordstroms the determination not to let Douglas have their place, selling out to Jeb's brother Harland instead, they wouldn't have the lovely home they'd worked hard to refurbish for their growing family.

No, Douglas Harper would have liked none of that. And it no longer mattered. Even Darcie had forgiven the man for the hurt he caused her family. For as she met John at the bay window in her mother's front parlor, gazed into his eyes, and exchanged wedding vows with him, she realized her heart had no room for hate. It was far too full of love for another man named Harper.

Darcie's heart soared with joy as Minister Turley pronounced them husband and wife.

John lifted her veil and raised her face to his. "I love you," he whispered.

"I love you, too," Darcie whispered back.

He bent his head, and they kissed, sealing their vows and assuring one another that they had made amends and started their future together.

A Letter to Our Readers

Dear Readers:

In order that we might better contribute to your reading enjoyment, we would appreciate your taking a few minutes to respond to the following questions. When completed, please return to the following: Fiction Editor, Barbour Publishing, Inc., P.O. Box 719, Uhrichsville, OH 44683.

1. Did you enjoy reading *New Mexico* by Janet Lee Barton?
   ❑ Very much—I would like to see more books like this.
   ❑ Moderately—I would have enjoyed it more if ______________
   ____
   ____

2. What influenced your decision to purchase this book?
   (Check those that apply.)
   ❑ Cover ❑ Back cover copy ❑ Title ❑ Price
   ❑ Friends ❑ Publicity ❑ Other

3. Which story was your favorite?
   ❑ *A Promise Made* ❑ *Making Amends*
   ❑ *A Place Called Home*

4. Please check your age range:
   ❑ Under 18 ❑ 18–24 ❑ 25–34
   ❑ 35–45 ❑ 46–55 ❑ Over 55

5. How many hours per week do you read? ______________

Name ____

Occupation ___________________________________

Address _____________________________________

City ________________ State __________ Zip __________

E-mail ______________________________________